CITY OF WIDOWS

ALSO BY NADIA HASHIMI

Sparks Like Stars

A House Without Windows

When the Moon Is Low

The Pearl That Broke Its Shell

CITY OF WIDOWS

A NOVEL

Nadia Hashimi

WILLIAM MORROW
An Imprint of HarperCollins*Publishers*

hc.com

FIRST EDITION

Designed by Nancy Singer

Library of Congress Cataloging-in-Publication Data

Names: Hashimi, Nadia author
Title: City of widows : a novel / Nadia Hashimi.
Description: First edition. | New York, NY : William Morrow, 2026. |
Identifiers: LCCN 2025037626 | ISBN 9780063423541 hardcover | ISBN 9780063423558 ebook
Subjects: LCSH: Women—Afghanistan—Fiction | Afghanistan—Fiction | LCGFT: Fiction | Novels
Classification: LCC PS3608.A78975 C58 2026
LC record available at https://lccn.loc.gov/2025037626

ISBN 978-0-06-342354-1

Printed in the United States of America

26 27 28 29 30 LBC 5 4 3 2 1

To the Aminis—lucky, lucky me to have a home with this family.

And to Afghanistan's daughters—to the ones who inspired this story. To the girls with wild dreams, the women who hold up half the sky, and the mothers of extraordinary grit.

To those who fought for their futures and those who continue to resist.

May you never stand alone.

Listen to the flute's lament,
Of separation, a forced absence:
Ever since I was cut from my bed of reeds
My song can elicit human tears
Bring me a heart ruined, hollowed
Let me sing of this lovesick sorrow
The distance from our origin,
Makes us long to be one again

—Jalaluddin Rumi (Mawlana),
thirteenth-century Sufi poet

CITY OF WIDOWS

Prologue

"Marjan," Kobra says slowly, suspending her name in the taut air. "You have not been honest with me."

There are a dozen eyes on Marjan, who instinctively takes a half step to the right, closing the gap between her and her daughter. She takes Hawa's hand, gives a gentle squeeze to the thin fingers. Hawa doesn't withdraw or resist, her fire tempered by this freshly unveiled peril in the sweltering heat of summer. It is the season of stone fruit, a hard pit in every belly.

The women have crammed themselves into this room, their numbers doubled by the shadows cast on the clay walls. They are here to bear witness. They are here to ensure their safety. They are here to gawk. Even the tightly swaddled infant holds her cries, waits on Marjan's reply.

Marjan tries to think quickly but she cannot find her thoughts, as if it is twilight in her mind as well. She needs only to choose one of the variations of her story that she has told in the past, but this is no easy feat. She has written, erased, and rewritten her story so many times that she has worn through the paper and vanished her own history. What had she told these women the first day she had climbed this hidden hill? She wishes she could ask one of the women in the room. Surely, one of them remembers.

"She should leave," someone says, a voice shaky with nerves. A murmur ripples through the room. Marjan feels the familiar sting of rejection. She's spent most of her life as an outcast. She reminds herself that she is a stranger to these women, a trespasser. She reminds herself that cornered mothers are dangerous creatures.

Something flutters in her belly, the anticipation of a fall. She feels as if she is high in the inky skies, readying herself to descend from a hovering helicopter with her freshly oiled firearm. On those nights, just before she put her hands on the rope, she always became acutely aware of her limbs, her head, her spine, her hammering heart, as if she were taking inventory of everything that could be lost if she wasn't smart, if she didn't remain vigilant. To the women in this room, she appears whole, but she is not. She will spend a lifetime grieving what she has lost because she chose to become a soldier.

The lights of the distant city flicker behind Kobra, like embers in the remains of a fire. The hill offers a unique view of the city, which has gone quiet these days; police trucks roll through the streets, driven by men who have their own laws, their own vision of order. People watch from behind curtained windows, some old enough to remember the last time they lived through this. Their heads bow, their shoulders slump. Their bodies recall the posture of submission needed to evade lashings.

"We have to think of our children," says another woman, and the dim room fills with the hum of agreement. "Especially our daughters."

"She is right," affirms another.

Marjan cannot remain silent. Recalling her training, she softens her voice.

"Please. I'm also thinking of my daughter. If we are found . . ." Marjan glances at Hawa, an instinctive gesture. She despises herself immediately for using her daughter to tenderize this clutch of women.

Hawa stiffens. She is reminded of the piteous looks she would get at the music school from the parents who had never sent their children to live in an orphanage. She has never, ever wanted to be regarded as a mascot for misfortune, and her mother knows this.

Hawa also knows her mother has never sounded so desperate.

"She is not one of us," a woman cries out, looking right and left at the widows of her community. "Our hill has been quiet for years, but our peace has not come easy, nor has it come cheap. I have three children to look after. The last thing I need is a reason for those brutes to climb up here and poke their filthy heads into my home. Do you think they will look past my daughter? A fifteen-year-old girl? Beware, ladies! Beware!"

A teenage girl lingers behind her mother, arms folded across her chest. Other mothers have similar fears. They know how easy it is to bring down clay walls. They sleep lightly. What if their children are sent to the families of their fathers? Will their boys be pulled into those trucks? Will they soon have weapons thrust into their hands?

Her face obscured by the dark, a woman begins to sob.

Kobra pulls her shoulders back and the ends of her headscarf, minty dots on a tawny fabric, skirt her hips. The lines on her face are more severe than they should be at thirty-five. She raises a finger; the henna-stained tip acts as a red light and halts the chatter. She has no officially designated authority here, no title or honorific, though her mother founded this small society and she has lived here most of her life. She has muddied her hands erecting walls and she has shared food. She has faced down corrupt police officers and settled quarrels. She has listened. The wealth of respect she holds is hard-earned, not an inheritance.

"I want to hear from Marjan," Kobra says.

The room awaits Marjan's reply.

In her lifetime, Marjan has been on both ends of an interrogation. She knows she is on the wrong side of the questions now. She closes her eyes, tries to hear the instructive voice that has guided her in her worst moments. When she was trapped in a forced marriage. When she spotted movement in the corner of her night-vision goggles. When she wasn't sure she could face another sunrise.

Where is that voice now?

Someone huffs, angry but not enough to violate Kobra's call for silence.

Marjan thinks of the climb to reach this city within a city, with its eroding steps and patched walls. Stepping into this place was like stepping into a gritty but mythical land. Marjan has been in spaces without men—a women's shelter, women's barracks, a maternity hospital. But those were stops on a journey, not a place a woman could call home. Marjan can almost see her neighborhood from the top of this hill. Are the birds perched on her balcony now? Are they looking at everything Marjan left behind? A tea kettle and sheets of music, a battered rug and a bar of lavender soap. These trinkets have swollen with value from the moment Marjan and Hawa left them all behind and fled to this scabrous hill.

Were it not for that one whisper in the wind, she would never have known this world existed, this world apart from men, this city of widows.

"Have you no answer?" Kobra asks.

"I will tell you why we're here," Hawa says.

Kobra raises an eyebrow. The women are still as a winter lake. From the beginning of time, people have sought refuge in the deep folds of a story, tragedy and triumph interwoven. We seek the hand-knitted comfort of a tale, particularly one steeped in the epic suffering of innocents, to hear of others who have been cheated by fate and tricked by friends and pierced by love's sharp arrow. The women lean in; the coven tightens. These widows are anxious, certainly. But they're also intrigued.

"Hawa!" Marjan protests. Their story was unwieldy even when she alone was the storyteller. What if Hawa gets it wrong? What if she reveals one detail too many?

Hawa looks unsurprised and unimpressed by her mother's reaction. They know each other as mothers and daughters do—all too well and not at all. Marjan thinks of the times she was silenced as a girl, all the decisions made for her.

At the bottom of the hill, the streets are crawling with vengeful men, patrolling and purifying a stolen city. Will they silence the women again? And if Marjan silences Hawa now, what will she have taught her daughter? Like everyone else in the room, Marjan's eyes are trained on Hawa, her daughter's youth marred by the shadows under her eyes. There has been no rest since the Taliban stormed into Kabul.

Marjan is reminded that their story is not exclusively hers and has not been since the day Hawa was born. She looks at her daughter and wilts, realizing that she will now yield their heavy history and their bleak fate to this young girl. She wants to scream, ashamed of the cruel inheritance she has bestowed upon her child. Marjan has endured much abuse and loss in this life, violence in all its many forms. But the humiliation burning through her body right now feels like a conspiracy of a higher order. She feels her faith slipping like water through cupped hands.

Hawa sees her mother's face flush crimson, her lip tremble. She wants to reach out and steady her, but she's also afraid to touch her mother, like the heat in her might sear Hawa's fingertips. She feels as if the world, her world, is only now coming into focus. Her senses sharpen. When there is more time, she will wonder if she has missed tendrils of smoke and movement in the shadows and dark clouds. She lets her gaze float from her mother to Kobra, to the thin lines on her face and the hard set of her jaw. She understands now that every leap and step and stumble she has taken in her life thus far has steered her to this place, to this moment, and to these words.

"My mother has made a lot of enemies in her life," Hawa says, her voice quavering like the song of an injured starling. "But I'm the reason we are in danger."

1

AUGUST 2, 2021

Marjan reaches for her water bottle only to find it empty. She's drained it more from nerves than thirst. Zarifa notices.

"Hey," she calls, getting Marjan's attention. Zarifa snaps a plastic water bottle in her direction, her half dozen bangles clinking on her wrist. Marjan grabs the bottle just before it hits the floor and mumbles a word of thanks.

"Well," Elaha begins, drawing their attention back to the reason they have all returned to this base, empty now that their American counterparts have gone. "Jenna called me from over there yesterday. You know I didn't like how direct the Americans were in the beginning, but now I appreciate it, even if it's bad news. She says the United States won't grant us any special visas. We don't qualify."

Six months have passed since the platoon's last mission, but Elaha maintains the authority of a captain, leading the conversation with Jenna and the other American women soldiers, their mission partners until not too long ago. Even when the platoon was at its most active, Elaha's leadership extended beyond the Hesco barriers that border the base. It was Elaha who decided which soldier needed additional target practice or extra sessions with the weights. She would check on her platoon members before and after missions and always volunteered to step in when needed. Now, with no missions ahead and no Americans around, Elaha has been keeping the platoon communicating via group texts. When one platoon member goes quiet, she messages individually. And when her messages go unanswered, Elaha knocks on doors.

Marjan looks around the room. The six women are spread out, some seated on folding chairs and two leaning against the wall. They are only a fraction of the entire platoon, but these are the women Elaha managed to gather to strategize around their options. Some have gone into hiding. Some are plotting their own escape routes.

When Marjan first joined the Female Tactical Platoon, she had felt utterly out of place in this training camp. She wondered if they'd made a mistake accepting her, even though she had passed their tests, physical and mental. She looks out the window. In the distance, she can see the tower that nearly undid her. She'd stood under its looming frame and heard the jeering, taunting voices she had to mute every morning. Those echoes threatened to violate the fragile barricades she'd built.

Worthless girl! Who do you think you are? You make a mess of everything you touch. Just look. You think you can climb this tower? Ha! You couldn't even take care of—

Elaha had pulled her aside and broken through the din.

If you have changed your mind, say so now and leave, she advised. *We will find another to wear your uniform. But I saw something in your eyes the first day you showed up that makes me think you have fight in you. So lace up and start climbing that ladder, because you need to learn how to get out of a helicopter without breaking those twiggy legs of yours.*

The ghosts are revisiting Marjan today, the ones who took her childhood from her. They are calling her by a half-dead name, clawing to pull her attention away from Elaha.

Marjan twists and untwists the cap on the water bottle. As a soldier, she has learned that nothing is clear in war. There are nebulous beginnings and endings to every battle and no clear winners or losers. The fight for this country started long before she donned a camouflage uniform and strapped herself into tan boots, and for a long while, she could have sworn she was on the side of the victors. Now it's evident she couldn't have been more wrong. When did the tables turn? Can anyone really keep score? Did they ever have a chance? Useless questions, all of them.

"What does she mean?" Zarifa asks. "My cousin worked as an interpreter for the Americans and he qualified. He and his family will be going to America as soon as they get through their interview. He wasn't even a soldier."

Marjan sits with her legs crossed, tapping out an anxious rhythm with one laced-up boot. Some days, she cannot believe she and Soraya dared to apply for the platoon positions. She thinks about where she was when she learned of the platoon, how miserable and broken she had been. *Naseeb* is her only answer, because now she cannot imagine doing anything besides this. This job might just have saved her life.

Soraya had been working at a fabric store, helping customers flip through bolts of velvet and linen and lace to pick out the right material for gowns or curtains. She spent her downtime sketching gowns she hoped would one day become couture pieces. She wanted to dazzle. She wanted to make others dazzle. She'd insisted on visiting the store with Marjan and Hawa on her day off to pick out fabric for an Eid dress.

They'd paused in front of an electronics store, one TV screen playing a rerun of a children's program and another running an advertisement for a female platoon. *I'm not a soldier,* Marjan had cried to her friend just a few days before. Neither woman had ever heard of such a platoon. Neither woman had any military experience. They'd never even held a firearm.

And yet.

Satin shimmers but I suppose camouflage has its own appeal, Soraya had mused.

Soraya's brother had been unenthusiastic, of course. Since their father had passed away, he had eagerly stepped into the responsibilities of being the man of the house, and to him, that started with restricting his sister's activities.

It's no place for a woman, Soraya, her brother had said.

Men rarely realize the great contributions they've made to emboldening women. Sparks of ambition had lit up Soraya's eyes. Just a few months later, she was pairing her camouflage uniform with aviator sunglasses and a bold lip.

"It's not the same for us. We worked for the Afghan army, not the Americans," Elaha explains.

"We didn't work for the Americans?" Soraya asks incredulously. "Who ran the base we trained at? Who trained us? They gave us targets and planned our missions. In the helicopter, I had one American on my left and another on my right," she retorts. "For God's sake, what did we ever do without the Americans?"

"I asked Jenna the same thing. She says she doesn't understand it either."

"Maybe Jenna needs to talk to someone else," Soraya huffs.

"You know she's doing everything she can," Marjan says, and Soraya's shoulders slump, her anger spent.

"I know she is," she mutters. "But things are getting worse here."

Marjan thinks of last night's program on Metra Media, the channel that covers the news with a focus on women's affairs. According to the anchor, Mina Noori, Taliban fighters had invaded homes in the north of the country. By phone, an anonymous woman shared that the Taliban had tossed a grenade into the home of a woman who refused to feed a dozen fighters. Her four children managed only to drag their mother's corpse out before the home was consumed in flames.

"Have any of you received last month's salary?" Zarifa asks. The women shake their heads.

Marjan thinks of the bills waiting on her. She is grateful to have a salary but wishes it weren't always so late. She budgets carefully, because everyone has heard that in some areas the soldiers haven't received a paycheck in months. Marjan keeps a notebook of expenses and income, a way for her to calculate precisely how worried she should be. Besides rent and groceries, Hawa needs new sneakers. She has grown since last year and will need a new winter coat soon. On the last page of the notebook, Marjan has a separate ledger for the rubab she saw in a music store, a handcrafted instrument with intricate inlays and delicate keys. Marjan had thrilled at the thought of this rubab in her daughter's hands. *Hawa will bring you to life,* she had thought, just before her eyes fell on the dizzying price tag dangling from a thread.

Drop by drop, the river is formed, her aunt used to tell her.

So on the back page of her notebook, Marjan wrote that number. Below it, she keeps a tally, a few bills stuffed into an envelope from time to time. A gathering of droplets, dreaming of running. When she last checked, she was only a few notes short.

"I spoke with the guy from the ministry about that. He told me it might be another two weeks—maximum," Elaha relays.

"Certainly. Maybe even sooner," Zarifa repeats, with sarcastic confidence. She slumps back in her chair, arms folded and a grim set to her jaw.

"How are your parents doing?" Elaha asks, because she knows Zarifa's paychecks pay for the three medications that keep her mother's failing heart from giving up completely. Her father is a diabetic with vision so bad that he cannot discern a five-afghani note from a five-hundred-afghani note.

Zarifa blinks rapidly, then sits up.

"They are managing," she says, unwilling to complain when she knows every woman here has her own burdens. She stands and begins to pace the length of the room. Marjan feels herself grow more tense as Zarifa tries to expel nervous energy. "They pray that God will protect Kabul. But we're the ones with the uniforms. Are we going to be called on to defend Kabul or not?"

Their missions continued after the Americans left but not with the same frequency. It has left Marjan with too much time. She's felt most unsafe when she's alone with her thoughts.

"I hate doing nothing," Soraya groans, then looks at Elaha. "It makes no sense to have us sitting around when we could be helping."

"I haven't received any orders from superiors," Elaha reports. "I don't know anything more than any of you know and we've all heard the same talk. We won't know until the president himself tells us if he's going to step down or if they'll form some kind of unity government."

"I may go back to college. There won't be any missions for us to go on if the targets are part of the government," Wahida says. She is the youngest of the group and the most junior. Wahida's family has asked her to leave the platoon behind, especially since the Americans announced they were tired of Afghanistan.

"What would you study?" Soraya asks. "I think you would be a wonderful teacher."

"Yes, teaching would be perfect if I had any patience whatsoever. Does this look like the face of a patient person to you?" Wahida asks. She swivels and leans forward to give Soraya a good look at the face in question.

Soraya laughs. "Not at all. Actually, you have the scowl of a butcher. Maybe that's a better option for you."

"At least butchers have meat on their tables," Wahida says, snapping her gum. Zarifa rolls her eyes.

"Be serious, ladies! What will become of us? What do you think, Marjan?" Zarifa asks, knowing Marjan will not sugarcoat her response. Marjan is naturally cautious, and realistic. When they descend upon a village in the middle of the night, it is Marjan who keeps her eyes sweeping the shadows for attackers. She does not trust a single piece of intel, and for good reason. The Americans mean well, but too often their intel is worthless.

"I'm not a politician. Your guess is as good as mine," Marjan replies. She checks her watch. "I need to get my daughter," she says. She is growing anxious being here and sitting still. She rises to her feet and walks out the door, past a row of Hesco barriers and empty barracks. She remembers the thrill she felt her first days here, her tongue tripping over the names of her American colleagues and the equipment, testing the limits of her body. She wouldn't have believed any of it possible if it hadn't been for the other women around her, women like Jenna and Elaha, who looked so at ease on these dusty grounds.

They had welcomed her, extended a hand to her when her ankle twisted on a loose rock during a training march, and taught her how to ignore the bitter remarks from the men in uniform, some of whom staunchly disagreed with women being allowed into the special forces. She spent so many years hiding from the world, shrinking herself to fit into small places and feeling like the only way to protect her daughter was to be apart from her.

Not one of her colleagues, perhaps not even Soraya, could fathom just how much the training had transformed her.

"Marjan, wait! I'll leave with you," Soraya calls out. She jogs to catch up with Marjan. Soraya wears large tortoiseshell sunglasses with round frames. Her lipstick is mostly gone now, transferred to a plastic water bottle. Marjan always feels like a peasant around Soraya. It has nothing to do with money; Soraya's glamour comes from her own creativity, a willingness to be noticed. In their first weeks of training, some of their American partners had been surprised to see the Afghan women show up with made-up faces—perfectly arched brows, winged eyeliner, powder. They couldn't make sense of it.

Can I ask you a question? Krista, a redhead from a place called South Carolina, had asked as she watched Soraya touch up her lipstick. *It's the middle of the night and we're geared up for a mission. Why do you bother with all of that?*

Krista had heard plenty of men grumbling about having women on base. They grumbled even more about having women anywhere near combat missions. Women were a distraction. They were weaker, and missions would suffer for it. What if they were captured by the enemy and raped? Krista wished the men who were so concerned about women being sexually assaulted by enemies would show the same concern for women harassed or assaulted by their brothers in uniform. So Krista and the other women downplayed their femininity. Hair pulled back. No makeup. More gym time. To be respected by the guys, they tried to act more like the guys.

Soraya balked at this.

People think you cannot be a woman and a soldier, she explained. *We have to show them it is possible. We are women and we are soldiers. That's why I dress the way I want to dress. I make my face the way I want it. And if I die, I die pretty.*

"This heat is too much for me," Soraya says with a sigh. Marjan knows, for her friend, there are many sources of heat. Her family has grown increasingly resentful of her role with the platoon. To avoid being called a family of traitors, they have lied to relatives and friends about Soraya's activities. It might have worked had it not been for those damning pictures.

"Soraya, you shouldn't be stuck here like the rest of us. You're the rising ambassador, aren't you? You should be in Europe speaking at that big United Nations conference. I still can't understand how the UN hasn't gotten you out of here by now."

Soraya scoffs.

"The United Nations doesn't have the power to blow its own nose," she says. Her plans are always derailed by some disaster, the first being her father's death. Law school became impossible when her brother lost the family's money attempting to launch a business. COVID foiled her chance to attend a global summit on gender. And now the Taliban seem to be putting her out of work.

"If we try to cross into Pakistan, we'll need to pay traffickers. Do you think your father's family will help you?"

"No," Soraya replies. She looks away, and Marjan gets the feeling she's working up the nerve to say more, but when she looks back at Marjan, her expression has brightened.

"How's Hawa doing?"

"She's fine," Marjan replies. "You know her. Hours spent away from the music school are hours wasted."

Soraya throws an arm around Marjan.

"Look at you! The mother of a musician, an artist. Does she get any of it from you? Did you ever dream of singing when you were a child?"

Marjan almost laughs.

"I was not that kind of girl," she says, recalling a time in her life when she would play soccer with the boys in the neighborhood. She wasn't Marjan then. She was Rahima and, for a spell, Rahim, a bacha posh. She has almost no nostalgia for her birthname. It wasn't a big deal to choose an alias. Women in Afghanistan were trained not to be too attached to their names. When they married, some would be given a new name by their husband's family. Women existed in relation to the men around them. They began their lives as "daughter of" and then were expected to become "bride of" and "mother of." Rarely did a woman exist for and of herself.

Without a husband, father, or son in her life, Marjan is a veritable ghost. Some days she questions her own existence.

"Well, good that your daughter's in Kabul. Everything will be okay, Marjan. In a few weeks, it will all be sorted out. We might not be soldiers if a few Talibs are brought into the government, but with our experience, maybe we'll end up working for one of those foreign organizations. Ask Ingrid. She can probably find you a job. Your English is much better than you think."

"Something's got you in a very generous mood today, Soraya. I'm not accustomed to these compliments."

"You can't handle too much sweet talk. You're like . . . like an emotional diabetic. I have to be careful with you," she teases. Marjan stifles a grin. It's true. Soraya is quick-witted, always laughing. Marjan feels like a dowdy schoolteacher next to her and sometimes doesn't know what to do with Soraya's affections. "Remember when I had to teach you to hug me back?"

Marjan hadn't realized she was recoiling at physical contact until Soraya had pointed it out to her.

Sister, are you okay? It's just a hug. I'm not kidnapping you, she had joked one day. But then Soraya had grown quiet. She was as perceptive as she was gregarious. *You don't like anyone's hands on you, do you?*

Marjan's guard didn't come down then. Her story unfurled slowly, and Soraya was the first person—the only person—privy to the entirety of it. Her history had sharp edges.

They have reached the bus stop. Soraya tents her hand over her eyes to shield herself from the sun's glare. Marjan wishes she had thought to bring a bottle of water with her. Even in this sweltering heat, she is grateful for the light. She prays Hawa will never experience the kind of darkness she has survived.

She steps onto the bus to return to her daughter and the life she has built for them together, an existence she never would have thought possible back when she first held her child.

Hawa. Marjan named her daughter after Eve, a woman created by God and without a father. Hawa is a ghost as well, an invisibility that her mother hopes will protect her from harm.

"I have a few American dollars too," a man says. "Come, come, and sit next to me."

Soraya and Marjan pretend they do not hear him. Half of soldiering is knowing when to fight and when to lie low, and city buses are sometimes even harsher territory than insurgent strongholds. Though the passengers on the bus didn't know what they did on the base, they were happy to make their own lurid assumptions. Their taunts were an impossible test. A woman who responded in kind was trashy, unbecoming. A woman who remained silent was almost admitting to the sin she was accused of committing. There was no winning, only less losing.

"I'm talking about the tall one," the man announces, then coughs into the already-stale air. He has his eyes on Soraya. People often do.

The bus jostles, and amid the crush of bodies, Marjan feels her panic rising. Were it not for Soraya's steadying presence, she might not survive these rides. Soraya has often told her the same. Marjan is grateful for her friend and terrified about that as well, because if there's one lesson this life has taught her, it's that nothing good remains.

She gives Soraya's hand a quick squeeze, then gets off the bus a bit early.

She makes her way down the street. Wonders if she should pick up some groceries or if she can pull together something from what they have. She is lost in thought when she realizes she is standing at the gates of the zoo.

Marjan regards the statue of the legendary lion, perhaps Kabul's best-known animal, near the entrance. Her namesake. People step right or left to move around her; some curse her under their breath. Others out loud.

Marjan fidgets with her headscarf and thinks of the girl she was before she took on this lion's name, a unisex name that meant "a precious stone."

Like a ruby or an emerald. Or a pearl. Back then, she was Rahima, the girl who was a boy and then a girl again.

She came here last year with Hawa and watched her daughter stare at the statue. She wonders even now what Hawa thought of the animal's likeness. She cannot settle on what she herself sees; the image changes and shifts before her. Is this a beast? A myth? A victim? Exposure has turned the bronze cast a soft verdigris, leaving touches of brightness only on the lion's nose, the tips of her ears, and the curl of her tail. Marjan can almost feel a puff of air, an exhalation from the lion's nostrils, a breath of petrified sorrow.

2

2010

Rahima. Her original name comes from the word for "mercy," one of the ninety-nine names of Allah. And derived from the same root is rahm, the word for "womb." But rahm is all she can hear in her name, and she resents it with all her body. She does not want to be a vessel for life. She has experienced so much cruelty in the past three years that mercy has become hard to recognize.

Rahima was not much older than Hawa when she slipped away from the Kabul apartment where she had been staying, guarded by her husband's men. She had tried to summon the confidence she had as a young bacha posh, those five years she had spent dressed as a son so that she could walk her sisters to school. Had those five years as *Rahim* really happened? She doubts her own memories of playing soccer and darting into shops in the bazaar and horsing around on the school playground. As a daughter, these behaviors would have brought shame upon her family. As a son, her assertiveness was applauded.

But then came her undoing. At thirteen, her opium-addicted father gave her and two of her four sisters away in marriage. Her mother, rendered feeble and numb by the same drug, mounted no resistance. For three years, Rahima lived as the fourth bride of Abdul Khaliq, a warlord. Rahima hated the man, but she had to admit he was clever, organizing the election of an obedient but unschooled wife to Parliament to advance his personal interests. Rahima had been her assistant, present only for her literacy. She might have survived that life, if her small son hadn't fallen ill while she was away. Somehow, the blame fell upon her shoulders, and it was made perfectly clear that Abdul Khaliq was preparing to bury her beside their son.

Rahima's escape had been harried. Dressed in stolen boys' clothing, she tried not to look over her shoulder as she opened one door and then another, finally stepping onto a sidewalk, into the light of day. She fully expected a hand to clamp down on her shoulder or for a familiar guard to step directly into her path.

Rahima arrived breathless at the location the American woman, a woman who supported female parliamentarians, had given her. Ms. Franklin had done a poor job of concealing her anxieties. Rahima saw her hands trembling as she gestured for Rahima to share her story with the two women seated before her. She hadn't realized she would need to organize a story.

Who were these women anyway? What if they turned her away? What if they called Abdul Khaliq?

There was no time for her questions. The two women were bombarding her with theirs.

What is your name?

Who are you running from?

What is your husband's name?

Do you have any children?

Where is your nearest family?

You will have to turn in all your personal belongings. Do you have a cell phone?

Rahima answered some, but not all. Ms. Franklin observed, intermittently squeezing her shoulder or offering an encouraging nod.

Within thirty minutes, Rahima was ushered into a car. Perhaps they told her Ms. Franklin wouldn't be joining them. If they had, Rahima hadn't heard them. She nearly jumped out of the car as it pulled away, fearful this was a trap and the driver was going to deliver her to the guards she had escaped, men surely aflame with anger that she'd slipped away on their watch.

Abdul Khaliq was not known for his forgiving nature.

Etched in her memory is the image of her hand on the car door handle as she debated hurling herself out of a vehicle that seemed to be collapsing in on her. She did not, but not because she chose to stay in the car. She simply lacked the will to leap out of it.

It would be years before she recognized that moment as the seismic shift that it was—the point in time she stopped feeling brave or capable of wanting something for herself. Deciding to run away from the guards might have been her last demonstration of agency. From that moment on, she was a paper bag blown about by a storm.

The driver must have sensed her nerves. He promised he was taking her to a safe place where women would care for her. Rahima had started to cry then, her head bowed so he would not see. He drove her through a set of gates, arriving at a large building. It looked like some kind of office, one without signage or other outward clues as to what it contained. A woman had opened the front door and led her inside while the car quietly retreated.

Marjan's heart hurts to think of her teenage self standing in the vestibule of that building. She cannot recall what the woman said to her, only remembers the pounding of her heartbeat and the cackling voice in her head warning that her husband would find her no matter where she went. No matter where. What made her believe a sixteen-year-old girl could escape a man like him?

Breathe. Breathe. Breathe.

It took nearly two hours for Samia's voice to reach her. Samia came dangerously close to giving up on her newest resident that day. She had seen women in all conditions and had an arsenal of different approaches. She began with her quiet, gentle reassurances—what anyone would use with a child. Finding Rahima impossible to soothe, she became stern, commanded her to calm down. Some women responded to harsh measures, tones they were familiar with and accustomed to obeying. When that failed as well, she left the room to give Rahima space. Standing in the hallway just out of view and listening to the girl gasping for air made Samia uneasy, though.

She hurried away and returned with the shelter's doctor, who put her hands on Rahima's wrist, pressed a stethoscope to her back, and echoed Samia's commands to breathe.

It seemed Rahima had forgotten how.

Finally, Samia spoke to Rahima the way a spent mother would speak to a child who will otherwise suffer the wrath of an even angrier father—harsh but with a merciful purpose.

Calm yourself or I'll send you back out to the street! I won't have the neighborhood thinking we're torturing someone behind these walls. I've got twenty-three other women to think about. Whatever safety you need, they need as well, so stop this huffing and puffing and breathe as God has instructed you to!

In many ways, entering the women's shelter was akin to being born again. Rahima learned to breathe anew, the way a newborn adapts from fluid to air. Her movements were clumsy. Her hands trembled. She startled so easily. She would wake with scratches on her arms.

Every face was a stranger, every conversation a confrontation.

Rahima was assigned to a room with a woman in her thirties with two children, an infant and a toddler. The woman would watch Rahima suspiciously and would tug on her daughter's arm if she began to wander across the room to Rahima's side. It hurt Rahima to see the children, to hear the little girl's tiny voice and follow her waddling steps.

She kept to her bed for most of the day, her face turned toward the wall.

Samia and other staff members would, from time to time, sit with her and ask a few questions. Rahima gave very little information, which they were accustomed to, just as they were accustomed to stories that shifted with time, some points affirmed and some retracted.

Where did you say your husband lives?

What kind of business does he run?

She had given them very little the first couple of days—her name, the name of a province, and the assurance that her husband was making every effort to end her life even before she ran away.

You must not contact anyone. No one can know where you are or you'll put everyone here at risk.

Rahima had no way to contact anyone. She had no phone and no phone numbers. The only person she wanted to reach out to was her aunt, Shaima, the single thread that remained to her life before she was wed to the warlord. Khala Shaima's visits were few and far between, but her aunt had kept her from feeling entirely lost. She would arrive at the compound for those brief visits, winded and sweating, one shoulder arched higher than the other by a wayward spine. Rahima wished Khala Shaima was sitting beside her now, telling stories of her brave ancestor, a woman who had stood guard over the king's harem.

You are strong like her, Khala Shaima had told her more times than she could recall. She could hear her aunt's voice echo in her mind, clear and insistent.

"I'm not like her," Rahima whispered while the world slept. She was most awake then, in the hour of spirits. "I'm not even like you. What am I supposed to do now?"

She listened but heard no reply.

During the day, the shelter thrummed with bickering, accusations, sniffles, footsteps, and milk-hungry cries. Rahima confined herself to her bed.

Samia grew impatient. One morning, she appeared in the doorway clucking her tongue.

"Enough is enough," she declared. "Get up this instant or I'll summon all the staff to pry you out of bed."

When Rahima did not respond, she called out for three of the staff members, including the woman who mopped the floors and cleaned the bathrooms. Someone asked Samia if they were to take her to the infirmary.

Rahima had relented then. She stood up only to be brought to her knees by a wave of nausea. Her roommate's daughter looked at the small puddle of bile on the floor and began to cry. Samia stood before Rahima, lifted her chin, and searched her face for a sign. She drew back and sighed.

"Oh, pure and perfect God, was this really necessary?" she muttered, lodging a cautious complaint against a silent overseer. The air was foul, sour, which only added to Rahima's nausea. She knew she had been pregnant when she was still at her husband's home. But the night he'd summoned her to his quarters and driven his foot into her abdomen, she'd been certain he'd ended whatever had started to grow within her.

In the small medical room of the shelter, the doctor dipped a thin paper strip into a cup of Rahima's urine.

The doctor didn't need to speak. The look on her face was confirmation enough.

Rahima let out a howl that slipped under the closed door, out of the clinic, and into the street, where it caused two women to pause their steps, but only briefly. As if they had heard a car honk or a door slam.

The cry of a girl wronged by the universe was hardly remarkable.

Rahima made fists of her hands. She wasn't done escaping Abdul Khaliq, but she would do anything necessary to salvage her life.

3

AUGUST 3, 2021

Ignore the noise, Hawa tells herself. *Focus on the music.*

She tries to keep her eyes glued to the page in front of her, but the slightest motion in the hallway pulls her gaze. When she brings her attention back to the sheet of music before her, she might as well be looking at splattered ink. She has to blink twice for the dots to reappear as musical notes.

The song calls to her, begs her to listen. Hawa wishes she could do just that.

Hawa spent her first year at the music institute getting to know the rubab, learning how to organize her hands and legs around the instrument and familiarizing her fingers with the tensions of the strings. She learned how to pluck notes and speak and read in a language new to her. She cannot recall when it happened, but somewhere in her journey, the notes turned into melodies and songs in the same way that flour and water become warm bread.

She knows this part of the song well, and her fingers move without hesitation, as if she's braiding hair. The music flows for a few measures, until she remembers the news anchor's reporting last night. The Taliban had taken another province and were going from house to house searching for anyone with connections to the Afghan government or army. When they played a video clip of a man suspended in air, his body taut as four Taliban each pulled a limb and a fifth whipped his back, Hawa's mother turned the television off and told her to forget what she had just seen.

Her mother has a habit of giving instructions impossible to follow.

Don't think about it. Concentrate only on your studies. Go to sleep.

She's lost her place in the music again; her fingers have frozen.

She considers, just briefly, throwing the plectrum across the room. Instead, she curses under her breath. This is the third time she's tripped up on the same note, and she's not in a forgiving mood, especially toward herself.

She sets the rubab on the carpet and digs her elbows into her knees. When Layma notices she's stopped playing, her strumming slows and the melody peters out.

Ustad Rafiqi sits up, suddenly alert.

"Hawa, why is your instrument not in your hands?" he demands.

"I'm sorry, Ustad. I keep forgetting to play that last note open," she says.

"And?"

"And it was the wrong note," she repeats, then realizes how short she sounds with him. "I'm sorry, Ustad."

Ustad Rafiqi nods.

"You are not as nimble on the frets with this song. I did warn you, Hawa, that it's a more complicated piece but you insisted," he reminds her. "Never have I met such a stubborn . . ."

He does not finish his sentence. Seated on the floor opposite his students, he rocks back and forth until he has assumed the proper cross-legged position, his right foot tucked into the angle of his left knee. He brings his rubab into his lap, holding it the way he might have held an infant. The curved body of the instrument rests on his right thigh and the neck in his left hand. He strums a long note—*Sa*—to begin the tuning process, turning the wooden pegs with his left hand while his right hand works the strings. He plucks first the long drones, then the fan of sympathetic strings, bouncing from sympathetic to drone as he ascends the musical ladder.

Then he begins the folk song, a ballad of ruby red pomegranates and a tease of spring romance. He plays it slowly, looking from Layma to Hawa to make sure the girls are paying attention to the finger movements. He shouldn't worry. Hawa would watch him for hours if it meant the songs would spill from her instrument as they do from his.

In the middle of a playful ripple of notes, he pauses and sets his instrument down.

"Ustad, why did you stop?" Hawa blurts.

"Does it bother you that I stopped?" he asks.

"Of course!" Hawa replies. She's blinking rapidly and frowning, as she does when she grows frustrated. She can hear her mother's voice in her head.

You cannot always let people know how you feel. They can use that to hurt you.

Hawa has taken this to mean she should hide her feelings from everyone, which she does with varying success. She certainly doesn't want to seem disrespectful to Ustad Rafiqi, a teacher and an elder. He raises an eyebrow.

"You should be bothered. The only thing worse than a shoddy note is no note at all. Layma was still playing, but you made her stop as well. Do not sacrifice an entire song for one wayward note. The music you are playing is older than our years combined. It has survived wars and drought and fickle hearts. It will survive your choppy renditions as well."

"I'm sorry, Ustad. I just wanted to play it correctly," Hawa mumbles, her face hot with embarrassment she feels for having given up so easily. She hasn't been herself today.

"And you will. You have two teachers in this room, my young musicians. I am one. The song is the other. Play it again and again, and it will guide you to the right notes. There is no higher professor of music than the song itself," her teacher promises, his eyelids fluttering.

Layma's been notably cool toward Hawa since the incident, so Hawa is surprised to see Layma shoot her a knowing glance. The girls both think it's true what the other students say about Ustad Rafiqi—he is too whimsical for this world, like some part of him never bothered to grow up. They've heard classmates imitate his way of speaking, closing their eyes and invoking metaphors involving the sun and the moon while lecturing on the importance of music. Hawa is just as amused as anyone else by his quirks, but she also worries that if Ustad Rafiqi finds out about the teasing, he will become a flattened version of himself.

"And so. Unfurl your fist and make sure you haven't crushed your shahbaz. Let's take the song from the beginning," he instructs them.

Hawa opens her palm to find three red indentations, marks from the edges of her plectrum. She and Layma begin to play the song. When Hawa reaches the same troublesome part, she focuses all her energies on the music.

Get it right, she tells herself. She opens and closes her fingers to shake the tension from her hand.

The second she realizes she's made it through without butchering the run, she's lost again. She can't seem to concentrate today and isn't sure why. Layma, two years older than Hawa, gives her an encouraging nod, and Hawa feels something loosen in her chest. Maybe Layma's not so mad anymore? Layma has been gracious about Hawa surpassing her in musical prowess, even though she's been playing the rubab two years longer than Hawa. The tension between them is new, and Hawa hates it.

Hawa returns to the song but looks up just long enough to see Ustad Rafiqi strum invisible strings with his thumb and right index finger, playing the song without the instrument. The melody twirls. It sounds like a ring of cheerful schoolgirls.

Hawa nails the note that tripped her up just a few moments ago but feels no relief. She wonders where she'll trip up next and questions the position of her fingers on the fret. She pushes to get to the end of the piece, but it's a bumpy ride. She's surely bruised these pomegranates along the way.

After the last note, Ustad Rafiqi appears pensive.

"Good, both of you. A bit more practice for fluidity. Layma, watch your tempo. You sometimes get ahead of yourself. And, Hawa," he says. Hawa looks up. "Better. Control your temper. Do not give up. Remember, this song is new to you. You need to spend time with it."

In the courtyard of the school, Layma bends down to tie her laces, and Hawa notices her sneakers.

"Those shoes look so good on you!" Hawa says.

Layma's sneakers are a pale blue with a thick white sole. She switches feet to retie her left laces, and Hawa spots the embroidered heart on the side of her sneaker. Her own feet inch toward each other, trying to tuck themselves out of view. Hawa's mother has promised her new shoes for two months now, but they cannot seem to afford shoes, even though Hawa's mother spends most of her time working. If her job isn't paying her, Hawa thinks, why does her mother continue to go? But of course her mother goes. She's always found work to be more compelling than time with Hawa. They've spent so much of Hawa's life apart that she's always somewhat surprised when her mother is around.

Layma responds but mostly avoids Hawa's gaze.

"My father just bought them for me. He told me I have to make sure my feet don't grow anymore because he won't be able to spend this much on shoes again," she says dryly. She has the cool demeanor of a teenager, someone with one foot in the world of adults.

"Do you want to eat lunch?" Hawa asks, and braces herself for what Layma might say next. There was a time when she didn't have to ask, when she and Layma would exit class and walk toward the cafeteria together. Hawa reminded Layma of her younger sister, she had said, and Hawa liked the idea of having a sibling, especially an older sister.

"I'm not really hungry," Layma says.

Hawa isn't hungry either. Her nerves are too rattled to have an appetite or to sit on what she's been wanting to ask Layma. She's not been the same since the video they made circulated.

"Are you very mad at me?"

"Mad at you?" Layma seems surprised at Hawa's question. "Why would you think I'm mad at you?"

"Because . . . you've not been talking with me much. I only see you in class and even there you don't say anything past salaam."

"I'm not mad at you. I've just been . . . thinking," she says, but this makes no sense to Hawa. Is she thinking so much that she can't look Hawa in the eye or have a conversation with her?

Behind Layma, a group of girls are playing a game of chase. On the other side of the field, boys are kicking a soccer ball into a goal marked by two cones. There are shouts and a dull thud as a foot connects with the ball. It was on this field that Hawa first met Layma, who noticed her standing against a wall and taking in the school grounds. Layma, dressed in the school uniform—a slate gray tunic and pants—wore her chestnut hair drawn back into a ponytail. Tiny wisps curled around her temples and the dainty dimples in her cheeks when she smiled. She looked like a perfect girl from a perfect family, the kind who would want nothing to do with a child from the orphanage.

Would you like me to show you around? she had offered, much to Hawa's surprise. She'd nodded, and Layma showed her the different parts of campus—the auditorium, the cafeteria, the classrooms, and the rehearsal rooms. She had pointed out the tabla instructor and warned Hawa that the mathematics teacher was the toughest at the school.

Layma thinks that Hawa chose the rubab because of her, but that's only partly true. Hawa first saw the rubab when Layma took her into the practice room and played a few notes on the instrument she was learning. To Hawa, it was the most honest, earnest sound she'd ever heard, a story from which she could not turn away. She became Layma's classmate.

"So you're not mad," Hawa repeats, feeling relieved. She was certain she had spoiled this precious friendship, the one that bordered on having an actual sister, like just about everyone else. Layma sits on the grass, her clasped hands hooked around her right knee. Hawa sits beside her, close enough for their shoulders to touch.

"It wasn't your fault, Hawa. I've already told you that."

"Yes, but I didn't believe you."

"Why wouldn't you believe me?"

Hawa blinks instead of admitting to her friend that she finds it hard to believe anyone. People speak so many untruths that she finds it prudent to be skeptical.

"Do you believe what the principal said this morning?" Hawa asks. The principal spent time during the morning announcements reassuring the children that despite the unrest in far parts of the country, Kabul would be safe from the militants.

Layma's eyes are fixed on the game of chase.

"Not at all. I've already told you. My father says there will be trouble if the Taliban become part of the government. But he also said there will be more trouble if they do not."

Hawa was once confused by this idea, but she understood it better after watching the neighborhood boys play soccer on a small patch of grass, which their apartment window overlooks. One boy, Nadir, went too far in his pushing and shoving and knocked a teammate's tooth out. The boys refused to let him join in after that, which worked until Nadir ran off with their ball and spoiled their fun completely. A week later, he was back in the games, pushing and shoving his way around the field.

"Do you regret the video?"

Layma scoffs. "The video wasn't the problem."

When the Ministry of Education announced that girls over twelve would no longer be allowed to sing at public events, the school's principal had organized a campaign of protest. Under the hashtag #IAmMySong, they posted videos of girls singing. Their voices were their defiance. Hawa had walked by a classroom where two girls were recording a video. She'd pulled Layma in to join her, because since that first day on the campus of the music institute, she had always felt her confidence buoyed by Layma's presence.

They made at least a dozen attempts, half of which ended with the girls in fits of giggles. They would clear their throats and start fresh, and finally created a thirty-second clip of a peppy, insistent song.

We are girls.

We are signs of spring, tall trees in the sunlight.

We turn stones into stars.

"You always forget that I'm older than you and that I make my own decisions," Layma chides. Her family had been supportive at first, but then the comments started coming in. "I'm glad we made the video. But my mother has given strict instructions to everyone in the family not to let me near a phone. As if I would want to post my face online again."

"My mother's still angry too," Hawa shares. "I didn't think so many people would be interested in watching a video of girls singing. And besides Sohaila, none of us even have a good voice."

Layma laughs.

"My father says people cannot resist a scandal. Imagine that. It's a scandal for a handful of girls to sing a song," she says. "What would they do if they saw the way Fatima dances?"

Hawa smiles thinking of the way Fatima mimics Bollywood dancers, batting her eyelashes and cocking her head to the side coyly.

The video had been seen by a few people and then hundreds. By the following day, it was being reshared by people outside the country, and other women were posting videos of themselves singing and using the same hashtag. The girls of the music institute had made enough noise that the ministry announced it was going to rescind its decision. Hawa felt powerful, like a strong politician or a movie star. Or a soldier.

Her defiance and short-lived fame did not impress her mother, though.

How could you be so reckless? she had yelled. She'd been on her phone, tapping and scrolling furiously, searching for ways to erase the video from existence, but it was too late. Even if the original clip had been taken down, it had been shared and reshared so many times that she would have had better luck ridding the streets of litter. She'd slid from anger into silent tears. Hawa had spent the day in her room feigning sleep and wishing her mother weren't so meek.

A soccer ball heads straight toward the girls. Hawa and Layma pitch their torsos in opposite directions and cover their heads with their hands.

"Basheer!" Layma screams when the ball lands just inches from her. "You play as if you're blindfolded!"

Basheer, the school's most gifted tabla player, shouts an apology. Another classmate claps him on the back. The girls cannot hear the teasing but watch the boys burst into laughter.

"If these sneakers weren't new . . ." Layma mutters, and Hawa feels her face relax into a smile.

Hawa has lived in an orphanage, away from her mother. She has also lived in three different homes with her mother, who, at work, is surrounded by soldiers. And yet, she has never felt as safe as she does here, behind the high walls that guard the music students from street view, inside the enormous building with its warren of classrooms, and among the teachers who speak in a language Hawa did not know existed until only two years ago.

She wonders how much more she can learn before she graduates from this institute. Will she rise like Rona, from playing a violin to holding a baton and conducting the orchestra? Will she play on grander stages than the one in their auditorium and hear the applause of a real audience?

Hawa hasn't even tried to imagine graduating from this institute, because this school is like a dream she does not want to end. She wonders if Layma feels the same, if she worries about what her life will be like when she is handed her diploma.

She opens her mouth to ask her friend about her distant tomorrows but her question is swallowed by a resounding boom. The school grounds shake. Hawa's classmates have become still on the field, resembling pawns on a chessboard. They are children, trained not only to recognize sharps and flats and chords but also to recognize the roar of a bomb and the rattle of gunfire, a refrain that sends them running into their sacred school for cover.

4

2010

If Rahima could have reached into her own body and clawed out the growing mass, she would have.

She curled into herself for a full week. Samia, softened by the news, let her be. When alone, Rahima would pound her fists against the small mound of her belly. The world expects women—even girls—to crave motherhood no matter the circumstances.

The son Rahima had lost, little Jahangir, appeared in her dreams, writhing with pain and fever. Calling her name. She tried to speak to him, to comfort him, but her words were locked in her throat. She'd thought she would not survive bringing him into this world. And though she breathed and walked, she wasn't sure she had survived outliving her son. She felt distinctly dead inside.

Lying supine, staring at a water stain on the tiled ceiling, Rahima felt the full weight of all she did not know. Her body was a mystery to her. She did not know if her parents, her sisters, or her sickly aunt were alive. She did not know how long she would be allowed to stay at the shelter or where she would go if she left. How long might she last as a beggar on the street, a ghost with a bundled child on her lap and an outstretched hand?

She existed on bits of bread and sips of tea. She was nauseated often. Her roommate must have complained, because she woke one afternoon to see the woman retrieving her daughter's doll from under the bed. All their other belongings were already gone, moved to a less offensive room.

The staff checked on Rahima, even the stocky woman who had cleaned up her first pool of vomit. Samia began insisting that Rahima join the other women of the shelter for at least one meal a day and forced her to bathe. She appeared one morning with a cup of sweetened tea and some clothes.

"These should fit you. You'll need to get out of what you're wearing and wash them. Hygiene is important."

"Please just leave me be," Rahima groaned. "I don't feel well."

She felt both cocooned and suffocated by the small room.

"Little sister, this is neither a hospital nor a palace. We are not your mother or your nurses or your maids. Time to rise and tend to yourself. Wake up. If you keep your eyes closed, you'll see nothing but darkness."

In Abdul Khaliq's home, little Jahangir had been Rahima's only source of light. She could still feel his small hands on her cheek, the gentle breeze of his breath on her neck, the twinkling smiles he saved for her alone. She resented anyone or anything trying to take his place.

That was the easier explanation for her despair, one she could use to self-soothe.

But there was more. This pregnancy felt like Abdul Khaliq's hands reaching across an impossible distance, his fingers curling around Rahima's neck and his breath in her ear. She said nothing of her condition to any of the women, but there were few secrets in the shelter and it was cheap therapy to ruminate on someone else's misery. She was certain the other women in the shelter could sense the resentment in her, that they could see what kind of monstrosity she was.

Rahima shuffled to the bathroom to relieve herself, hobbling as if her ankles were shackled.

Two weeks into her stay, Samia drew a red line.

"I've called the woman who begged me to take you in and told her I would accept no other referrals from her," she said.

Rahima squeezed her eyes shut, tried to drive Samia's voice away.

"She told me you were a lion of a girl," Samia remonstrated. Then she crouched to be close enough to Rahima that she could whisper and still be heard. "Where is that lion? Have you let this sorry jungle tame you already?

Do you think you are the first girl to have lived this life? Hardly. But you are one of the few to have a chance like this, to be in a place like this. Don't squander it."

To Rahima, it sounded as if her aunt was speaking through this woman, reminding her of the women who had suffered and endured before her. She could almost hear the wheeze of her aunt's uneasy breathing.

"Get up, wash your face, and be ready. We're going for a walk," Samia commanded, her words sharp as a blade.

Rahima obeyed.

When Samia threw a chadori over her, Rahima's heart began to pound. The rules of the shelter had been made clear on the first day, and one of those rules was that no one was permitted to leave. There was no such thing as a stroll into town. But Samia led her past the gate and into the narrow streets.

"Where are you taking me?" Rahima asked. Was Samia kicking her out? She wanted to apologize, to promise to be better.

They moved through small streets, passing by a government building. Rahima thought of the women she had met sitting in the Parliament building not far from here. The world was so much bigger than her husband's compound, she had learned. Some of the people she met were good, and some were corrupt. Some were a bit of both.

And now, untethered from her husband and having thrust herself into the immensity of this universe, Rahima felt quite small. She told herself to find comfort in that feeling. The smaller she was, the easier it would be to hide from Abdul Khaliq. She needed to be little more than a speck. Invisible. She was grateful for the privacy the chadori offered her.

Rahima caught flashes of color through the mesh of her chadori, the yellow of taxis and a street cart piled high with red tomatoes, emerald green cucumbers, and bulbous purple eggplants. When they came upon the Kabul River, a trough running through the city, they followed its path.

Samia stopped at a place Rahima had never seen. Looming brick columns framed teal gates. Rahima read the sign with wonder. Samia had brought her to, of all places, the zoo.

"Have you been here before?" she asked.

"Of course not," Rahima said. She could have laughed. Did Samia think she had run from a life spent in parks and gardens?

Rahima may not have been familiar with the zoo, but plenty of other young families and clusters of men were strolling through the grounds. She spotted a group of boys standing in front of a rectangular plinth with a bronze statue of a lion. The beast was resting on its side, his head straight and eyes fixed on the trickle of new visitors coming through the entrance.

One little boy stood before the plinth on his toes, his fingertips just barely reaching the lion's mane. When he reached out to pet the statue, his friend standing behind him let out an explosive roar in his ear. The startled boy nearly fell over, which had the other boys with them doubled over with laughter.

"Wait till I get you . . ." the boy cried out, giving chase and abandoning the statue.

"Do you know the story of Marjan?" Samia asked.

Rahima shook her head.

"Marjan came to this zoo in 1978. Chucha, a lioness, joined him shortly afterward. There was a coup that year, which was the beginning of so much fighting. No one was paying attention to the zoo when the country was busy defending itself from Russians first, then fighting each other once the Russians left. In all those years of war, the animals here suffered, even Marjan. Their only saviors were the people who had worked for the zoo, people like my uncle, who risked their own lives to care for these beasts, even after their salaries stopped. My uncle would gather from the markets what butchers and vendors could not sell. He kept Marjan and Chucha and all these animals alive, barely."

Rahima stared directly into the dark hollows of Marjan's eyes as Samia spoke.

"Things were ugly during the civil war. Anyone who could, left. This zoo fell right on the frontlines. When one group took control of these streets, their warriors ravaged the zoo. They killed some of the animals and roasted them over open fires. My uncle thought of these creatures as his children. He nearly lost his mind then."

"Was Marjan killed by a rocket?" Rahima asked. The story had piqued her curiosity. Stories always had, she realized, thinking of the ancestral tales her aunt Shaima would tell her.

"No, Marjan survived, but he suffered at the hands of an idiot. In the nineties, a guerilla fighter wanted to prove his bravery, so he went into their den and touched Chucha. The fool had forgotten that lions are territorial and even more proud than Afghans. Marjan killed him. The fool's brother returned the next day, hungry for revenge, and threw a hand grenade into the enclosure. It exploded in Marjan's face, blinding him in one eye. A few keepers did what they could to stop the bleeding, to bandage his wounds. My uncle held his mangled face in his hands and cried into his fur. He thought he would lose his beloved lion then."

Rahima did not want to hear any more about Marjan. It became even harder to breathe under the chadori. Samia must have sensed she was losing her audience, because she quickened the pace of her story.

"But Marjan survived with only one eye and saw the Taliban take Kabul in 1996. When some Taliban fighters visited the zoo, they launched stones at Marjan. My uncle stepped in again and reminded them that our beloved prophet respected animals."

"What a dismal life," Rahima said, thinking both of the lion as well as Samia's tenderhearted uncle.

"Dismal, yes. But Marjan became a legend. This beast survived a coup, a Russian invasion, and bombings from the mujahideen, the Taliban, and the United States. This lion came to represent our struggle, our survival."

Rahima did not feel like she was surviving. The word was a poor fit for her condition, but she could not yet envision herself in any better condition.

"What became of him?" she asked.

"Ah, good question. Marjan died of old age one night. My uncle and six other men laid him to rest with the dignity of an elder. Hundreds came for his funeral. Can you imagine such a thing?"

Rahima, who had seen stray dogs kicked in the street and songbirds in cages, could not imagine such ceremony for a lion.

"Some who suffer inspire pity. Others simply inspire," Samia said. "If it's pity you're after, good luck finding much in the shelter. No one comes to us because they've had it easy. Some stay a short spell and some stay longer. Everyone leaves eventually. So think carefully about what you make of your time here. How do you want to leave this place? Do you want to be stronger, prepared to be your own provider? Or do you want to become one of the women you see begging on the street with a drugged baby beside her?"

Rahima felt a wave of nausea rising in her. She willed it away. It would be disastrous to vomit under the tent of the chadori.

Samia mistook her silence for contemplation. She turned to face Rahima directly.

"You are young. There is much fire in your eyes."

Rahima could tell Samia meant well, but she was simply tired of listening to the woman talk. And the only fire in Rahima was the one burning in her esophagus. Samia probably gave the same rehearsed speech to all the women who arrived at the shelter's doorstep.

Rahima could bear it no longer.

"Help me get rid of this," she pleaded. "There must be a doctor or someone who can help."

Samia was silent for a beat, her expression flat.

"Is that what you really want?"

Rahima nodded.

Samia chewed her lip. "It's not legal, you know. Unless your life is in danger."

"I would not be in the shelter if my life were not in danger," Rahima replied.

"That kind of danger doesn't count." Samia sighed. She stared at the bustle of traffic in the street before turning back to Rahima. "Let me talk to someone I know."

Rahima nodded with measured gratitude.

"I think it's time to go, Marjan," Samia said, then caught herself. "Goodness, so much talk about Marjan, I've called you by his name. Let's get back. Please don't breathe a word about this to anyone."

Rahima felt Marjan's eyes on her back as they left. She stole one more glance over her shoulder but could hardly see the zoo's entrance, her vision limited by the blue mesh. Two steps more and she mistook the backfire of an engine for the sound of a detonation and nearly tripped over her own feet.

5

AUGUST 3, 2021

"Where is she?" Marjan calls out before she's even fully opened the door to her apartment.

"She's resting. She's fine," Ingrid assures her. "And you? You weren't answering your phone but it appears you're alive and well too."

"Alive, yes," Marjan replies as she relieves her shoulder of the weight of her bag. The black backpack lands with a thud in the corner of the room, onto the unraveling fringe of a rug. Ingrid doesn't bother getting up from the makeshift office she has set up in Marjan's living room. She remains reclined against the overstuffed cushion against the wall, her laptop open and a cup of tea perched dangerously close to the keyboard.

"The blast was close to the school but not that close. Thankfully."

"Thankfully," Marjan murmurs. To be thankful for a bomb falling on a street corner instead of a music school has to be a new spiritual low, but she keeps this thought to herself.

On the television screen, a man and a woman sit stiff-backed and perfectly made-up behind a news desk. They speak with the distinct inflections of newscasters—the steady tempo, the practiced lift and fall and pauses. The melody is the same, but the lyrics change each day. Ingrid lowers the volume.

"Anything you care to share?" Ingrid asks, uncrossing her legs. Her hair is pulled into a messy knot, speared by a pencil, and her button-down shirt has a web of creases, evidence that she's been restless despite her loose clothing.

Marjan shakes her head. Ingrid knows better than to ask again. Her Afghan friend is tight-lipped about what happens on the platoon's missions. She's even more tight-lipped about her life before she donned a military uniform.

"You could have sent a message. I hate wondering if I'm going to spot your face in the wrong place." Ingrid waves a disgruntled hand in the direction of the television.

"I texted you after the bombing."

"Yes, but it's been a few hours since then. I heard there was more gunfire."

"Ingrid, if I die, I promise you'll be the first person I'll call," Marjan vows.

Ingrid doesn't laugh. She has a right to be peeved, but Ingrid also knows Marjan would have called if she could have.

"This is dead," Marjan says, pulling her phone out of her pocket and setting it on the table. She's been meaning to buy a new battery but had faith that this one would last at least another month. By then, her paycheck would come through, and she could feel a bit more comfortable spending on something besides food and rent. Her rare show of optimism hadn't served her well.

"The guy I know will give you a good deal on a new one," Ingrid says. "Let me know when you want to stop by his shop. Lucky for you, I'm willing to stay here with Hawa while you get this fixed."

"I am lucky," Marjan confirms, her way of expressing gratitude to Ingrid. It's because of Ingrid that she can leave this apartment on a Monday and return on a Tuesday without worrying too much about leaving Hawa. "How is she?"

Ingrid steals a glance at the closed door behind her. She shrugs. Marjan crosses the room and stands beside the door, listening for the sound of stirring within. It is six o'clock in the evening, far too early for Hawa to be sleeping. She reaches for the doorknob.

"She's okay," Ingrid says. "She's got her period again. I don't think she slept much last night, so I've let her be."

Ingrid, despite herself, has superb maternal instincts. Then again, her instincts around all kinds of people have allowed her to continue to walk straight in a city that tilts and swerves under the feet of its inhabitants. Two years ago, when her organization's programs finally found a rhythm in this country, her bosses had wanted to pull her out of Kabul. She had refused, stating she wanted to see a bit more progress before she could entrust the program to someone who would have to begin from zero, acclimating to Kabul's bureaucratic trapdoors and hidden passageways.

Marjan was relieved. She wouldn't know what to do without Ingrid.

Marjan presses her ear to the bedroom door. She opens it slowly, not wanting to wake Hawa but also hungry for a glimpse of her daughter. She sees only the gentle curve of her back, like a river stone, and the spill of dark hair on a pale yellow pillow. Marjan cannot resist touching the end of a strand and hears her daughter's soft exhale. She is struck yet again that there was a time when this girl's head would fit in the palm of her hand. When she could carry the sum of her in her arms.

Marjan recalls a verse from Kahlil Gibran. *Between what is said and not meant, and what is meant but not said, much love is lost.* It makes perfect sense to her, and yet she knows that if she were to try to explain it to her daughter, she would do nothing but muddle the meaning.

Through the thin cotton of Hawa's pajamas, Marjan traces lines on her daughter's back. M-A-D-A-R and H-A-W-A. Hawa stiffens. Her sleep is featherlight, and Marjan chides herself for ignoring this. Motherhood is but a series of mistakes.

"Were you spelling something on my back?"

"I didn't mean to wake you," Marjan replies. Hawa sits upright.

"You're back," she observes.

"I am," Marjan replies. She tries to read her daughter's expression, but Hawa moves her head by degrees and lets her hair hide her face. "How are you, sweet girl? I missed you."

"Fine."

"Were you scared today?"

Hawa frowns.

"Of course not. The explosion wasn't even that close."

Marjan winces at this, at how accustomed her daughter has become to bombings. When did that happen? Was it after the sixth or seventh bombing in Kabul this year? Was it after the one that detonated by the hospital or by the university?

Had it not been for the message from the school that all students were safe and unharmed by the bomb outside the defense minister's home, Marjan would have run straight there.

She's okay for now. It's best to wait, Forozan had cautioned. Marjan wanted to snap back that Forozan wasn't a mother and should refrain from offering advice. But she also knew Forozan was right. The streets would be dense with rescue efforts and redirected traffic. She decided to take the school's advice and allow the dust to settle.

Marjan puts an arm around her daughter and is relieved Hawa doesn't pull away. She is soft with slumber and lets her slim frame fall against her mother's chest.

"Where were you today?" Hawa asks, her question a test.

"I was at the base," Marjan says, choosing her words carefully. "I came from there only a few moments ago."

"Are the soldiers preparing for a battle?" Hawa asks.

"They are," Marjan says because she wants her daughter to feel safer. She wishes Hawa had seen the base back when it was alive with training exercises. She would have preferred fast roping and ruck marching to looking at pictures of Taliban fighters parading through cities on the other side of the mountains. Last month, an Afghan commander reported to Bagram Air Base, only to find the electricity off and the Americans gone without so much as a farewell.

Before you know it, we'll see the flea-bitten, lice-infested Taliban taking up seats in the Parliament, Zarifa had predicted. She speaks with confidence Marjan envies. Marjan knows she's right too. She has no faith that the government will protect her platoon.

"Some. But mostly going over supplies and reviewing reports."

Marjan has always struggled to balance protecting and preparing

Hawa. But seeing Hawa thrive among the children in the music school, seeing her make music at this young age has made Marjan hope that maybe Hawa doesn't have to be so prepared for terrible things.

"You think I'm too young to understand, but I'm eleven, Madar-jan. Do you know plenty of people would consider me an adult?"

Marjan feels a stab in her chest, thinking of herself at Marjan's age, when her name was Rahima. She was hardly two years older than her daughter is now when she was dragged from her parents' home and into the high-walled compound of a man old enough to be her father, a man with three wives and a brood of children, some close to her in age.

She knows all too well how willing some people are to pluck unripe fruit from a tree. Somehow, she survived those nights pressed under a warlord, but she will die before she lets anyone think Hawa is old enough for such misery.

Then again, maybe this is the moment she should tell Hawa about those punishing years. Maybe it would help Hawa understand her mother better.

Marjan had crafted what she thought was the simplest story for her daughter. She told Hawa that, far from Kabul, she had been married young and into a family that spoke with fists and lashes. When her husband suddenly died from an illness, the family wanted to marry her to one of her husband's brothers. Marjan realized she was carrying Hawa only after she had run away.

So they do not know about me?

No. And if they knew, they could try to take you. They would have the right.

What about your family? Why did they not help you?

They could not. They were very poor. In health and in finances.

Do you ever speak to them?

No, we lost touch.

And my father. Was he a terrible person as well?

Many people respected him, Marjan had said. She sensed that answering this question truthfully might make her daughter want to excise some part of herself, and she knew there was nothing worse than feeling damaged. *Hawa, janem, it's not helpful to think about what's behind us. We need to keep our eyes on the path ahead.*

She has tried so hard, at work and at home, to give Hawa everything she deserves.

"Madar? Are you really going to tell me nothing?" Hawa's voice cuts through Marjan's thoughts. The past two days have caught up with her. She's exhausted, her throat dry.

"I'm going to wash up, then I'll start cooking. Ingrid said you have your illness. Is it bothering you?"

Hawa recoils at the question. This is only her second time bleeding. Her first blood came three months ago and took both mother and daughter by surprise. Marjan realized too late that she hadn't prepared her daughter, just as her mother hadn't prepared her. She didn't think she would repeat the mistakes her mother had made, but here she is, tripping on the same stones.

Hawa pulls her knees up to her chest and looks away. Her neck flushes with discomfort.

"I'm fine," she says.

"I'm glad to hear it. Get some rest," Marjan says gently, and retreats before she can say anything else she'll regret.

In the living room, Ingrid shoots her a knowing look. She has already gathered her computer and her papers. She bends down to retrieve her mug as well.

"You're leaving? I'll make dinner soon," Marjan offers, though Ingrid hardly ever seems hungry. She lives off instant coffee and foods that come in crinkly foil bags. To Marjan's knowledge, she's never cooked anything more than an egg.

"Perhaps you've forgotten, Marjan, but I'm paying rent for a lovely little apartment just down the hall," Ingrid teases.

"Thank you for staying with her," Marjan says. Her words feel inadequate. Ingrid squeezes her arm, returns the mug to the kitchen counter, and opens the door.

"It's none of my business, Marjan," she says. She has one foot in the hallway when she comes back in. "But when I was Hawa's age, I told my mother school was a waste of time. I was convinced I could teach myself more by reading magazines. My mother was so frustrated with me. I wouldn't listen to a word she said, and she thought the only answer was to send me somewhere to fix my behavior."

"Like Afghanistan?"

Ingrid laughs. "Like boarding school. But maybe Afghanistan would have been a better choice. Maybe I've sent myself here to fix what's broken in me. I mean, we're all a little broken inside, aren't we?"

Marjan smiles wanly and closes the door behind her friend. She retreats to the bathroom and removes her clothing, one piece at a time, letting the garments form a small heap on the floor. She looks at her body, at what she hides from the world and her daughter. Her slim frame deceives. The trainings at Camp Scorpion have made her limbs stronger than they appear.

Blisters and wounds have left darkened dots and dashes on her feet, her arms, her torso. If she allows herself, she can feel a dull ache in her leg; her bones hold her story too. Inches below her navel, a horizontal line of raised skin bisects her into before and after. Here and there. Hurt and healed.

Marjan wishes she could show her daughter her strength without revealing her scars, but separating one from the other would be like trying to collect plain water from steeped tea. She cannot blame Hawa for keeping her at arm's length. Marjan told herself that it was necessary and temporary for Hawa to stay among orphans and other children whose families could not provide for them. She would be happy with the colorful toys and the carefully arranged cots. She would sleep so well that she wouldn't cry at night.

Marjan has told herself a thousand lies and told her daughter a thousand and one. She showers and then retrieves her duffel bag from the bedroom and goes through the small bundle of documents for the thousandth time. The contents haven't changed. She still does not have passports. She thinks of the hours she spent last week standing amid the crush of people at the passport office, only to be told that she cannot obtain a passport for Hawa without a tazkera. And to obtain a tazkera for Hawa, Marjan will have to present a birth certificate or two witnesses and the father's consent. Marjan had declined a birth certificate when Hawa was born.

Birth certificates intentionally did not bear a mother's name until only a year ago, and many still grumbled about the impropriety of seeing a woman's given name on an official document. They seemed to fear that merely by knowing a woman's name, a stranger would be able to conjure her body, envision her hair, her hips, and everything in between.

Only fathers were named on birth certificates when Hawa was born, and Marjan would not list Abdul Khaliq. She would have had to make up a name, and at the time, that felt like it would bring her only more trouble. She didn't want to be tied to any man, real or imaginary.

A passport now seems impossible, and yet without one she and Hawa are left with the worst kinds of options. Hiding in flour sacks in the back of a truck. Trusting their lives to human smugglers. Looking for holes in guarded borders.

Marjan seethes. Without a man to validate her existence, she is a shadow and so is her daughter.

And that's when she hears it. One voice, at first. She is still. It is late and the city is tense. Maybe she was mistaken.

Then a second call erupts and a third. Marjan feels a tingle on the nape of her neck. Something is happening. She turns off her living room light and steps into the warm night air on her balcony.

Allahu Akbar! Allahu Akbar!

"God is great," the voices call, multiplying with every repetition. The Taliban have usurped the phrase, manipulated the devotion into a battle cry.

Allahu Akbar!

Marjan's hands grip the balcony railing. Across the way, others are gathered on their balconies as well, birds perched on branches. She looks down and sees, down the street, a swell of people. She stares hard, unnerved by the sight. But as they approach, she realizes this is no ragged bunch of militants. These are people, mostly men, but women too. Fists in the air, eyes to the sky, they are marching and chanting. The people on the balconies, the people on rooftops have joined their chant. A woman waves a flag, the red, black, and green stripes rippling in the night.

Allahu Akbar!

An impromptu orchestra sings a plangent harmony, a defiant melody.

Marjan squeezes the railing. Hawa has joined her on the balcony, unsure what's happening.

"What's happening, Madar-jan?"

Marjan looks at her daughter's face. She tries not to see her husband in the shape of Hawa's eyes, the color of her hair, but his genes seem to be pushing harder and harder to stake his claim over her young body, her rosebud life.

Allahu Akbar, her husband had said when their son was born.

"Allahu Akbar!" she shouts into the night. Hawa looks up at her, astonished. Who is this woman beside her? Her mother takes a deep breath and once again bellows: "Allahu Akbar!"

Marjan's voice grows, taking on a bold and defiant timbre as she harmonizes with a city determined to reclaim the beloved, a city that is more than a little broken inside.

Marjan feels her daughter's shoulder touch her side. She sings for the both of them, willing her voice to reach the stubborn stars.

6

AUGUST 4, 2021
METRA MEDIA

From his place in the shadows, the producer adjusts his earpiece. The lighting, the sound, the camera—all are in position to capture Mina Noori's every word. He signals the cameraman, who nods in reply.

The music is mechanical, with a hint of urgency. The program begins as it always does, with a twenty-second spin through images of women in various corners of Afghanistan: a women's handicraft market in the north, three female cyclists on an isolated road, a classroom full of schoolgirls, and a female member of Parliament standing behind a podium. The music fades, and there is one final transition to a solitary figure sitting behind a paneled wooden desk, her legs hidden from view, her eyes stealing one last look at the papers in her hands. She is wearing a burgundy dress with cuffs of embroidered trim. She is immaculately presented, from her blush-colored headscarf to her mauve lipstick, to her expertly shaped brows.

"Esteemed viewers, welcome again to tonight's program, where we bring you news from around the country and beyond. I am your host, Mina Noori of Metra Media.

"Two days ago, President Ashraf Ghani acknowledged that the

departure of international forces that had begun in May has sparked renewed Taliban offensives, with large swathes of territory falling to the insurgent group. In his address to a special joint session of Parliament, he announced he had directed the ANSF to implement a military strategy that would achieve stability within six months.

"Last night, the people of Kabul took to their balconies and rooftops and to the city streets in the hundreds to thousands for a collective chant of 'Allahu Akbar.' Many said they wanted to send a message to the Taliban that they do not have an exclusive claim to God. One man carrying the tricolor flag past shops and restaurants told us tonight's chants were also meant to show the popular support for the Afghan National Security Forces and to boost morale as they battle to win back insurgent-claimed areas and to defend vulnerable territories from Taliban incursions. Similar demonstrations have occurred in Nangarhar, Khost, Kunar, and Bamiyan provinces, with images flooding social media and inspiring other regions to join. In some areas, volunteer militias have formed, with people taking up arms to help the ANSF push back against Taliban advances."

Mina Noori looks directly into the camera, her shoulders pulled back and her voice steady despite the grim announcements she is sharing. The screen splits then, and Mina Noori shares the square with another woman who is joining the conversation from what looks to be an office. There are books and a framed Afghan flag on the shelves behind her.

"My guest tonight is Latifa Hamdard, a senior spokesperson from the office of the president. Miss Hamdard, thank you for joining the program tonight. The Afghanistan Women's Chamber of Commerce and Industry recently conducted large-scale surveys of women-led entrepreneurship. As we continue to hear of regions being taken by the Taliban, what are your top concerns for these women in business?"

Latifa Hamdard clears her throat and adjusts her posture. She has positioned a ring light behind her computer's camera to make up for the paucity of light in the room. Latifa does not share Mina's love for the camera. Maybe because the camera is not as gracious to her as it is to her host. She was assigned this program instead of her superior, a man who felt Latifa would do a better job conveying the message to Mina Noori. She doesn't have time to regret agreeing to come on the program, because Mina's viewers are waiting on her to answer the host's question.

"We conducted a survey this year. We have over seventeen thousand women-owned businesses. These businesses employ over a hundred thousand people, mostly women, and make a significant contribution to the national economy. Clearly, the offensives launched by the Taliban are disrupting local businesses, but we remain confident that our Afghan National Security Forces will restore order to those areas. It is our priority that women are not deprived of opportunities to earn a living for themselves and their families. This is a matter of importance to our national economy, not just individual households."

Mina nods in that way she does before she gets to the heart of the matter. And she always cuts to the heart of the matter. Her viewers, mostly women but also growing numbers of men, tune in for this precision, this refusal to waste anyone's time with obvious talking points or pleasantries.

"Miss Hamdard, many women used their own savings to launch their businesses. Some received grants from international donors, programs managed by major entities like the World Bank. These may be microloans, but cumulatively these are sizeable funds. Now it seems we may be facing a Taliban integration with our government. How confident are you that the president will not compromise on promises made to women? How secure should these women entrepreneurs feel?"

Miss Hamdard blinks rapidly. She curses the man who put her in this position. She wants to scream to Mina the truth she knows in her heart. Instead she pinches the flesh of her thigh with two fingers, punishment for the false hope she gives Mina's viewers, for the cover she provides for her superiors.

"The women of Afghanistan should know that their economic well-being is nonnegotiable," she says, and waits for Mina's next question.

"And what of their rights? Many believe that we will see a hybrid government in the near future, with Taliban integrated into our ministries, our

Parliament. How will this administration ensure that women's rights are maintained in such an arrangement?"

Latifa recalls entering her supervisor's office yesterday, noting that the small square frames holding pictures of his family had gone missing. On his chair was the open mouth of his leather bag, filled with manila folders and the small green wallet that held his travel documents. He wasn't the only one with a bag packed. But if word were to get out that the Taliban had the government on the run, what would that do to the city? To the nation?

She thinks of her two children. Her son has a mind for numbers and begged her for a computer he could take apart and put back together. Her daughter is about to enter high school and already dreams of attending law school. She faces Mina and swallows hard.

"As you know, we are not the same country that we were in the nineties. We are not a country divided by civil war. The Taliban must understand that this is a new century, an egalitarian era. As women, we will accept nothing less than the rights enshrined in our constitution," Latifa vows to the blinding light, to the unblinking eye of the camera, to her daughter listening intently at home.

7

2010

"Good morning, little sister." This is what Samia had taken to calling Rahima. If she had intended to disarm the pregnant teenager, her strategy worked. Rahima was finding it impossible to remain stoic and silent around Samia.

"From now on, call me Marjan," Rahima announced.

Samia was seated at her desk, an invoice in one hand and the fingers of her other hand poised over a calculator.

"Did you say you want to be called Marjan?"

Rahima nodded. "I cannot keep my name. It's too dangerous."

"I see," Samia said, nodding. "And why is that?"

Rahima takes a deep breath. She has rehearsed her answer in her mind, preparing for this moment.

"My father gave me to a very powerful man. And that man would never forgive me for shaming him."

"Hm. And does this man have a name?"

Rahima looked at the crack in the floor beneath her feet. She was expending great energy to distance herself from those memories. She did not have much to spare.

"No matter," Samia declared with a wave of her hand. "Your name is more important. It seems the story of the lion made an impression on you. After all that happened to that poor animal, you still wish to take on that name?"

Rahima felt a heat in her cheeks. What seemed like a good idea yesterday now felt childish, and she had no business acting childishly. Who would choose to take on the name of a beast? She was only three steps into Samia's small office. She could retreat and let Samia get back to her calculator and papers, but no. The name Marjan translated to "precious stones" and made Rahima recall the singular line of Mawlana's poetry her beloved Khala Shaima had whispered to her the last time they were together.

Seawater begs the pearl to break its shell.

Rahima wants to be that small pearl. She wants to be Marjan.

"I think it's quite a fitting name for you," Samia mused. "It will serve you well."

Rahima felt a wisp of encouragement. Could a name lift her out of this feeling?

"And in other matters," Samia asked at half volume, leaning in. "Have you had any bleeding yet?"

It had been four days since the midwife handed Rahima the packet of pills.

Is it a sin? Rahima had asked.

Let me tell you something, the midwife had said bitterly. *If the mullahs were at risk of pregnancy, they would take these pills and wash them down with a shot of liquor.*

Back at the shelter, Rahima had sat on her bed with the aluminum sheet and a glass of water for thirty minutes before she drove her fingernail through the foil and extracted the first pill. She placed it on her tongue, took a gulp of water, and swallowed hard. The water went down, but the pill stayed in her mouth.

She wanted to sever herself from the man who had violated her thirteen-year-old body, from everyone in that compound who had treated her like chattel, and even from her parents, who had thrown her into the fire to keep their heads in clouds of opium.

She had no explanation for why she spit the pill out or why she sent the other pills down the drain. She could not admit this to Samia, who had gone so far out of her way to take her to the appointment. “Not yet,” she said, hoping Samia would understand her meaning.

“Well, it’s in God’s hands now, Rahima,” Samia said. She closed the notebook she had been writing in and corrected herself. “No, not Rahima. Marjan. Marjan. I suppose I can get used to calling you this name. But you’ll also have to get used to answering to it. Do you think you can do that?”

Rahima nodded. Marjan nodded.

A light breeze made the blades of the potted spider plant dance on the window ledge.

Marjan.

The lion’s story *had* made quite an impression on her. She wished she could revisit the statue that had greeted her in the entrance. She wanted to hear the story again, to learn more about Chucha and how the lions lived when they were together.

Marjan.

She knew in a contest of strength, a girl was no match for a lion and never would be. She only wanted to know how a ferocious creature could survive a grenade to the face, how the lion could have recovered from both a devastating injury and the knowledge that there were those who wished him dead.

“How long can I stay here?” she asked Samia, who had already reassured her on the first day in the shelter that she would not be asked to leave until she became an adult and indicated she was ready.

“For as long as you need,” Samia said. The line sounded rehearsed, and Marjan could picture her telling other women the same.

“But what does that mean? One month or three months? One year?”

Samia detected her insecurity and folded both hands on her desk to show Marjan she had her full attention.

“You are still young. The organization will support your stay here until you can provide for yourself. Or if relatives or friends decide they want to take you in,” Samia explained. “We can discuss this later. There really is no rush. You should be focused on yourself right now. Think about what kind of life you want. These are important first steps."

Footsteps echoed in the hallway, slow and deliberate.

Marjan turned to see who was approaching Khanum Samia's office. A young woman appeared in the doorway. Wisps of light brown hair peeked out from under a forest green headscarf. She held in one arm a baby who could not have been more than a year old. A stuffed travel bag hung from the opposite shoulder, a counterweight.

"Khanum Samia," she said softly. The baby looked into the office and then back into the hallway.

Samia looked at the bag and sighed heavily. She shook her head.

"I'm sorry, Khanum Samia," she began, without even looking at Marjan.

Samia let out a light groan.

"Are you certain you want to leave? I may not be able to bring you back," Samia warned.

"There is no other way," the woman responded, turning to the baby on her left hip. "He says this was all foolishness. Nothing serious."

"You are not supposed to have a phone in here. How did he get through to you?"

The woman's head bowed under an invisible weight.

"I needed to hear my mother's voice," she admitted. "I begged someone to let me use their phone. I did not tell her where I was, though. I swear on my life. I just knew my mother would be so worried about me. And he'd been there the day before to tell my mother this. And anyway, it's only a matter of time before he demands his son."

Marjan already knew that in the very rare case of a divorce, custody of the children went automatically to the father. She thought of one of the women she had met while she scribed in the Parliament. Marjan was mostly an eavesdropper unless she was called upon by her sister wife to read or write something for her.

Do not expect men to write laws that benefit women, the parliamentarian had once muttered while watching a man argue against having a mother's name listed on a birth certificate. *If God Himself cast a vote that advanced the basic rights of women, these men would accuse the Almighty of blasphemy.*

"Rahim—" Samia had begun, then stopped herself. "Marjan. Why don't you go back to your room and we'll continue this conversation later?"

Marjan obliged, then turned to walk out. When she passed the baby, he leaned his head into the crook of his mother's neck and whimpered. Marjan slipped past the woman, who had the same cinnamon eyes as her sister, Parwin.

Being forced into marriage had been too much for Parwin, who was timid and gentle. From time to time, Marjan would wake from sleep in a cold sweat, having dreamed of her sister's final moments. Parwin, glistening with the cooking oil she had poured over herself, flames climbing up her body like hungry serpents.

Though she hadn't seen it happen, the images haunted her. And what of her younger sisters? She didn't know if they had been married off as well.

Marjan looked at the hallway, thought of the many rooms on this floor and the one above it, of the many women and children who found shelter here and the countless who would never be saved by this space.

There were so many ways to lose someone.

8

AUGUST 8, 2021

The morning sun bathes the insides of Hawa's eyelids in orange light. The neckline of her cotton pajamas is damp with sweat, and she wants to be out of these sticky clothes. Her eyes flutter at the familiar sound of her mother's teaspoon clinking against her glass like the chime of a triangle, a small heap of sugar dissolving into her green tea.

Hawa sits up and rubs the sleep from her eyes. Just as she starts to rise, she spies her mother's black duffel bag by the small wardrobe. It wasn't there last night but it is now, too plump to be empty. Hawa walks to the bag, unzips it, and finds her mother's pants and shirts are inside, rolled up neatly. There's also a clear plastic sheath containing folded papers, a bundle she's never seen before.

"Hawa? Are you up?"

"Yes, I am!" she blurts, jolted by her mother's voice. She zips the duffel and arranges the straps over the zipper to make it look untouched. Marjan opens the door to find her daughter only folding her bedsheet.

"Good morning," she says. The tea in her cup is bright and eager, the color of tulip stems.

"Good morning," Hawa replies.

Marjan's prepared a glass for her daughter as well, hers with a splash of milk, because she wants her daughter's bones to be strong enough to hold her body up. Hawa takes a sip before setting the glass beside the lamp on the small table in the corner of the room. She hasn't quite bought into her mother's belief that hot tea can cool a person down. She thinks this might just be what people without ice makers tell themselves.

"I slept too much. Why didn't you wake me?" Hawa asks her mother, reaching into the wardrobe to retrieve fresh clothes.

"Because you looked tired."

Hawa blinks twice. Her mother has never said such a thing.

"But I'll be late for school," she replies.

Marjan shifts her weight.

"You know, Hawa, you could stay home for today," she says. She tries not to sound alarmed . . . or alarming.

"Why would I do that?" Hawa asks. It's a fair question.

"Hawa, you hear and see everything. The situation is getting worse by the day. I don't want to wonder where you are if something were to happen."

"My math teacher said that we cannot hide from danger. It will find us anywhere if it is our naseeb."

At this, Marjan huffs. There are some phrases that should have exhausted themselves into extinction long ago, she thinks, and this is one.

"Your teacher should stick to teaching math and you should make sure you think for yourself."

Hawa bristles. Her mother is not in the habit of speaking harshly about Hawa's teachers.

"Did something happen?" she asks.

Did I do something to make you angry? is what she means.

"No, no, nothing," Marjan reassures her. "No, I'm just . . . I didn't sleep much last night. I thought it would be good to rest today."

"I have nothing to do here," Hawa replies. She doesn't see why she should stay home and watch her restless mother, when her teachers and friends and her rubab are at school. Even after the bomb detonated two blocks away from their campus, the principal refused to cancel classes. The students were relieved. Sitting at home felt like an undeserved punishment.

Marjan senses her daughter won't budge.

"Fine. But first listen to me, Hawa. Do not talk to anyone at school about this, but I'm trying to get us out of the country. If the Taliban reach Kabul, it may not be safe for us."

"But isn't everyone coming to Kabul? Where would we go?" It is true. People from the provinces have swarmed into Kabul, fleeing the militants storming into their villages.

"We would have to leave the country," Marjan explains. "But we don't have passports yet."

To Hawa this sounds like fantasy. She was enchanted by the possibility of traveling to distant countries with the school's orchestra, but she cannot imagine living anywhere but in this city. Hawa is not accustomed to seeing her mother flounder, unsure what to do next.

"But, Madar, if we don't have passports—"

"I don't know yet but I'm working on it. There are some people trying to help us, but please don't talk about this with anyone at school. I just want you to be prepared in case our situation changes."

"And what about Ingrid?" Hawa asks.

"Ingrid will be okay," Marjan says. "She has her passport. She only needs to get on a plane."

Hawa had meant to ask if Ingrid could help them, since Ingrid often did. But her mother's response leaves her more unsettled.

"Who is helping us? Is it Americans? I thought they were all gone."

"They are gone," Marjan confirms quietly.

Hawa wonders, as she slips into her school uniform, if she should stay home with her mother. What if her mother decides it's time to leave, and she hasn't packed? What if she's still at school?

Something buzzes in the corner of the room. Her mother's phone is connected to the outlet with a cord that is starting to fray. It's probably a text from Khala Soraya. Hawa unplugs the phone to take it to her mother but stops when she sees the preview of the message on the screen. There's no contact name, just a number.

If he finds you, he'll find out about her.

Hawa reads it again, unsure what this could mean. She unlocks the phone with her mother's code and taps on the messaging app, but as she's swiping, her mother appears in the doorway.

"Who's going to be looking for you?" Hawa asks.

"What?"

Marjan's eyes fall on the phone that fills the small palm of her daughter's hand.

"You should be getting ready," she says, and takes the phone from Hawa. She reads the text and shoves the phone in her back pocket. "Put your shoes on. Let's go."

"But the message . . ."

"It's nothing," Marjan insists, but something in her daughter's face urges her to offer more explanation. "He's someone from one of the ministries, checking on our work. Are you ready to go?"

Hawa says nothing.

"Hawa, please." Marjan reaches for her headscarf, folded neatly on the dresser. Hawa lets out a disgruntled huff.

"I'll put my shoes on."

They walk down two flights of stairs. From behind apartment doors, signs of life seep into the communal hallway—the sounds of television programs and children bickering, the smell of cigarette smoke and fried eggs.

Outside, the neighborhood seems as it does every other day.

"You don't have to come with me," Hawa tells her mother. "Everyone else at school walks by themselves."

"That's not true," Marjan replies as she always does when Hawa requests to walk alone. Marjan takes her daughter's hand and they walk together, passing concrete blast walls painted with political slogans and edgy graffiti art.

"Who is hiding?" Hawa asks.

"What do you mean?" Marjan asks. "Is this about the message? Who knows. Probably some paperwork missing or something like that."

Hawa looks at her hand, firmly clasped in her mother's, as if Marjan is afraid Hawa will run into the street. Her mother is so different with her now that they live together. She's not as timid as she was when she would visit the orphanage, bringing small gifts—butter cookies, pink hair clips, a set of colored pens. By the way Hawa reacted, Marjan could not have guessed that Hawa kept those treasures under her bed and pulled them out at night, while the other girls slept.

Marjan is dressed in a black tunic and jeans. Her headscarf is gray with thin black stripes, and her lace-up boots look like they could be part of her military uniform, though they are not. Hawa finds herself comparing her mother to the other women she sees in the street or the mothers who bring their children to the music institute. Some are cloaked in chadoris, but others dress in kaftans or long-sleeve blouses over slacks. Hawa tries not to stare at a woman wearing an emerald tunic over navy pants that taper at the ankle. Nearly everything Marjan owns is gray or black. Hawa wonders if her mother was always this way or if her father's death sapped the color from her.

They weave through throngs of people, the sidewalks louder and busier than usual. When they near the park, Hawa nearly trips on her own feet. A swell of people, families and rings of men, have gathered. Some sit on bundled carpets. One child is perched on a bag of rice that outweighs him. A teenage boy sits on the ground, his head between his knees. Hawa spots a mother with a swaddled baby in her arms and two children at her side. A doctor crouches, presses her stethoscope to the child's chest. Just behind the doctor, Hawa sees a bag of serum tied to a tree branch. She follows the plastic tubing but loses it behind the shuffling bodies.

"There are so many," she says to her mother. "What will happen to them?"

Marjan can't help but pause, taking in the new mass of refugees in the city. A journalist arranges himself in front of a woman with a baby perched on her hip. Behind him, a second man holds a small video camera. The journalist asks the woman a question and directs her to speak into the small microphone he holds before her. The woman's eyes flit from the man in front of her to her child. She pulls her navy headscarf across the bottom of her face, trying to find a way to be both seen and not exposed.

"Yes, they took eight people from our home. They found out there were police officers in our family and stormed inside. My uncle tried to fight them off. We wrapped the bodies with whatever we had in the house. My husband's brother stayed behind to bury the dead."

"And do you know anyone in Kabul?"

She shakes her head.

"I have never been here before. We came because we were told nowhere else is safe. We have nothing to eat, nowhere to sleep, and nowhere even to . . . to catch our breath. I didn't want to come here but what choice did I have?"

The journalist thanks her for her comments. He swivels, searching the crowd and settling on Marjan. In two steps, he is in front of her, and the cameraman, trained to keep close, is right behind him, camera on.

"Sister, you look like you're taking your daughter to school. Would you care to share a few words about what you're seeing in Kabul today?"

Marjan recoils, pulls Hawa away from the camera's eye with a tug so strong Hawa winces. They hurry away from the sleep-deprived faces and different dialects.

Hawa is afraid her mother will want to turn around and go back to the apartment, but she does not. *No looking back* is her forever refrain. *Only forward.*

They pass the zoo, where the statue of Kabul's famous lion rests regally at the entrance. Hawa is amused that her mother shares a name with this creature. Her mother calls it a silly coincidence, but Hawa sees a familiar quiet strength in the statue's eyes.

"Hawa, come away from the road," Marjan warns, scowling at a driver who has veered so close to them that he might have clipped the back of her boots.

When they reach the gates of the music institute, Marjan pauses.

"Be good. I'll be here when school is dismissed," she says, then embraces Hawa tightly and kisses the top of her head.

It has been less than a week since the bomb shook the campus. Hawa wishes she wasn't so rattled but knows her classmates are too. The students keep one ear on their lessons and the other listening for the next blast. They hold their instruments but not too tightly, because they may have to throw them aside and run for cover.

Even with all these concerns, a bombing that bloodies the street is not Hawa's biggest fear.

"Hawa? You're staring. What is it?"

Hawa shrugs and says a quick goodbye to her mother. She doesn't want to speak her thoughts aloud. But the thought echoes in her head, building to a deafening crescendo as she walks away from her mother and enters the school grounds.

Don't leave me behind again, Madar-jan.

9

2010

Rahima, now Marjan, grew more and more convinced she'd made the wrong choice. She would have asked Samia about it, but Samia had gone north to attend her nephew's wedding.

Marjan was terrified that Abdul Khaliq would come for her if he learned she was carrying his child. On the day Samia was due to return, Marjan slipped down the hall and checked her office every hour. On her third visit, she stood in the hallway looking through the glass window of the door at the empty chair and her vision blurred with tears.

"Don't just stand there," Samia called out, coming around the corner. She was carrying a cardboard box large and heavy enough to put a bit of a waddle in her step. "Open that door for me."

Marjan did as she was told. Samia grunted as she set the box down on her office floor and clapped the dust off her hands.

"Now, tell me how you've—" Samia stopped short. "What's this? Are you crying?"

Marjan bit her lip. Now that Samia was here, she felt tongue-tied.

"Sit down," Samia said, taking her by the shoulders and guiding her into a chair. "And tell me what's happened."

"Nothing has happened," Marjan said softly.

"Then what are you crying for, silly girl?"

"I . . . I was scared."

Samia's face grew serious. Why did she think she could spend so much time away from the shelter without something going wrong?

"Scared of what? The pills? What did you do with them, you foolish girl?" she asked.

Marjan buried her face in her hands. "I threw them in the toilet. But I shouldn't have and I didn't know how to get back to the midwife and . . ."

Samia groaned.

"Okay, okay. Let me think," she muttered. "Go to your room and I'll come to you once I've gathered my thoughts."

Marjan did as she was told. That's all she ever did these days, she realized. She ate what was offered to her. She kept her room tidy and waited her turn for the bathroom. She stayed inside the building most of the time and didn't even think of venturing off the property.

Two hours later, Samia entered her room, grim-faced.

"The midwife says too much time has gone by now for pills. She says you will need a small surgery."

Marjan's chest tightened.

"No, I don't want to go back to the clinic," Marjan said.

"There is a doctor who helps our clients. She is excellent."

"No. There is no need."

"So you want to remain pregnant?" Samia asked, looking confused.

"Please tell her thank you," Marjan said. She heard footsteps coming down the hallway, and her voice melted to a whisper. "But I won't need anything else."

"But you know this means—"

"Yes, I know," Marjan said, cutting her off. She wished so desperately she could talk to someone. Khala Shaima. Her sister, Shahla. Even her mother. She had no one. Even when she was trapped in her room at Abdul Khaliq's compound, she knew her khala Shaima would occasionally appear at the gate insisting on a few minutes with her niece. No one would come to visit her in the shelter. When she ran away from her warlord husband, she cut herself off from everyone. She was a planet flung out of orbit.

"What should I do?" she whispered to the empty room.

Marjan wrapped her arms around her belly and felt a demure flutter within, the presence of something fledging. Something small. She did nothing, in denial that this, too, was her shaping her naseeb.

The days dragged on. Marjan tried to keep herself occupied with the classes they offered at the shelter, but then a couple of months passed and the other women in the shelter began to eye her growing belly with curiosity. One day, in the shared restroom, Marjan found herself standing at the two adjacent sinks alongside a woman with restless green eyes. When Marjan cleared her throat, the woman flinched. She looked to be in her thirties, with a nose that bent just below the bridge. Though abuse was what gave all the residents of the shelter an entry pass, few women had visible scars. This woman was one of the unlucky ones.

She had been found alone in the city, Marjan had overheard. The police used to take women like her, women who may have been raped or abused, to the police station, where they ran the risk of being imprisoned. But the organization running the shelter had petitioned the government to bring the women to the shelter instead.

"You are carrying," the woman said, and nodded in Marjan's direction. It sounded somewhere between a question and a statement.

"I am," she admitted. She'd not breathed a word about her condition to any of the other women at the shelter, and the question caught her off guard.

The woman nodded again, her suspicions confirmed.

"I can always tell," the woman said. A bitter smile bloomed on her face. "Even before someone starts to show, I can tell. There's something in the cheeks, the eyes. And other things too. I can just tell things about people from looking at them. My mother used to joke that God must whisper to me in my sleep."

She filled her cupped hands with water and splashed her face three times, her fingertips starting at her hairline, curling down her jawline, and meeting at the point of her chin.

Marjan's brow furrowed. She did not like feeling so transparent. She rinsed her hands and dried them on the towel she had draped around her neck. She would come back later to bathe, she decided.

"Want to know what else I can tell?" the woman asked, just as Marjan reached for the doorknob. Marjan hesitated, then turned to face the woman, who cocked her head to the side, her face wet and glistening.

"What else?" Marjan asked.

"I'm sorry to tell you but you're carrying a girl," the woman replied. And then, for a long second, her eyes locked on Marjan's. "And she'll be the end of you."

She slipped past Marjan and left the bathroom. Marjan leaned against the door, gathered herself, and returned to her room.

She was reluctant to join the other women in activities after that but knew she had to find something to do with her nervous energies.

Iqra, Khala Shaima had told her. *It means "read," my brave girl. "Iqra" is the first word of the Quran, the preeminent command, a sacred first step.*

So Marjan read every newspaper she found in the shelter and borrowed from Samia anything she could find in her office—a booklet on grant writing, a manual on accounting, a real estate leaflet. When Samia realized Marjan's specific hunger, she began stopping by the local bookstore on her way in and asking the sellers for their top recommendations. The vocabulary was a struggle, of course, so Samia picked up a bilingual dictionary for Marjan too. That was how Marjan came to have a handful of children's books in English, as well as Jane Austen's *Pride and Prejudice* and a Farsi translation of Paulo Coelho's *The Alchemist.*

Marjan had been learning English even while she served as her sister wife's scribe in Parliament. She found the children's books manageable, but the language of Austen confounded her. Samia had told her it was a popular read among Kabul's young women, so she kept the book, determined to one day be able to decipher it.

It was in *The Alchemist* that Marjan felt the electricity of words. She liked the idea that the desert had a language and the warning not to die of thirst just when palm trees appeared on the horizon. She liked the idea of God revealing the future only so that a person could change it. She sat up in bed at the idea that the universe might just conspire on behalf of her dreams.

The Alchemist, somehow, felt like a continuation of the stories her khala Shaima had told her about her ancestor, Bibi Shekiba. Outwardly, they had little in common. Bibi Shekiba came from a village and, by turns, found herself dressed in men's clothes and serving as a harem guard in the royal palace. In *The Alchemist*, a shepherd boy and a wandering Englishman find themselves at the foot of a pyramid. But, Marjan realized, those were mere details. What tied them together was faith that something better was yet to be discovered.

She needed that frisson of hope on days when the familiar kicks in her growing belly reminded her of the little boy she had lost. Her dreams became more vivid. Jahangir appeared more frequently, in Abdul Khaliq's courtyard. In a Kabul alley. On the banks of a gurgling stream. Always just out of reach. Marjan woke with tears sliding down her cheeks on many nights, terrified of the universe's cruelty.

Despite Samia's pleas, she had refused to visit the midwife until her seventh month. That was when she learned that the prophecy of the woman with the broken nose had been correct. She was having a girl. Two months later, Marjan felt her back tightening, her belly squeezing, her breaths growing quick and shallow.

Marjan tried not to fill the shelter's clinical room with her groaning, but the pain was too great. Had she really done this before? The pain drove out all memory, commanded all her attention.

The doctor stood between her legs one moment and then by Marjan's shoulder the next. "We need to get you to the hospital," she said, as she doffed a bloodied glove. "The baby is not where she's supposed to be."

The baby is not where she's supposed to be.

This Marjan understands.

At the hospital, Marjan saw faces hidden behind pale blue masks, then squeezed her eyes shut against it all. They placed a mask on her face, and she heard a whisper of air. What a strange scent. The room blurred and faded.

Marjan thought she'd already met her end, until the ache across her abdomen awakened her, brought her back to this punishing physical world. Her limbs were heavy, her mouth dry. She sensed she was not alone before she opened her eyelids.

When the figures around her reached under her arms to sit her up, the movement sent a jolt of pain across her lower belly. Marjan reached to touch the stitches on her abdomen, but a nurse grabbed her wrist and pulled down Marjan's hospital gown to hide the incision.

"Are you ready to hold your daughter? She's a bit feisty but otherwise perfect," a nurse said.

Indeed, it was a girl, pink and crying. She was still sticky with vernix and a clipped cord stuck out from her belly button. Marjan examined her from head to toe for defects and found none.

"Everything moved so quickly. I'll come back for your paperwork. Do you have a name for her?"

Marjan had not chosen a name. She hadn't done anything to prepare for this baby. She was already a terrible mother to this child. What name could she give to a little girl with such a twisted beginning?

"We need some fresh air," the nurse mumbled, then went to open the door.

Air. Hawa.

The name came to her then, sweet as baby's breath. Besides "air," Hawa was also the name of the first woman in the story of humankind. What if her daughter was the beginning of a story yet untold? What if she came from a place of purity? Marjan liked that the Quran spoke of God creating Hawa, albeit from a rib of Adam. Hawa had no mother to speak of, but Marjan felt that was somehow apt as well.

She whispered the azaan into her baby's ear, something a father would do to welcome a newborn into the fold. Marjan hoped her daughter would never yearn for a father.

Marjan's first experience with motherhood did little to prepare her for the first weeks with Hawa. This child was nothing like Jahangir, who cried when hungry but was easily soothed. Hawa's cries were shrill and impatient. Every time Marjan moved, she thought her sutures might tear apart. The shelter's doctor gave her pain medication, which only helped a little. Marjan, stiff and groaning, positioned Hawa against her breasts to nurse and changed diapers and rocked her daughter, but oftentimes Hawa could not be soothed.

In her fourth month of life, Hawa wailed less and slept for three-hour stretches at night, but she was still quite adept at demanding attention. Marjan's incision had healed and she could move without pain, but she was depleted and would fall asleep with Hawa in her arms or sleeping at her side.

She would have lost her mind if it hadn't been for the quieter moments with Hawa. Her babbling and cooing sounded like music to Marjan, like the precise vocalizations of a ghazal or playful notes on a stringed instrument. Lying on her back, she would pound her fists against the mattress and laugh, delighted at her own percussive sounds.

Hawa's sleep breathing, quiet and rhythmic, could lull Marjan into a nap as well.

By six months, Hawa was sitting up and eagerly stealing bites of her mother's food. Marjan watched her gum pieces of bread, butter crackers, and mashed fruits. *Iqra,* her aunt and the Quran had directed, and so Marjan read to her daughter, sat outside with her to get her sunlight and fresh air, and explained to her all the sights and sounds that could be seen or heard from the courtyard of the shelter. In front of the building were a few climbing vines and small shrubs. Judging by the plants in Samia's office, this humble landscaping was likely her doing. In the evenings, Marjan liked to take Hawa to breathe in the sweet and heady scent of the night-blooming jasmine. There was a small cage with a canary outside, and Marjan would shoo away the mischievous boy who would rattle the cage and delight at the bird's panicked fluttering.

In Abdul Khaliq's home, she had not had the luxury of time with her newborn. She had been expected to return quickly to her heavy load of domestic chores in a household with three sister wives and all their children, as well as a merciless mother-in-law who treated her like a drudge. Here, Marjan was responsible for her own laundry and caring for her child, but the shelter had a cook and people who came to clean the building. Women spent their time learning skills they hoped would give them more independence after they left the shelter—embroidery and tailoring, jewelry making, and literacy.

Marjan was ever aware of the threats to this quiet existence. But she also knew that she could not stay in the shelter indefinitely. At some point, she would be asked to move into the halfway house, though Samia refused to give her a timeline. Marjan learned, by observing and overhearing, that women going through a divorce or women who had been raped might stay at the shelter six months to a year. She had already lingered longer than most and grew anxious at the thought of being asked to leave.

So she read to Hawa, sat across the room from her to encourage her to crawl, and reminded her again and again that she was brave and strong. She also recited the story of Bibi Shekiba from start to finish, leaving out some of the harsher details of the abuse she suffered.

"You have no father," Marjan whispered into her daughter's ear just as she had whispered the azaan. This was an equally important indoctrination. "You need no father and you have no father. I will do everything for you."

Slowly, Marjan became comfortable bringing Hawa to interact with some of the other women in the shelter. There was always turnover. Every week a reticent woman with wide-eyed children would enter seeking refuge and another woman would either reconcile with her husband or complete the terms of a divorce and dare to live independently.

She would stay here, in this home for women hidden within a city of men, until the day it was decided she could stay no more. Then what was she to do? How would she care for herself and a child?

She will be the end of you.

Marjan laid a sleeping Hawa on a piece of foam on the floor. She slipped into the bathroom to quickly bathe herself. Undressed, she was confronted with her body. Her incision had healed, though she could still feel a tugging from the inside at times. Pale, pink hash marks reminded her of the sutures that had held her together. Marjan traced the raised ridge below her belly, the path the blade had taken to cut her open, to lift this child from her womb. Where had the blade first entered? Marjan's fingertip ran the length of the scar and back, unable to tell the beginning from the end.

10

AUGUST 8, 2021

METRA MEDIA

The producer drags the back of his hand across his forehead. He has never had much tolerance for heat. Mina, on the other hand, seems immune to these suffocating temperatures. Even after twenty minutes under the lights, her face shows not a bead of sweat. He's never wanted to be in front of the camera anyway. He is good at his job, he knows. He should really be at a bigger station, one that can afford to pay its staff a decent salary. But he also knows that he has never worked with someone like Mina Noori. When she's not in front of the camera, she is plowing through emails, squeezing acquaintances for scoops, interviewing people over the phone, or stewing in verses of contemporary poetry. Viewers love it when she recites a memorized quatrain or inserts a literary reference into her program.

"Esteemed viewers, since the capture of Zaranj, the Taliban have continued to press further into the north, and in the last twenty-four hours, other major cities have fallen into the hands of the insurgents. We have confirmation that the provincial capital Sheberghan has been captured along with the province of Jawzjan. Heavy fighting was reported throughout the city, and while Afghan National Security Forces launch a counteroffensive to reclaim control, it appears Taliban fighters have taken over a number of government buildings. Furthermore, today brings us word that three additional provincial centers—Sar-e-Pol, Kunduz, and Taloqan—have been taken over by the Taliban after several days of intense fighting.

"Families packed the bare essentials and fled the city of Kunduz, moving through clouds of panic and smoke as fires raged in several areas. One local resident told us that since the Taliban had arrived, the city had come to a standstill. While some shops burned, others closed down, and people were going without water or food. An Interior Ministry spokesman announced on social media that the counteroffensive efforts were making significant progress and that many areas of the city had been recaptured and that many insurgents had suffered injuries or been killed at the hands of the ANSF.

"Residents have also reported that the Taliban broke into the local prison and released captured Taliban soldiers along with other prisoners. Across social media, video clips showed inmates fleeing. Afghanistan's human rights commission sharply criticized the Taliban for abuses and violence perpetrated against civilians. A young man revealed to us the fresh wounds on his back after he was captured by the Taliban and lashed publicly while two men held him by his wrists and ankles.

"An attack in Kabul yesterday claimed the lives of two men and wounded another. Lawyer, radio voice, and journalist Toofan Omari of Voice of Paktia was killed returning to his home yesterday. Notably, his radio station dedicated half of its time to coverage of women's issues and news, and Agha Omari partnered with other media institutions to support free media in the country. The attackers also killed a prosecutor from the attorney general's office.

"Thus far, no individual or group has claimed responsibility for the attack, though government officials believe it was carried out by the Taliban.

"Meanwhile, in southern Helmand, journalist Nematullah Hemat was abducted from his home by Taliban fighters. Without knowledge of his whereabouts, his family and colleagues are in a state of panic.

"Concern grows across the country as deliberate attacks continue to claim the lives of journalists, health-care workers, police officers, and other civil servants. In the past year, more than thirty journalists and media workers were killed or abducted by extremists. This, on top of the targeted assaults against health-care workers, police officers, civil servants, and judges, has spurred growing alarm across the country. Women in these professional roles have been especially at risk. Among notable women with positions of authority or influence or significant visibility, many feel they could be next."

The producer wonders how Mina can continue to be a public figure in such a time. He thinks of the great courage all these slain or assaulted women and men must have summoned to continue their work each day. How many viewers are learning not to follow in their footsteps? How many others will die trying?

Mina looks back to the camera. Only the producer, who has come to know the anchor's countenance and rhythm better than anyone else, detects the subtle clench in her jaw. It's gone before he can name what he's just seen. He reaches for his mug of tea, tepid and bitter, and listens to Mina close out the program just as she has been doing for the past two years.

"Valor may shorten a life in harsh terrain, but like a rising sun, it lengthens the shadow she casts. Long live the glorious memories of our lionhearted women and men. Dear viewers, this concludes our program for the evening. As always, may God be with you all and, inshallah, may I come to you tomorrow as the bearer of brighter news."

11

2011

Marjan looked up from her embroidery work to check on Hawa. She had, inch by inch, crawled to a corner of the classroom, where two toddlers were rolling toy cars on the thin carpet. The women sat cross-legged on the floor, squares of fabric in their laps. Hawa was drawn to others, especially children. Her eyes would widen at the sight of a child, and her small hands would bounce up and down with excitement. Marjan kept to herself. She feared a slip of the tongue or a familiar face would reveal her whereabouts to Abdul Khaliq. Besides, she didn't want to become entangled in the petty squabbles that erupted almost daily in the shelter.

Marjan knew her next step would be a halfway house. There, she would be expected to work so that her wages could help pay for her living expenses. She needed to learn skills that would earn her a living. She found embroidery to be incredibly tedious, but she persevered because options were limited in this shelter funded by unimaginative international donors.

The world seems to think all Afghan women can stitch and that stitching is all Afghan women can do, Samia had griped.

Marjan, seated under the window, checked the back of her fabric. She pulled her needle through and felt the thread snap.

"Damn it," she whispered. The woman next to her shot her a look, and Marjan sighed. She reached for the spool of crimson and lifted her needle to rethread it.

The silver spine glinted in the slant of daylight.

"You're pulling too hard," the woman cautioned. "That's the third thread you've snapped."

"It's the second," Marjan corrected. The instructor looked up from the front of the room.

"Ladies, need help?"

Marjan shook her head. The instructor was a petite woman in her forties hired by the shelter to provide instruction twice a week. Her mother had once been a seamstress for the country's last queen, and her daughter carried on her craft with the pride of one who has been touched by royalty.

From her, Marjan learned about the various styles of embroidery from around the country. ZanjeeraDozi came from the Dari word for "chain" because the next stitch was looped through the previous one, like links in a chain, to create geometric and floral patterns. PukhtaDozi styles originated in Uzbekistan and used satin stitches to create large-scale embroideries, even tapestries. The Hazara style embroidery was called Tarshumar, mathematically precise and delicate stitches on silk or cotton. The patterns were grounded with rectangular footprints or triangles lined up like arrowheads.

Then there was the Khamak style, which originated from Kandahar, in the south. The instructor noted that the best Khamak artisans used very thin needles to make complicated and intricate motifs that would decorate the yoke of a tunic or the cuff of a sleeve. Though they sewed on higher thread count fabrics, they knew just how to finesse the satin threads or untwisted silk floss so that they did not tug or pucker the garment. They did not use frames or hoops or tracing paper. Their craft required eyeing a midpoint, then carefully counting stitches so that their glossy diamond pattern would bloom symmetrically toward the outward boundaries. They worked carefully from the back of the fabric, making sure the pattern looked the same from either side of the cloth.

"In the world of textiles and design, Afghanistan is known for this craft," the instructor had told them at the beginning of that day's lesson. "Our embroidery tells a story. When you become more practiced, you can learn the different motifs that represent our different regions and traditions. Beyond the geometric shapes, you can learn rosettes, sun and stars, almond leaves, and pomegranates. I'll pass around this embroidered panel of a dress so you can see the detailed work. Pay attention to how the small, round mirrors and metal coins are attached as well. These catch the light and make dresses shimmer. And you'll see that it also has tulips stitched into the design, just like the ones you'll be working on today. These flowers represent fertility."

The tulip was a single-stalk flower with petals and leaves of pale blue rhomboids and small rust-colored triangles representing the stamens. Below the flower, the same rust-colored satin thread had been used to create a zigzag border with a pleasant sheen. It looked simple enough, constructed of geometric shapes.

"And, ladies, look at this piece I brought in to show you an example of a ram's horns pattern," the instructor had said, holding up a small boy's shirt. It was so beautifully crafted, Marjan thought it might have been intended for a child born into a wealthier family, one touched by providence.

Hawa started to babble. The two toddlers had grown restless. One was tugging on his mother's arm and the other was standing by the door, threatening to leave. On her own, Hawa had moved into a sitting position. She was wearing a onesie with a faded cartoon sun on the front and sweatpants that were meant for a one-year-old. Some of her clothing came from the growing babies of the shelter. The rest came from donations or, rarely, were purchased from secondhand stores with earmarked shelter funds.

How would Marjan buy clothing if she didn't have the shelter supporting her?

Marjan looked ruefully at the square of cloth in her hands, the stitches overlapping and lumpy instead of neat and flat.

God will provide, people loved to say. But wasn't there ample evidence in the streets that God very often did not provide?

She would have to work harder than anyone else. She would have to be more careful with her sewing, less harried. She was a daughter of Afghanistan too. Even if she had not learned needlework sitting at her mother's or grandmother's feet, surely she carried some knowledge of it in her bones.

She pierced the fabric from the back, pulled the thread through, and drove it back into the cloth to make the next leaf. She repeated her steps until she had made a small triangle, this one more refined than the others.

She felt her spirits buoyed. She only needed to slow down, to concentrate. Maybe she could start a small business embroidering prayer caps or tablecloths. She could work from her own home and—

"Oh, God! What's happened to her?" someone shouted.

Marjan looked up. Her head spun around, trying to figure out which of the women had sounded the alarm and why.

"Pick her up! Pick her up!"

Marjan's heart pounded in her ears to see a woman on her knees, crouched over the spot where Hawa had just been sitting.

Hawa.

She dropped her needlework and couldn't scramble to her feet fast enough, so she crawled, hand over hand like she was drowning, to reach her daughter, who was in the arms of another woman. She had one hand on Hawa's chest and was pounding her back with the other. Hawa's face had gone pale, her eyes open wide, though her eyelids fluttered with every blow to the back. There was a thin line of drool at the corner of her mouth. The silence nearly stopped Marjan's heart.

"Hawa? Hawa!" she cried, grabbing her daughter.

"Dear God," someone began to wail.

"She's choking!" another called out.

The realization cut through Marjan's stupor like lightning through clouds. She stuck her finger in her daughter's mouth, searching the soft space for an obstruction. Hawa wasn't fighting her, Marjan realized with dread. Her daughter had gone even more pale; her eyes were still open but that wild, wide-eyed stare was no longer there. Her tiny hands, which were usually busy with discovery, lay loosely at her sides. She felt more like a doll than a child.

"Hawa!" Marjan screamed. She moved her finger again, sent it even deeper into her daughter's throat in desperation. This time she felt something on the tip of her finger. She swept the object up and brought it out and felt her daughter jerk in her arm, her body shudder. Marjan held her up to look at her face. Hawa grimaced, her head lolled to the side, and she groaned lightly as if waking from a deep slumber.

Someone put a hand on Marjan's shoulder.

"God spared her."

Marjan became aware she was panting. She looked to the floor, to where she had flicked the object she'd pulled from her daughter's mouth. It was a small, round mirror. It must have fallen off the adorned dress panel the instructor had passed around. Hawa's eyes were always on the lookout for a plaything.

Hawa blinked slowly, her grimace turning into a cry. Marjan pulled her daughter to her chest, felt the reassurance of Hawa's warm breath against her cheek, and cupped the back of her head with her hand.

"Forgive me," she whispered.

"Turn your back for a second and the worst can happen," someone murmured.

Marjan thought her chest might burst.

She wanted to scream at everyone in the room, to disperse the blame, but her throat was tight with the hard lump of guilt.

Why hadn't she noticed her daughter pick up the mirror? Why had she let herself get so consumed by a stupid needle and thread? Did she really think anyone would pay money for her attempts at the craft?

The women were sharing stories of their own children's brushes with injury or death. Everyone had them. Why else would birthdays be such cause for celebration?

Marjan heard the echoes of her mother-in-law's voice.

Because of you, your son is gone, said with a crooked finger pointed at Marjan.

With Hawa in her arms, Marjan left the room. Her unfinished embroidered tulip, the symbol of fertility, remained on the floor.

12

AUGUST 11, 2021

"Hawa," Marjan whispers. "It's time to wake up, Hawa. Just like we talked about last night. Hawa? Are you awake?"

She is now. Barely. It was four o'clock in the morning, and Hawa was in the thick of a nettling dream. She was on a small stage with a handful of her classmates, their faces blurry but for Layma's. Someone urged her to hurry. The audience was waiting for the music to start, but when Hawa looked down, she realized her lap was empty, tragically light. There was no rubab to play.

"Please, Hawa," Marjan pleads. Hawa rolls onto her side. She slowly realizes her mother's voice had infiltrated her dream.

"If we wait much longer, the lines will be very long," Marjan says. She is no longer whispering. The passport office has been swarmed with people desperate for documents. Some have taken to laying a blanket on the sidewalk and spending the night outside the office doors.

Hawa sits up, the mist of her dream evaporating as yesterday's conversation comes back to her. Her mother has said before that they needed to leave Kabul, but it never seemed like a real plan. Now it's an emergency, an absolute. Hawa's not sure what will happen to them if they fail. She rubs her fists against her eyes so hard that Marjan grabs her wrists.

"Okay, okay," she says. "I'm up."

Hawa stands. She reaches for the light switch, but her mother stops her.

"We don't need to let all the neighbors know we're awake," Marjan says. She lights a small candle, and Hawa moves quickly and quietly, dressing herself by its glow.

Marjan paces the room. In such a small space, pacing amounts to spinning in circles. It is dizzying to watch, so Hawa focuses on fixing her headscarf.

"Madar?" Hawa whispers.

Marjan is looking at the glowing screen of her phone, perplexed. She begins tapping.

Hawa goes into the small kitchen, a galley where only one person can comfortably stand. She pours herself water and takes a sip.

Her mother always seems to be elsewhere, even when she is close enough that Hawa can hear her breathing. When she can convince her mother to watch a sketch comedy show on television, Hawa notices the stretch of time it takes for a joke to make her mother smile, as if the humor has further to travel before it can reach her. Sometimes it does not find her at all, and Hawa feels the smile on her own face dissipate.

It's only when Hawa is ill that the chasm between them vanishes. Marjan's hand lingers on her daughter's forehead. She peppers her with questions and spoon-feeds her tea with crushed ginger and expensive threads of saffron. She pulls the blanket over Hawa's shoulders and brushes her bangs to the side with a feathery touch. She is quick to take her daughter to the clinic down the road, where the doctor presses the cold bell of the stethoscope to her chest and tells her to breathe deeply. Marjan searches the doctor's face while Hawa stares at her mother's. Hawa's energies are slow to return so that Marjan is always late to realize that the cough, the fever, and the stuffy nose have long gone.

When Hawa is not ill, her body finds other ways to draw her mother near. She takes to bed with a headache. She picks at old scabs. She barely touches her dinner. None of it is intentional but it works. A species survives only because the young have the gift of adaptation.

"If you're wondering why I didn't just leave you with Ingrid and go to the office alone, it's because I don't know what they will tell me. If they demand to see you or want to take pictures, it's better we are both there. We don't have time to wait on these lines twice."

Hawa's eyes have adjusted, opened by the intrigue of the hour and her mother's determination to accomplish what seems like an impossible task. It is rare to find women living alone in this world. Hawa wishes she had more family, a father and siblings and aunts and uncles. But she also swells with pride to think that her mother does the work of two parents. Sometimes she takes out the photograph her mother keeps tucked in her belongings, a photo of seven women dressed in military uniforms, firearms at their sides. Her mother is in the middle, somber-faced, while the other women smile brightly. The photo is from a training exercise, her mother had told her. Even soldiers who spend their days battling paperwork must know how to hold a weapon. She wishes her mother were more of a warrior, instead of a worrier.

Marjan locks the apartment door behind them. They move down the stairwells and slip into the quiet street. City lights glow against an indigo sky. Hawa hears the sharp bark of a dog, but she cannot tell if the beast is around the corner or ten blocks away. Sound reverberates against the concrete blast walls of the city and the facades of buildings, obscuring distances.

"Madar, how long do you think we'll have to wait?" Hawa asks.

"I'm not sure. Let's get there and see what the line looks like," Marjan says, checking the time on her phone. She opens up her messages, and Hawa tries to peek at the screen. "Where is he?" she mutters.

Hawa's mother paid a taxi driver handsomely to pick them up at this hour. They were to meet the driver just beyond the borders of the apartment complex, but there are no cars around. Moth-eaten clouds sneak past a sliver of a moon as the minutes tick by.

"What if he does not come?" Hawa asks. "Will we still go?"

Marjan bites her lip. She doesn't answer her daughter's question. Hawa prepares to ask again, when her mother's phone buzzes.

"Damn him. He says this road is blocked. We have to get to him," Marjan relays.

She holds Hawa's hand tightly in her own, watching the shadows. The streets have become treacherous in the past couple of years. Kidnappers and thieves. Young men floundering without jobs, looking for shortcuts. Feral dogs who rest by day and roam by night. Hungry and resentful, they travel in packs.

A man passes on a bicycle. He stares long and hard at the mother and daughter, and Hawa feels her heart thumping even after he's ridden past them. He is still visible when he laughs inexplicably. Hawa's mother leads them across the street, picking up her pace. Will the man circle back? She listens for the susurration of the bicycle's chain.

Hawa yearns for the azaan, wishing a call to prayer would awaken the city and send people into the streets.

"What if he's left?" Hawa asks.

But the taxi sits at the corner, lights and engine off. Marjan and Hawa make their way down the sidewalk, a network of interlocked gray pavers under their feet. Marjan approaches the driver's window first. The driver rolls down his window and nods at Marjan.

"Salaam," Marjan says, keeping her tone formal. He responds in kind, makes no mention of his tardiness. "You were supposed to be here ten minutes ago."

"Forgive me," he says. "I was praying."

The taxi driver's face is mostly in shadow, but Hawa feels in her gut that he is being spiteful. Hawa notices the white curl of an earbud and the glint of a silver chain on his neck. He rests his arm on the open car window, the sleeve of his checkered shirt rolled up to the elbow. Marjan's eyes shift to the back of the car and then to the street. Hawa knows what's making her mother hesitate. She's warned her daughter often to be wary of men, to avoid getting into a room or even a conversation with one. Her mother has not told her what a man might do to her, but Hawa never felt the need to ask. Her body seems to know and stiffens when she sees something primal in a man's stance or his eyes. She pretends not to hear the comments some men make to the women who pass them, especially those who wear a dash of lipstick or shoes with a bit of a heel.

"Shall we go then?" the taxi driver asks.

"Yes." Marjan looks at her daughter, then at their apartment building. She runs some kind of calculation and decides to get into the back seat of the car.

The taxi driver adjusts his rearview mirror. When his eyes meet Hawa's, she instinctively looks out the window, into the dark streets. The car merges onto the main road, the one that will lead them southwest to the passport office. The driver reaches across the gear stick and plucks a tall, red aluminum can from the passenger seat. He pops the tab of an energy drink.

"Why is her father not with you?" he asks with a nod in Hawa's direction. "Has he already left the country?"

Hawa sees her mother's jaw tense and feels the muddle of feelings she always experiences when the question of her father comes up. She has next to nothing of him, not a single picture and only the vaguest of stories.

Marjan does not respond to the taxi driver's question. She rests one hand on her daughter's knee and keeps her eyes on the surroundings, alert as the soldier she cannot admit to being. Hawa sits up straight and pulls her shoulders back, mimicking her mother's posture. The daily congestion has not yet begun, so within minutes they arrive at the passport office. People mill around the building, mostly men.

"It's not a good idea to come here alone," the taxi driver says.

"I've hired you to drive, not to counsel me," Marjan replies.

"You're only paying for the ride. I won't charge you a cent for the advice," the driver says with a laugh.

"It's worth less than that," she mutters.

Hawa hides her smile with her hand.

"If you're unsuccessful at the passport office, don't worry. I am happy to drive you around. And you don't need to sit in the back seat either. It's a better view of the road from here," he says, and it's evident he thinks himself quite clever. He doesn't see the harm of flirting. It gives a truly virtuous woman a chance to demonstrate her character and it gives the less virtuous the pleasure of his company. Kabul is full of noble women, but that won't deter him from his quest.

Hawa can almost feel the heat coming off her mother's body. She knows her mother is biting her tongue, and she wishes she wouldn't. She likes it better when her mother fires back at people, wiping smirks off faces with a few words. Hawa is happiest when her mother is a sharp pin, pricking at a world of hyperinflated egos.

"Here is fine," Marjan declares, then turns to Hawa. "Get out of the car." They've reached the passport office, the entrance blocked by a growing cluster of people. The line trails along the side of the building and down the sidewalk. How long have these people been here? Hawa wonders. Her mother takes her by the hand and leads her toward the tangle of people. Some have black plastic bags in their hands, thin and crinkled. One man appears to be sleeping upright. It is not hard to find Soraya.

"There she is!" Hawa calls out, relieved to see her aunt. Soraya waves them over from a couple hundred meters away. She is wearing a khaki coat that cuts at her knees and cinches neatly at the waist with a belt. Her makeup is understated, a better fit for the hour and purpose of their outing.

"Sorry we had to drag you out of bed," Soraya coos, pulling Hawa in for a tight embrace and planting a kiss on her cheek. Hawa loves so much about Khala Soraya, the way she can speak of the scandal of a mismatched outfit with the same energy others give to politics. And when Khala Soraya leaves lipstick imprints on her cheeks, Hawa slips into the bathroom to see what the touch of color looks like on her face, to see if she can look pretty too.

"I don't mind," Hawa says, ever eager to please her vibrant aunt.

"You're such a good sport, my lovely. And maybe you'll bring us some luck today."

Soraya steps back so that they can say hello to her brother, Temur, who has been standing behind his sister, scrolling on his phone. Temur nods at Marjan and Hawa, presses a hand to his chest, then returns to his phone.

Two people further back in the line grumble loudly about Marjan and Hawa jumping the queue.

"We're one family," Soraya calls out loudly. She dismisses their complaint with a wave of her hand. "She's my husband's second wife. Temur, tell them."

Temur cuts his eyes at his sister then turns away, clearly embarrassed. Soraya is colorful, with or without her lipstick.

"More people show up every minute," Soraya shares. "We can't even see how far back it goes now. Have you heard anything from Jenna?"

Marjan shakes her head.

Updates move up and down the line. The Taliban have claimed more territory, closing a border crossing into Pakistan. People forced from their homes have gathered under tents far enough away to escape the sounds of gunfire. A media director was executed while at the masjid for prayers. It's not all dismal. There is the occasional spot of encouraging news. The military's special forces have won back a major city.

"We have a good army. They'll win it all back, you'll see," someone says loudly. "And who wants America here anyway? I'm tired of their bombs and puppet presidents and midnight raids. Let them find another country to use as a testing ground for their weapons."

Soraya and Marjan stiffen. Hawa senses they're avoiding each other's gazes, concealing any reaction to what's been said. Hawa wonders if Soraya hides as much as her mother does. Marjan's instructed Hawa not to mention to her classmates or teachers or neighbors that her mother is in the military and to never admit that her mother's been trained by American soldiers. Some see ties to the American military as boasting, others as betrayal.

"Khala, what if the office doesn't open?" Hawa asks.

While Soraya searches for an answer, the sound of the azaan ripples through the air. Prayer is better than sleep, the muezzin promises. Hawa has heard plenty of prayers standing on this line.

"The office will open because it has to, my doll," Soraya says, finally finding words. "Say a dua that we'll have our turn today. God listens to the prayers of children. Your heart is pure, more than any adult's by far."

Pray for what, exactly? If they get these passports, where will they go? America? The thought terrifies Hawa, who has never been more than two hours outside of Kabul.

She tries to pray in silence, but the doubts and questions swirling in her head drown out her thoughts. If she cannot hear herself, is there any way to imagine that God can hear her? She inches closer to her mother and waits for the timid dawn to displace night.

13

2012

One week before she was scheduled to move out of the shelter and into the halfway house, Marjan stopped sleeping. Utterly alert at night, she heard every cricket, every distant car sound, every hiss of an old pipe. During the day, she found herself nodding off while she was folding laundry or even while she was spooning mashed rice and lentils into Hawa's eager mouth.

The lack of sleep frayed her nerves. One moment, she would marvel at her growing, thriving daughter and feel determined to succeed if only for her. A moment later, she would realize the price of milk and oil and flour and be racked with terror that she would fail as a mother. She was a passenger on an erratic flight, awed at her soaring height one moment and throttled by the turbulence the next.

"It doesn't make sense," she told Samia. "Sometimes I think I'm capable and sometimes I fear I'll fail at everything. Which do I believe? Which is true?"

"Ah, sweet girl, everything is true!" Samia laughed. "You are right to be terrified. And you're right to feel capable. The trick is to feel both without letting it jam you up too much. Being afraid that you won't provide for your daughter will push you when you need to be pushed. And you'll need to feel capable on those days when you realize this city is made of more walls than doors and you've got to convince people that you deserve a chance. And one more thing, my darling. All of this is infinitely harder alone. Find yourself a circle of women, even if that circle is very small."

What Samia said made logical sense but did little to temper the highs and lows of Marjan's moods. She resigned herself to living with the head spin, hoping she would grow steadier with time. She was still a teenager and younger than any of the other women in the shelter. She'd kept to herself, which meant she'd not heard their stories, hadn't learned from their experiences. She was expert at meeting their questions with a shrug of her shoulders, a sudden headache, a need for sleep.

Their first weeks in the halfway home tested Marjan in every way. She and Hawa had to share a room with six other women. Their sleeping quarters were a single large room with metal-framed bunkbeds lined against the walls and three large windows that drenched the space in light. The room had an eggplant-colored carpet with white lines running across it in a zigzag pattern. Marjan didn't mind that it wasn't traditional. It was the kind of machine-made carpet that was sold off giant spools and lacked warmth. But the real issue was that it felt rough as burlap and made her feel like she was going cross-eyed whenever she opened her door to enter the room.

To Marjan, the women seemed listless. While they all had run *away* from abusive homes, very few were running *toward* anything better. They cared for their children and made small talk and sometimes even revealed the lives they had dreamed of for themselves in their youth, before something essential had been beaten out of them.

She thought of the women she met in the Parliament when she was accompanying her illiterate sister wife, the one who had been placed there as a puppet for their warlord husband. Those women moved and spoke as if they were up against a ticking clock. She remembered one parliamentarian who narrowly survived her car being struck by gunfire, then returned to a voting session with bandages covering where glass had sliced through her skin. She thought of her beloved Khala Shaima, crippled but still bright as a summer day. Marjan felt her feet drag, her thinking slow. Her own fire was dampening, slipping into a winter of the soul.

So when she met Aneesa, she did not pull away.

"Ah, God bless those fat little feet!" Aneesa cheered when she saw Hawa. Aneesa had already been living in the halfway house when Hawa moved in. On Marjan's second day at the house, when all the other women were tied up with classes or work, she shared her own story.

Aneesa's husband had both a heavy fist and a taste for liquor, a combination that meant two years of misery for Aneesa. On the eve of her sister's wedding, on a night for women and henna and dancing, Aneesa had put on her finest dress and done up her makeup. She was taking their toddler with her. She was sure her husband would spend the evening doing what he usually did, scrolling through mindless videos on his phone and snacking. She had tried not to look too excited to be heading to a party for once, but there must have been a bit too much cheer in her voice when she called to their daughter, Roqia, that it was time to put shoes on.

His fist hit the coffee table first. That was her only warning, and it hardly gave her enough time to process what was happening before he slapped her across the face so hard that he sent her spinning. Her daughter watched her mother's skirt twirl like that of a dervish, as tiny coins sewn onto the hem lifted and fell. With one more blow, her husband slammed Aneesa's head against the wall and she crumpled to the floor in an unconscious heap.

Aneesa never made it to the party. She didn't make it to the wedding either. She woke in the middle of the night still on the floor with a massive headache. Roqia had fallen asleep next to her; her cheeks bore the tracks of dried tears. The next morning, Aneesa made her husband breakfast and carried on as if nothing out of the ordinary had happened. This was tragically easy to do.

Her family had been furious with her for not coming to the henna party and the wedding. Her thin excuses about not feeling well had left them only angrier.

Four days after the wedding, her sister showed up at her house to make clear how betrayed she felt. She took one look at Aneesa's battered face and realized what had kept her sister from coming to her henna party. They plotted her escape, and within forty-eight hours, Aneesa found herself in the shelter with her daughter. The team at the shelter had tried to work with her husband, to rehabilitate them as a family and talk about nonviolent communications. They quoted verses from the Quran that required husbands to protect their wives. They reminded him that the prophet himself never struck his wives.

He laughed. What did a bunch of women know about the prophet?

Talaaq, talaaq, talaaq! he had shouted, as he waved a thick finger in her face. And with the word "divorce" repeated three times, he formally severed their union.

The only silver lining was that, despite his right to claim their daughter, he had no interest in being responsible for her. Aneesa and her daughter were more comfortable in the halfway house than they had ever been at home. Aneesa was working as a seamstress in a high-end fashion boutique. They both slept better and smiled more, and Aneesa was hoping to soon find a place for them, a life she could never have imagined before her marriage.

Hawa stood up, took a few steps toward her rag doll across the room, then looked over her shoulder to confirm her mother was bearing witness to this triumph. Her cheeks were round, still cherubic. The colic of her first months was a distant memory. It was almost as if she had gotten all her crying out of the way so that she could spend her time smiling and babbling now.

"She must have grown tired of all that rug burn from crawling on this carpet," Marjan said.

Aneesa laughed.

"Watch out. She'll be outrunning you soon," she warned Marjan. Aneesa did not know that Hawa was not Marjan's first child. They knew her only by the simple story Marjan had grown accustomed to telling—a widowed woman who had escaped an abusive family of in-laws.

Aneesa and Marjan became friends, both of them young and determined. Roqia was two years older than Hawa. They held hands and shared toys. The sight made Marjan miss her four sisters, especially Parwin.

She wondered if there would be any reunions with her other sisters or family members in this life. She didn't see how it was possible. She feared any attempt to get in touch with them would signal her whereabouts to Abdul Khaliq.

"You know, Eid is only five days away," Aneesa said. "Do you have any plans?"

"Oh, maybe I'll take Hawa to the park. She loves playing in the grass and watching the water fountains. I think she's just earned herself an ice cream too."

"You both deserve an ice cream," Aneesa advised. "Will you visit anyone?"

Though they were similar in so many ways, Aneesa's situation differed from Marjan's. She still had her parents and siblings to deal with, her uncles and even a grandmother. Her divorce had brought sufficient shame to their family. They refused to magnify it by having her move back in with her parents, and still encouraged her to try to reconcile with her husband. This stung Aneesa, but she understood. She couldn't bear to cut herself off from her family. They still cared for her and doted on her daughter.

Marjan shook her head.

"I have no one in Kabul. But it's okay. It's better this way," she said. A month ago, she had worked up the nerve to send a letter to her khala Shaima. She had signed it Bibi Shekiba, the ancestor whose name only her aunt would recognize. She was certain Khala Shaima was worried about her, and Marjan wanted to put her mind at ease. Marjan didn't share her location, so there was no way for her aunt to respond, no way for Marjan to know if she ever received the letter or if she was even still alive.

"Maybe we can visit the market and pick up new clothes for the girls?" Aneesa suggested.

Marjan liked the idea. She had just started working as a teacher in the halfway house. She wasn't earning much, but it was the first time she had earned anything at all, and she quickly learned that she relished the feel of paper bills between her fingers. She was practically floating with joy, as if they had given her wings instead of a few colorful afghanis. That was, of course, until they reclaimed some of that money to pay for the living expenses of the halfway house. She didn't mind, though. She liked feeling capable of paying her way, something she had only ever seen men do.

She and Aneesa made the trip to the shops themselves. Marjan was terrified of being in public and was constantly looking around for familiar faces or to see if anyone was noticing her. She wore her headscarf so low that it hooded her face from view. Aneesa came from the outskirts of Kabul. Her ex-husband's family stayed close to home, so she was less concerned with running into anyone connected to her married life.

In a small shop tucked between a bank and a shoe store, they found pale blue satin dresses with skirts of blue tulle. Silver threads around the waist and neckline added enough sparkle to make the small gowns look regal. The dresses were utterly impractical. Both mothers knew it. Still, they looked at their daughters and decided they would be frivolous on this holy occasion, the holiday of Eid coinciding with this first taste of independence. They walked back to the halfway house, giddy from the indulgence.

"This is all your fault," Aneesa proclaimed. "I swear I was planning on buying her a winter coat."

"Oh, really?" Marjan laughed. "I wasn't the one who pulled the dress off the rack. I walked right past it and was looking at those cute little sweaters with the green buttons."

"Is that so? As I recall, I'm the one who talked you out of buying them those tiny matching purses," she chastised playfully.

They put the girls into the dresses as soon as they got back to the house. Three of the other women who lived at the halfway house watched with disapproving frowns. One mother took her two children and left the room. She had neither the stomach nor the wallet for such antics.

Aneesa and Marjan sat the girls side by side on the carpet, posing them for portraits they had no way of taking. Marjan just stared at her daughter as her small fingers felt the stiff tulle, as she looked up at the older girl beside her.

"They look like little dolls! God protect them. If only they had a grand party to attend. Oh, I have an idea!" Aneesa exclaimed, rising from the floor.

"Just remember, this was all your idea!" Marjan called after her, giggling.

She still wore the smile when the feeling hit her. Grief was a rogue wave, and Marjan had turned her back to the ocean.

Jahangir, a child more beautiful and precious than she could ever have hoped for. It was unimaginable that she would never hold him again, that he was not here for this Eid. That he had hardly been old enough to know what Eid was when she lost him. That he would never see another Eid or any other day. Marjan could almost hear the music of his laughter. She could almost feel the silk of his curly hair.

"What is it? What's happened?" Aneesa asked, startled to find a pink-eyed Marjan holding a hand over her mouth to stifle her sobs. Aneesa put an arm around her, pulled her close. The girls had wandered off, lured by a stray balloon left behind by another child.

Marjan shook her head. Aneesa pressed her.

"You can't keep everything inside. Believe me, it feels so much better to let it out," she said.

Marjan felt something swell in her chest then, uncontainable. Afraid it might crack her open, she told Aneesa about Jahangir, her firstborn and the brother Hawa would never meet.

"This world is too cruel. How you must have suffered! Will you tell Hawa about him?" Aneesa asked.

"I don't think I can," Marjan said. "And I don't see what good it would do for her to know."

"I suppose." Aneesa sighed. "God is good, no? To give you Hawa after what you suffered."

Marjan nodded. Losing her son had weathered her. There were shadows under her eyes that weren't there before, even with the abuse she had suffered. She looked older than her years and struggled to feel joy without guilt. Her son was never too far from her thoughts. Everything Hawa did for the first time sent her back to Jahangir's first year.

Aneesa treated her a bit more delicately after that. Marjan hadn't been looking for pity but appreciated the kindness of a friend. She had been so busy fumbling through the logistics of this new life that she hadn't realized how lonely she felt. Marjan and Aneesa ate together. They groused about the conditions of the common bathroom and took their daughters outside to play together.

"If we get real jobs, we can afford a real place to live," Aneesa said as they fed the girls bowls of rice with lentils. "I'll watch the girls while you go to work and then you can look after them when I go to work. We'll be able to afford a decent place, too, with both of us working. I'm a much better cook than you, so maybe you do more of the cleaning."

"You really think two women can afford a place in this city? People say rents have doubled in the past few years," Marjan huffed.

"It's true but we'll lean on each other and we'll find something," Aneesa insisted.

"No one will want to rent to two women coming out of a shelter. People will think our shame is contagious," Marjan whispered.

"We'll tell them we're both widowed," Aneesa replied defiantly. "It's very believable. This country is full of them. And we might as well be widows. Our husbands are dead to us."

Marjan pinched a small morsel between her thumb and two fingers and pressed it into Hawa's open mouth. It occurred to her that her mother had hand-fed her in the same way, then stood by while she was given away to a warlord only twelve years later. She dabbed at her daughter's mouth with a wipe. Hawa batted the cloth away and smacked her lips, hungry for more and trusting that her mother would give her what she needed.

14

AUGUST 11, 2021
METRA MEDIA

Mina watches for her producer's cue. In the distance, she sees the show's opening playing on a television screen. She wonders how many people are watching and rubs her fingertip across her front teeth one last time. The new tube of lipstick she purchased goes on a bit too creamy, and she already gets more critiques and analyses of her face than the Mona Lisa.

Her producer raises three fingers. Then two. He points at her.

"Esteemed viewers, welcome again to tonight's program, where we bring you news from around the country and beyond. I am Mina Noori of Metra Media.

"The crackle of gunfire echoed through Farah Province all day yesterday. Residents have kept to their homes for safety, unclear whether the Afghan military forces will be able to fend off the approaching insurgents. Witnesses reported that Taliban fighters had paraded the mangled corpse of an Afghan soldier through a central road. The insurgents drove through the town in Humvees and Ford pickup trucks brought here by the Americans, firing into the air and declaring to residents that the area was now under their control.

"In addition to the northeast region of the country, much of the north has also succumbed to Taliban advances. While warlords plan collaborations with the Afghan national forces to push back the Taliban and reclaim territory, violence continues to plague communities and the number of wounded soldiers increases.

"Civilians who fled Taliban advances spoke of schools burned down and revenge killings. Shariah law was declared by Taliban leaders, and women were advised that they should dress in full hijab when in public. President Ashraf Ghani traveled to Mazar-e-Sharif to buoy the spirits of the Afghan National Security Forces as they set out to defend the largest city in northern Afghanistan."

Mina wonders if the grim updates she's just shared are being received with the same placidity with which she's just delivered them. She wonders, too, if her placidity might be part of the problem. Is she lulling people into a false sense of stability or is she demonstrating admirable stoicism?

"And in world news, we move to Algeria, where rampant wildfires have claimed forty-two lives," she reports, feeling the room warm by degrees.

She spends the taxi ride home counting her blessings. Her parents are in reasonable health and fair spirits. She has an education and skills that can never be taken from her. And, above all, she is grateful her travesty of a marriage left her only with disgrace, and no children to worry over, no tiny hands to hold as they take their first steps across this untamable earth.

15

2012

The days were growing shorter, and evening winds danced through the courtyard carrying whispers of winter. Marjan had nearly forgotten about Hawa's laundry drying on the clothesline. She'd come out to retrieve her still-damp pieces in case it rained overnight. Marjan paused to scratch at her ankle. The mosquitoes found their way to the tiniest sliver of exposed flesh.

The door to the halfway house creaked open. Marjan looked up from her basket to see Aneesa's figure illuminated by the porch light. She stood on the step with her arms folded across her chest and her head lowered.

When Marjan approached her, the gathered laundry in her arms, Aneesa still didn't look up. A crown of white moths flitted above her head, mistaking the glow of a cheap bulb for the moon. Gauzy wings orbited the brightness then fell away, disoriented.

"Are the girls okay?" Marjan asked.

Aneesa sniffled. She pressed her fingers over her eyes and shook her head. The girls had both come down with a cold two days back. Maybe Aneesa had caught it too.

"Yes, they're both still asleep."

"Then what's happened?" Marjan asked.

Aneesa shifted her weight uncomfortably.

"He wants me to come back," she said.

Marjan stood in stunned silence. She knew right away who Aneesa was talking about, even if she hadn't mentioned any names.

"Are you sure? How do you know?"

"Yes. He went looking for me at my family's home," Aneesa said. She fished a crumpled tissue out of her pocket and dried her nose.

"After all this time? But he divorced you!"

"He's denying he ever said it."

A heavy silence hung between them, for the truth was that Aneesa's word was no match for her husband's.

"I thought I was free. Marjan, I can't go back to him. Every other day he finds some reason to . . . to . . . I just can't go back."

Marjan put a hand on Aneesa's arm.

"What did your family say?"

A bitter laugh escaped Aneesa's lips.

"That I should be grateful for a chance to go home. That I've brought too much shame on them being in this place. He's convinced them that these shelters take women in and then turn them into prostitutes. I told my mother a thousand times it wasn't true, and she reminded me that it doesn't matter if it's not true. It only matters that it was said."

Marjan's heart sank. It was too easy to sully a woman's character. There was no need for evidence. An accusation became a conviction as soon as the words were uttered, and there was nothing a woman could do to prove herself innocent. There was no path to redemption.

"But what he did to you that night . . ." Marjan's words drifted away, meaningless.

"He told them I was very sharp with him and laughed when he asked what time I was coming home. And that it's normal for husbands and wives to argue sometimes, which of course my father was not going to dispute," Aneesa said bitterly. "My husband doesn't love me. He just doesn't like that I've not gone crawling back to him."

Aneesa wasn't the first woman to face the prospect of returning to an abusive home. Far from it. The staff at the shelter worked with families with the goal of reconciling. It would be ideal to restore a woman to her home so long as it was a safe situation. And many women felt compelled to return home, either because of their children or because being on their own in a world of men was too overwhelming.

"What did you tell them?"

"That they can all go to hell. And that I refuse to go back to him," Aneesa declared, wiping her tears away.

As if she had uttered her final word on the matter, over the next few days she did not bring it up again and refused to speak about it when Marjan inquired if she had heard anything more.

Marjan was relieved. She did not want to think of her best friend returning to a husband who had left her nearly lifeless on the floor. And she was more relieved to see that the staff of the halfway house did not push Aneesa to reconcile with her husband. They respected her decision and believed her when she said there was no safe return for her.

One evening, late into the night, Marjan heard Aneesa's sheets rustling. Neither one of them was getting much sleep.

"Aneesa?"

"Mm?"

"Did you really tell your family that they can all go to hell?"

"No," she whispered. "But I most certainly thought it."

Aneesa continued in her daily routines as usual. The other women in the halfway house did not detect any changes, but Marjan noticed that Aneesa's eyes would glaze over when she watched her daughter playing or flipping through pages of a storybook, pretending to read. She would poke at her food, and her steps were slower, laborious.

Again, Marjan was awakened in the night by the sound of Aneesa's restless movements.

"Are you all right?" she whispered in the dark.

Though Marjan was sure she was awake, Aneesa didn't respond.

In the morning, Aneesa put on a smile and helped her daughter dress. She kissed the top of Roqia's head. Marjan wondered if she really had been asleep and was putting her husband's nonsense behind her. In the afternoon, they brought the girls back to the room, hopeful that they would take a nap and give their mothers a few moments to themselves. While they played, Aneesa mended the torn knee on a pair of Roqia's leggings. Marjan was working her way through a chapter of *Pride and Prejudice*, which she was stunned to discover was about five unmarried sisters, their vexed parents, and the finicky suitors circling their lives. The Bennet girls weren't children, of course. And they weren't being forced into brutal marriages. Still, Marjan was stirred by Elizabeth's spirit, her self-assuredness.

What are men to rocks and mountains?

Marjan was about to share the line with Aneesa when someone knocked on the door of their room, then entered.

"Aneesa?"

Marjan and Aneesa both looked up.

The woman standing in the doorway was a social worker who checked on the halfway house residents from time to time. She beckoned Aneesa, but Aneesa shook her head. Marjan watched with confusion.

"It's important that I speak with you." The woman's tone was gentle but firm.

"I'm busy," Aneesa said. Her hands trembled as she pierced the patch with her needle.

"Aneesa."

Aneesa set her work down with an exaggerated huff. She rose and walked to the hallway to have a private word with the woman. She returned a few moments later, her expression darkened.

"Is everything all right?" Marjan asked, though it was evident nothing was all right.

"He wants to take her," Aneesa muttered.

Every woman in the halfway house, every woman in Kabul, every mother in Afghanistan knew that in the rare case of a dissolved marriage, the law sided with men on the issue of custody. It didn't matter that Aneesa's husband had knocked her unconscious or that he'd nearly killed her in front of their daughter. If he wanted Roqia, the courts would give him Roqia.

"This is too cruel," Aneesa moaned.

That night, Marjan wondered what she would do if Abdul Khaliq were to show up at the halfway house tomorrow demanding his child. Would she hand Hawa over? Would she go back to Abdul Khaliq so that she wouldn't be separated from her child?

Aneesa refused to lose Roqia.

She packed her bag and became one of the countless women who chose the lesser of two evils. Marjan and Hawa followed Aneesa and Roqia to the halfway house's front gate. Marjan hugged her friend tightly.

"If things are bad, just come back. Don't be afraid to leave," Marjan reminded her, though she knew it would be nearly impossible to gather the courage to leave a second time. "We'll be praying for you and Roqia-jan."

Aneesa nodded, her eyes glistening. She did not want to break down, especially with Hawa and Roqia watching.

"Yes, pray for us. And I'll be praying for you and Hawa-jan. Don't give up. I want to hear that you've gotten yourself an apartment with your own bathroom and kitchen, something in a tall building. You'll tell me about your job working somewhere . . . somewhere important. Not a dress shop, for sure, but somewhere important. You're so clever and young."

Marjan laughed bitterly.

"Promise me," she repeated, blinking back tears. "Promise me you'll come back if things get bad."

Aneesa pointed to the sky above, where dithering clouds occupied most of the slate-colored sky. Winter was drawing near.

"God as my witness, I will do my best."

Marjan kissed Roqia's face.

"Be a good girl," she whispered. Roqia nodded. Her five years of life had already taught her how vital it was that she behave. She knew, in her still-growing bones, that this world did not tolerate a disobedient girl.

Marjan, with Hawa on her hip, stood on the concrete steps of the halfway house, watching her friend walk out the gate as the first drops of rain landed on her head.

16

AUGUST 15, 2021

The knock on the door comes just as Hawa is pouring herself a glass of water in the kitchen. She immediately looks to her mother.

"It's Khala Soraya," she explains, seeing the alarm on Hawa's face.

Hawa breathes out in relief. She hasn't seen Khala Soraya since they left the passport office, defeated. After hours of waiting, someone emerged and announced that the office was going to close and would not take any more applications for the day. The news whipped the crowd's anxieties and frustrations into outrage. Marjan pulled Hawa close, trying to shield her from the shouting, the cursing, the pointing of fingers. The stray dogs, lazy from their midnight prowling, watched the unrest with disinterest. It came as no surprise to them that people could be feral too.

Soraya bursts in, pulling her sunglasses and headscarf off in one sweeping motion. With her other hand, she pulls Hawa to her in an embrace.

"My little songbird, how are you?" she asks, kissing the top of Hawa's head. She is affectionate but not her usual bubbly self.

"My mother won't turn on the news. What's happening out there, Khala Soraya?" she asks. "Are the Taliban in Kabul?"

Marjan shoots Soraya a warning look.

"Stop trying to hide things from me," Hawa gripes. "Well? Are they attacking the city?"

"No," Soraya says. "But they've taken Kandahar. What we thought might happen slowly is happening quickly. We thought we had months, or weeks, at least. We do not. We've got to move now. Jenna is calling me in a few minutes with instructions. Marjan, please tell me you're ready."

"It won't take me long," Marjan promises.

Soraya nods, her impatience evident. Hawa has never seen her act this way. Today is not just another day, she thinks.

"Are we going to the airport, Madar?" Hawa asks. Despite her mother's attempts to shield her, she's seen chilling footage on the television, the crush of bodies trying to squeeze themselves through the gates of Kabul airport.

"When the moment is right—" Marjan starts to say, but Khala Soraya cuts her off.

"The moment will never be right."

Soraya walks into the living room, looks out the window onto the street below. Her hair is pulled up in a loose bun that still looks refined. With her hands on her hips, her elbows are angular. Insistent.

"Soraya, you've seen the same warnings I have," Marjan says.

"What warnings?" Hawa asks, but her mother only raises a finger, as if she'll answer Hawa's question in a moment. She won't, of course.

"Yes, I've seen the warnings about the airport, but I've also seen the warnings about the whole goddamned country," Soraya retorts.

"Who of our group has gotten through so far? Only one. And you know what she described."

People trampled. A pregnant woman fainting in the heat. A man lifting up his baby, offering him to the American marines guarding the walls of the airport as if he were making a sacrifice to the gods. They took the baby, but then came warning shots from the Taliban and the family was swept away in a surge of movement—the baby on one side of the wall, his parents on the other.

"It's completely unsafe," Marjan says.

"If it's safety you're looking for, staying in Kabul won't help you. It's just a matter of time, Marjan. You know this as well as I do." Soraya's caution echoes like a single plucked note in a silent room.

Marjan takes slow, deliberate breaths. She needs to think. She looks around her apartment, at the few possessions she has gathered, at the space she managed to secure for her and her daughter. No one wanted to rent to a single woman with a daughter.

But Elaha, the platoon captain, used her brother's connections to put in a good word for her here. Marjan and Hawa have slept side by side in the bedroom, dreaming and resting and rising. Hawa's school uniform is folded neatly in the dresser Marjan purchased from a neighbor. In her cabinets are the three glass plates and four mugs she purchased with her first paycheck as a soldier. She is reluctant to leave, she realizes. Maybe she's letting emotions cloud her judgment.

"Khala Soraya's right. We need to get on one of those planes," she tells her daughter. "Maybe by the time we get there, instructions will come through."

Soraya's purse rumbles on the table. She quickly digs her phone out of her bag.

"Is it Jenna?" Marjan asks.

Soraya looks at the screen and shakes her head.

"No, it's my brother. Just one second," she says, turning away as she answers the call. She takes a couple of steps toward the kitchen, though it gains her no privacy. "Yes? No, I'm not there yet. I promise if I get through the gate, I'll beg someone on the inside to add your name. Okay. Yes, I will. Just please don't answer the phone if he calls. You cannot let our idiot cousin get into your head."

Soraya hangs up the phone and mutters something Hawa cannot make out.

"Your brother?" Marjan asks.

Soraya nods.

"Yes, my brother. My cousin has been calling me everything from a traitor to a harlot ever since I joined the platoon. And my brother has apparently stopped thinking for himself. He told me I was dishonoring our dead father. But now that he sees I might have a chance of getting onto a plane because of my work, he doesn't seem too upset to be the brother of a 'harlot.' Maybe I should tell him that's the code phrase to get across the gate—*I'm a harlot!* I'd love to see him wave his arms and shout that for the world to hear."

Hawa's ears are burning. She has never heard Khala Soraya use such language.

"Toba, toba," Marjan says, repenting on her friend's behalf. Soraya is suddenly aware of Hawa and covers her face with one hand. She groans but doubts this is Hawa's first encounter with the word. It is too handy, like a slim pocketknife that lives in a man's pocket and unfolds to reveal its many tools, its many uses and functions. It can discredit, silence, shame, and maim a woman. It is a red target on a white wall.

"Forgive me, my sweet," Soraya says, squeezing Hawa to her. "It's just hard to fight every hour of every day. If I were my father's eldest son, my cousin would not dare open his foul mouth to say a word about me. Instead, this idiot, who cannot tell a hammer from a nail, feels he has the right to tell me what I should or should not do. In his mind, I should have been given away as a bride long ago, before I could become a problem."

Hawa may sometimes want to pound the wall in anger for the life she has not had—a father and siblings, an extended family with cousins, grandparents, aunts, and uncles. She has never attended a wedding or had her hair brushed by a grandmother. She has never been carried on anyone's shoulders or touched a stubbled cheek. She does not have a brother to walk with her in these streets or a grandfather to tell her she is the light of his eyes.

But Hawa also knows she has been spared other experiences. She cannot name them specifically, but she recognizes them when they crash-land at her feet. Soraya's brother calling her a harlot is one of those moments, even if she is not entirely certain what a harlot is. She senses that, of all the ways a woman can be wicked, it is the worst way. She is grateful that Soraya's brother is not her brother or uncle. She is grateful that her mother has only herself to answer to.

Two phones chime at once. Marjan and Soraya both swipe their phones open and stare at their screens. Hawa tries to read their expressions. Does she need to gather her belongings too? She wishes she could talk to Layma. She wonders what her family is doing.

Her mother surveys the apartment. There's something odd about her breathing, as if she's having trouble letting go of the air she's taken in.

"We can trust Jenna," Soraya says, one hand on Marjan's forearm. "Remember, one bag. Stay light."

Marjan nods.

"You have fifteen minutes," Soraya says.

"We'll be ready in five," Hawa's mother says as she takes her daughter by the hand and leads her into the bedroom. She grabs her duffel bag. "Hawa-jan, we don't have time. Empty your school bag and pack a few pieces of clothing, tops and bottoms. Essentials only."

Hawa's heart races. She has so many questions. If they leave now, will they ever come back? And how can she possibly fit everything into her schoolbag?

"I . . . I don't know what to . . ."

"Hawa-jan, tops and bottoms. Come on. Not too many pieces. Pick out your favorites."

Marjan rifles through the bundle of papers she's pulled out of her duffel. Satisfied, she sets them aside and plucks two more shirts from an open dresser drawer.

"Soraya, can you bring me the phone charger? It's next to the television."

Soraya delivers the cord, coiled and compact. Both phones chime again. Soraya reads through the messages they are both receiving.

"What are they saying?" Marjan asks as she stuffs two pairs of rolled-up pants into her bag.

"That we need to go to the airport now."

Hawa watches her mother's movements, steady and focused. She feels both a bit assured but also a shade unnerved.

"Hawa, bring the toothbrushes and toothpaste from the bathroom."

Hawa feels outpaced. She cannot keep up with this tempo. Leaving in five minutes? What about the rest of their belongings? What should she start with? Isn't there a different bag she can use? Her schoolbag is small. It will never hold everything, her drawing book and colored pencils, her green pencil case with two compartments, the clothes her mother allowed her to pick out for herself in the secondhand store, the stuffed bear she is too old for but cannot let go, the beaded bracelets Ingrid gave her. Should she pack her sheet music? She wants to tell her mother that she needs more time, a bigger bag, more information, she needs . . . she needs . . .

She needs her mother's help, but she's choking on the words. She stares at the stuffed bear in her hands, fingers the two dainty buttons sewn onto its fuzzy chest, feeling like one of them might be lodged in her throat. She is tugging at the collar of her shirt, hungry for air, when her mother enters the room.

"Madar—"

"Please, Hawa. I need you to help me now," she pleads.

Hawa swallows her words. She keeps her eyes on the rug and nods.

17

2012

After Aneesa's departure, Marjan curled into herself like an autumn leaf. She shouldn't have let herself get caught up in someone else's dreams. It was best to concentrate on preparing for a life outside of the halfway house, a life in which she would be solely responsible for her daughter in every sense of the word.

She tried not to think about Aneesa. They had no way of communicating with each other and hadn't even bothered to make flimsy promises of doing so when they bid each other farewell. And Marjan wasn't the only person in Afghanistan to endure perpetual goodbyes. People who fled during the Soviet invasion might have thought they would return after the conflict, but then came the civil war and the Taliban. Hope of reunions diminished. Bags packed, people held on to their parents and siblings longer in that final hug before escape and touched each other's faces. Parents kissed their grown children as if they were school age again. Children pressed their lips to the palms of their grandparents' hands. Life had never been guaranteed, but the whistle of rockets signaled a tipping of the odds in mortality's favor.

Marjan couldn't work unless someone else cared for Hawa. She needed to rely on the other women in the halfway house, but she kept her relationships transactional and flat. She was polite enough. Her aloofness was readily accepted in a community of women who had been scarred by the people closest to them.

She found a restaurant willing to hire her, thanks to a good word from

Samia. The job was in the kitchen, julienning carrots and peeling garlic and chopping onions until her eyes felt like they had been set aflame. She wasn't trusted with the serious cooking, though they did allow her to blend the chutneys and to flip the eggplant as it fried in vegetable oil. The grease splatter and heat caused her face to break out, but she dared not complain. The work was reliable, paid decently, and kept her out of public view. She saved every penny and took home with her any food that would otherwise have been discarded. Often enough, the owner sent her home with enough food for two.

One month turned into three, three turned into six, and before she knew it, a year had gone by. Marjan was growing comfortable in her new life, accustomed to the rhythm of her days and the weight of the struggle. Hawa was thriving, turning words into sentences and becoming the darling of the home, since most of the other children were older.

Marjan was so busy during the day that she could hardly think an hour ahead. But at night, while the world slept, she tried to envision her future. The halfway house was a stepping stone, but to what? And the restaurant was a job that barely covered her expenses now. Could she go back to school? She watched girls her age dressed in school uniforms or carrying satchels heavy with books and imagined a day when she might fall in step with them. She would be more than happy to stay up all night studying if it meant she could hold a diploma in her hands and know that she would be able to support herself and her daughter for the rest of her life.

Marjan's brooding wasn't the only reason she lost sleep. Hawa seemed to come down with a cold every few weeks. It would start with a bit of fussing and pushing away food. Then her cheeks would flush with fever, her nose would start to run, and she'd be racked with coughing fits. One Ramadan, in the dead of winter, a tenacious flu made its way around the halfway house, passed from child to child.

Marjan knew it was only a matter of time. When Hawa came down with the illness, the hacking cough was so persistent that she didn't have the energy to play with her favorite toy, a red ball with blue stitching. Marjan touched her daughter's chest and felt the heat of her small body.

She gave her a spoonful of the red fever-reducing elixir one of the other mothers had recommended to her. Hawa had pushed away her white rice, setting her head down on a pillow instead. Marjan offered her water and juice, but Hawa pushed the cup away. She changed Hawa's clothes, opting for a lighter shirt so that Hawa wouldn't feel so hot. The coughs cut through the stillness of the night, sharp and relentless.

It was when Hawa's breathing changed that Marjan became alarmed. Hawa's breathing, the rise and fall of her chest, had once been the rhythm that lulled Marjan to sleep. But on this night, she heard a strange whistling coming from her daughter.

She was immediately taken back to her son and the malady that had claimed him in her absence. What if this wasn't just another cold? What if Marjan was ignoring something more sinister, just as her mother-in-law had when Jahangir had fallen ill?

Marjan tried to stay calm. She checked the clock on the wall. It was two in the morning, if this devilish hour could be called morning. Could this wait? All she could hear was the soft whistle in every exhalation of Hawa's shallow breaths.

Marjan went down the hall to Husna's room. Husna had three children and had been at the halfway house the longest. She made it her business to know as much as she could about the other women, recording in her mind every sordid detail of their abusive and dysfunctional family dynamics. Marjan avoided her for this very reason. In fairness, Husna was an open book about the abuse that had forced her to pick up her three children and seek help at the shelter. She could not imagine why anyone wouldn't want to vent about their misfortunes. Husna was always available, deeply sympathetic, and rather shameless.

And this was your sister-in-law? Dear and pure Allah, what a scoundrel.

My husband slapped me for flirting with my son's teacher at school. Imagine that? I saw the man once on the street. Was your husband terribly envious too? Did he ever accuse you of sins he himself was committing?

Were you terribly constipated when you were pregnant? It took me nine months to have the baby but even longer to take a shit.

There were benefits to having a busybody in the house, a woman who inquired about every illness with more interest than a medical student. On top of that, she was an experienced mother.

Marjan knocked on Husna's door. Impatient, she opened it enough to make out four sleeping figures on floor mattresses—Husna and her children.

"Husna-jan? I'm so sorry to disturb you," Marjan whispered into the room.

Husna inhaled sharply, roused from sleep.

"Who's there?" she whispered back.

"It's me, Marjan. I'm worried about Hawa."

Husna snapped her comforter off and stood, as if she'd been summoned to an official duty. She followed Marjan back to her room and touched Hawa's damp forehead. She put a hand on her chest and felt the rise and fall, heard the soft whistle. Hawa began to cough again, tight and hard.

"She is breathing hard, poor thing," Husna said, clucking her tongue. "Has she been this way all day?"

"No, not like this," Marjan said, though as soon as she uttered the words, she wondered if she was right. Maybe she had been breathing hard, and Marjan hadn't noticed. Guilt snaked around her chest and squeezed. Hawa groaned and rolled away, as if she wanted these two makeshift nurses to allow her to sleep.

"My youngest coughed like this once. He had pneumonia. Nearly killed him," Husna said. "You should take her to the hospital."

Marjan threw herself into action. She packed up Hawa and began the moonlit trek to the hospital. Hawa was not so easy to carry now that she wasn't an infant. Marjan shifted her from one arm to the other and walked quickly but carefully, terrified that she would trip on the rough streets and send them both crashing to the ground.

At the hospital, the nurse checked Hawa's temperature and asked Marjan how long she'd been ill. A doctor came in and asked a few more questions while he pressed a stethoscope to Hawa's chest. With a lighted scope, he peered into her mouth and ears and pressed on her belly. He watched Hawa's chest and belly rise and fall with every heavy breath, then gave her back to Marjan.

"We'll need to give her some medications to help her breathing. Are you familiar with asthma?"

Marjan shook her head.

"It's a condition that makes it harder for children to breathe," he explained, then asked the nurse to bring in two medications. She nodded and left.

"Is it fatal?" Marjan asked.

"No, not if it's treated." He noticed that Marjan's hands trembled slightly as she fussed with the buttons on Hawa's sweater. "Where is her father?"

Marjan's hands tightened around her daughter. Why was he asking? She could only come up with sinister reasons.

"My husband dropped me off on his way to work," she lied.

Marjan was ashamed to be a single mother. She was also ashamed that she felt that way. She felt slightly better telling people she was a widow, but the word didn't feel natural to her. Abdul Khaliq was too alive in her mind. She saw him coming around every corner and heard his taunts in her sleep. He was a grenade with its pin pulled.

"Very well," the doctor said. "I hope he'll be free soon. He'll need to pick up the medications she needs for her breathing and her ear infection. Let me teach you about asthma because it is likely this will happen again."

The pediatrician was right. The asthma returned every time Hawa caught a cold, which seemed to happen with the same frequency as the appearance of a new moon. Marjan kept a pouch of Hawa's medicines by her bed and learned the signs and symptoms of her illness. Six months later, the pharmacist could almost guess what she needed before she said a word.

"Antibiotics again or steroids? Or are you out of the inhaler?" he asked.

The medications took a big bite out of her income, as did her absences from work. Early winter was a particularly rough spell with a virus that had Hawa barely able to keep her food down. When one child in the halfway house came down with a runny nose or stomach flu, it would inevitably pass to every other child. Neither one of them slept much at all. Marjan was in a fog when she dragged her feet into the restaurant one afternoon, leaving Hawa with her very reluctant babysitter, Husna.

"You're late," Elyas announced as she walked in.

"I know and I'm so sorry," Marjan said. She had grown to respect her boss. He had taken a chance on her at a time when she couldn't bring herself to trust anyone. He always respected her space and never made idle conversation. He was all business with her, which she appreciated. As underwater as she felt, she still didn't want to be coddled.

"You were late yesterday as well," he reminded her.

She nodded, feeling a slight burn in the back of her throat. Was she coming down with something too? First chance she got, she would steal a pinch of salt from the kitchen and gargle with salt water, as Husna had recommended.

"I know and I'm so very sorry," she repeated. She hoped she sounded sincere. Sleepless nights had worn her out. One hour before work today, she'd inadvertently dozed off while Hawa napped. She woke to the sound of Hawa coughing and realized she should have been out the door ten minutes earlier.

She probably wouldn't sleep much tonight either, even though Hawa was breathing easier today. The social worker had informed all the residents of the halfway house that they had run out of funding. They had three weeks to find shelter for themselves. Husna was planning on returning to her father's home, two provinces away. Her family was less than thrilled at the prospect of being the talk of the neighbors, but her father had suffered two heart attacks and didn't resist as he might have just a few years earlier. He'd decided he could use another caregiver in his senior years.

"Forgive me," Marjan promised, her voice shaking. "It's been a rough week. Hawa's better, thank God, but I'll have to find a new place to live by the end of the month. This job means so much to me. I won't let you down again."

Elyas sighed heavily. He knew only that she was widowed and shared a home with several women. She hadn't told him it was a halfway house, though he might have assumed as much. He started to walk away and then turned back.

"Maybe there's a place you could stay," he suggested. "There's a room for rent with two young women. I'll give you a number. You make the call."

The thought of leaving the halfway house both terrified and excited Marjan. She craved independence and would love to get Hawa out of that cesspool of germs. But how was she to manage work and a daughter on her own?

Her manager scribbled a phone number on a napkin and handed it to her. Marjan tucked the paper into her pocket and vowed to call immediately after work that night.

Hawa, I promise I'll give you the home you deserve, Marjan thought to herself. It was the first of many promises to her daughter that she would not keep.

18

AUGUST 15, 2021

They wait for the sounds of gunfire from the city outskirts, for signs the national army is engaging the approaching Taliban, but none come. Perhaps the entire city has been fooled, Hawa thinks as she, her mother, and Soraya sit in the back of a taxi driving through a perfectly sunny and panic-stricken Kabul. The women are busy on their phones, reading messages and tapping out replies. They cannot trust any reassurances; they will not ignore any warnings.

But where are the Taliban? Hawa watches people dashing about. She takes a closer look and sees what she hadn't noticed before. Shops have closed their doors. There are too many children with backpacks scurrying to keep up with their parents.

The ATMs have not worked for the past couple of days. People are swarming bank branches, desperate to extract their cash. Marjan was one of them yesterday, one among hundreds. Two men emerged from the bank shouting for the crowd to disperse as there was no money left in the branch. This only made the crowd push harder toward the entrance.

Earlier, Hawa watched her mother retrieve a plastic pouch she kept tied to a pipe under the kitchen sink. Hawa noted the frown on her mother's face when she finished counting the cash she had squirreled away.

The back seat is cramped and the seat cushions so thin that Hawa wonders if she's sitting on the chassis. Trapped between her mother and

Soraya, she scoots forward to get a better view of the city. She can hear the low drone of fear vibrating through Kabul.

The traffic light turns red. Hawa looks out the window and realizes they've stopped at the entrance to the shopping plaza where her mother had taken her to buy a new dress for Eid, where she had stiffly refused to buy Hawa a doll that came with a bottle of vanishing milk. *You don't need a toy like that,* she'd snapped when Hawa had pleaded. Something in her mother's voice made Hawa burn with shame for having asked.

A dark green pickup truck pulls up next to them. The government's insignia and the word "police" written in both English and Dari decorate the passenger door. Hawa's eyes drift to the truck's open window. She comes face-to-face with the midnight eyes of a bearded man wearing a bright orange vest. In his lap is a rifle, its barrel sticking out the window and toward the open sky. Behind him are at least three more men, along with the driver and two more in the front seat. Two more men in turbans sit in the open bed of the pickup, their backs to the truck's cab, a stark white-and-black flag of the Islamic Emirate hanging over them.

"Dear God. Soraya, cover yourself," Marjan hisses. She and Soraya pull their headscarves across their faces. Hawa's mother draws her close. The taxi driver mutters a prayer.

The men look gleeful, like boys on a holiday. The man with the orange vest laughs at Hawa's gaping mouth. He slaps the side of the truck, pumps a fist in the air, and points at Soraya. He nudges the man sitting next to him, who then leans over to get a good look at them.

Marjan knows what Soraya is thinking. They both have with them paperwork that identifies them as members of the Afghan army as well as certificates from the Americans honoring their collaborative service. Kabul's air carries the smoke of so many documents like these set afire by people who did not want to risk being caught with them. Identities and degrees and careers have been turned to ash. But Marjan and Soraya made the risky decision not to destroy the evidence of their work or the documents they need to prove their lives would be in danger if they stayed.

"Just drive!" Marjan hisses at the driver.

"Sister, be still. Wolves smell fear," the driver says just loud enough for them to hear. He keeps his eyes straight ahead and silently curses himself for picking up these passengers.

Hawa hears her mother's heart pounding through her chest. Or is it her own? What's become of the police department? Have all their vehicles been commandeered by the Taliban? The taxi driver feels foolish to stop at a red light. Yesterday's rules seem incongruent with today's reality.

To their relief, the truck full of Talibs rolls past them, the driver with a phone to his ear. One man in the bed of the truck fires two celebratory shots into the air. Hawa flinches, twice.

The taxi moves forward again; the driver keeps his hands steady on the wheel. "Sisters," the driver says. "Do you think you will be able to get on a flight?"

"We hope so," Marjan says.

"But do you have passports? Visas? I hear they're only letting through people who have paid someone off," he continues.

Soraya looks at Marjan again. Caution. Half of Kabul is desperate for travel documents.

"Isn't that the story of our lives? We will try our luck, just like everyone else. God is merciful," Marjan says, still holding Hawa against her chest.

"If you know how I can get passports, I would appreciate it. I have three daughters and two sons. My wife has family in Germany and I have family in the United States. We've been trying but we cannot get passports or visas. If you know of anyone, any way . . ."

"I wish I did," Soraya says. "May God keep you all safe."

"My daughter is sixteen," he adds, continuing his plea. "We heard the Talibs want lists of unmarried girls and widows, anyone between fifteen and forty-five years old, for their fighters to take as brides. Is it true or not? I do not want to find out. If you are going to America, please take her with you! She could stay with my brother there. She's a bright girl and would be no trouble to you at all. We could pick her up now. It wouldn't delay us more than a few minutes."

His passengers grow quiet, stilled by his desperation. Would Marjan send Hawa with strangers if that were the only way to get her out of this country? If she found a way, would she send her daughter over the airport walls alone and onto a plane bound for God knows where?

"If I believed I could help your daughter," Marjan says softly, "I would take her. But I am not sure my daughter and I have any chance at all."

Soraya looks ready to burst into tears. There are so many girls to save.

His cell phone rings. Soraya's phone pings. Alerts ricochet. The taxi driver puts his caller on speaker phone.

"Ghani has fled!" the caller announces. The president?

"What? When? Are you sure?" the taxi driver demands.

"Yes, yes! He and all his people took off in a helicopter. There's no one left in the presidential palace. They're all gone!"

"That God forsaken son of a dog," the taxi driver exclaims.

From the way Marjan's staring at a message on her phone, Hawa can tell she's reading confirmation of this news.

"And where is our army?" the driver demands. Soraya and Marjan exchange a glance. He curses the president again and tells the caller he'll phone back in a few moments.

Soldiers in the provinces have gone without pay for months, the women know. They've been left without bullets. They may have had the will to fight the Talibs but could hardly do so without ammunition.

Marjan stares at her phone. It's a message from Krista.

New warnings just now. ISIS threat at the airport. I hear no one's getting through the gates.

"God damn them!" Soraya says, her words a ball of fire. It is not clear whom she is cursing. There are so many contenders. She looks from Hawa to Marjan, her face clouded with an uncertainty that was not there only a few moments ago.

"What's happened?" the driver asks. Marjan doesn't answer. She's too busy trying to hide her fear from her daughter, too busy trying to judge whether to risk the airport when they've just received a warning, too busy watching Soraya's steely resolve falter.

"Stop the car, please," Marjan calls.

"At your service. Extra charge for stopping," the driver replies as he spins the steering wheel, pulls the car to a stop on the side of the road, and pops the tab on an energy drink.

Marjan and Soraya exit the vehicle and meet at the trunk of the car. They can feel the heat emanating from its shell. Hawa follows.

"What do you think?" Marjan asks Soraya.

They are not far from the airport. It is evident from the number of people they can see holding duffel bags. An occasional suitcase. Just down the road, families are perched like birds on the thick concrete curbs. A woman shouts at someone in the distance, a baby in her arms. The air is inhospitable.

"I don't know. We're damned no matter what we choose," Soraya says. She turns away and shouts, releases a burst of compressed air from her chest.

Marjan meets the driver's eyes in the side mirror. He's watching them, counting the minutes and recalculating their fare. She tries to slow her thoughts.

"It's not impossible. Let's think tactically. That's what we learned as FTPs. We need a real plan," Marjan says, trying to tame the situation. For every mission, she was equipped with maps, night-vision goggles, guns. Even candy to win the trust of children.

"What kind of plan?" Soraya shouts, whirling around to face her. "The only plan is for us to run through a mine field and try to convince a soldier staring into an ocean of people that we deserve to be saved!"

"Soraya, lower your voice," Marjan warns.

Soraya digs into her purse and extracts the plastic envelope of documents, evidence of their service as FTPs. She thrusts them into the air, proof that she, too, has made sacrifices to the gods.

"For God's sake, Marjan. Do you really think anyone is listening?"

Marjan's head spins. She grabs the papers out of Soraya's hand and throws her arms around her friend. Only the wrong people will cock their ears. Their role in the military is both their hope for salvation as well as the reason they are being hunted.

"Today's not the day," Soraya whispers. "We can't ignore the warning."

Hawa looks from her mother to Soraya and back again, understanding the grim truth that only one of these women is right.

19

2014

The three-bedroom apartment was on the third floor of a building near Kabul University. Marjan sat in the living room across from two young women, distant cousins of Elyas, the restaurant owner. Afternoon light fell through the window and nurtured a pothos plant, its heart-shaped leaves trailing the length of the sill.

Hawa sat on her mother's lap, eyeing the two women. They had come to Kabul for their studies. Wana had straight black hair, was taking credits toward a theology degree, and let her cousin do most of the talking. Farrah was studying for an undergraduate degree in economics. Her dream was to work for the government and maybe even be named head of a ministry.

"My cousin Wana," Farrah explained, "she will soon be teaching at a university somewhere and will become one of the leading names among the world's scholars of Islam."

Wana blushed at her cousin's confidence in her.

"God willing," she said, then turned the attention to Marjan. "Our cousin told us you're a very hard worker. And your daughter is precious, mashallah."

Marjan smiled meekly.

"It is your eyes that are beautiful," she replied, as was customary for such a compliment. Meanwhile, she was distracted by the miracle that was two young women deep in their studies and choosing careers. What would it be like to be a roommate here? Would she finally find her way back to school?

"Our cousin told us about your . . . your husband," Farrah said. "May God forgive him and grant his spirit peace."

Marjan looked down.

"Yes," she said, accepting Farrah's condolences.

"And my cousin and I both are so impressed with your strength, raising this daughter on your own," Farrah added. "We hope this arrangement can work out. The room is very small and doesn't have a window, but it's yours if you'd like it."

They stood and opened the door to the apartment's unoccupied bedroom. Wana flipped a switch and a single overhead bulb lit up. It was much smaller than the rooms at the halfway house but would fit a single mattress and the two bags that held all their belongings.

Marjan cleared her throat. She tried to imagine herself living here, frying an egg for Hawa in the small kitchen and walking past textbooks and pencils.

"I would like to say yes this very second but . . ." Marjan began to explain the most difficult part of her decision. Hawa tugged on her hand and said she wanted to leave. Marjan put a finger to her lips and begged her to be quiet. "I don't know if your cousin mentioned, but I will need to find someone to look after Hawa while I'm working. Maybe there's another mother in the building. I will have to ask around."

"Yes," Wana said. "He told us about your daughter. And maybe we can help here and there until you find someone. Farrah is the baby of her family and has just learned to fry eggs, but I practically raised my younger siblings."

Marjan flashed a shy smile. She looked around the apartment again at the irrefutable evidence of freedom within this space—the cat key chain on the console table by the door, the short stack of books next to the floor cushion, the framed picture of Wana and Farrah hanging on the wall. All of this and two young women who were willing to help her with Hawa? Marjan could hardly believe her good fortune.

"Mama, let's go," Hawa said, eyeing the two women. "Let's go outside."

"And the rent?" Marjan asked.

They were not asking for much, given the size of the room. Marjan did some quick math in her head. With what she earned at the restaurant, she might just be able to cover her share of the rent as well as food, Hawa's medications, and a few other small costs here and there. Even the most austere life was expensive.

She had to make it work. The halfway house was closing down for good. Its location made it too valuable to rent out to a charity group. She and Hawa risked being out on the street if she didn't find somewhere to live. She would talk to people in the building and see if there were small household jobs she could take on while Hawa was with her to help make ends meet.

"I think . . . I think I can do it," Marjan said, her head still stuck on the numbers.

When her response was met with silence, Marjan was brought back to the moment. She realized she wasn't exactly making herself the most appealing roommate.

"So, maybe . . ." Farrah looked like she was trying to figure out how to say something diplomatically. When Marjan saw their concerned looks, she realized she was on the verge of losing this chance.

"I mean, it's great. I will take it," she said with sugary enthusiasm. "I'm so grateful."

"Wonderful!" Farrah cheered.

"We'll be glad to have you here," Wana added.

Two weeks later, Marjan packed up their belongings in luggage that had been given to her by Samia and said goodbye to the women of the halfway house.

"Husna-jan, I can't thank you enough for all your help with Hawa," Marjan said. "You've saved us both so many times."

"Look at me, getting all misty-eyed! I'm going to miss you, by God!" Husna said, laughing at her own emotions. "So tell me more about these two young women you're going to be living with. One's studying religion, you said. And the other? Do they have boyfriends? Are they pretty? I bet their figures aren't as nice as yours."

Marjan laughed. She disappointed Husna with her vague responses, but Husna forgave her.

"Maybe this is a good thing," Marjan wondered aloud. "Maybe we need to be pushed out of this place so we can get on with our lives."

"Ah, yes. Let me get on with my brilliant life," Husna agreed. She removed her tortoiseshell hair claw and ran her fingers through her hair, loosening the waves. Then she gathered her hair into a fresh twist and held it in place with the hair claw. Marjan wanted to tell her she was beautiful. She was still young and had a long life ahead of her. But she had three children to mother and would forever carry her divorce around her neck like a yoke.

"Things are different now, Husna. My aunt used to tell me stories about one of my ancestors. She had the worst fortune. The absolute worst. But she refused to give up on herself and made something of her life. She shaped her own naseeb. You can do that too."

"I'm not sure why you're only now telling me about her. It sounds like you've inherited her hardheaded genes and I'm glad for you. I don't know what I've inherited from my ancestors other than these hips. I hope I will not pass on too much of my shame to my children. And I will pray for both of us. Maybe even more for you. You're a troublemaker, Marjan, and before you shoot me one of your looks, know that I mean that as a compliment. Your story is just beginning. One day, later in life, if I'm lucky enough to see you again, I want you to keep me up all night telling me about the life you made for yourself. Make it like the movies. A lot of action. Comedic scenes throughout and a bit of drama. Oh, and don't forget the romance!"

Marjan laughed out loud at that last one.

"Take good care of my little doll," Husna said, kissing the top of Hawa's head. "I'll be praying for you both. Don't forget to pray for me and my children too. That's all we can do for one another."

Marjan's first week in the apartment was full of adjustments. Hawa kept asking to go home, and Marjan tried to find ways to make the apartment feel like home, even as she tried to minimize their presence around her new roommates. At first, Hawa clung to her mother anytime she was around the two new women in her life. She was comforted by their easy demeanors but seemed to miss the presence of children. Farrah and Wana cooed over Hawa, delighted to be around a child but not fully responsible for her.

"Hawa!" Farrah would call out. "Come and share this rice and spinach with me. I made too much. Your mommy can give you a bath afterward."

True to their word, Wana and Farrah looked after Hawa while Marjan was at the restaurant. She worked only three evenings that week, a schedule coordinated around their availability.

"Oh, now, aren't you putting on a good show!" Farrah exclaimed when Hawa raced to meet her mother at the door. Something between a run and a waddle, the excitement made Farrah laugh. Even solemn Wana would delight at the way Hawa would sway and clap while they watched music programs on television.

In the hours Marjan spent at the restaurant, her mind was on her daughter. What if Hawa was being irritable with Farrah? What if Wana got so caught up with her reading that she lost track of Hawa? What if she put something in her mouth and choked just as she had in the shelter?

After each shift, Marjan practically ran off the bus, down the street, and up the stairs to return to her daughter. She was on edge, imagining all the terrible things that could possibly have happened in her absence.

"Marjan, I need to tell you something. But first promise you won't get angry," Farrah said one day while Marjan was removing her shoes at the door. She was breathless as usual and held a bag of leftover food from the restaurant for her and Hawa to share.

"Why would I get angry?" Marjan asked. "What's happened?"

"Nothing's happened," Farrah said, shaking her head. "That's exactly what I wanted to tell you. You're quite panicked, and really the worst thing that's happened while you were gone is that I ate an extra slice of this cake and won't fit into my pants in the morning. Please, Marjan. Everything is fine."

Everything is fine. Everything is fine.

She repeated Farrah's reassurance to herself, let it echo in the cavern of her mind where nightmarish memories hung like stalactites.

Everything is fine. Everything is fine.

She turned the volume up, needing to drown out the tinny, insistent voice that whispered to her while she slept, while she pulled a brush through Hawa's hair, and while she stood in the heat and steam of the restaurant's kitchen plucking chaff and stones from uncooked rice: *Do you feel that little rumble under your feet? Something's coming. Something's coming and you won't be ready for it.*

"If Elyas replaced you with a statue, I wouldn't know the difference," the chef barked at her. "We've got a stew to prepare!"

Marjan blinked herself back into the moment, just as Elyas poked his head into the kitchen to see what his chef was fussing about this time. She squared herself in front of the wooden cutting board and tightened her grip on the knife.

Everything is fine. Everything is fine, she repeated with gauzy conviction.

Marjan slid the blade through an onion, halved the glistening orb, and waited for the familiar sting of its vapors to draw tears from her eyes.

20

AUGUST 15, 2021
METRA MEDIA

"Esteemed viewers, welcome again to tonight's program, where we bring you news from around the country and beyond. I am Mina Noori of Metra Media."

Mina's voice is somber, flattened. It is the voice of a doctor announcing a child has not survived a virus. For the first time, she struggles to look directly into the camera's lens.

"Today is a tragic day in our nation's history. Despite all the reassurances from our president and his cabal of officials that Kabul would defend itself from a Taliban conquest, our city has fallen."

Mina lowers her head briefly to conceal her trembling lower lip.

"Thousands have flocked to the airport in hopes of securing a flight out of the country. We received reports today that President Ghani and his people, in what people are calling an act of extraordinary cowardice, fled from the presidential palace in helicopters to an unknown destination. Ghani made no public announcement and his whereabouts remain a mystery. Afghan army forces usually stationed at the airport were nowhere to be found by this afternoon, very possibly disappearing into the city after hearing that the president had absconded. While the public does not have the president's resources, they do have a mighty will and many muscled their way into the airport, breaking through barriers and moving past American soldiers. The Americans have maintained control of the airport, while the Taliban have set up several checkpoints along the road that leads to the airport. They seem to be letting through some people with proper travel documents, but they have also violently turned many away. The heat has resulted in exhaustion and dehydration. The area near the airport has already claimed many lives.

"The chaos at the airport has also resulted in separations of families. Recently, a family passed their infant son into the hands of an American soldier at the airport. It was another thirty minutes before they were able to get through the gates themselves. They could not find their child inside. Relatives reported to us that the parents were told the two-month-old had likely already been flown out of Kabul and that they would be reunited in the near future."

Mina takes a deep breath. The desperation to escape is nauseating and well-founded. She is a young woman in a country of young women. War, poverty, and disease have made for abbreviated lives, which means that most Afghans have no recollection of the previous Taliban regime. Still, their brutality is well documented. Young women who have grown up with the opportunities and relative liberalism of Kabul can't fathom living under such a regime. For God's sake, Mina has her own news program named after the Zoroastrian deity, the protector of covenants, light, truth, and justice. Mina has been free to talk about whatever she pleases and criticizes any member of government whose hypocrisy needs to be examined in the daylight, even if talking has resulted in little change.

But there will be no free speech in a country of mandatory beards. Schools closed for girls. Public executions. Whips lashing at exposed ankles or painted fingernails.

It is already hell to be a woman in this country. Afghanistan is consistently ranked as the worst place on the planet to be a woman. A woman has to be willing to be insulted and ridiculed if she wants to have a career.

So many women she has interviewed in government, women in charge of making laws and representing districts, have told her in confidence that they've had to negotiate their curfews with their husbands. If her headscarf slips two inches while she is on-screen, Mina can be assured that someone on social media will call her a whore. Hell, they call her that even when her headscarf hasn't moved. And how many women are tolerating abusive marriages because divorce would strip them of custody of their children? On her way to the studio today, Mina felt the urge to scream. That same urge overcomes her now, the camera fixed on her face.

Instead, she straightens her spine. She is a professional journalist, and she will do her job.

The cameraman can sense she might fall apart. He decides he will turn the camera off if she does. No need to expose her vulnerability to her viewers. He thinks of her as a sister and feels a duty to protect her, though she would probably scold him for his old-fashioned thinking.

"Taliban soldiers have been roaming the streets of Kabul in police vehicles. And surely by now, esteemed viewers and fellow countrymen, you have all seen the photos and videos of Taliban fighters roaming the rooms and halls of the presidential palace. They posed for pictures, bearing rifles in the rooms reserved for the nation's leadership. We may not have had the highest regard for those who worked in the palace, but we most certainly should have held sacred the order, structure, and civility those spaces represented. Today, civility was lost."

"We have heard and confirmed from knowledgeable sources that the American ambassador was flown by helicopter from the embassy to the airport. Embassy staff have been destroying sensitive documents as they abandon their post and wait for their evacuation from the country. It seems even the Americans did not anticipate that the Taliban would trespass into the capital this quickly. Though, esteemed viewers, you all surely remember that the language of the withdrawal agreement the Americans signed with the Taliban conveyed that they did, in fact, anticipate the Taliban assuming a role of authority. They only misjudged the timeline."

Mina looks straight into the camera. She took a risk in launching her own show, and she did it just so she could have moments like this, opportunities to infuse her own views into her journalism. Her following practically built itself, and while she doesn't read all the comments on her social media, she's read enough to know her work is appreciated by many.

"Beloved viewers, today we are a country without a president. For the past twenty years, the west fought the Taliban on our soil, and today, they partner with them to control the crowds of citizens rushing the airport to flee a homeland that has fallen to these same Taliban. I want to be optimistic, but as a student of our history, it is hard to be so. The past is the future. The days ahead will reveal how dark our world will become, how much we will lose. I pray for your safety and well-being and will continue in my duty to report the truth. When our so-called saviors have all left, when the dust of those planes has settled, may God leave us some dignity."

21

2014

Living with Farrah and Wana felt like freedom to Marjan, felt more like a life she might have dreamed up. One semester ended, another began. She was living with two women close to her age, two women who had become the circle Samia had encouraged her to find. She knew, though, that Wana and Farrah needed quiet and peace to study. To keep them from growing resentful of Hawa's many questions, her playful antics, she made a habit of taking Hawa out in the early evenings, when it was just dark enough to see the moon.

"It looks like a balloon!" Hawa exclaimed.

"She's full again. That means another month has gone by," she explained to Hawa as they walked back toward the apartment. "Remember when there was just a wink of light, so skinny we could hardly see it? Look at her now, letting her whole face glow."

Marjan was beginning to feel a kinship with the moon in that way. She was beginning to recognize that she went through phases as well, those quiet revolutions. She understood the waning moon. There were times she wanted to hide from the world, to curl up into a silent ball. And then there were times when she walked along the high walls that surrounded the university with her daughter by her side that she felt so full of light, she might fill the sky.

She bore witness to the waning, but she was buoyed by the waxing. She was in that phase of lunar replenishment the week the temperature dropped. Before long, she would need a winter jacket for Hawa. Wana had found her work with a local seamstress, adding embroidered patterns onto sleeves and necklines. To prove herself, Marjan was asked to copy an embroidery pattern onto a swatch of cotton. Marjan stitched carefully, checking and rechecking her work against the colored sketch the seamstress had given her. She ripped out more stitches than she put in for the first hour, unsure of herself. But her finished product won her the job, so she dedicated her early mornings, while Hawa was still asleep, to stitching. She thought of Aneesa often and wondered how she was faring.

Though Farrah and Wana were gracious about looking after Hawa while she worked, Marjan did her best to keep out of their way when they were home. She stayed in the confines of the room as much as possible and kept Hawa occupied with coloring books and crayons she purchased in the market. She taught her to count to ten on her fingers and made her repeat the letters of the alphabet after her. Marjan hadn't had much schooling, but her literacy had made all the difference in her world. Without it, she might still be living under Abdul Khaliq's roof, enduring his abuses. Without it, she wouldn't be able to read the newspaper or signs in store windows. Marjan was determined to teach Hawa everything she knew. She could hardly wait for the day that she could walk Hawa to school and watch her enter the gates with other children. She wanted her daughter to feel at home in a classroom, to impress the teachers with her handwriting and knowledge.

Of this, Marjan was certain. By her third birthday, Hawa could recite the alphabet and knew the sounds each letter made. Marjan would trace simple words onto her palm—"water," "give," "dog," "rain," "milk"—and she would recognize "water," "give," "dog," "rain."

On this day, Marjan thought she would try something new.

H-A-W-A, she traced onto the soft flesh of her daughter's hand.

"Hawa!" she cried, delighted to recognize her own name. "Another one!"

M-A-D-A-R, she spelled next.

"Maaa . . . maaa . . ."

"Madar," Marjan filled in. And as she reviewed the sounds the letters made, she closed Hawa's fingers over the invisible letters so that she could linger there in the warmth of her daughter's hand.

Hawa stood in front of the television. It was the hour of her favorite programming, a music show with a rotation of the country's best vocalists performing against an electric backdrop of bright purple and green lights. A neon Pepsi sign hung prominently in the corner. Today's singer was a man in his early twenties, maybe. He sported a trendy goatee and wore a burgundy velvet blazer with a black lapel over dark-washed jeans. He held the final note of the verse, his chin pointed to the spotlights above the stage. He pointed to the keyboard player, whose fingers danced over the white and black keys. The singer adjusted his aviator sunglasses and swaggered across the stage, his feet in step with the song's upbeat tempo.

Hawa burst into applause.

"He's her favorite," Wana noted.

"He's *your* favorite," Farrah said, which made Wana blush. "She's only clapping to be polite. This man is a walking disco ball. Are his shoes made of gold? His watch is so big, I can tell the time from here."

Marjan watched Hawa bend down to pick up a yellow barrette she'd spotted on the rug. She tried to press it onto her head with so much force that her whole body leaned to the right.

"Come, let me help you with that," Marjan said, smiling. Hawa walked to her mother, who noticed that her leggings no longer reached her ankles. Were the pants shrinking or had she grown that much already? She was thriving in this life, with regular meals and fewer roommates and her mother teaching her words and numbers. Marjan clipped her bangs to the side and planted a kiss on her daughter's head.

"Okay, lovely people. Time for me to go deliver my paper to my dictator of a professor," Farrah complained. "He gave us less than a week for this assignment and I absolutely cannot have this class bring down my grades. If I get anything less, my father will demand I return home. I had to beg to be here and they only let me come because they knew I would be living with this saint of a woman, our theologian. Little do they know . . ."

"Farrah, you're impossible," Wana complained.

Farrah cut her eyes at her cousin. "You're the most dangerous kind of woman, Wana, and I love you for it. A woman who knows the scripture better than the mullahs. She'll have them tearing their beards out soon enough. Inshallah!"

Hawa laughed at the image.

"What about you, Marjan?" Wana asked. "Have you considered enrolling in university studies?"

Marjan felt her neck grow warm. She had told her roommates that she'd been married off young but hadn't been precise, nor had she mentioned how early she'd been forced to abandon school. Would Wana still think Marjan could survive a university class if she knew she'd never even been to high school?

"Maybe someday," Marjan said bashfully. She stole a glance at Hawa, her honey-colored strands sparkling in the slant of autumn light falling through the window.

"Come visit the campus with me," Farrah said. "It will inspire you to feel like a student again."

Marjan looked at the digital clock on the side table.

"I have to leave for work in forty minutes," she said. Elyas had given her so much grace, she did not want to be late for work.

"We'll just walk through," Farrah said. "I'm not asking you to sit in a class with me. And Hawa's busy with her favorite show anyway. Is that okay with you, Wana?"

Wana had already retreated to her usual position, her feet curled under her, a textbook on her lap and a yellow highlighter in her hand like a spear in the grip of a hunter.

"Go on, it's no problem at all. I'm going to let her dance until she falls asleep," Wana said. Marjan thanked her and went to her room to grab her purse, before kissing Hawa goodbye.

Farrah opened the door and led the way. Marjan had walked all around the university campus, the street lined with pine trees that stood guard like straight-backed soldiers, painted white from the waist down to protect their bark from pests and the scorching sun. Farrah talked about the research she had done for this global business class, and Marjan pretended to understand the technical terms she used. As they approached the main gate, Marjan stayed close to Farrah, half expecting someone to call her out for trespassing. Surely, she thought, everyone could see that she did not belong here.

But nothing happened. They walked through the open gates and entered a world thrumming with activity. Students walked along the wide cement paths, some alone and some in groups of three or four. There were postures unique to this world—the asymmetry of a student weighed down on one side by a bag full of texts and notebooks, the forward lean of a student late for class, and the tilted head of a student caught up in a stimulating conversation. A bicycle chimed and laughter echoed behind Marjan as she took in the size of the buildings. Each discipline, Farrah explained, had its own space on campus.

The air felt different here, suffused with purpose and optimism. Marjan had trouble focusing on what Farrah was saying. She was intoxicated.

"This is where the department of economics holds most of its classes. Do you see those last two windows there?" Farrah asked, pointing to the end of the building looming before them with tall, rectangular windows on the facade. "That's where my professor's office is. Come, let's go."

"I could just wait for you by those benches," Marjan demurred. She wouldn't mind a chance to be still and take in the surroundings, the students crisscrossing the lawn. Marjan's mind was moving forward and backward at the same time, remembering what it felt like to sit in a classroom as a child and wondering what it might feel like to walk through those heavy doors.

"Don't be silly. Come with me," Farrah said, pulling Marjan by the elbow and leaving her with no option but to follow. They entered the building and went up a flight of stairs. "I hope he's in his office."

A young woman dressed in jeans and a long white button-down shirt must have overheard Farrah. Marjan was most taken by the brightness in her eyes and the bold lip color she wore, the same shade of pink as the flowers in the mulched bed in front of the building. "He's stepped out but has a note to leave your assignment on his desk."

"Oh, thanks for the warning," Farrah said to the other student. "Marjan, I'm going to drop this off and we can be on our way."

Marjan stood in the hallway by a bulletin board, grateful that she could appear busy reading flyers about job announcements and computer-repair services.

From down the hall, Marjan heard distant shouts. Curious, she took a couple of steps toward the stairs.

Then came the pops, the unmistakable eruption of gunshots followed by screams and loud thuds. They were coming from behind her, the long hallway in the opposite direction of where Farrah had gone.

"What is . . . Oh, God. Farrah. Farrah!"

Marjan understood then. They were all primed to understand what was happening. Just weeks ago, gunmen had stormed a different university in Kabul. Last year, they'd attacked an office where tuition assistance was distributed. Marjan ran down the hallway. She heard glass shattering and looked over her shoulder. There was no one there, at least not for the moment.

She opened the door to the office she'd seen Farrah enter, a windowless space that barely had enough room for a desk and a bookcase against the wall.

"Farrah!"

Farrah stood in front of the professor's desk. She appeared stunned, her mouth agape and her eyes wide.

"What's happening?" she asked.

A loud boom rattled the building, shaking away all doubt about what was unfolding around them. Farrah's hands flew over her ears.

Marjan closed the door behind her and darted to the other side of the professor's desk. She shoved Farrah into the kneehole, hidden from view by a laminate panel. She grabbed a pair of scissors from the desk and then crouched to the ground.

Marjan heard movement in the hallway. It was the slow, casual pace of the footsteps that sent a chill through her bones.

They held their breath, tried not to make a sound.

A door opened nearby. More gunfire erupted, this time treacherously close. There were shouts and long groans, the sounds of metal clattering, chairs scraping against the floor. The sounds were barely muffled by the closed door, and the smell of gunfire and smoke seeped into the professor's office.

Farrah and Marjan sat facing each other, hands holding their knees.

"Should we run?" Farrah whispered.

Marjan shook her head. They were too close, whoever they were. Hiding behind this desk was their best chance, maybe their only chance.

They spent the next thirty minutes trying to block out the sounds coming from across the hall.

"We need to get out of here," Marjan said. She stuck her head into the hallway to assess the situation.

"No, no, no," Farrah refused, her voice a whisper. "We can't go out there!"

Marjan saw no one and realized the gunman or gunmen must be on the other end of the building. Marjan didn't want to be stuck inside this small room, two sitting targets.

"The hallway is empty going down the stairs. We need to get outside!"

Marjan grabbed Farrah by the arm.

"Quickly," she said. She pulled Farrah into the hallway. The screams and shouts continued. Two figures burst into the hallway. Farrah started to scream, then clapped a hand over her own mouth. These were students too, terrified and seeking safety. One was the young woman who had told Farrah to leave her assignment on the professor's desk.

They raced down the stairs, legs trembling. Farrah's headscarf fell away.

More gunshots.

Marjan heard a shout behind her and turned to see one of the other students had fallen. She was struggling to get back on her feet.

"You've got to move," Marjan barked as she helped the young woman to her feet. She took a step but yelped with pain when she put her weight on her left foot.

"Farrah, get on the other side of her," Marjan ordered. Farrah did as instructed. Marjan and Farrah each clasped hands with the injured woman, who grimaced and nodded. She leaned on their forearms as they went down the six steps to exit the building.

The campus lawn was a scene of chaos. People running toward the perimeter, hands over their heads. Marjan led Farrah and the woman away from the building and toward the street. The university was the target, and they needed to get as far away from it as possible.

More shouts.

They were approaching the campus gate when Marjan turned around and saw two men with blunt-cut military vests over their clothing. One had a brown cloth tied around his head and covering his face. His narrowed eyes sent a chill down Marjan's spine. The men were about to enter the building the woman had just fled when one of them turned his attention to the group of students and staff running toward the university's exit.

Marjan darted to the right, pulling their trio toward a row of thick shrubs.

"Down!" Marjan yelled as she pulled Farrah and the other woman behind the wall of green. More shots rang out. One man stumbled, then fell face forward onto the ground. From where they were crouched, Marjan could see a bloom of red on the back of his shirt.

Marjan peeked through the shrub and saw that the gunmen had entered the building. Gray smoke floated out from broken windows, jaws of shattered glass. On the right side of the building, Marjan saw a figure opening a window. She saw the man consider the distance to the ground, look back into the classroom, and then take a leap. He landed with a thud and a cry, then scrambled to his feet. Lopsided and limping, he ran away from the building.

"They're inside. We run now," Marjan ordered. The trio took off toward the exit, arms linked and eyes on their surroundings. They made it through the gate and onto the street, where soldiers with rifles on their shoulders guarded the walls of the school. A tank rolled down the road, passed the procession of evergreen trees, the silent witnesses to the day's madness. They felt safer in the presence of armed forces, their breathing steadied. Marjan's forehead was damp with sweat, as were her clothes.

An ambulance wailed, maybe a block away.

"God, why?" Farrah yelled. Her classmate leaned her back against a tree, one foot off the ground. She put a hand on Farrah's shoulder.

"Are you okay?" Marjan asked her, struggling to catch her breath. The air was acidic and thick and made it harder to breathe.

"I wouldn't have made it," she said, her face drawn. Her partially smeared lipstick emphasized the pallor of her face. Her hand shaking, she dug her phone out of her pocket, probably to let her family know she had made it out.

Marjan had no one to call, no one waiting on word of her well-being. She had only Hawa.

The wail of the ambulance grew louder.

Marjan wanted to run to the apartment. She wanted to wrap her arms around Hawa, because it felt like only then could she be sure she'd survived this bloody event.

"I need to go," she said. She started to walk, then broke into a jog. But the gunfire and grenades had only been an opening. As she rounded the corner, a deafening blast sent her stumbling into the street just as the ambulance turned the corner.

There was suddenly a bewildering distance between Marjan's feet and the ground and not nearly enough time to set the world right.

22

AUGUST 19, 2021

"Madar, what is an FTP?" Hawa asks.

They are both relieved and disappointed to be back in their apartment. Marjan is looking out the window, searching the streets for answers. All she knows right now is that they were not the only ones to try to leave. Marjan noticed two neighbors returning to the building with bags this morning. She's also seen the Taliban walking around on foot, armed patrollers in multiplying numbers. It's an infestation.

"Where did you hear that?" Marjan asks, wondering if she heard her daughter correctly.

"When you and Khala Soraya were talking," Hawa recounts.

Hawa has always been a curious child, and though she asks many questions, she also learned at an early age to be skeptical of the answers she received.

"Oh, that's an abbreviation for our jobs," Marjan offers.

"What does it stand for?" Hawa asks.

"I forget the exact English words. Something about finances . . . Oh, is that Ingrid?" Marjan says, spotting a familiar figure approaching the building. The temperature will reach ninety degrees later today, though it feels that hot already in the confines of the apartment.

Hawa joins her at the window.

"She looks like she's in a hurry," Hawa observes. Marjan wonders what the latest is with Ingrid. Most foreigners have already cleared out. The embassies, the aid organizations, the contractors. Ingrid should have been gone by now, but she's almost as stubborn as a native Afghan.

The city is still reeling. The president flew off without a word. The Taliban have taken over the palace. The new world order has yet to be fully revealed. Marjan heads to the door to meet Ingrid in the hallway.

"Hello, my friends," Ingrid says. There's a hint of resignation in her voice, a touch of guilt. Ingrid has no reason to feel badly that she has a way out, though that does not mean Marjan does not envy her.

Hawa runs over and throws her arms around Ingrid.

"Beautiful girl. How are you?"

"I thought maybe you were gone already," Marjan says. "I knocked on your door earlier."

Ingrid shakes her head. She pulls her headscarf off and pulls a folded paper from her handbag to fan herself.

"It's hot as hell," she mutters. "I'll be leaving soon. I've just met up with a couple of colleagues. They're terrified. Our organization is trying to figure out how to evacuate them but everyone's saying it's damned near impossible. Our government's accepted a dozen asylum cases already but there are so many more."

The same conversation is happening in more homes than anyone can count in Kabul. Everyone who had any connection with the toppled government, the one that was seen as a puppet of the Americans, is feared to be a target for the Taliban. Anyone not in lock step with their extremist views is an infidel, especially the women who had dared to rise to positions of authority. Now that the Taliban has taken over all the government buildings, they have access to all the records and files of everyone who was on the government payroll, which includes Marjan and Soraya and every other woman who served in the FTP.

"They're right to be afraid," Marjan says. The past two years have been deadly, the Taliban ramping up their violence across the country even as they engaged in talks with the Americans. They were launching attacks on hospitals and military bases. They assassinated a provincial leader of the Afghan Independent Human Rights Commission and women judges who had put their fighters in prison. For all the compounds the Afghan military and their American counterparts had searched, for all the targets they had turned in for interrogation and detention, it seemed the country should have been safer.

"I cannot stand to see you still here, Marjan. What have the Americans said about getting you out?"

"They are trying," Marjan replies.

Ingrid looks livid.

"Trying? Isn't that lovely," she snaps. She is flushed, and Marjan wonders how much of it is from the heat and how much is from frustration. Marjan should be wild with rage, but she hasn't the time for it now.

"You must push them. You must keep trying," Ingrid tells her.

"I will. And you will leave when?" Marjan asks.

"Maybe tonight," Ingrid reveals, and Marjan feels a knot in her stomach. "They will let me know when the transportation is arranged. I am supposed to always keep my phone on me and wait for the call."

"Madar!" Hawa yells, her voice coming from the bedroom.

"What is it?"

"Madar, come here!" Hawa calls again. Marjan and Ingrid step into the bedroom and see Hawa standing by the window, looking down into the walkway around the building.

Three Talibs are standing together, one with a cellphone to his ear. Two are wearing peran tumban, baggy shirts hanging over loose pants cinched at the waist by a drawstring, and the third is wearing camo pants and a black tunic. Their turbans are shades of gray. One Talib looks up and sees Marjan before she can step back from the window.

"God damn them," Marjan whispers. Her heart is pounding. Why are they outside her building?

"I'm going to my apartment," Ingrid declares. "It is better if they do not see me with you."

Marjan nods, though she knows standing next to Ingrid is not what makes her most at risk for Taliban wrath. She has been warned again and again that the Taliban have ransacked homes, broken television sets, and searched through personal belongings to track down their enemies.

Marjan races to the duffel bag.

"Madar, what are you doing?" Hawa asks.

"My child, we have to be ready. If they come here to ask questions, tell them you study at the public school. Say nothing of your music. We will tell them I am a secretary in an office. Say little and cover yourself."

Marjan pulls her documents out of the folder. She cannot get out of the country without these papers. She may not survive the next ten minutes if she holds on to these papers. She looks around for a place to hide them but remembers the pictures she saw online of a home that had been searched. Even the long, low cushions of the living room had been torn open.

What will they do with Hawa if they find Marjan out?

Marjan tears apart the papers that identify her as a member of the FTP, the Female Tactical Platoon, and flushes them down the toilet. A part of her dies as she does so. She is left with a plastic badge, one that will not even bend in her hands. She hurries to the kitchen to bury the badge underneath the soiled paper towels and potato peelings in the trash bin. She hides her national ID card under the flowerpot on the balcony. On its own, the ID card doesn't incriminate her, but she cannot risk them taking it from her. The ID card might be her only path to a passport. Lastly, she silences her phone and stashes it in the package of menstrual pads in the bathroom.

Thump. Thump. Thump.

"In the name of the Islamic Emirate, open this door!"

Marjan freezes. Hawa looks especially small in the corner of the room, as if she's shrunken in size.

"Open it!"

Marjan peers through the peephole. The Talibs are one door away, at the neighbors'. She grabs her headscarf and long, black abaya from the coat hanger and throws them on.

"Who lives here?" a man barks. Marjan can hear Abed, her neighbor, trying to speak calmly. Abed and his wife own a small flower shop ten minutes away. His wife smiles whenever she sees Marjan or Hawa, but she rarely has interest in anything more than small talk. The story Marjan has shared with them is the same one she has shared with Hawa's school: Marjan works as a secretary in a trading company. She is a widow but has some family on the other side of town. Hawa's father died before his daughter could get to know him. Marjan suffers from health issues and is sometimes hospitalized for a day or two.

This last bit helps explain her absences and, she hopes, will keep people from gossiping about her. A sick woman is barely a woman, she learned from watching severe scoliosis turn her khala Shaima into a specter.

"God as our witness, our business is flowers. Nothing more. Please, our children are frightened."

"Madar, will they hurt them?" Hawa asks. Marjan looks over her shoulder.

"I don't think so," she whispers, shaking her head. She turns back to the peephole and almost jumps when she sees a Talib's face enlarged by the rounded glass. The door rattles under his heavy fist.

"We order you to open this door!" he shouts.

"Let me see the paper," someone behind him says. "Maybe it's this one."

"I thought he checked the list. Does he even know what he's doing?"

Marjan takes a deep breath. She motions for Hawa to go into the bedroom.

There is more pounding but this time from the bottom, as a boot strikes the door.

Marjan has already assessed her situation. They are too high up to leave through the window. She has a couple of knives in the kitchen, but it's unlikely she'll best three armed men. She has to be smarter than them.

"In the name of God," she calls through the door. "Please. I am a woman alone with a child. I am trying to maintain my honor and cover. Please understand."

There is a burst of cursing.

"Open the door!" the Talib shouts, punctuating his command with a kick so strong it nearly takes the door off the hinges.

Marjan has no choice. She turns the knob slowly and opens the door a crack. A dust-covered boot wedges itself in the gap as the Talib shoves his way into the apartment. Marjan takes two steps back, catches herself on a side table.

A second Talib enters. They reek of cigarette smoke and sweat. Marjan keeps her gaze on the floor and the end of her headscarf pulled across the bottom half of her face.

"What's your husband's name?"

Marjan has debated how to answer this question. After what she heard from the taxi driver about the Taliban wanting lists of widows, she does not want to risk them knowing she has no husband. Offering a name is also troublesome. What name should she give? What if they ask a neighbor and someone contradicts her story?

"Zabiullah," she says. The less information she gives, the better.

The Talib asking the questions looks past her.

"And that's your daughter?"

Marjan whirls around, alarmed to see Hawa standing just outside the bedroom door, her delicate face framed by her headscarf. She resists the urge to cover Hawa with her body.

"Yes, that's my little girl," Marjan confirms.

"And your husband? What work does he do?"

It occurs to Marjan that if this soldier goes into her bedroom and pokes through her things, he will find not a single article of men's clothing. Not one shirt.

"He's a mechanic," she says. It is hard to find a profession that will not offend them.

"Hey, a mechanic!" the Talib calls to the man behind him. "Just what we need!"

The Talib lingering in the doorway takes another step in; his eyes, dark and skeptical, sweep the apartment before they settle on Marjan.

"Sister, think before you speak," he warns. "Because we know someone here worked for the army."

Marjan's heart pounds. This is not a random visit. They have information that has led them straight to her door.

Marjan is acutely aware of how petite she is compared to these men.

She thinks back to the day Khala Shaima had visited her at Abdul Khaliq's compound. She'd come for the Eid holiday with a basket of cakes and sweets. The night before, Abdul Khaliq had summoned his youngest wife to his chambers. Khala Shaima shook her head at the bruises she could see, knowing there were more she couldn't.

Why did God bring me here to die? she had asked her aunt. *Why such a cruel fate?*

I don't accept that this is your fate. Like the biscuits we have with our tea, no naseeb is shaped without the press of your fingers, her khala Shaima had told her as they sat in a corner, Jahangir playing between them.

But Khala Shaima, I'm too weak, Marjan had cried into her trembling hands.

Silly girl, Khala Shaima said. *Look at me. I've been weak all my life. Where else would I get such strength from?*

23

2014

"No, your mommy can't hold you right now, but, look, we're going to sit right next to her and you can hold her hand," Wana said to a very sullen Hawa.

It was barely twenty-four hours since the brutal attack at the university. Farrah and Wana had brought Hawa to the hospital to see Marjan. The ambulance hadn't expected Marjan to tumble into its path. The impact fractured her shin bones. Two medics gathered Marjan and loaded her into the ambulance that had struck her alongside a student with a blood-soaked shirt wrapped around his head wound.

Marjan was triaged and, hours later, underwent surgery. She woke to find her left leg elevated and in a thick plaster cast. In this room, Marjan was one of three recovering patients, each separated from one another by a pale blue curtain.

Hawa's eyes lingered on the cast, on this new mother who refused to rise from bed and wouldn't even pick her up. Marjan tried to make space on the stretcher for Hawa to sit next to her, but there was a bag on a pole beside her and a plastic tube that fed fluids into her vein. She struggled to move herself a few inches.

"Let me see if I can help you," Farrah said. The movement sent a shock of pain through Marjan, and she yelped despite her best efforts to remain stoic.

"Mommy, let's go home," Hawa whimpered. If they were back home, surely her mother would act like her normal self. She wriggled her way out of Wana's arms and stood by the door, insistent.

"I can't go home yet, janem," Marjan tried to explain. Her mouth was so dry, her head still foggy.

Hawa looked disappointed. Farrah took her to the plastic chair by the bed. She opened a game on her phone and handed it to Hawa, who took it with less than her usual enthusiasm.

"I thought it was the end," Farrah said, her eyes puffy. She hadn't been sleeping well since the attack. Wana slid her arm around her cousin.

"God had mercy on you both," Wana said.

Is this mercy? Marjan wondered, her mind still a flashing reel of images from the attack. She had heard the ambulance coming around the corner, heard the siren getting louder. But she couldn't have guessed that moments later she would be in that very vehicle writhing in pain.

"How long will you be here?" Wana asked.

"Just know that we will look after Hawa," Farrah interjected. "You don't have to worry about her at all."

Marjan blinked back tears. She didn't have words for her gratitude and didn't know how long she would have to rely on her roommates to care for Hawa.

"Yes, it's not like we'll have classes again tomorrow. How long do you think before the university reopens?" Wana asked her cousin.

"Well, the other campus closed for seven months after they were attacked," Farrah said softly. "My mother almost didn't allow me to come to the university because of that one."

Maybe classes would resume in a month. Maybe two. Some classrooms had gaping holes in the ceiling and walls that looked like the cratered surface of the moon. Floors were splattered with blood and debris.

Hawa cried when Wana suggested it was time to leave. Marjan squeezed Hawa's hand, begged her to be a good girl, and promised to come home soon. She thanked her roommates with words that fell short. Once they had left, she sobbed herself into exhaustion.

On the order of the nation's president, and to the surprise of anyone who had seen footage or images of the aftermath, the university reopened the campus and resumed classes just two days after the attack. The decision was meant to signal resilience and a refusal to be deterred by terrorists, despite twenty-four dead and thirty-one wounded. Some students were eager to go back. Farrah was not one of them.

The doctors told Marjan she would be released in a week. Farrah and Wana juggled caring for Hawa and awaited her return. But a series of unexpected events derailed everyone's plans.

Marjan developed a fever. It turned out she had a bladder infection, so she was started on antibiotics. No one could have predicted that she would have an allergic reaction to the medication. Her body was aflame with hives. The itching beneath her cast threatened her sanity. The doctors changed her medications and added some new ones to quiet the reaction. They even removed the cast to check the condition of her skin and applied ointments. When Hawa returned with Wana and saw her mother's puffy face, her arms covered in raised, red markings, she cried.

"I'm fine," Marjan tried to tell her daughter. "It's nothing."

Hawa, a child who would sit rapt for story time, did not believe this tale.

"Mommy, we go home," she insisted again and again.

"Don't bring her again," Marjan whispered to Wana. She was desperate for every second with her daughter, but the visits distressed everyone. "I should be better in two days. Maybe they'll even let me go home."

Two days later, the hives had started to play a game of peekaboo. They would disappear for a spell, then reappear. The doctors told her that sometimes the reaction went on, a persistent rebellion in the body.

Days later, Wana came to visit Marjan on her own and rested a hand on her friend's. Marjan could see Wana had been picking at her cuticles.

"Farrah's been struggling. She puts on a brave face but that's all it is, a mask for the world. She's terrified that the terrorists will come back."

It had taken seven hours for the military to gain control of the university grounds. All four attackers were killed. The bodies of the murdered students were returned to their families, and the injured were left to do the hard work of healing.

Marjan didn't blame Farrah for her fears. The first couple of nights, when she was floating on a morphine high, her dreams were racked with images from the attack. Blood on walls. Gunshots echoing in her ears.

"Her parents have arranged for her to go back home. They think she needs some time," Wana said quickly. "And the same goes for me. I mean, I'm fine, but my family has decided that the universities in Kabul aren't safe for us. For now, anyway."

"Oh," Marjan said, her stomach dropping. She should have seen this coming. Her roommates would be leaving the apartment, an apartment she could not afford on her own even while she had been working. And with a broken leg, it would be weeks before she could go back to the restaurant. Elyas would hire someone else to take her place, if he hadn't already.

"Now," Wana said, with concerted positivity, "we both know that you're not yet able to look after Hawa. We found a good solution, a temporary solution. There's a really lovely place for children. They have a swing in the yard and games and teachers. They provide warm meals."

"But where . . . How soon are you both leaving?" Marjan had so many questions. She didn't know which to ask first.

"In two days," Wana admitted.

Marjan's head, heavy with thoughts, fell back on the pillow.

"How will I take her to this school and bring her back? They haven't said when they'll release me. It doesn't matter. I'll just . . . I'll leave."

"No, that's the wonderful thing about the place we found. Hawa could just stay there. They have beds for all the children, and the women who look after them are very kind. You can take your time and recover."

"What kind of school . . . Wana, what is this place you've found?"

"It's an orphanage, but there are many children there with families. Some just cannot afford to provide for their children for the moment. They come and visit them, and the children are doing so well. They have classes and activities. They sing songs and play games together. You should see it. It's very sweet."

"No, no, no. I can't send her there. She's going to stay with me. I'll ask them to release me. They will have to," Marjan said.

"My friend," Wana said gently. "You need time to recover. And the apartment will be . . . will be difficult for you on your own."

"An orphanage," Marjan whispered. She wanted to protest. She wanted to be outraged at Wana for even bringing up the possibility, but her leg ached and her scalp itched and her bladder was full. If she couldn't manage her own basic needs, how could she possibly look after Hawa?

She cursed herself for going to the campus with Farrah that day, as if a girl who had never seen a high school classroom had any business visiting a university campus.

The nurse looking after Marjan that evening was a round-faced woman with almond-shaped eyes and soft hands.

"My goodness, I thought you were finally turning the corner but your skin is angry and red again today! I'm going to see what we can give you now. We'll get you through this. God is merciful."

Marjan could not wait for mercy. She needed to stand up. She had to find a way out of this mess. She needed . . . she needed to be stronger.

She had been knocked down before, but never like this.

When the nurse offered her pain medication that evening, Marjan refused the chalky white pills. She wanted to feel the war raging in her body, to endure the wounds and let the pain summon her back to the fight.

24

AUGUST 19, 2021
METRA MEDIA

For the sixth time, the producer asks Mina if she's sure she wants to proceed with a broadcast. He tells her she doesn't have to put herself at risk to report what others are already reporting.

Seated behind the desk with her notes in front of her, Mina tells him he's welcome to leave if he is concerned about his own well-being. She says she will understand if he goes. The producer runs both hands through his hair and mutters something incomprehensible. Mina asks him—dares him—to repeat himself.

"You know, I was speaking out of concern for you, but even if I weren't, it's not a crime to think of my own well-being. I have a wife and young children," he says.

Mina sets her pen down, lays a hand over it, and presses her lips together. People are quick to remind her that her existence is of lesser value because she does not have a husband or children. It is a cruel calculus.

"Since my job is all I have, I might as well do it," she responds tartly.

The producer huffs. He wishes she wasn't so damned sensitive. He's never told her, but he thinks she is one of the smartest and most courageous journalists on the air. He would be proud to see one of his daughters grow up to be like her—professionally, that is. (He could not abide the shame of a divorced daughter.)

"Let's get on with it, then," he says, and spins a finger in the air to propel them into action. "Camera? Camera!"

The cameraman is distracted, his mind on the urgent phone call his mother received from his fiancée's family last night. They drained two thermoses of tea trying to figure out how to handle the demands they firmly but politely made. He swings the round eye of his camera back to Mina and waits for the countdown.

"Esteemed viewers, welcome again to tonight's program, where we bring you news from around the country and beyond. I am Mina Noori of Metra Media."

The cameraman keeps the camera trained on Mina's face. His eyes flit to the producer, who watches Mina, his expression grim.

"Despite reassurances from the leaders of the top banks in the country, the economic crisis continues, with account holders trying desperately and all too often unsuccessfully to retrieve their hard-earned savings from bank branches. ATMs are not functioning and there are grave concerns that the currency will be further devalued by the political instability. The acting governor of the national bank has fled the country, but on social media posts, he has stated that since the Taliban are on international sanction lists, the majority of the ten billion dollars of assets, frozen by the United States, will not be accessible to them. Year-end disclosures by the bank listed $362 million in foreign currency cash held at the bank's central offices and branches, as well as at the presidential palace. All of these are now controlled by the Taliban. In addition, the national bank's vaults located in the presidential palace and central office held nearly $160 million in gold bars and silver coins, a collection of two-thousand-year-old Bactrian gold jewelry and coins. Nearly twenty-one thousand artifacts that had been presumed lost during the previous era of Taliban rule were recovered from a secret vault in the central bank's basement in

2003. The Taliban have not yet indicated how they will handle archaeologic treasures."

Mina is quoting numbers the cameraman can hardly fathom. And what will happen to the money he has scraped together over the past two years? For the past year, he has been saving his wages, because his future in-laws have made clear that a lavish wedding is required to show their friends and family that their daughter is marrying into a successful and respectable family. They want to invite three or four hundred of their closest family and friends to celebrate in a grand ballroom with an architectural ceiling, ornate plaster patterns backlit with LED lights, gilded columns, and dining chairs covered in white cloth with sashes of green tulle. Though they had agreed to the engagement, they would not permit a nikah until the wedding. It was their way of ensuring the groom's family did not try to get away with a cheaper marriage before God only.

He does not blame them. His own parents demanded the same when his sister was getting married, insisting on three arches of roses for the stage instead of one and for two extra lambs to be slaughtered for the dinner buffet.

But last night, his future mother-in-law had revealed a new plan.

We can have the wedding when the chaos settles, but let's have a small nikah as soon as possible. This weekend, even. Better they be married now given the new . . . climate. I'm sure you agree.

Panic is driving decisions these days. Families don't want their daughters left behind if a groom manages to flee the country. And this is a terrible time for a young woman to be unmarried.

His mother agreed, of course. In four days' time, he will sit next to his fiancée, and they will each sign their names to the marriage contract. They will be husband and wife, no matter who is in charge of the country. But even a small nikah means getting the immediate family together. His siblings. Her siblings. Their closest aunts and uncles. He has nearly three thousand dollars in the bank but was only able to get out two hundred when he went to the branch. Maybe he'll get lucky at the bank if he goes again. He would hate to ask his brothers for cash.

"And in other news, the Taliban have ordered all women's shelters to close. Schools remain closed as well, with children and parents left wondering when they will reopen and whether the Taliban will allow girls to return to school as they seem to have indicated they would during talks with Americans. But as we've noted in previous broadcasts, the U.S. agreement with the Taliban made no mention of women's rights, human rights, or ensuring girls had equal rights to education. The city's national music institute has also closed, and as can be seen in these photographs, the school's instruments were destroyed, a signal that the Taliban regime currently occupying the presidential palace is not far removed, ideologically, from the Taliban of the late nineties. This does not bode well for women and girls, or anyone who believes in freedom of speech and individual rights. Yesterday, I spoke with young students who went to school only to be turned away on order of the Taliban."

Mina looks down as they roll the clip of her interviewing a girl dressed in a black school uniform, a white headscarf tied primly under her chin. She is sobbing into the camera, her sullen-faced classmates around her.

"What sin have we committed? Why are we being punished?"

The cameraman looks to the producer, thinks of babies. With marriage comes children, sons and daughters. His sisters were all top students. He cannot imagine keeping a little girl away from a classroom. Maybe he won't have daughters. Maybe things will change by the time he has to worry about any of this.

The first Taliban regime lasted five years, a destiny cut short by the military might of the United States and her NATO allies. But how long will this Taliban regime last now that the world has grown weary of battling them?

You have all the clocks but we have all the time, the Taliban had warned the American generals.

"Dear viewers," Mina says, and takes a deep breath. It is impossible to report these updates without wondering if this will be her last time addressing her audience. "This concludes our program for the evening. As always, may God be with you all and, inshallah, may I come to you tomorrow as the bearer of brighter news."

25

2014

"Greetings! May I enter?"

Marjan didn't bother looking up to see who was asking. Nurses didn't announce themselves, and she no longer expected anyone now that Farrah and Wana had left Kabul. She expected the visitor would walk past her to the other patient in the room, a woman who was going to have a tumor removed from her arm tomorrow. There was no privacy in the shared room beyond the thin curtain that veiled them from each other.

Another knock.

Marjan screwed her eyes shut. She had just practiced walking on crutches for twenty minutes, and the effort had left her exhausted.

"Hello! Marjan?"

At the sound of her name, Marjan opened her eyes. She did not recognize the woman standing in the doorway. She wore a black jacket and a headscarf in a beige-and-black checkered pattern. Her lips were a vivid raspberry color.

"Yes?" Marjan sat up as much as she could. This had to be about Hawa. Maybe the woman was one of the caregivers from the orphanage. Hawa had been there ten days already, and Marjan had only spoken with the director on the phone a couple of times. "Is my daughter all right?"

"Your daughter? Oh, I'm not . . . Let me introduce myself. I don't blame you for not recognizing me. I was a mess that day. My name is Soraya."

And then Marjan knew why she looked familiar. She was the girl with the injured ankle, the one she and Farrah had helped escape from the building. Soraya took two steps into the room and stood at Marjan's bedside.

"I wanted to come sooner. I should have come sooner. I want to thank you for everything you did that day. You could have left me but you didn't."

"It was nothing," Marjan said quietly. "How is your ankle?"

"Better, thank you," Soraya replied. From behind the blue curtain came a low groan and the sound of the hospital bed creaking.

Marjan remembered her manners and pointed to the plastic chair. Soraya took a seat, folded her hands on her lap.

"I didn't know Farrah other than being in the same class," Soraya said. "I had to ask around until I found someone who had her number. We lost four people from our class that day, so everyone is devastated. I've never attended so many fatehas in one week. Anyway, I finally connected with her and she told me you were here."

"I'm so sorry. You didn't need to trouble yourself coming all the way here," Marjan said, because it seemed the right thing to say. Looking at Soraya's face, her neat appearance, made Marjan even more self-conscious. She felt stale and greasy from lying in a hospital bed, and her skin was splotchy from the persistent hives.

Soraya's tone softened.

"It's no trouble. I very much wanted to see you. How are you doing?" Soraya asked.

"I'm fine. I mean, it's been one thing after another but I'm getting better. All these medications are making my face swell," Marjan said, her hands touching her face self-consciously.

"I know people who have paid good money to have their lips plumped up the way yours are," Soraya whispered. "The clinic isn't far from my home. Kabul's most successful doctor, I swear."

The comment was so unexpected, Marjan laughed.

"Forgive me." Soraya smiled. "I don't mean to make light of what you're going through. It was devastating what happened to you. I feel so terrible about all of it."

"You shouldn't feel that way. None of this was your fault," Marjan replied.

"I don't know if that's true," Soraya said. "See, I keep thinking about what I could have done different that day. Besides being so damned clumsy on the steps, of course. I don't know why it took me so long to pull myself together. And if I had thought to go through the offices and out the back door . . . maybe I wouldn't have fallen on the stairs. And maybe you would have been long gone by the time that bomb went off."

"It's also possible that you would have walked right into one of them," Marjan said.

Soraya brushed her bangs away from her face.

"Have you been able to sleep?" she asked.

"Some," Marjan replied.

Soraya nodded, expecting as much.

"Me too. I wake up a few times every night. It's not always a nightmare either. Sometimes I just find myself awake. How much longer until you're released from the hospital?" she asked.

Marjan wasn't sure.

"Well, I hope it's soon. I expect the food here must be quite terrible." Soraya pulled a plastic container from her purse. "So, I brought a little something. This is my mother's roat. She made it this morning and I thought I would bring you a bit."

"That's kind of you," Marjan said, accepting the offering. "Please thank her for me. May your mother's hands not ache."

"Oh, her whole body aches all the time, but that doesn't stop her. My father is no longer with us and my brothers struggle to hold down jobs. On top of everything else, she has me as a daughter."

"Is that so terrible?" Marjan asked.

"I've rejected three suitors, can't cook to save my life, and forget my prayers all the time," she said.

"Allah forgives easily," Marjan reassured her.

Soraya laughed. "I hope so. Farrah told me about your daughter. I hope you don't mind. It must be so difficult to be away from her."

"I will get her back the day I get out of here." Marjan had said the same to the orphanage director, wanting her to know she wasn't planning on giving her daughter up.

"Of course you will," Soraya agreed. "Your daughter is lucky to have such a brave mother. You might have been the only person who had their head on straight that day. I keep thinking about that too."

"That's not how I remember it," Marjan replied. "I didn't feel like I was thinking straight at all. And I didn't feel brave at all. I was terrified."

Soraya leaned forward.

"But, Marjan, that's precisely what makes you brave. We were all terrified. Farrah told me she froze up. But you were thinking for all of us. And you weren't about to let us give up."

Soraya was just being kind, Marjan thought.

"Have you gone back yet?"

"I have," Soraya said. "They held our class in a different room. There is still so much to clean up. And even besides all the damage, it was just hard to be there. Someone dropped a stapler and I was ready to dive under the desk."

"So you were there despite your fear. I think you would call that being brave, no?" Marjan asked.

Soraya hid a smile.

"Or stupid. Only time will tell," she said, and then her tone turned serious. "I've had to fight to go to school. Most of us are fighters. And you look like a fighter to me. You even have a lion's name! Do you know about the lion who lived in our zoo?"

"Yes, I've seen the statue," Marjan says softly.

"So tell me, you lion of a woman, where will you go when you leave here?"

Marjan sighed heavily. On the other side of her bed were two duffel bags that held all her belongings. Farrah and Wana had packed for her. It hadn't required much effort, since she and Hawa had so little. They'd even dropped off Hawa's clothing at the orphanage.

"I don't know," Marjan said. "I mean, I don't know yet, but I'll figure something out."

"Farrah said you don't have family in Kabul," Soraya said.

Marjan nodded, and to her surprise, Soraya didn't ask her anything else about her family.

"Farrah also said your daughter is a firecracker of a girl. Now, she doesn't know me at all, but I would love to meet this child. If you want to write her a letter, I could go read it to Hawa. Or I could record a video message from you on my phone and play it for her. I could take her some roat and play some music for her. I hear she loves the singing programs on television, just like me. Do you think she would like a hardheaded khala paying her a visit?"

Marjan's ache for her daughter dwarfed the ache of her broken bones. The orphanage director seemed thoughtful and kind, but Marjan had no idea how Hawa was really faring there. If Soraya had coaxed a laugh out of Marjan today, maybe she could lift Hawa's spirits as well.

"I would really appreciate that," she said, embarrassed to ask such a favor of this woman she barely knew.

"Great! And let's do a video message so she can hear directly from you." Soraya promptly pulled out her phone and tapped on the camera app. Marjan sat herself up, tried to smooth down her unwashed hair, and tried not think about what her face might look like. Soraya tapped her phone, and Marjan started to speak.

At Marjan's request, Soraya deleted the first seven attempts at a video message. She finally settled for a brief message in which she did not try to explain her absence.

Hawa jan, my sweet daughter, more precious to me than a breath. I know I'm far from you but I'm thinking about you all the time and I hope that I will be with you very soon. I miss you. Please be a good girl. Soon I will . . . I miss you so much.

"A career in film might not be your destiny, but the lighting is terrible in here and you didn't have much time to prepare a script, so maybe we shouldn't make final decisions today," Soraya teased, tucking her phone into her bag.

"I don't know why I fumbled so much. I'm sorry for the trouble,"

Marjan said, surprised to find herself already looking forward to seeing Soraya again. It wasn't easy to find reasons to smile in here.

"Well, I caused you some trouble. You're allowed to cause me some trouble," Soraya replied, rising from the chair and shouldering her handbag. "That's what friends do."

26

AUGUST 19, 2021

Hawa watches her mother limp across the living room. Why is she limping? Hawa would ask if she thought she was capable of speech, but for the moment she is not. The Talib's eyes follow her mother, who looks shrunken in his presence. The Talib whom Hawa saw while they were in the taxi was at least separated from her by the car's window. This one moves comfortably around their apartment, his boots leaving dirty prints on their burgundy carpet. Hawa has never seen anyone enter a home without removing their shoes.

The Talib looks at the framed Quranic verse on the wall. As he moves toward the small television in their living room, Hawa takes a step backward. Her mother is at her side now, nudging her toward the bedroom. The Talib is standing before their narrow three-shelf bookcase. Hawa keeps her schoolbooks on the bottom shelf, along with a pencil case and a box of markers she has not yet opened. He looks at the top and middle shelves, at the books her mother has collected.

"Whose books are these?" he demands. The Talib behind him looks up from his phone briefly. He is growing impatient, moving in and out of the apartment as if he is eager to bang on another door.

"Those belong to my husband," Marjan replies meekly. She knows all too well how to play the part of a docile housewife. "I'm not to touch them ever."

"What does he read about?" he asks, picking up Marjan's paperback copy of *Pride and Prejudice*. The title is written in scrolling letters and bears no images that would give away the story.

"He tells me they are about history," she says, as if she has no way of confirming this. "And business."

What are men to rocks and mountains? Elizabeth had exclaimed.

Marjan feels this in her bones as she watches the Talib drop the book to the floor.

Marjan detects resentment. She is willing to bet he cannot read. The education of a Talib involves time spent reciting verses of the Quran, naming God's enemies, and firing weapons. Not long ago, word got out that a Taliban leader was displeased with the increasing literacy among their bands of fighters. Nothing good could come of too many men who could read and write, he warned. And besides, throughout history, men kept track of their women, sheep, and weapons without so much as a sheet of paper.

"Call your husband. Tell him to come home now," the Talib orders.

"Forgive me, but I cannot. He does not permit me to have a phone," Marjan explains. The Talib does not bat an eye at this claim.

"If there's nothing here, let's go!" the other soldier calls from the kitchen. He emerges with a butter cookie. Marjan had purchased a tin for Hawa, a special treat for the high marks she received last quarter. Hawa had decided to allow herself one every Friday to make the tin last longer.

"Give me a cookie!" the Talib near Marjan demands. His partner nods his head in the direction of the kitchen, telling him to help himself.

"Let's go. This cripple doesn't have anything helpful to offer us," he says, a sprinkle of crumbs and sugar crystals caught in his beard. But the closer Talib has his eye on the bedroom.

"Out of the way," he barks at Hawa, who steps fully into the living room and stands by her mother. Marjan winces at the violation of her private space. She hears him taking steps around the small room, imagines what he might be looking at. Her clothing on the bed. Their duffel bag in the bottom drawer of the dresser. Hawa's hairbrush by the window. She thinks of her ID under the flowerpot and tries to control her breathing.

She hears the soft protest of rickety drawers and tossed belongings.

"Find anything interesting?" the other Talib asks. Even more footprints that will have to be swept away. He is taller than the man in the bedroom. Marjan and Hawa both recoil at the sharp smell emanating from his body. Hawa starts to cough, and Marjan sidesteps the man and practically shoves Hawa into the bathroom.

"Excuse me, my daughter is unwell. Some kind of lung infection, but I cannot afford the medications," she says woefully.

As soon as the bathroom door closes, Hawa coughs again, sensing she should go along with her mother's lie. She presses her ear to the door and tries to hear what the men are saying. For a few moments, there is nothing but heavy footsteps and mumbling.

Then Hawa hears a buzzing sound.

Her mother hasn't completely silenced her phone. Hawa coughs again to cover up any other sounds the phone might make. She gingerly opens the small cabinet, reaches into the package of sanitary napkins and extracts her mother's phone. She silences it and then wonders if she should try to get help somehow. She cannot call the police. She knows this much. But she feels desperate to let someone know that her mother is in the living room with two Talibs.

Khala Soraya would know what to do.

Fingers trembling, Hawa unlocks the phone and goes to her mother's messaging app. She is about to search for Khala Soraya's name when she notices a message from an unnamed number.

You will be in grave danger, sister. The men have already shaken hands with the new masters. They will get what they need from this arrangement, as they always do. I am not the only one who thinks of you often. Do what you can to save yourself and your daughter from him. If I do not send you another message, it will only be for your safety.

Who is thinking of her mother often?

She does not understand what she's read. She starts to tap out a message to Khala Soraya, ready to hide the phone in her underwear if a Talib were to barge into this small space.

On the other side of the door, Marjan still holds the tip of her headscarf across her face. She keeps her eyes averted, maintains her timidity.

"The man has to come home sometime," the Talib says. "If it's him, we'll get him. Let's go."

He's just emerged from the bedroom with one of Hawa's sweaters caught on his boot. He reaches down, growls, and rips it off, tossing it aside with a child's petulance.

"Tell your husband we'll be back. He'll have to answer for himself," he vows. The two Talibs walk out then. Marjan counts to five and then tiptoes across the apartment and quietly closes the door. Like Hawa in the bathroom, she presses her ear to the door, trying to hear if they are approaching Ingrid's apartment. She hears their heavy footsteps on the stairs and breathes a sigh of relief.

"Madar?" Hawa calls out. She pokes her head out of the bathroom, her face drained of color.

"Come, my sweetheart," Marjan whispers, arms open. Hawa lets herself be embraced, wants to confirm that her mother's arms still have the strength to wrap around her. Hawa's mind is racing. For some reason, she had not anticipated that the Talibs roaming the street would breach the privacy of their home. What else could they do? Then there was the curious text message on her mother's phone and her mother's behavior around the Talib foot soldiers.

"Why were you limping?" Hawa asks, clearly confused by her mother's act of weakness.

In her mind, Marjan hears echoes of her crippled aunt's laughter. Even now, she can remember the look of distaste on her father's face whenever he would come in to see Khala Shaima sitting in their living room, her crooked spine pressed against the cold wall of their home. No man ever asked for her hand. She was pitied, dismissed as something other than a woman. But in overlooking her, they had both underestimated her and liberated her. It was Khala Shaima who had the freedom to visit Marjan even after she had been married off to Abdul Khaliq. In those visits, Khala Shaima fed her niece stories of their ancestor, the legendary Bibi Shekiba, who was disfigured, orphaned, abused, and yet found her way to become a guard of the king's harem.

Those stories and her blood ties to Bibi Shekiba were the sustenance that kept Marjan alive in the worst of times. She could not have prayed for a more precious inheritance.

Marjan is struck by the realization that in trying to protect her daughter, she is depriving her of that very gift. She must find a way to share the lessons, even if she does not—just yet—feel it is safe to share the stories.

What are men to rocks and mountains?

What are men to girls and women? Marjan thinks.

She has worked hard to make sure her daughter always has a warm coat in the winter, crisp notebooks for the first day of school, and fresh vegetables to help her grow. She has purchased for herself only the barest necessities. She has worn the same clothes for years. In their kitchen, they have two plates, two mugs, one pot, and one frying pan. She chose this apartment because she wanted to give Hawa the safety of neighbors, the appearance of financial stability. She has taken Hawa to bookstores and gardens, wanting her to feel the freedom of ideas, the comfort of birdsong, the taste of indulgence.

She has provided well for her daughter. She has also deprived her.

With the Taliban roaming the streets around them, Marjan feels the pressure of time. Her heartbeat is a ticking clock. She looks into her daughter's eyes, pools of wonder.

"Sometimes," Marjan says, hoping her explanation will make sense, "sometimes we must keep our strength hidden. It's better if they believe we are weak."

"How long before they stop believing?" Hawa asks, still holding on to her. It is plain she is her mother's daughter, because Marjan is wondering the same.

27

2014

Marjan spent almost four weeks in that hospital. She had stopped asking to be released once it hit her that she had nowhere to go. If she showed up at the orphanage, where would she take Hawa? Would they sleep on the street?

The doctors and nurses would have sent Marjan out the door sooner, but word had gotten around that she had saved two other students during the university attack and that she was a young, widowed mother. Marjan never complained. She asked very little of the nurses and channeled her energies toward her recovery. She didn't want assistance. She needed to be able to get around on her own.

A wisp of a girl surviving such an attack? God truly is great.

I haven't seen anyone so determined. I should complain less about my aching feet.

Marjan's phone had been destroyed in the accident, and she wasn't all that mobile yet, making it next to impossible to search for a room and a job to go with it. She forced herself out of her shell and approached doctors, nurses, and other hospital employees.

If you happen to know of a small room for rent or anyone hiring, I would appreciate it. I can do embroidery, I've worked in a restaurant, and I'm a quick learner. Sorry to trouble you, but I really need to get back on my feet.

"It's embarrassing," she told Soraya. "I feel like the vegetable man, pushing my rickety cart down the road and shouting to the neighbors about onions and peppers. Up and down the hallways of the hospital, I'm announcing my problems. *Needs a job! Needs a room! Here's a girl who needs a job and a room!*"

Soraya laughed.

"I didn't know you had such a commanding voice! Maybe you just need a couple sacks of potatoes to get you started."

"If I only had a pushcart," Marjan mumbled.

"Well, let me show you something to brighten your day. I stopped by the orphanage on my way here to check on our little butterfly. I took the best pictures!"

Marjan practically burst into tears as she took the phone into her hands. Hawa's face filled the screen, her cheeks pink with delight and her hair in two precious pigtails. She was looking at something out of view, a smile across her face.

"Keep swiping," Soraya encouraged.

In the next picture, Hawa was sitting on a carpeted floor with two girls who looked to be slightly older than her. Between them was a pile of crayons, coloring books, and a small stuffed animal. Marjan swiped again and came to a video. She hit play.

Show me what you've made, Soraya said, and Hawa was happy to oblige. She walked toward the camera with a piece of paper in her hands and held it up for Soraya to see.

I made a moon and this is a girl.

Is this girl sitting on the moon? Soraya asked.

Hawa nodded.

What's her name? Is her name Hawa?

Hawa turned away, hiding her bashful smile.

This is the most beautiful drawing! Do you want to say anything to your Madar-jan? You know she misses you so much!

At the mention of her mother, Hawa's face grew solemn. She tried to take the phone from Soraya's hand, tried to find her mother on the screen.

Oh, no, I haven't called her. I'm so sorry, I wish we could but . . . oh no. Come, come, sweet thing.

Soraya's recording ended there. Marjan took in a long, slow breath.

"She just got a bit emotional. She's very busy there, Marjan. She's strong like her mother. But thankfully, way more talkative than you."

"I was talking to somebody yesterday and they mentioned . . . there might be a place you could stay," said Zarmina, a nurse who had a pleasantly round face and earnest eyes. She was chronically late and rushed so much that Marjan often heard a faint whistle in her respirations.

Zarmina had Marjan's full attention.

"Really?"

"Possibly. My father knows a businessman. Agha Rasuli. He travels between here and Dubai. His wife just had her first child and they are looking for help. They have an extra room in their home."

"Help them with one child?" Marjan asked, curious.

"I know," Zarmina replied. "But wealthy people spend their money the way they want to. He's actually a very nice man and just wants to take good care of his wife and child."

Zarmina tried to slip her pen into the pocket of her top, but instead it slipped out of her hand and dropped to the floor with a clink. When she rose from retrieving it, her face had turned red. "Just think about it. I know it might not be the best—"

"Can you call him now?" Marjan asked.

To Marjan's relief, Agha Rasuli wasn't bothered by her ongoing recovery.

You don't exactly need to chase after a newborn, he'd joked. And he was pleased to hear that Marjan had a little girl of her own. The experience made her a qualified candidate.

On the day Marjan was discharged from the hospital, Agha Rasuli sent a taxi for her. She was delivered to the Rasuli home, a two-story structure in an area of town reserved for the well-to-do. Marjan stood on her crutches with one duffel bag in each hand. The privacy walls and home itself were painted a salmon color, the metal door black with ornate gold accents.

"Come in, come in," Agha Rasuli said, stepping back so Marjan could enter the yard. She prayed she wouldn't drop a bag. A narrow staircase led to an upstairs balcony attached to the house. Agha Rasuli led Marjan through a ground-floor door and into a spacious room with floor cushions on three sides of the room. The fourth wall had built-in shelves surrounding a large-screen television backlit by the sapphire glow of strip lights. The shelves were empty save for a copper vase and a couple of framed photographs.

"Zargul! Come here, would you?" Agha Rasuli called up the stairs. Marjan tried to plan how she might climb those stairs. Luckily, her cast started below her knee. "You can leave those bags there for now," he said to her.

Relieved, Marjan balanced herself on one foot and leaned over to set her bags down instead of dropping them.

"Zargul? Where are you?" he called again. He spoke and moved fast, Marjan observed. She understood he would expect the same of her.

A woman appeared at the top of the stairs with a baby in her arms, impervious to the urgency her husband seemed to feel. The stairway received no daylight, and the overhead bulb flickered for a second, but only Marjan seemed to notice.

"She's sleeping," Khanum Zargul whispered over the baby's head, shooting her husband a pointed look.

"Why didn't you set Leeda down, then?" her husband muttered. "Anyway. Zargul, this is Marjan. We'll need to show her around here and then take her to the room behind the house. She's quite capable, I hear, and will be even more so when she is finally out of that cast."

"Very well. Come on up," Zargul said.

Marjan managed to climb up with one hand on the railing and one crutch under her other arm. Zargul showed her to their sprawling bedroom with gray lacquered furniture and a tufted headboard in gray velvet. In the corner stood a white wooden crib with a satiny pink bumper tied to the railings and a plush fitted sheet on the mattress. She pulled open the drawers of a dresser to show Marjan where they stored Leeda's diapers and clothing.

"And in the kitchen . . ." she said, exiting the room. She stood in the hallway and looked at Marjan. "Let me know if you need to sit down."

"No, please go ahead. I'll follow you," Marjan said.

The kitchen was three times the size of the galley kitchen she had shared with Wana and Farrah. It hadn't occurred to her that a home kitchen could or should be larger. Honey-colored cabinets were set against a creamy backsplash with a horizontal strip of gold metal. Two glass milk bottles sat on the gray granite counter.

"Here is the baby's formula, but she prefers when I breastfeed her," she said. As if stirred by the mention of a feeding, Leeda started to fuss. "Why don't you go back downstairs and my husband can show you to your space? I'm going to change and nurse her."

"I could help if you—" Marjan started to offer, but Zargul was already gone.

Marjan was terribly thirsty. She would have loved a sip of water but didn't want to overstep on her first day. She went back downstairs and found Agha Rasuli standing outside, bidding someone a jovial goodbye on his cell phone.

"Back already?"

"Yes, Leeda-jan needed a feeding," Marjan explained.

"It would have been nice if you could have done that feeding. But let me show you to your room," he said, before Marjan could explain that she had offered to help but had been turned away. She was reminded of her first days at the restaurant, before Elyas understood just how hard she was willing to work.

Behind the two-story house was a separate structure, a single room with a floor cushion, a coffee table, and a box fan. There was a simple bathroom but nothing else. It was more than enough for Marjan. "I'll let you get yourself situated, then come back into the house. You can wait in the living room upstairs for instructions from Zargul."

Marjan wanted to ask Agha Rasuli right then and there when she could bring Hawa to live with her, but she didn't want to appear too needy. She was here to help them, not the other way around. While the baby slept, Marjan folded and ironed clothes. Only when she had finished that task did she work up the courage to ask if she could have a glass of water.

"The cups are in that second cabinet," Khanum Zargul said. "Will you be able to manage?"

Marjan thanked her, then drained an entire glass standing over the sink. When she finished, she refilled the glass and took another look at the kitchen. There were crumbs and sticky patches on the counter that she had noticed earlier. The sink was half full with dishes and two baby bottles. With a bit of balancing, Marjan washed and dried the dishes. As quietly as she could, she opened cabinets and drawers until she figured out where everything went. She wiped down the counters, then hung the damp cloth on the edge of the sink.

Marjan was determined to prove to the Rasulis that they had not made a mistake in hiring her.

Marjan woke the following morning praying Agha Rasuli or Zargul would bring up Hawa so she wouldn't have to ask. She washed up, dressed, and rapped on the door to the house. When no one answered, she knocked a bit harder. Agha Rasuli let her in.

"Today will be your first full day and a chance to see if this is the right job for you," he said.

Marjan bit her tongue. Were they just testing her out? She supposed they had a right to be wary. She walked into the kitchen and found the breakfast dishes in the sink, along with a greasy frying pan and cracked eggshells. She busied herself once again. She found a broom tucked behind the refrigerator. She found that she could sweep with her right hand if she planted her left hand on the kitchen counter.

With her crutch under one arm, she went down the hallway and tapped lightly on the bedroom door. There was no answer. She raised her hand to try once more but instead put her ear to the door. She heard nothing.

Marjan remembered how exhausted she'd been in those first few months with Hawa and decided not to wake Zargul. She thought about sweeping the living room, but hunger distracted her. She listened for sounds in the hallway, then slowly opened the fridge, cringing at the loud sucking sound the door made as it opened. There was one glass container with meat stew, another with sliced red onions and herbs, a tub of yogurt, a half dozen eggs, uncooked ground beef, and a liter of juice. What could she eat that they would not miss?

Her stomach growled, embarrassing her.

She found a paper bag with a few squares of day-old flatbread, dry but satisfying.

Zargul emerged from the bedroom halfway through the day, a pink-faced infant in her arms. Marjan offered to feed or change Leeda, but Zargul demurred. Marjan didn't blame her for it. She remembered the velvety feel of her babies at this age.

"I think it would be best if you focus on the housework," Zargul said, eyeing Marjan for a reaction.

Marjan had learned much about people from being a wife to her husband and being under the thumb of his other wives and his hawkish mother. A man expected obedience from all the women in his life and, depending on his station, obedience from a few men too. Women also wanted deference, but they had to look for it in dark corners. If they found themselves standing over the right woman, they too could experience that heady high.

Marjan didn't flinch or recoil. She reacted with muscle memory.

"Yes, Khanum. I'll get started on the clothing first so it has time to dry on the line. I think I saw some detergent in the closet."

Zargul nodded—satisfied, but not sated. No one ever was.

For the next two days, Marjan worked as hard as she ever had in her life. She washed and cleaned and dusted and peeled and pushed away the feeling that she was again a thirteen-year-old drudge in Abdul Khaliq's house. She was not that girl, she told herself. She was a mother fortunate enough to have found employment with a well-to-do family. No one had raised a hand to her. They hadn't even raised their voices. On top of that, Zargul had let Marjan know that she could set aside portions of food for herself when she cooked their meals. This should have been obvious, she insisted, when Marjan had gently asked if she could step out to get some food.

Marjan only needed to be patient. She could feel their eyes on her, following her movements and checking on her work. She needed this couple to realize she was worthy of their trust and goodwill before she asked when she could bring Hawa to the house.

If she hadn't been so certain that she'd been fulfilling her duties and then some, she would not have dared rap her knuckles on the doorframe of Agha Rasuli's office.

Agha Rasuli sat behind his desk in the small upstairs office. He was looking intently at a computer screen. On the shelves of the lacquered bookcase behind him sat a printer, a few books, and so much paper, some in folders and some in small piles.

"Yes?" He was squinting at his screen and tapping at the keyboard.

"I am sorry to interrupt your work but I need to ask you something. I have been away from my daughter for so long," Marjan said, trying a slanted approach to her request.

"Mm-hm," he said without looking up.

"And I need to see her," Marjan said softly. "I need to see her today."

"Oh? Has something happened to her?" Agha Rasuli asked, looking up.

"No, well, I mean, I don't know. I have no way of being in touch with the . . . the school." She hated calling it an orphanage. An orphanage was for orphans.

"Don't you have a phone?"

"I do not," Marjan said. Didn't he remember that she had used Zarmina's phone to speak with him? "It was crushed by the ambulance the day I was injured."

"You could use Khanum Zargul's phone to call the orphanage," he offered. "You should think about getting yourself a phone, though," he said. "There's a mobile store not far from here, next to the flower shop."

"I do want to replace my phone, but I can't afford one at the moment. That's why I was so grateful for this job," Marjan said, seizing the opportunity to talk about something they had yet to discuss—her wages. "When I'm able to bring Hawa here, I will be paying for our food and anything else we need."

"When you bring . . ." Agha Rasuli said, then let out a huff, his hands steepled. "Marjan, I think you have misunderstood. We brought you here to help with Leeda. This is a place of employment for you."

Marjan felt her insides tighten, bracing for impact.

"But Zarmina-jan had told you about my daughter," she said.

"Of course she did. She told us that your daughter was being cared for elsewhere and that you needed a job and a place to live. We thought this would be the ideal situation for you."

"But . . . but my daughter needs me."

Agha Rasuli pushed himself away from his desk, folded his arms across his chest, and looked at Marjan in utter disbelief.

"Surely, you understand that a child needs more than just the presence of a parent. If you're not able to purchase a phone, how do you imagine supporting her right now?" he asked.

"Well, we have not yet discussed my wages." Her voice trembled. She took slow breaths, trying to steady herself.

"Your wages," Agha Rasuli repeated. He pivoted in his chair, turning to stare at the name of God written in calligraphy on parchment and displayed on the wall in an ornate gilded frame. "Marjan, we have promised you room and board here. Surely, you're aware of the value of these benefits?"

Marjan realized she had been blind, so inexplicably blind. Her heart pounding, she tried to formulate a response. He wasn't wrong. Room and board was valuable, and she had no other options.

"With all due respect, sahib, I appreciate that you have given me a place to stay. I'm . . ." Marjan faltered. "Maybe there is additional work I could do to earn money. And I promise you, my daughter is quiet and well-mannered. I would never allow her presence here to interfere with caring for Leeda-jan. Leeda-jan will always be my priority, along with all the other household tasks. You have seen that I am capable. I promise I am capable of even more."

Agha Rasuli paused to consider her offer, then tilted his head to the side and pressed his hands to his chest.

"The last thing I want to do is get between a mother and her child," he said, and Marjan felt a bubble of hope in her chest. "So you'll have to decide if you want to keep this job or find another way to work and be with your daughter. But we simply cannot have another child in the house."

28

AUGUST 22, 2021
METRA MEDIA

Mina is breathing heavily as she enters Sonbul Café. Once upon a time, she would have undone her headscarf at the door in one graceful sweep and, with a smile, signaled the owner, Tabassum, for her usual order—a slice of carrot cake and a cup of saffron tea. Her steps are cautiously defiant now. Too many of her colleagues have gone into hiding, disappeared by choice or by force. She is here to prove to herself that she is not yet among the vanished, that she is present still.

"Mina!" Tamina embraces her, pulls her into the space. It is her birthday they're celebrating, though no one is in a festive mood. Pop music plays softly from a small speaker on a corner table, and Mina thinks of the previous birthday parties she has attended for her colleagues, when they could dial up the volume on the music.

"I hope you didn't have any trouble getting here," Tamina adds.

"No more than anyone else," Mina replies, nodding at the other women already in the space. She stood shoulder to shoulder with many of them in last week's protest, carrying signs with messages like "Freedom, Bread, Work" and "Let Girls Learn." They'd been thrust into the dark ages.

You are an intellectual and well-spoken too, but make no mistake, plenty of people are watching just to see your pretty face, her eldest brother once said. By all standards, he was a good man, well-read and with a sharp sense of humor. He loved his wife and treated her well. He was a gentle father to his children. He was ready to help when a relative was in need. But he was somehow forever between jobs and often complained about all the employment opportunities that the Westerners had created for women only.

They'd barely spoken in the last year, not after a conversation that ended with Mina seeing red.

Women's this, women's that, he had groused. *As if half this country isn't men. A woman can marry a breadwinner. What the hell is a man supposed to do?*

I wonder if a man might be afraid he'll have to do more than the bare minimum, Mina had retorted.

The only thing I wonder is why your husband didn't divorce you sooner.

Her brother always went for the lowest hanging fruit, which, in Mina's case, was a pointed mention of her divorce.

Dear brother, at least you and I agree that we live in an unfair world, Mina had told him. *Maybe we should leave it at that.*

I've encouraged my daughters to go to school, Mina. Don't get all self-righteous on me. I'm not one of them.

Mina had nearly screamed then. His daughters hadn't even started high school yet. How low had he set the bar for himself as a father?

She looks at the bulletin board behind a table of food. It is full of pinned notes, square flags of pink, yellow, green, and blue with messages of love and friendship. One has the imprint of a kiss. Mina smiles to imagine a young woman pressing her lips to the paper and leaving a token of affection on this wall of mementos.

A kiss is a sacred protest, the paper reads.

It is a small gathering of young women. Mina greets the others with light kisses on cheeks and lingering hugs. She asks after every individual in their family by name, and when she's finished making her rounds, she takes a seat by the window with a cup of tea. For an hour or two, they will pretend they are unfazed by the upheaval in their country.

Mina loves this café. Immediately after her divorce from a man who guzzled his income and hers, a man who cozied up to the very people Mina was reporting on, Mina went through a period of seclusion in her brother's home. It was short-lived. Her brother had told her she could stay as long as she liked but Mina thought it would be better for everyone if she found a place for herself. Her apartment is not far from this café. Tabassum was outside cleaning the windows one day and invited Mina to try a pastry. It was a café just for women, she explained. Inside, Mina had found a cluster of women gathered at each table, much like the hyacinth blooms after which the café was named.

Tabassum's customers are the women of Kabul. Mostly married, some uninterested in marriage and some eagerly seeking romance. Most have jobs, but a few steal away for an hour while their children are in school. They are teachers, activists, artists, and owners of small businesses. They come here to sip chai, to rant, to whisper about sweethearts, and to indulge in a water pipe out of the view of their families.

They are here today to celebrate a friend's birthday, their gathering a form of preemptive protest.

Tabassum emerges from the small kitchen with Tamina's birthday cake on a gold platter. It is a round cake decorated with white frosting, chocolate ganache dripping down the sides. Tabassum wears a white apron tied around her waist, and her hair is in a bun on the crown of her head. She wears a black shirt with a purple hyacinth embroidered over the left breast pocket, the café's logo. Good thing Tabassum had opted for hyacinths when naming and decorating her storefront. If she'd had pictures of women outside, she would have been painting over them as the beauty salons had done before the Taliban arrived. Tabassum smiles when her eyes meet Mina's.

"How are you doing?" she asks.

"Well enough, I suppose," Mina replies with a shrug. "And you? How have things been here since last week?"

Sonbul Café was where Mina and a handful of other women organizing the protest had gathered last week to discuss their plans. They didn't want too many details floating around on messaging apps. While the Taliban clung to stone-age ideologies, they also fully embraced modern technology. They were dependent on them, really. They issued official statements and flooded Twitter with propaganda. They managed to obtain contact lists and send threatening messages to WhatsApp numbers of former military and government workers.

"I don't know if I'll be able to keep this place open for much longer," Tabassum admits. "I've always been the baker, the server, and the cleaner here. I can't be the only customer too."

"Your customers will be back," Mina offers, but her optimism is forced. Tabassum knows it. She squeezes Mina's hand, tells her to try the food, and returns to the kitchen.

Mina doesn't have much of an appetite, but she wants to be able to compliment Tabassum sincerely. She stands and walks toward the long table set up with small bites of food.

Just as she passes the front door, it swings open and she is violently knocked off her feet. She hits the ground hard, landing on her hip.

"Attention!" a man's voice bellows. Mina looks up. Four Talibs have stormed into the small café. They take up nearly half the space. Mina is so close to the one standing above her that she can see the individual hairs of his beard and the scratches on the barrel of his rifle.

"Get up," the first Talib orders as he kicks at Mina's feet. She scrambles to rise, her mind racing. Will they recognize her? Will they check her phone and find pictures from the protest? She would sooner die than be the reason her family is punished by these animals. The women are adjusting their headscarves, doing their best to hide their faces from the intruders.

Everyone is on their feet. Mina wills them all to be strong. She thinks of all the broadcasts she has done, her face on television screens talking about the way the Americans were mistaken to engage in cozy talks with the terrorist group. She had, as any good journalist would, named names, and she surely has no friends among the Taliban leadership. She eyes the back door.

She considers making a run for it to spare the others from being punished for their ties to her. Would the Talibs chase her? Were there more outside?

"Shut up!" a Talib with a whip shouts into the face of a young woman Mina doesn't know. "We know what is happening here. You bitches and harlots are up to no good. Shame on all of you. Shame on your families. Stand up in a line. We will find exactly what deviant acts you are hiding."

"But we have done nothing," someone pleads. "We have only come for a birthday."

One Talib eyes the birthday cake. He elbows the man next to him and nods in the direction of the cake. He carries his weapon casually but with a hand close to the trigger. Mina decides against running.

"Stay calm," she whispers to the young women on her right and left. "Do not give them a reason."

Another Talib slams the speaker to the floor, cracking it in half and silencing the music. He walks over to the bulletin board on the wall. Against the colorful flags, he looks even more stark and joyless. The paper kiss catches his attention. His turns back to the room, scowling and freshly validated.

Having heard the ruckus, Tabassum emerges from the kitchen with a large scarf draped over her head and shoulders. A Talib barks at her to join the line the others have formed against the long wall of the café, and she obliges in a hurry.

The Talibs consider the women. One takes out his phone and walks down the line, recording their faces. The young women look away, shielding their faces. He brings the phone close to each of them, grabbing them by the chin when they try to look away. The Talib's whip cracks against the table. The clap jolts the women and sends two glasses to the floor, where they burst into shards.

"Do you admit you have come here for sinful reasons? Do you admit you are a prostitute? Look into the camera and say it now."

There is crying. Mina tries to steady her breathing. Her body is tense, her skin prickled. She is aware, as is every woman in this room and every woman on the streets and every woman in her home and every girl on a city bus, of the catastrophic damage that can be done to a woman at a man's hand. She does not fault these young women their practical cowardice, their false confessions. She is almost relieved to hear them, voices small and breaking, give in to the Talib's demand. These are the very definition of white lies, are they not?

"And you. Do you confirm you are here to sell yourself in sin?"

Mina looks straight into the Talib's phone. His is a fair question, she realizes. *What are you willing to do with your body?*

"Turn the camera around if you want to see the face of a sinner," Mina says. The blow to her face sends her to the floor for the second time, her mouth meets a shard of glass. She tastes blood on her lips.

When she lifts her head, she sees a smear of red on the café floor. It is true, she thinks. A kiss is a sacred protest.

29

AUGUST 23, 2021

"I will talk to everyone I know. I will keep trying," Ingrid vows, holding Marjan's hands. She delayed her departure for four days to see some work through but cannot postpone leaving any longer. She is moments away from being picked up by a van that will take her to the airport. "Promise me that you'll stay safe."

The clock ticks. The Americans had declared that they would be out of Afghanistan by September 11, the anniversary of the worst terrorist attack on American soil. *How poetic*, Jenna had said. The Taliban have given the Americans until the end of August, and despite the director of the CIA flying in to meet with one of their leaders, this is their red line. Any delays will result in unspecified consequences. The American embassy has been evacuated. Bases and equipment have been abandoned. The Americans will be gone by the end of the month, eleven days earlier than September 11.

The real enemy is the more elusive Islamic State group, the Americans insist, and the Taliban will help them in this new, more urgent fight. It is perplexing to the living, confounding to the dead.

Marjan squeezes Ingrid's hands and nods.

"We will be fine," she promises, more for her daughter's benefit than Ingrid's. The Talibs have already tied this apartment to someone in the Afghan army. Now that they have access to all the biometric data of the government, it won't be long before they return with more detailed information. They'll have her picture, her name. They may even have a record of all the missions Marjan went on and all the Talibs she helped put in prison. How many of them are running free now, released from prison?

It is Hawa's turn to say goodbye to Ingrid.

"I don't want you to go," she says. Marjan watches her daughter hug their neighbor tightly. Marjan is both in awe of this bond and slightly envious of it. She pulls Hawa back gently because she knows Ingrid is too kind to let go. They watch Ingrid slip down the hallway with a suitcase and a large bag. Hawa moves to the window to watch Ingrid get into a van as soon as it pulls up.

Marjan turns to her phone. There are new messages in the group chat with Jenna and the other American women from the Cultural Support Team.

How are you ladies doing? When I hear from my contacts, I'll let you know which gate is open today. Ts control the checkpoint but they're letting people through if they have travel documents. Looks like U.S. command is working with them to secure passage.

And we're supposed to trust them? Georgia, another CST, had replied. Soraya had painted henna onto her hands during one of their hangouts. She'd been slower to warm to the Afghan women but was now very protective of them and had been working with Jenna to pressure anyone they could find in Washington to help the FTP.

It's part of the deal, Jenna wrote back.

The women were on the base together the day the details of the American-Taliban agreement were released. After two decades of fighting, the Americans would leave. They would help secure the release of five thousand jailed Taliban fighters and vowed not to interfere with Afghanistan's domestic affairs. In exchange, the Taliban would not shoot at Americans on their way out.

Whole lot of blood and treasure for nothing, Georgia writes now.

I'm pissed too, but for our sisters, let's keep this chat on task, Jenna encourages. A moment later, Georgia deletes her previous message. Marjan realizes that the American soldiers must have a chat for themselves, just as she and the other FTPs do. "Shoulder to shoulder"—that is how they describe the way Afghans and Americans fought together against the Taliban. And it is true. But it is also true that they are not exactly the same. Marjan does not resent the difference. It's just a matter of circumstance. They are two different blooms in a shared pot.

Will the messages from these American women dry up one day? How long before the memories of their shared missions become hazy in the minds of the Americans? How long before they forget the names and faces of their Afghan sisters?

"Madar, where will we go?" Hawa asks her mother. She has repacked her bag three times already. As small as their lives are, so much will be left behind. These are regrets not yet realized.

"We will figure it out," Marjan promises, but Hawa is unsure. Where could they possibly go in this city? Hawa wishes they were like everyone else in Kabul and had uncles and aunts and cousins to turn to. But they have no one.

"Can we stay with Khala Soraya?" Hawa asks. She is as close to family as they have, and Hawa likes the way Khala Soraya makes her mother seem more at ease. Where her mother is anxious and reserved, Khala Soraya is vibrant and spontaneous.

"No, we can't," Marjan replies. "That's out of the question. She lives with her family, her brothers and their wives and children."

It's more than that, though. Marjan feels something in her loosened by the threats around them. She needs Hawa to understand this world if she's going to survive it.

"And, Hawa, Khala Soraya is family to us but that does not make her brothers family to us. It will always be a problem for us to stay in a man's home."

"I know, Madar," Hawa says. She has learned lessons that were never taught.

"We will find a safe place," Marjan repeats. She has made this promise a half dozen times today, even though she has not yet figured out where that place might be. "Let me call Soraya. I need to check on her too."

Marjan steps into the other room to make the call. Soraya's brother and cousin are wearing on her, she can tell.

Soraya picks up on the first ring. With everyone glued to their phones, there are few missed calls these days.

"What's happening?" she asks, skipping the formalities.

"Ingrid left. We're packed." Marjan lowers her voice. "I can't stay in this apartment much longer. It's just a matter of time before they come back."

"Where will you go?" Soraya asks.

"I'm thinking about trying the shelter," Marjan said. She's already told Soraya about the place she lived in the first year after escaping Abdul Khaliq.

"But I heard they closed them down."

"They couldn't all close down so quickly, could they? I have to try."

"You think you'll be safe there?" Soraya asks.

"If they're looking for soldiers, they won't think to look in a women's shelter," Marjan explains. "And we don't need to stay there long. Jenna and the others will get us through the airport soon."

"They're trying. There's no guarantee that it happens," Soraya replies.

"You know what we say: For every mountain, there is a path," Marjan says.

"I don't know about that, Marjan," Soraya says, a slight tremble in her voice.

"What do you mean? You don't sound like yourself."

"We had four Talibs here today."

"Oh, God," Marjan says. She sits on the edge of the bed.

"I hid in an armoire and my family told them there was no one in the army in our home, but the Talibs wouldn't believe them. They were searching the house and throwing things around. I was so lucky they didn't find me. They came so close."

"Oh my God, Soraya."

Marjan knows exactly how her friend must have felt in that moment, being a breath away from Taliban retribution.

"They didn't find me and it made them furious. They took it out on my brother. My mother was crying, begging them to stop. They beat him terribly and now . . . now it's just confirmed for him that I am to blame for everything. They're starting to think that my cousin is right. That the moment I put on a soldier's uniform, I started to shame the family."

Marjan's heart sinks. Cursed are the women who like walking against the wind, women eager to break with tradition. Soraya and Marjan are these women, as are all the women in the platoon. Soraya has a natural eloquence and charisma. The Americans were taken by her early and nominated her to an international delegation on women's rights. In a conference coming up in Europe, she was to be one of the global ambassadors advocating for equality across the world.

A few of the female soldiers come from families proud of their daughters' achievements. Soraya's mother might have been proud of her if she weren't hammered with warnings that her daughter was dragging their family through the mud.

"Look, I'm going to visit the shelter. And if it looks like we can hide out there until we can get to the airport, maybe . . . maybe you should join us."

"It's bad enough that the Taliban are driving us out of our country. I won't have my cousin drive me out of my home," Soraya says defiantly.

Marjan makes her promise she'll call if she needs anything. Soraya makes her promise the same.

"Remember, I caused you some trouble once. So I owe you, friend," Soraya says.

Marjan lets out a laugh. "Soraya, you're the best kind of trouble."

When she hangs up, Marjan turns around to find Hawa standing in the doorway. She's no doubt heard most of the conversation.

"We should leave. There's a place I want us to check out," she says to her daughter.

"Is Khala Soraya going to be okay?" she asks.

Marjan nods. "Khala Soraya is one of the strongest women I've ever met," she tells her daughter. It was Soraya who helped her, even after training ended, increase her fast roping speeds so they could get out of the helicopter and find cover quickly. And it was watching Soraya, carrying twenty pounds of gear, grit her teeth and push through the last mile of a hike that inspired Marjan to push harder. "If you only knew how strong she is, you wouldn't worry about her."

"You're strong and she worries about you," Hawa says as her mother walks past her and into the living room.

The comment startles Marjan. Hawa had said it so quietly that Marjan almost didn't hear her. She wonders briefly what else she might have missed.

"I suppose it is natural to worry about people, even if we think we're very strong," she says. "I worry about you all the time and you're one of the strongest people I know."

"But I'm not strong at all!" Hawa protests.

Marjan shakes her head.

"The video you and your friends made at school, that took courage and strength."

Hawa looks surprised.

"I thought you weren't happy that I was in the video."

"I wasn't happy about it, but I respect that you took a stand." She touches Hawa's face. There's a bit of Parwin in her smile, a touch of Marjan's mother in the way she wrinkles her nose. There's a bit of Abdul Khaliq in her eyes, too, but Marjan no longer fears this. Her daughter couldn't be more different from him.

Marjan's phone buzzes with a message. She swipes her phone and reads a message that sends her heart racing.

Be careful. He is looking for you.

She tucks her phone into her bag, tries not to let her face betray her. Hawa is alarmed enough.

"I didn't want to say goodbye to Ingrid. I don't want to leave this apartment," Hawa says. "Why does everything have to change?"

Marjan nods. She thinks of the many farewells she has said, the many people who have come and gone from her life.

This life is a guesthouse, a man once told her. He'd broken into her heart with Mawlana's verses. She cannot recall the lines, but the essence stayed with her. *Sorrow may spoil your joy, even as it sweeps your house clear and readies the way for a new delight.*

Hawa and Marjan both take a look at the apartment they are leaving behind once more. Just before they cross the threshold, Marjan walks back and takes the two terracotta planters from the windowsill. She cannot bear to think of her mint and delicate cilantro leaves withering in her absence. She leaves them outside the neighbor's door and then shoulders her bags.

Marjan shuts the door behind them and starts to walk down the stairs. When she turns around to check for Hawa, she sees her daughter already has a foot on the step behind her.

"I am with you," Hawa says to her mother.

In the stairwell with cinder-block walls, their footfalls sound like the pattering of rain on a hot roof. Like anxious fingers drumming a tabletop. Like twin heartbeats swimming toward synchrony.

30

2014

Having the cast removed felt like being liberated from a cage. Marjan's leg was stiff and her skin flaky, but the doctor reassured her that diligent stretching and walking would restore her strength and flexibility. Until then, she would walk with a bit of a limp.

The Rasulis had agreed to start paying her a bit of pocket money, though nothing close to a salary. As soon as she had scraped together a few bills, one day Marjan asked Zargul if she could wrap up her duties a bit early so that she could pay her daughter a visit. Zargul had readily agreed. Marjan understood that Zargul didn't care for her presence, though she seemed quite content to have the housework off her shoulders. She'd let Marjan use her phone a couple of times to call the orphanage but always hovered close by. Meanwhile, Hawa had become extremely agitated on the phone, and the staff at the orphanage suggested maybe she needed some time to adjust before she could handle hearing her mother's voice.

Marjan climbed into a rickshaw and gave the driver the name of the neighborhood where the orphanage was located. He asked her a second time if she had money for the fare and only started down the road when she showed him a small fan of bills.

Marjan folded the end of her headscarf and pressed the doubled layers over her nose and mouth, but the bitter exhaust from the many cars on the road seeped through and caused her throat to itch. Despite the concrete walls and veils and threats, this was an utterly permeable city. Smoke. Resentment. Fear. Violence. Nothing could be contained.

Marjan wished Soraya could have been there with her. She and her mother had traveled to the provinces for a funeral. She had left a week ago and wouldn't return for another month. The distance made Marjan realize just how much she had come to treasure Soraya as a friend. She found this both comforting and unnerving. Her friendships had all been brief, the goodbyes abrupt and painful. She wondered if she should just tolerate the loneliness, if that would guard her from hurt. She pushed the thought away. Maybe things would be different this time.

The air cleared as the rickshaw began to reach the city limits. There were fewer cars and shops. They passed a cemetery, a hillside scattered with tombstones of all shapes, jagged edges and pointy tips. Children ran across the graves, dodging tombstones as if they were players on a rival team. Their laughter floated down to the street, breaking through the rickshaw's rumble.

The rickshaw driver's phone didn't have GPS, and Marjan did not have a phone, so they were reliant on the directions given to Marjan by the orphanage director. The roads were haphazardly arranged in this district, and Marjan had to step out of the rickshaw twice to ask someone on the street if they knew where the orphanage was located, but neither person could help. When she asked to stop and ask a third person, the driver asked for his fare and sped away. Marjan stood for a moment, trying to decide on a direction, when a woman came around the corner.

"The orphanage?" she said when Marjan stopped her. She pointed to a yellow structure peeking out from behind a privacy wall. "If you were any closer, you might have tripped over a child."

The building sat at the end of a street, announced only by a faded, wooden placard by the gate. Marjan knocked three times on the door, then stepped back. She was so eager to see Hawa again, she worried her knees might buckle with anticipation.

The gate swung open, and Marjan was greeted by a woman wearing a cheery green headscarf and a bright smile. Marjan wondered if she'd been expecting someone else. Her expression did not change, though, upon seeing Marjan.

"Salaam! Can I help you?"

"Yes, please. My daughter, Hawa, is here. I've come to see her finally. I've been unable to come sooner," Marjan said, embarrassed by her absence. They all must have thought her a terrible mother.

"Oh, yes. Come, come! I'm Atefa. We spoke once on the phone," she said, waving Marjan in and shutting the gate behind her. Marjan entered the private yard of the building. A concrete walkway led to a two-story structure with large windows and two fluted columns on either side of the entrance. On either side of the walkway were rosebushes dotted with pink blooms and sunflowers, tall and vigilant guardians.

"I'm so glad you're well enough to come. Hawa-jan is a brilliant child and she's been thriving here. She's made so many friends. We've actually just gathered the girls for a birthday celebration and she helped set up the tables. She's so mature, more like a child twice her age!" Atefa boasted.

Marjan wanted to push past Atefa, to run down the hallway and toward the sound of children chattering and find her daughter.

"Here they are!" Atefa said, stopping at an open door on the right. Marjan saw a cluster of girls, some younger than Hawa and some in their early teens, with paper plates in their hands. They were gathered around a folding table in the center of the room, atop which sat a half-eaten sheet cake decorated with white and pink frosting.

"Hawa? Hawa, I'm here!" she called out. Half the girls turned to see who was calling one of the youngest among them. Marjan stepped into the room, her eyes searching for and then finding her daughter.

From behind other girls, Hawa emerged like a sunflower leaning toward the light. She ran into her mother's open arms. Throats tight, sobs barely contained, they clung to each other while the other girls watched. Hawa had grown, Marjan marveled. Even in these two months, she appeared taller, older. Marjan kissed her daughter's cheek and brushed away tears that might have been hers but also could have been Hawa's.

"Let's step into the next room," Atefa suggested, aware of the audience.

Many of the other girls also had family members who would pay them visits, mothers who would come with small gifts and big kisses. But emotional reunions could trigger others, even a girl who just missed her mother more on that given day.

Two doors down, Marjan and Hawa sat side by side on a round rug, the classroom walls around them painted sky blue, with geometric shapes in pale green. The shapes were cartoon characters with angular limbs, round eyes, and smiles shaped like crescent moons. A stack of plastic chairs was parked in the corner of the room.

"Why didn't you come before? I've been here so long!" Hawa cried.

"I know, my love, and I'm so very sorry! If I could have come sooner, I would have. I had to stay in the hospital for a long time to get better."

Hawa looked her over then, as if searching for the wounds that would justify her mother's absence. She could see nothing, of course. That was the problem with healing. It was too easy for others to believe there'd never really been an injury.

"I've missed you so, so much. I've wanted nothing more than to hear your voice and put my arms around you," Marjan said, cupping her daughter's face in her hands.

Hawa smiled, warmed by her mother's attention and relieved that she'd not been abandoned. The orphanage staff hadn't bothered to tell Marjan that Hawa cried often, especially in the first few weeks. Or that she continued to wet the bed and sometimes grew so frustrated that she tore through sheets of paper with angry scribbles, snapping crayons in half. These were normal behaviors for children in an orphanage, after all. Every child went through an adjustment period, and it did no one any good to dwell on it.

"I hear you've been doing so well here! My smart girl, I'm not the least bit surprised."

"The teachers are nice," Hawa said. "I like the songs."

Marjan smiled. Singing was a sign of joy, wasn't it? She couldn't imagine a sad child singing.

"Will we go home now?" Hawa asked.

"Home?" Marjan asked, as if this wasn't all she was thinking about too. She had practiced this conversation with herself, the spurious excuse she would offer her daughter for why she would not take her home this very minute. "I wish I could do just that, but we can't go back to the apartment with Farrah and Wana. They've left and won't be coming back to Kabul. I am staying somewhere that will not allow children. I'm working very hard to earn enough money so that we can live somewhere together."

How much money did Marjan need to walk out of this building with her? Couldn't she just take her daughter's hand?

"Do you live in a hospital?" Hawa asked.

"No, not anymore. I live in a home. I have a small room to myself. I work at that home. That's the only job I could find for now."

Hawa sat on her hands.

"It's a home but not for children?"

"There's only one baby there. My job is to help take care of the home and that baby. But no, they won't allow any other children. And believe me, I begged them."

"You take care of a baby?" Hawa asked.

"I . . . I do," Marjan confirmed, knowing that Hawa was hearing she was capable of being a mother, just not to her.

Marjan, flustered, tried to change the subject. She asked Hawa to show her some of her drawings or schoolwork. Hawa went to the wall and retrieved a green folder. She handed the folder to Marjan, who opened it gingerly, extracting one page at a time and lingering on each worksheet, marveling at each drawing. Marjan was astounded by how much Hawa was learning but also felt her daughter's eyes on her. She had a debt of attention to pay.

Atefa returned and asked Marjan if she wanted to see the rest of the orphanage. Hawa led the way this time, pointing out the long rooms lined with metal-framed bunk beds. Her room was a patchwork of mismatched rugs, curtains, and blankets. Hawa pointed out her bed. She pointed to the bed of another girl, a friend she had made.

An hour went by quickly. As did a second hour. The sun had dipped below the horizon, and Marjan knew she had to leave. Hawa saw her look at the clock on the wall.

"Don't go. You can stay here," Hawa offered.

"They won't allow me," Marjan said gently, Hawa's small hands in her own.

"Can I go with you? Just for tonight?" Hawa asked.

Marjan was grateful for Atefa, who knew just when to intervene.

"You had a wonderful visit with your dear mother and she can come back soon, but it's time to say goodbye. Dinnertime and then bedtime."

"You can stay here with me."

"My love, if I could—" Marjan tried to hug Hawa, but as soon as she touched her daughter, Hawa stiffened. A switch flipped in her.

"Mommy, don't go! Don't go don't go don't go!"

Marjan tried to calm her daughter; she tried to find the words that would make Hawa understand. She stammered. But even if perfect words could have found their way into her mouth, it wouldn't have mattered. Marjan was drowned out by Hawa's cries, by the crescendo of her anguish. Atefa knew what to do. She gave Marjan a nod and turned herself into an anchor, wrapped her arms around a flailing Hawa, spoke into her ear, and held on tightly until Marjan was out the door, down the hallway, and on the other side of the metal gate. Panting.

Marjan's departure was swift. Cowardly. Had she just run away from her daughter? This was why she had stopped asking to speak to Hawa when she called the orphanage, as well. Every conversation had triggered a storm of emotions in Hawa, and it took the orphanage staff a couple of hours to settle her.

The skies had darkened. Every passing headlight seemed to shine directly onto Marjan's face with the intensity of an interrogator's beam, revealing the truth of what she was and, most important, what she was not.

31

AUGUST 23, 2021
METRA MEDIA

Mina shouldn't be online. Nothing good comes from scrolling through comments on social media, but she cannot help herself.

The chatter around her latest post is mixed. Most comes from within Afghanistan, but she also has viewers around the world, her dispersed compatriots. They watch her from all corners of the globe, tethered to their homeland by a rope that grows longer by the day.

Dear God, why is our country so doomed?

I knew this would happen. Our politicians are money-grubbing snakes.

At least now there will be peace.

Mina wants to scream. Peace is not the absence of war. It is the presence of security and justice, and she feels anything but safe right now.

They've destroyed our beautiful religion.

Have you idiots forgotten what the so-called heroes did to our people?

The commentor has posted a link that Mina clicks, against her better judgment. It leads her to a video of a Special Forces pilot and a talk show host.

MOAB. Mother of All Bombs. We love our acronyms, right? Now, that's not really what the letters stand for, but it sure does describe the beast pretty well and it's a hell of a lot more fun to say than Massive Ordnance Air Blast.

It was nearly twenty-two thousand pounds of deadly force, a green pencil-shaped explosive with a yellow tip and powerful wings.

Why would anyone name a bomb a mother? Mina had wondered. A mother created life and a bomb—did the Americans not realize what bombs did to life?

Mina's tea grows cold as she listens to the pilot recount the bomb dropped over rough terrain in Nangarhar Province at 7:32 p.m. local time on April 13, 2017. The bomb slid out the rear cargo door of a Lockheed MC-130 and detonated above the old soapstone mines where Islamic State militants were believed to be holed up in caves. The mushroom cloud could be seen for miles.

The MOAB was an air-blast bomb, which unleashed its wrath midair when a proximity fuse on its nose ignited the warhead. It caused a crunch of air pressure that could and would wipe out life within a nine-block vicinity. In the video, the pilot walked through the technical sequence of events.

The bomb detonates in the air, atomizing the fuel it carries. A secondary explosion ignites the atomized fuel.

While other bombs created shrapnel or fragmentation, the MOAB destroyed with a tsunami of pressure. It turned people inside out, blew their lungs out of their mouths with such force that there were no remains to retrieve. No bodies to count.

Nothing to bury, but plenty to grieve, Mina thinks grimly. She wants to stop the video, but there's something deeply honest about the way this man was speaking, and honesty was so rare these days.

It's twice the size of the Daisy Cutters used to clear jungles and make way for helicopter landings in Vietnam. But it's also smaller than a bunker buster.

The American president had been asked if he'd authorized the use of the bomb, and he said he had given the military total authorization. *That's why they've been so successful lately,* he had said.

Lately.

Had the president been talking about the operations in Afghanistan or was he talking about other places Americans were dropping bombs? It had been a busy few months. Nearly sixty Tomahawk missiles fired into Syria. An airstrike in Iraq that killed more than a hundred civilians. But the conversation was not about the dozens of small bombs, the ones that flew under literal and metaphorical radars. This one was about the bomb that came with alpha energies, the matriarch of all bombs.

It's more of a message, really, the pilot explained.

What's the message? the host asked.

That we're willing to use unprecedented force to win this thing. That we're doubling down. That we're not quitting until we are victorious. We've got to get into their headspace. So much of war is psychological. Shock and awe, you know. Flex a little muscle and scare 'em off.

Hell yeah.

The Americans declared that they had taken rigorous precautions and conducted extensive surveillance to avoid civilian deaths. They claimed, and the Afghan government confirmed, that no innocent lives were taken in the attack. The host didn't bring up Daniel Hale, the former U.S. Air Force intelligence analyst convicted for disclosing that nearly ninety percent of Afghans killed in airstrikes were unintended targets. Or the unofficial acronym for children killed in error: TITS. Terrorists in training. Why bring it up? Everyone knows war is messy.

Villagers about two kilometers away reported feeling like they were bombed. A farmer lost two cows. Homes had windows blown out.

Mina remembers the parliamentarian from Nangarhar talking about the teacher who had been killed by the blast, along with his son.

Thirty-six ISIS fighters were killed in the attack, the Americans declared. Hang on, new information coming in.

The number was a moving target.

Fifty-one. Eighty-two. The final count was ninety-six.

ISIS reported they did not lose any fighters, but terrorists were not to be trusted. What about the teacher and his son?

He's right about one thing, Mina thinks as she tries to rub the tension out of her temples. *So much of war is psychological.*

32

2014

Marjan was eager to return to the orphanage, to prove to her daughter that she wasn't being abandoned. She also went back for those precious embraces with her daughter. She had to admit, Hawa was doing quite well in the orphanage. Peals of laughter rang out in the colorful hallways. The children were learning English, math, and even a bit of science. She was eating well and had been taken to a clinic for vaccines.

Marjan and Hawa sat in the garden outside, under the smiling faces of the sunflowers, yellow petals dancing in the breeze. Other girls peeked through windows and around corners, curious to see Hawa's mother. Some of their mothers came to visit, as well. Atefa wouldn't say how many of the girls were actual orphans and how many simply came from families who could not afford to care for their daughters.

"Who takes care of all these flowers?" Marjan asked.

"Khanum Atefa. But we help her too. I give them water and pick off the yellow leaves. And we planted seeds, too, in dirt and soon mine will grow a stem and I'll water that too," Hawa said, her eyes twinkling.

Why hadn't she ever thought to plant seeds with Hawa? It seemed like such a simple activity to do with a child. She smiled brightly, told herself to be grateful Hawa was having the experience here.

They went inside, and Marjan looked at the clock. Hawa noticed and stiffened.

As if possessed by a djinn, Hawa darted out of the classroom, down the hallway, into the courtyard, and out the gate.

"Hawa? Where are you . . ." Marjan didn't understand at first. She walked into the hallway, where the evening light spilled into the vestibule at the school's entrance. When she saw the open door, she understood and broke into a run, nearly tumbling onto the dirt street outside the orphanage. She looked left and right, calling out her daughter's name.

Marjan went around the corner, scanned the area, and, seeing nothing, turned around and jogged in the opposite direction. The small road had branches. Should she go left or right? Marjan heard a dog barking. She ran toward the noise, terrified she would find Hawa struggling to free herself from the jaws of an aggressive beast.

"Hawa!"

But the neighborhood was a maze, and Marjan's ears could not track where the barking was coming from. She turned and turned again. The barking stopped. Marjan's chest hurt. She was out of breath and trying to think straight.

Atefa came around the corner.

"What's happened? Where did she go?" she asked. Marjan could only shake her head. "Let me look around. I'll have a couple of the older girls help me too."

Marjan started to walk toward the school, her eyes blurred with tears. She hadn't done Hawa any favors coming here today. Just this morning, Hawa had drawn a picture of a cat sitting on the branch of a tree, a waxy sun placed in a sky colored with two shades of blue. Her cheeks were plump and her spirits bright—until Marjan showed up.

Marjan reached the corner. The small street intersected with the main road, cars going east in one lane and west in the other.

Tires screeched and a horn blared.

Marjan followed the sound and saw a small girl standing just a few feet from the hood of a black sedan, a face-off. Rickshaws and cars swerved around them.

"Hawa!"

Marjan dodged cars. She ran into the street and put her own body between the car and her daughter, throwing up one hand to thank the driver. He looked equally angry and shaken. How close had he come to plowing down this wild child? He drove the heel of his palm into the horn one last time, then yelled as Marjan pulled Hawa toward the side of the road.

"What kind of mother are you? Teach her to cross the street if you're not going to pay attention to her!" he shouted.

Marjan fell to her knees and hugged her daughter tightly.

"Hawa! Don't you realize what could have happened to you? Never, ever do that again!" she shouted, her voice quavering. Hawa was saying something Marjan couldn't make out over the whooshing sound of her own heartbeat in her ears, over the rumbling traffic.

Take me with you, Mommy, Hawa had pleaded, but her words went unnoticed.

Marjan wiped her cheeks and stood up, ignoring a passing woman who was shaking her head. She could go to hell, Marjan thought, even while she cursed herself for not finding Hawa sooner. For not realizing her visit today could trigger a bigger tantrum. For everything she'd done to arrive at this moment.

They walked back to the orphanage. Hawa, petulant and silent. Marjan the same.

She walked through the orphanage gates with Hawa, steeling herself for another outburst. But Hawa pulled her hand out of her mother's tight grip and ran straight into Khanum Atefa's arms.

Marjan watched for a moment, then left without saying goodbye to Hawa or Atefa, the image of Hawa's small body just a breath away from being crushed by a vehicle seared into her mind. She sobbed shamelessly on the ride back to the Rasuli home.

Two days later, Soraya stopped by. They walked into the market to have a cup of tea together in a café owned and staffed by women. Soraya had declared this her favorite place in all of Kabul, as if she had occasion or the money to try many places. The setup was simple. Small round tables. Wooden chairs. Skinny glass vases holding a single red rose. On the wall was a board where patrons could post notes—confessions, promises, jokes.

Across the road was a restaurant called King's Palace, its recent opening announced by a yellow banner in the window. Soraya caught her eyeing the sign, a picture of an ornate throne. Marjan thought of the stories her khala Shaima would tell of her ancestor, the woman who had been a guard of the king's harem. It was hard to believe an orphaned girl could have risen to such a role. She wondered, for the first time, if her aunt had made the whole thing up.

"I see you eyeing that fancy place. One day, when we finally get some jobs that pay us reasonably, we're going to put on our finest clothing and indulge in a most elegant dinner there."

"I'm sorry to disappoint you, my friend, but I'm wearing my finest clothing right now," Marjan said.

"Not tomorrow, silly. Sometime soon, and by then we'll have new clothes. Maybe some handsome suitor will treat me to a new wardrobe," she said, and winked. "And maybe that handsome suitor will have a very good-looking brother."

"You love a fairy tale, don't you?" Marjan laughed, turning her attention to the wall. The café had a sign on the wall, rotating verses from dead poets. Today's words came from Kahlil Gibran.

Your children are not your children . . . They come through you but not from you.

Over steaming cups of green tea, Marjan worked up the courage to tell Soraya about her recent visit.

"There she was, standing in front of this car that could have . . ." Marjan could not finish her sentence. She didn't need to.

"My God," Soraya said, putting her hand over her friend's. "How terrifying for both of you!"

Marjan's mind flew back to that scene, the one she had returned to countless times in the past forty-eight hours. Here, in this room of women and poems, in this space of whispered secrets and bold hopes, it occurred to Marjan that the expression on Hawa's face had not been one of fear—it had been the hard stare of defiance.

Dear God, Marjan thought. *Who is this child of mine?*

33

AUGUST 23, 2021

Marjan slips into a thin, black cloak. After sunglasses, a face mask, and her chadar, there is nothing left to recognize. Even Soraya would wonder. Hawa is dressed in a navy tunic with small flowers on the collar, gray slacks, and a gray chadar. They are out in the open, and it is a most uncomfortable feeling for Marjan.

Her military training has taught her to avoid exposure, to watch her back, to move swiftly, to find cover, and to scan her surroundings for potential threats. From behind her tinted lenses, she looks for anyone who might be eyeing her. She moves from one side of the street to the other to make sure they are not being followed. She tries to anticipate the unanticipated. She thinks through what she will do if a Talib accosts them. If there is a bombing. If the text messages she has received are to be believed.

The text messages.

Marjan is taken back to the one mission that nearly cost her her life, the one in which she flaunted protocol and risked everything. Only Soraya knows the truth about what happened on that mission. She didn't breathe a word to anyone else—not her American sisters in arms, not the Rangers, not the other FTPs, and certainly not the commanding officers who listened to her debrief without suspecting she had hidden something from them.

Was it her naseeb to be assigned that mission? Was what happened there a choreographed event? It had felt unrehearsed and chaotic in the moment, but her aunt had told her once that life's design was revealed only in hindsight.

"Stay close to me. Keep your head low," she tells her daughter.

The city feels like it's been drawn from memory. Everything is where it was before, but nothing is the same. They pass by a beauty salon, the faint image of a woman in full makeup and an elegant updo still visible beneath two coats of white paint. A small café has its curtains drawn, making it impossible to tell if the restaurant is open or closed. There are hardly any women on the street, and the ones present appear in a hurry to be behind closed doors again.

Hawa does not know exactly where they are going, but they are approaching her beloved music school. She wishes today were like any other day and she could slip through those gates and into the instrument room. Being this close, she can almost feel the fret under the pads of her fingers; she can almost hear a plucked string tremble at the sound of its own poetry.

Sometimes Ustad Rafiqi would forget he had students in the room, and they would listen to him speak directly to the rubab:

Its wood and skin and strings long-dried,
From where does this lush sound of love derive?

They near the music school's entrance, the thick concrete walls separating the space from the rest of the city. Hawa thinks how strange it feels to walk purposely past the gate when just a few days ago she would have been flustered to be even a few minutes late for the first class of the day. It must be close to noon. She wonders if she'll hear the lunch bell, the signal that the government-sponsored lunch was about to be served. Without a government, there would be no lunch.

"Do you think anyone is inside?" Hawa asks.

"No," her mother answers. "It's closed."

Hawa bites her lip. She thinks of the instrument room and the piano-practice sign-up sheet. She has in her pocket the laminated card she needs to present to borrow a rubab for an hour of practice. She feels the corners with her fingers, the slight frayed edge of her proof that she belonged to the school and the school belonged to her.

The gate is open. She only wants to look. She slides her hand out of her mother's grip and adjusts the straps of her backpack. Her mother appears deep in thought, as if she's trying to decide if they'll go right or left at the end of this road. Hawa looks around and confirms there are no Talibs patrolling the area, only a handful of people who seem unaware of their presence.

She wants to go in for just a moment, maybe to pick up a sheet of music or to see if Ustad Rafiqi has stayed behind.

"I will be right back," Hawa says to her mother as she darts through the half-open gate. Her mother's eyes go wide.

"Hawa!" Marjan calls, then bites her tongue. She does not want to draw attention. She follows and spots Hawa crossing the quiet yard and approaching the concrete steps of the main building.

Marjan feels herself slow. Is there a sight more haunting than a deserted school? She might as well be crossing a cemetery. Her bag, slung over her shoulder, thumps against her flank as she speed-walks, trying to catch up with her daughter. She is not bothered by the weight. She and the other women routinely hiked five miles carrying a full load of gear over rugged terrain to train.

Don't you get hot in that headscarf? Georgia had asked. She wasn't the only one wondering. Marjan wasn't sure why women who didn't blink at deadlifts or ten pounds of gear would be so taxed by a square of cloth.

"Hawa!" Marjan calls again, a bit louder now that she is off the street, but Hawa is already through the door. She enters the atrium and lets the door close softly behind her. The pictures from the spring concert have been torn from the wall, shredded.

On her left is the piano room, a soaring chamber for small performances. It was in this room that Hawa sat center stage with her rubab and performed a song with only a tabla as an accompaniment. Marjan had been desperate to take pictures on her phone, to capture this impossibility of her daughter shining among children who were the descendants of Afghanistan's finest musicians. The woman seated beside her had tsked at her fidgeting.

Just enjoy the music, she'd advised. *It will all be over too soon.*

It is possibly the truest statement ever made.

The notes burst with emotion, then slowed, a flock of birds taking flight.

You were incredible, Marjan had wanted to shout. The coy smile on Hawa's face told her she knew it to be true.

But now, standing in the doorway, Hawa gasps at the horrific sight. She jumps when her mother's hands touch her shoulders, as Marjan takes it in as well.

Two legs of the music school's piano have been shattered, the instrument kneecapped, humbled. The top has been bashed in, a broken smile with white teeth scattered across the floor. A bass drum speared. A rubab, neck snapped and strings torn. Music stands piled like tinder. A half dozen ruptured tablas, stabbed through the thick black syahi, a once-unblinking eye. Only a high hat remains standing, bearing witness.

Hawa doesn't realize she's crying.

She picks up the splintered rubab. She thinks, for the first time, that its shape resembles a long teardrop. One of the tuning keys has been snapped off. She finds the wooden peg nearby, carved in the shape of a clover, and pockets it. She touches the torn goat skin of a tabla, traces the edges of the ruptured syahi.

In the first weeks, Hawa and her classmates were introduced to the sounds and necessary care of various instruments. Hawa recalls a boy named Haroon, who was eager to begin drumming.

Ustad, should I powder the tabla? he had asked, holding the white container of talcum powder above the drum.

Put that down. You should do nothing until you know what to do.

Though he had chastised Haroon, he appeared to have appreciated that the boy's misstep had given him an opportunity to do what he loved best—teach.

Look at the tabla. What is it made of, this husk, this skin? Animal, fire, tree, metal, passion. You hear all of it in the music.

Hawa cannot imagine what kind of monsters would do such a thing to instruments. She regrets her impulsive dash into the school. She's then struck by a more terrifying thought. What would these monsters do to people who played these instruments? She understands suddenly why her mother reacted so harshly to the video she appeared in.

Hawa's heart thrums in her chest. She is ready to leave. She is ready to run. She looks to her mother, standing grimly behind her.

"One day . . ." Marjan starts to say. But she can make no promises. She has seen too much, both as a girl made into a wife and as a soldier on missions. She thinks of the mission that went wrong, the terrified woman she found sleeping among the livestock because that was what she was to her husband, chattel.

It will all be over too soon.

She takes her daughter's hand. Time is compressing. They need to keep moving. Marjan turns them toward the door. They slip past the fallen photographs, their footsteps echoing, filling the columnar space. Marjan has a hand on the door leading outside and is about to push it open when she looks through the glass pane and realizes there's a figure on the other side.

Marjan claps a hand over her daughter's mouth and spins them, partners in a desperate dance, so their backs are to the atrium wall. They are still as the instruments. Willowy necks. Fragile skins. Unblinking eyes.

34

2014

Marjan held Zargul's phone to her ear, aware she was being watched. Zargul insisted Marjan stay nearby in case she received an important call. After seven rings, Atefa answered. Marjan introduced herself, humiliated by the necessity of calling her daughter at an orphanage in front of a mother who was, at that same moment, nursing her baby.

"Oh, hello!" Atefa said. "While we bring her to the phone, let me update you. She was ill last week with a sore throat. We took her to the clinic and the doctor saw an ear infection along with very large tonsils. I remember you told us she'd been sick frequently as a child. The doctor said it's possible she'll need surgery to have her tonsils removed."

"Surgery?"

"Not now. Just a warning in case it happens often. And before you worry too much, please know that we have funds set aside for these kinds of emergencies, and we will of course keep you updated."

Marjan looked up and saw Zargul had stopped rocking the baby. She turned her back away from her employer, her face flushed.

"Is she coming to take me home?" she heard Hawa ask.

Marjan's head fell to her chest, heavy. She heard Atefa's muffled voice telling Hawa that was not yet possible.

"I don't want to talk to her. No, no, no!"

Marjan closed her eyes, tried not to fall apart. Atefa tried again to put

Hawa on the phone but to no avail. She returned to the line, and in a low, gentle voice suggested it would be best to connect another time.

"Of course," Marjan said, quashing her devastation. She could feel Zargul's eyes on the back of her neck.

Marjan thanked Zargul and placed her phone on a side table near her without meeting her eyes. It felt hard to breathe, so she mumbled something about seeing to the laundry and left.

All around her were reminders of the life a child was meant to have. The Rasulis had been married less than two years and looked nothing like any marriage Marjan had ever seen. Her own marriage had been an assault. Abdul Khaliq's other wives had also cowered under him. The women she had met in the shelter were there because they'd been beaten by their husbands.

It wasn't that Marjan hadn't met good men. She'd met plenty. The restaurant owner. The customers. The man at the bakery and so many of the doctors and staff at the hospital had all been gentle, respectful people who most certainly treated their spouses with kindness and respect. Her father had been an affectionate family man before opium transformed him. Marjan had always wondered how different marriage could be if a woman were married to a decent man.

Agha Rasuli seemed to be a decent man. He was tender with his wife. He loved their daughter and often held her in his arms, asking her again and again in a wistful voice if she'd missed him while he was away.

I missed you too, my darling, he would say when the corners of Leeda's tiny mouth turned up.

Marjan would have to remind herself not to stare.

Both parents cooed over Leeda, marveled at how fast she was growing and every new, miraculous feat. She saw Agha Rasuli run his hands playfully over his wife's backside when he didn't know Marjan was in the room. She caught Zargul smiling at their wedding picture, framed and displayed on the shelf of a glass curio.

But she also sensed Agha Rasuli was easily frustrated by Zargul. If she asked more than three questions, he would huff with exasperation. And Zargul was a woman with a lot of questions.

What time are we invited to your sister's home this Saturday? Look at this spot on Leeda's leg. What do you think it is? How much did that suit cost? When will you show me the designs for the restaurant? What should I make for dinner tomorrow? Don't you think this material is too rough for Leeda's skin?

Marjan saw the way husband and wife would sometimes cut their eyes at each other, the tight smiles. She sensed the words held back because she was on the other side of a wall. She tried to make her work visible and herself invisible. The sooner she could earn enough money to afford some choices, the better.

Three weeks into her employment, Marjan once again knocked on her employer's door while he sat at his desk.

"I'm sorry to disturb," she said softly. She could hardly recall when she'd last spoken in her full voice.

"Yes?" he said, looking up.

Marjan took a deep breath, emboldened only by the depth of her desperation.

"Agha Rasuli, I am very glad for this position and hope that even in my short time here, I have proven that I am willing to work hard."

"Yes, I have noticed."

"I wanted to ask if you've given thought to the salary for this job. I do not mean to ask for anything more than what is fair, and I realize that having my own room is generous and the pocket money has helped a lot. But I do have other general expenses."

Agha Rasuli looked directly at her. "That's quite forward of you."

She lowered her gaze. Was there another way to go about this? Would he have preferred her to speak in hints and signals? She waited for him to go on.

"I hope you don't think me an unfair man. I'm certainly not. The type of business I'm in, I've met all kinds of people."

"Of course," Marjan said, only because she felt obligated to say something.

He rapped his knuckles on his desk.

"I was going to speak to you about this," he said. Marjan wanted to believe him. She really did. "I've just been tied up with so many meetings. I'm doing the work of three men right now. Launching a business is quite consuming."

Marjan nodded.

"I suppose a weekly salary is reasonable," he said. He rose halfway from his chair and extracted his wallet from his back pocket. He counted out a few bills, counted them a second time, then stuck his hand out. Marjan did not want to seem overly eager, so she crossed the room in two slow steps and accepted the bills from him.

"Thank you," she said. "I will continue to do my best. It is a pleasure to care for Leeda-jan."

She turned to take her leave, but Agha Rasuli called her back.

"I want to speak to you about something. Marjan, my wife comes from a very . . . respected family," he said, choosing his words carefully. "They are accustomed to certain standards and reputation. They're concerned about . . . chatter. I am not, of course. I told them that you had experience working in very refined restaurants and came highly recommended."

Marjan tried to keep her expression neutral.

"And it's important that they understand you are here as an employee, nothing more," Agha Rasuli said. "I'm sure you can appreciate how sensitive these situations are for me, her husband. Anyway, I'll have a salary for you on a weekly basis. Thank you."

She nodded, her face flushed with embarrassment, though she'd done nothing wrong. She could be ruined by a whisper, a finger pointed in her direction. The best way to protect herself, she knew, was to make sure Zargul felt more beautiful, more powerful, more capable than her at every turn.

Each day, Marjan tried to achieve the unachievable, to please Zargul without irritating Zargul.

"Leeda's asleep finally. I don't think she'll wake again until much later," Zargul said a week after Agha Rasuli's vague warning to Marjan. She was standing in the doorway of the square kitchen, watching Marjan dry her hands on a faded kitchen towel.

"I noticed the yogurt was almost finished. I could make some more," Marjan offered. "I know you like to have some with your dinner."

"That's not necessary at this hour," Zargul replied.

"It's still early. And it would be no trouble," Marjan insisted. She should not have.

Zargul shifted her weight on her feet. Her expression soured.

"I do not like yogurt and I do not want yogurt," she said flatly.

"Of course," Marjan agreed, though she knew this was a lie. Earlier today Marjan had watched Zargul drag a piece of bread around the inside of her yogurt bowl to get every last bit.

Marjan folded the kitchen towel and hung it from a metal hook to dry.

She slipped by Zargul, felt her eyes on her back as she walked down the stairs. She pulled the door closed behind her and ran through their exchanges that day, trying to recall if she had done anything especially troublesome. Early in the mornings, Zargul seemed relieved to turn Leeda over to Marjan. She would retire to her room and then emerge midmorning having changed her clothes, tamed her hair, and dabbed a spot of color on her cheeks. This morning was no different. Marjan had changed Leeda out of her soiled diapers, washed the baby bottles, and swaddled and rocked her when Leeda began to whine sleepily. Marjan sometimes felt ashamed when she found herself enjoying a moment with Leeda. What kind of mother could smile while she was away from her own child?

Marjan looked around her room and realized she'd forgotten to bring anything to eat for dinner. She'd not eaten anything all day and was too hungry to wait until morning. She decided it was best to return now rather than disturb the couple in the evening.

Marjan entered the main house and was halfway up the stairs when she overheard Zargul speaking to someone. She spent most of her time on the phone, so this wasn't surprising, but Marjan froze when she realized she was the subject of Zargul's conversation.

"He keeps telling me he's hired her so I can get rest, but I know that's not the whole truth. He's having a hard time getting investors for his restaurant. He hired this girl just to make it look like he's so successful, that he's got money for servants and hoping that will get people to believe in him. I feel like a fool, Mariam. He made himself out to be this hotshot businessman like our father and uncle but I don't think he can even afford the tablecloths for a restaurant in Dubai. And now I'm stuck with a . . . a ghost walking around my house."

Zargul let out a groan. Marjan closed her eyes. Mariam was Zargul's sister. This was a conversation no one was meant to hear.

"I'm not exaggerating! She is like a ghost. No living person is this quiet. She even whispers when she's talking to the baby. I swear she's trying to haunt us. I need my privacy, my space. And I know my darling husband will turn this around on me one day. He'll probably complain that he had to hire her because I'm not able to manage a home and a baby. Just be sure you know if Ali's money is real before you make big decisions. Trust me, not all boyfriends should be husbands."

Zargul giggled. Marjan retreated, stepping quietly down the stairs and out the door.

In her dim room, Marjan sat on her floor cushion and stared at the wall. Maybe Zargul was right. Maybe she was an apparition. She had no family. She had no bright future ahead. She might as well not have a single bone in her body or a drop of blood in her veins. No wonder this life did not feel like life.

Marjan lay down and rolled onto her side. She pulled her knees to her chest. Tears slid from the corners of her eyes and darkened the fabric of her pillowcase.

35

AUGUST 23, 2021

Hawa sees the outline of the man on the other side of the music school's main door. She understands why her mother spun her around so forcefully.

The man has not yet entered, though. It's hard to tell through the frosted glass, but it looks like he is facing the schoolyard and pointing at something. Are there others behind him? How many?

Marjan considers their options. Behind them is the vandalized chamber hall, the destroyed instruments. She tries to remember if there was anywhere to hide in that room, any second exit. Why didn't she notice? She should have noticed.

"Is there a way out through that room?" she whispers in Hawa's ear.

Hawa shakes her head.

"Is there another door somewhere?"

Hawa's eyes widen.

"There's a window in the ustad's office," she whispers back to her mother.

Marjan nods. The founder of the music school, a man with a doctorate in musicology, has an office diagonally across the hall from where they stand. It's less than ten meters away. Marjan grabs Hawa by the hand and crouches, but it's too late.

The front door opens. Marjan has nowhere to go but back into the chamber hall. She pulls Hawa with her, ducks into the hall just as the man enters the atrium. He does not shout, so he must not have seen them. She looks around the room again and feels her heart sink. She might as well have kept her daughter in the atrium. This chamber hall, with its tall white walls, is an open field. They cannot hide behind a few scattered folding chairs. And because it was designed with acoustics in mind, there is not a single window. Every sound they make will be amplified. There is a single bass speaker in the corner, large and heavy.

What are the chances this man walks past the chamber hall without looking in?

Marjan cannot take that risk. She needs a diversion.

"Stay here," she whispers to Hawa, then takes a step toward the door. Hawa tugs on her arm, tries to pull her back. She shakes her head, vehemently disagreeing with her mother. Marjan peels her daughter's hand off her arm. Hawa's eyes are wet with tears.

"Let me find out who he is. Go hide behind that speaker. Go!" Her whisper is barely audible, but Hawa is propelled by the urgency in her mother's voice. She tucks herself and their bags into the triangular hollow behind the speaker.

Marjan steadies herself. She has a plan, albeit a lousy one, that will buy her a couple of minutes at best. She will be the diversion, making sure Hawa does not catch this man's attention. She needs to find out who he is so that she can navigate an exit around him, lead him away from her daughter.

She adjusts her headscarf, takes in a deep breath, and enters the atrium. The man is not there. For a split second, Marjan thinks about darting back into the chamber hall, grabbing Hawa, and making a dash for the door, but before she can do so, the man appears in the doorway of the music school's front office and his eyes lock on Marjan's.

She assesses him quickly. He has a cellphone in his hand but no weapon. He is three or four inches taller than her, slim and dressed in a dark blue long-sleeved shirt and a pair of jeans. He has dark features, hair that is thick and wavy on top and tapers to a close buzz cut. He is clean-shaven, which gives him a youthful appearance and, more important, signals to Marjan that he is not one of the Talibs. She sees curiosity in his eyes.

"Who are you?" he asks, looking from the stairs to the far end of the hallway behind Marjan. She is concealed behind her sunglasses, her shape hidden under this loose cloak.

"I wanted to ask you the same," Marjan replies. She is looking around as well to see if anyone entered with him. "The school is closed. Why are you here?"

"Seems we both have good questions," the man observes. "Okay, I'll go first. I heard there had been some destruction of equipment at this school. I wanted to see for myself. And why are you here?"

"Why would you want to see for yourself?" Marjan asks, skipping over his question. "Are you a music teacher here?"

A note of laughter escapes his lips. It disarms Marjan, melts some of the tension in her shoulders.

"Not at all," he says. "Sister, I work in journalism. I'm here to see for myself what they have done. I'm no threat to you. So, tell me now. Why are you here?"

Marjan reevaluates him, considering this information, and it makes sense. He looks like a journalist, which is an utterly unscientific conclusion to come to, but she feels fairly confident about it.

"Who else is here with you?" she asks.

"I'm here alone. And you?"

"Why do you care about the music school?"

"Are you sure you're not a journalist?" He sighs. "You certainly ask more questions than you answer. I'm here alone to take some pictures and document what's happened."

Marjan nods. "My daughter went to school here. We were just passing by."

"We?"

But Marjan has already turned her back on him and is in the chamber hall. She calls her daughter's name, and when her timid head peeks out from behind the speaker, Marjan beckons her to come. She leads her into the hallway, telling her a journalist is here. He has, of course, followed her into the chamber hall, where he begins to cluck his tongue at the sight of the destruction.

"Here it is," he says with a sigh. When he sees Hawa, he raises a hand in greeting and then turns back to Marjan. "Before you go, can I just ask a couple of questions? Have you heard any discussions about whether the school will reopen? What instrument was your daughter learning here? How does she feel about the school closing?"

It is time to leave. Marjan cannot risk Hawa saying something that makes the journalist connect her with the protest video she was in.

"We need to leave now," Marjan says. Hawa looks uncomfortable.

The man has his cellphone out. He is taking pictures of the instruments from different angles, trying to capture the brutal way they were attacked.

They are almost out of the chamber hall when Hawa stops short and turns around.

"Without music, I feel lost," she says to him, her voice breaking. The man looks up, bites his lip. She has cut right to the heart of the story with this admission.

"Without music, we are all lost," he responds. Hawa nods. She senses decency in this man and is glad he is here taking pictures of the terrible things that have been done to her school.

Marjan pulls on her daughter's arm, moves her into the atrium, through the door, and into the schoolyard again. They are soon back on the street with their bags.

"Are you okay?" she asks Hawa.

"I'm fine," Hawa says, and Marjan breaks a little, because Hawa has been telling her since she was just a little girl that she was fine when she most certainly was not fine. When she most certainly should not have been fine. She remembers the days she would visit Hawa in the orphanage, showing up on weekends with the other mothers to make sure her daughter didn't forget her. To kiss her daughter's cheek and breathe in the sweet smell of the top of her head.

She cannot think about this now. She needs to get to the shelter and off the streets before a Talib stops and questions her. They are getting closer. She could try to catch a taxi, but from here they will be moving through smaller side streets.

"Stay close to the curb," she warns her daughter. She is always warning her daughter of something. She wonders if it is as exhausting for Hawa as it is for her.

It has been a decade since Marjan left the shelter. Once she moved into the halfway house, she never returned. It was not a place that accepted visitors and, besides, returning would have felt like a regression at a time when she was determined to move onward.

But she knows this block well, even though much has changed. Beyond the walls, she can see the second stories of two homes that have clearly been built with imported dollars and designs. Just past those homes, she sees the familiar entrance to the shelter, the building still unmarked and forgettable.

Marjan looks over her shoulder. She remembers how careful Samia and the staff were about keeping the building's location and purpose a secret and hopes that they've been able to keep it open despite the orders to shut down. Marjan cannot hear any sounds from within either, but that is not unusual. The whole city has quieted. She knocks softly on the gate. After a moment, she knocks again. Three loud raps.

Marjan wishes she had Samia's phone number, but numbers have changed over the years. She has no way of getting in touch with anyone from the shelter. She tries to recall where the intake office was, but it was over a decade ago, and she wasn't recording these details at the time. She has no steps to retrace.

"This is where I was born?" Hawa asks, while Marjan is trying to decide how long to wait before knocking again. She's tempted to try to scale the wall and apologize later, once she and Hawa are safely on the other side.

"Yes," she says. "I came to this place when I was expecting you. The people here helped me a lot. It was not an easy time."

Hawa takes a couple of steps back, stretches her neck, and tries to see over the privacy wall, but the wall does its job well.

"How old was I when we left?" she asks her mother.

Marjan bangs on the gate with the side of her fist. The metal rattles.

She hopes the sound is drowned out by the distant rumble of passing cars, the sputter of a generator, and the shouts of children.

"You were about a year old. You had just started walking," Marjan says, then presses her ear to the gate, listening for any sound.

"Why did you have to come to a place like this?" Hawa asks. "Why wouldn't your family take you back?"

"My family had a lot of troubles. I've already told you," Marjan says. She pounds again on the gate, this time with enough force that Hawa can feel it in her feet.

"Even your sisters?"

"My sisters had their own troubles," she mutters. Is it possible she's standing outside the wrong building? She looks up and down the street, tries to see if there's another building that looks familiar.

"You think my father's family would still be terrible to you now? Maybe they've changed," Hawa wonders aloud. She is uncomfortable seeing her mother like this, banging on doors where no one seems to be home. Looking over her shoulder. Passing herself off as a cripple. "Lots of people change with time. Maybe they could help us."

"They haven't changed," Marjan says.

"How do you know?" Hawa asks.

"Because I know. They haven't changed and we can't run to them. You'll just have to trust me, okay?" Marjan snaps. She's suddenly aware of her volume and closes her eyes for a beat to reset herself. She has another idea and looks around the frame of the gate. "They must have cameras out here. Maybe they can see us?"

Two doors down, a gate opens and a woman emerges with a prayer shawl draped over her shoulders, chestnut brown with a paisley pattern. She appears to be in her fifties, but it is hard to tell. People are aged by much more than time.

"Who are you looking for?" the woman calls out.

Marjan straightens her shoulders, clears her throat. She elbows her duffel bag, trying to tuck it out of view.

"Sorry. Didn't mean to disturb you," she says.

The woman eyes them both, mother and daughter with bags on their shoulders and faces flushed with heat.

"There's no one there," the woman says, her eyes flicking to the gate Marjan has been banging on.

"Are you sure?" Marjan asks. "Do you know the people inside?"

"There's no one inside," the woman repeats. "Understand? You should leave."

Marjan understands that this woman knows exactly what type of facility is behind these walls. What if she is just trying to protect the residents of the shelter by driving her away?

"I know this place. My daughter and I just need to speak to someone," Marjan begins, her tone soft and pleading.

"Everyone is gone," the woman hisses. "Do you hear me? They were forced to shut down. There's no one left. Don't believe me? Climb the walls and see for yourself!"

She spins around and disappears into the confines of her home, leaving Marjan and Hawa to process her warning.

"Madar?" Hawa's voice is small. Timid.

"Give me one second," Marjan mumbles. She needs to think. Her throat is dry, and the heat is getting to her. Hawa must be thirsty too. And hungry. Marjan checks her texts.

Jenna and the other CSTs have sent a few messages, asking their Afghan counterparts to check in. There are warnings about security around the airport. Credible threats of an impending attack. Marjan shakes her head. She thinks of how many missions they carried out with half-baked information, a single name or a description that could have fit dozens of men. How much should they believe? Maybe this rumor is meant to drive the masses away from the airport so that a select few can get through.

Marjan calls Soraya. She needs a strategy and is too flustered to come up with one on her own right now.

"Where are you?" Soraya asks, skipping all formalities.

"We came to the place I told you about but a neighbor says it's closed. No one's answering the door," Marjan reports.

"I believe it. Those women have probably ended up back with the people they ran from."

Marjan turns away from her daughter. She is certain that if she'd been sent home from this shelter, she would not be alive today.

"Soraya, I think I have to go back home. I don't know where else to go."

"Be careful, Marjan," Soraya warns. "Listen, they didn't show my brother any mercy and he wasn't even the one they were looking for. They have all our files. Oh, Marjan. I can't stay here any longer."

Marjan has never heard Soraya sound so shaken.

"I'm supposed to be writing my speech for that conference in Europe about women's empowerment," she whispers between sobs. "If that meeting was a month ago, I would have been out already."

Marjan's eyes blur with tears. While Elaha keeps them all in line and communicates plans, Soraya is the red balloon of their platoon. She is the one who makes jokes as they gear up for a mission. She is the one who helps everyone unwind after a debrief. And in the planning of their escape, Soraya has been the one to insist a door will open. Marjan wishes she could put her arms around her friend.

"Soraya, it will be okay. Look at the skies. The planes are still leaving. Jenna and the others, they'll find a way. We just have to stay safe for a little bit longer."

The line is quiet but for a sniffle.

"Soraya, don't give up. It doesn't suit you," Marjan chastises.

"You're right, you're right," she says. "Ugh, I've made such a mess."

"With your mascara? Yes, I bet you have," Marjan replies.

"If I die, I die pretty," Soraya says softly. Her mantra.

Marjan turns to see Hawa watching a pigeon, gray with white markings, walk around. The bird tries to fly, but only one wing flaps, and it's not enough to get off the ground. It walks away from Hawa, then reverses direction. "Look, my beautiful friend, I've got to get us off the streets. I'll call you when I figure something out."

"But, Marjan, your apartment isn't safe," Soraya warns.

"I know. We won't go there," Marjan promises. "Neither is your home.

There's one other place—the one Ingrid told me about. I'm going to check it out and let you know."

"Good idea. I'm going to try the bank once more. Then I've got to get my mother's medicines before I leave. If you run into any trouble, promise you'll call me?"

"That's what friends do, right?" Marjan asks. "You promise too?"

"Promise."

She hangs up and chews her lip. Where can they go? She can't afford one of the hotels where people from out of town stay, and she is certain the Taliban is keeping a close eye on those premises anyway.

Hawa's back is turned toward Marjan. What did she hear? Marjan tries to remember what she has just said to Soraya. She calls her daughter's name and is surprised to see she holds the injured pigeon in a nest she's made of her two hands. Hawa strokes the bird's neck with a fingertip, the iridescent feathers flashing green and violet. She brings the bird to her, coos in its ear. Sings for it a song for the flightless.

36

2014

Marjan heard the door, then the voices. As he often did, her employer had returned home with guests. Zargul, who had just stopped into the kitchen to pick up a bottle for Leeda, rolled her eyes and slammed a cabinet door closed. She left the room muttering something under her breath.

"Marjan, are you there?" Agha Rasuli called from halfway up the stairs.

"Yes, I'm here," she called back.

"Tea, please. We have company."

"Yes, of course," Marjan replied, and filled the kettle with water. "How many?"

"Four!" he answered, then went back downstairs to rejoin his guests.

Marjan ground two cardamom pods while she waited for the kettle to whistle. A few minutes later, she assembled her tray and tried to turn on the lights on the stairway. She had to flick the switch twice before it came on, lighting the precarious journey down the steps. She moved slowly, praying the thermos wouldn't topple over and send the teacups crashing to the ground. When she reached the bottom step, she let out a sigh of relief and took in the guests. The men had settled into a corner of the room opposite the television, their backs against the wall.

"The location is great. I have bids from two construction contractors. Haroon, you have a few friends in the business as well. If you can find me someone who can beat these numbers, I'll give you a cut of the difference," Agha Rasuli said. He sat on a floor cushion with one knee bent, his elbow resting on a cylindrical pillow. On seeing Marjan enter the room with the tea service and a tray of dried fruits and nuts, he gave a faint nod of approval.

"Maybe. How about a room to stay in when I go there? I love those marina views," Haroon replied, tapping on his phone and scrolling. "I took some amazing pictures from our last trip."

"You were supposed to delete those pictures," Agha Rasuli teased, his voice lowered.

"You're a married man. I'm not," the friend with the beard interjected. "I think it's time we go back and . . . I don't know . . . find an electrician? Or buy the kitchen appliances? Saboor, you want to help us find an electrician?"

A man with round, black-framed glasses smiled politely.

"I don't think I'd be very helpful with any of that," Saboor replied.

"Don't scare him off," Agha Rasuli warned. "I am trying to convince Saboor to manage the hotel once it's opened. I want the same level of class that he brought to Serenity Hotel."

"But remember, it's Dubai. People don't just want clean towels and windows. They want to stay somewhere . . ." Haroon searched and landed on an English word to convey his meaning. "Sexy. You know what I mean?"

Marjan crouched down and set the tray on the carpet. She kneeled, threw the end of her headscarf over her shoulder to conceal her neck, and kept her eyes averted. She was intensely aware, as any young woman would be, that she was alone in a room with four men. She didn't need to look at them to know they were watching her. She reached over to place a steaming cup of black tea in front of one of the guests. The cup rattled in the saucer.

"Must be an earthquake," one of the men joked. There was laughter. Marjan poured a second cup. This time she set the saucer on the carpet first, then set the teacup onto it. She did the same for the third and fourth cups. She set the dried fruits and nuts in the middle of the men and placed next to it four small porcelain plates.

"Listen, friend," one of the men said to Agha Rasuli. "Let's set something straight right now. You are not permitted to speak to my wife. If you let it slip that you've hired someone for the household, I'll lose all my hair."

A cellphone rang. The man named Saboor excused himself and stepped outside to take the call. Marjan gathered herself and went back upstairs. She pushed her headscarf off her head and lifted her hair off her neck. The kitchen had been warm all day. She opened the window, hoping to catch a breeze, and heard a voice.

It was the man named Saboor, she realized. The kitchen window was just over the door to the receiving room where the men were drinking tea.

"Did the doctor say anything else?" she heard him ask. He stepped into view then, walked toward the back of the house where her room was and then back toward the entrance to the home. She had barely looked at the men while she had served the tea. She couldn't see his face from here but saw that he was neatly dressed. Navy slacks and a striped dress shirt with sleeves rolled up. He paced in camel-colored loafers.

"All right, Madar-jan. I'll be home soon," he said. "And I'll stop by the pharmacy on my way, I promise."

Two birds flew past the window then. The movement drew Saboor's eyes skyward, where he spotted Marjan watching him. She pulled back from the window with a start. Did he think she was spying on him? Her face was hot.

"Marjan! Close that window, will you? I don't want flies in the house again," Zargul said. She heard the voices from downstairs then, heard Rasuli laugh and call someone a womanizer. Her brow furrowed. She moved to the top of the stairs, then looked at Marjan. "You know, I've finally gotten Leeda to sleep. You can leave for today."

"Are you sure? I can stay to clean up after the guests."

"No, it's fine," Zargul said with an encouraging wave. "You've done plenty today. Truly."

It was unlike her to fret about Marjan working too hard. She clearly wanted to eavesdrop on her husband without any witnesses. Marjan nodded and walked past Zargul down the stairs. She hoped she would spot Saboor seated with the men again, but he wasn't there. She opened the door and found him standing, looking at his phone.

"Excuse me," Marjan said as she tried to slip past him.

"Oh, I'm blocking your way," he said, realizing she was there. "Apologies."

Marjan smiled politely, still trying to keep her eyes averted.

"I hope I wasn't too loud on the phone," he said, pointing to the window. Marjan felt the heat creep up her neck again.

"No, not at all. I was just getting some air."

"I think I needed some air too," he said, smiling. "I'm not really accustomed to these kinds of conversations."

Marjan saw a softness in his eyes, an honesty.

"Neither am I," she said.

"Of course not," he agreed, as if he knew something about her just by looking at her. "Are you going home now?"

"Yes, but not . . . I stay in those quarters back there," she replied, pointing to the structure behind the house. When she saw his brow furrow, she felt she needed to say more. "It's a convenient arrangement. I'm very grateful."

"Do you not have family in Kabul?"

Marjan shook her head.

"What is your name?"

"Marjan," she said, and with that she landed on the other side of an invisible line. She should not be having this conversation. Even now, she should issue a polite goodbye and walk to her room. Even while she worked at the restaurant, she'd avoided conversations with the men who came in as customers and the waiters and kitchen staff. She sensed a different energy around Saboor than most men. Something sincere.

"I'm Saboor," he said. "Like the stone."

Marjan felt a memory shake loose.

Her aunt had told her about the magical black stone, a confessional stone that absorbed the hardships whispered to it by troubled people. The stone, though magical, was not without limits. It would one day explode under the strain of all it had taken in, an event that would be the harbinger of an apocalypse.

"Do people confess their heartaches to you?" Marjan asked.

"So you know the legend!" He sounded pleased. "They do, actually. And I hold it all in. No cracks thus far. No leaks."

"I'm glad you're in one piece."

He laughed, surprised at her humor. She held back a smile.

"As far as I can tell. So if you ever need to unload yourself of troubles, you know who to call," he said, pointing to himself. There was a beat of silence between them, and in that pause Marjan came to her senses.

"It was nice to meet you," she said.

"And you," he echoed. She had taken two steps toward her quarters when he called her name. She turned around.

"Would you be willing to hear my troubles sometime?" he asked. "Even a stone needs someone to talk to."

Marjan looked at the ground. What was he asking? She shook her head.

"That's not possible. I don't even have a phone," she said, fumbling for a polite excuse.

"Is that true?" he asked. His boldness caught Marjan off guard.

"It's very true. I had a phone but it was crushed in an accident."

"What kind of accident?"

"An ambulance drove over it."

"What was your phone doing in the street?"

"It fell from my hand when . . ."

"When what?"

"When the ambulance hit me."

"You were hit by an ambulance?" he said slowly, looking her over as if he expected to find signs of injury. "But you're better now?"

"Thank God," she said.

"You do look well," he said, then cleared his throat. "So, how did you end up working here?"

Marjan saw the flutter of the kitchen curtain in the window.

"I should go," she said. Zargul would not take kindly to her chatting with one of Agha Rasuli's acquaintances.

"Of course," he said. "See you next time."

Marjan felt his eyes on her as she disappeared around the back corner of the house and entered her small space.

Two nights later, Marjan lay on her floor cushion, trying to fall asleep.

Agha Rasuli's guests were in no rush to leave, and Marjan knew there would be many glasses and plates to gather in the morning. The sound of pop songs drifted from the house, down the small walkway, and into her solitary room.

Marjan heard a knock. Startled, she sat up. Maybe it was Agha Rasuli asking her to come in and help with the guests. Or maybe it was Khanum Zargul needing help with Leeda. The baby had coughed a few times in the afternoon.

"On my way," Marjan called out. She rose and reached for her head-scarf. She moved quickly, especially eager to keep her employer happy now that she was receiving a salary. She reached the door and opened it just a crack, enough to receive directions.

But there was no one there. Marjan stuck her head out a bit further, and still saw no one. She wondered if the knocking she'd heard had been anything more than a drumbeat from the late-night gathering. Relieved, she started to pull the door closed when she noticed a small paper bag on the ground. She picked it up and brought it inside. She sat on her mattress, the pale light of a gibbous moon filtering through her gauzy curtain.

Inside the bag was a piece of paper, a mobile phone, and a charger. She unfolded the paper and found a message penned in blue ink, a smudge on the bottom of the page.

A small gift, a patience stone of a modern sort. I hope you'll make good use of it.

Marjan turned the phone on. There were no text messages, no pictures in the gallery. The phone was clean except for a single contact.

Saboor.

Marjan turned the phone off and set it beside her. The music's tempo quickened. Marjan removed her headscarf, suddenly thirsty. Something in the night shifted, and it was unlikely Marjan would get any sleep.

37

AUGUST 23, 2021

"Is it much further?" Hawa asks. Afternoon has given way to evening, and the sky is draped in a lavender haze.

"I don't think so," Marjan replies. In the back of the taxi, beads of sweat drip down the nape of her neck. Her shirt clings to her body.

"Do you want a sip?" Hawa offers her the can of orange soda Marjan bought her. Hawa noticed her staring into her thinning wallet and insisted she wasn't thirsty. Marjan takes a sip to absolve her of any guilt. She licks her lips, tastes the salt and the sweet together.

"We must be close," Marjan says.

Marjan's commute to the base and her errands around town never brought her to these city outskirts. If Ingrid hadn't talked about it, Marjan never would have known the City of Widows existed. The taxi driver had not heard of it, which was fine with Marjan. More than fine, actually. Invisibility was the goal.

Hawa looks out the window. Marjan is surprised to hear her humming softly. It is not a cheerful melody. It is a hymn of exhaustion and melancholy. It takes her a moment to recognize the song and recall the lyrics, sung in the slow baritone voice of the mustached singer whose first instrument had been the mandolin. The music school had made of her daughter a girl who sang songs decades older than herself.

I've heard from here you'll soon depart
To sing the anthem of another city

Hawa drains the last drops from her can of soda. They pass a hospital, one of more than two dozen in this city. This one is four stories tall, with windows of ocean blue reflective glass. Marjan takes her phone out and sees she's gotten a new message from the unnamed number. She taps on it.

Are you all right? I saw a video of the airport and it looks like madness. He is in Kabul, asking questions. I do not know more than that. God be with you, sister.

Marjan stares at the screen. She taps out a reply.

We are okay. Looking for somewhere safe to be and hoping for a departure. I am praying for you and your children too. Please let me know what you hear about him. And stay safe. Don't forget to erase these messages.

"Madar?" Hawa's voice breaks through her thoughts.

"Hm?" she says absently. She reaches over and squeezes her daughter's forearm, confirms her presence for Hawa and Hawa's presence for herself. "What is it, jan?"

"Who is in Kabul?"

Marjan turns her phone over as her pulse quickens. The taxi pulls over at the end of the cricket field, the perimeter marked by a metal fence. In her mind's eye, she sees the chicken wire of the coop at her husband's compound. She remembers draping wet shirts on a clothesline and her mother-in-law clapping the back of her head for . . . for . . . What had her mistake been that day? She cannot recall. She, a thirteen-year-old bride, seemed unable to do anything right.

"What do you mean?"

Hawa huffs and points at the phone in Marjan's hand.

Fatigue has made Marjan sloppy. Her phone is close to dying, and she doesn't know when she will be able to charge it again.

"We're here, Hawa," she says as she hands the driver a few bills. "Come out on this side, away from the road."

Hawa slides out behind her mother, slings her bag over her shoulder, and looks up and down the block. She is curious about the cricket field, a spot of green in a neighborhood of mostly newer buildings. It is quiet here too. Cars roll past with their windows down, desperate for a breeze in the sweltering heat.

"Why don't you tell me anything?" Hawa asks. "You treat me like a baby but I'm not."

"I know you're not a baby," Marjan says. Hawa is not wrong. Her questions are not wrong. The timing is wrong.

"Hawa, janem, we need to find this place, and once we're off the streets and somewhere quiet we can talk. Understand? We've been moving all day and I know you're tired."

"I'm not tired," Hawa mutters, then goes silent. She is exhausted, of course. Her feet are hot in her sneakers, and though the heat might have stymied her appetite some, she needs more than an orange soda.

He is in Kabul.

Marjan knows this is true. She can feel Abdul Khaliq's proximity in her bones, a low thrumming. It's not his face that she remembers most. It's the weight of him, the feel of his beard, the viselike grip of his hand on her arm.

You're not a little girl anymore. You are a grown woman. You are a trained soldier from an elite platoon. He could not imagine the things you have done.

They walk a kilometer, circle the area, and search between buildings in case there is a hidden alley that leads to this hidden city.

"Where did Ingrid say it was?" Hawa asks, leaning against a young plane tree.

Marjan shakes her head. She called Ingrid earlier, but her call went to voicemail, so she sent a text asking Ingrid to call her back. Urgently. She takes out her phone to check again for messages.

"Oh, God. It's dead."

Hawa toe-kicks the ground twice. A commandeered government jeep rolls by, the stark black-and-white flag of the Taliban empire flapping in the wind. A Talib leans out the window, grinning at pedestrians as if he's a football fan whose team has just won the World Cup.

"Let's try once more in this direction," Marjan says, pointing north. There is more traffic on the road in this area, which is comforting but also disconcerting. Marjan finds herself searching faces, her gaze snagging on men of a familiar stature and build, on men who might be eyeing her. Abdul Khaliq could be anywhere in this city of millions, but the density and sprawl of Kabul bring her no comfort.

If he could be anywhere, he might be right behind her.

"Are you looking for me?" a man asks Marjan. He approached from the opposite direction on the sidewalk and must have noticed her wandering eye. He exhales a cloud of cigarette smoke into her face. Marjan pulls her headscarf across her nose and mouth and quickens her step, pulling Hawa along with her.

"Madar, look," Hawa says, pointing to a young boy carrying a blue plastic bag sagging with the weight of groceries. He wears a gray vest over his navy tunic and pantaloons. His sandals slap against the ground as he walks. Is he seven or eight years old?

When he disappears between two buildings, Marjan and Hawa follow. They leave the street and turn into the same unpaved alley, a path that has a slow, winding ascent. The boy has a head start. He is at least forty meters ahead of them and again goes out of view as the path makes a sharp turn behind a small brick building with a roof of corrugated tin.

"Let's see where this goes," Marjan says. She feels the pulsing trepidation she would feel on night missions, not knowing what or who she would encounter on the other side of a wall. They spot the boy again, a blue figure against a khaki landscape. He looks over his shoulder, sees them, and then continues on his way.

"Wherever we go, I will have to tell people why we are hiding. Hawa, I need you to go along with the story without questions. Understand?"

Hawa suppresses her rebel spirit and nods.

They are climbing now; the path widens. The apartment buildings are out of view. The contours of these clay homes are different. The contours of these lives are different. On the right, there is a solid wall over which float the sounds of everyday life—a spoon banging on the edge of an aluminum pot, the squeal of a mischievous child, the splash of water in a plastic jug. White pipes emerge from the earth serpentlike, make sharp turns, and breach the wall of a home. Other pipes are open to the air, mouths agape.

"Is this the place?" Hawa asks.

"I don't know," Marjan says. The climb steepens, reminds Marjan of the training treks she went on with her platoon. Mile after mile, with Soraya urging her to pick up her pace.

It's hard to keep up with you, Soraya. And somehow your lipstick isn't even smudged.

This brand makes everything else feel like cheap crayons. I told you to try it.

Lipstick doesn't look right on me. Makes me feel like I'm trying to be beautiful.

How dare you speak those words! Do you want Hawa to speak that way of herself? Whether you like it or not, whether you mean to or not, you are training her to be like you.

Marjan looks at Hawa, uncomplaining even as her breathing has grown heavier on the uphill. She has made a small soldier of her daughter now. A small, beautiful, unwitting soldier.

There's a blue metal railing on their left, the color of the chadaris that float through the markets and down the sidewalks. The rails insert into crumbling concrete. The boy glances once more over his shoulder before ducking under a torn white tarp tied to two rusted nails lodged into the brick of the walls on either side.

Marjan tries to look over the tarp, to see what might exist on the hill on the other side of this makeshift barrier.

"Are you sure?" Hawa asks her when Marjan lifts the corner of the tarp. Marjan nods at her daughter.

"Hello?" she calls out. They are nearly at the top of this hill. She looks through the hole and sees that the path and walls continue on the other side. The little boy is gone. Though the barrier is nothing more than a square of ragged plastic, Marjan knows even tarpaulin walls are put up for a reason. "Hello? Is there anyone here?"

She signals for Hawa to cross under the tarp with her.

They continue up the path. Twenty meters along the path, the wall gives way to a red door and a window obscured by a layer of dust. The door swings open slowly, and it feels like a warning. Marjan pulls Hawa behind her.

A woman, solid as a pillar, fills the frame. She examines the intruders with kohl-lined eyes, arms folded across her chest, and a black woolen scarf draped loosely over her head and shoulders.

"Are you in the habit of trespassing?" she asks. There's not a hint of emotion in her voice.

Marjan feels her face grow warm. She is embarrassed, both at her intrusion and by her desperation.

"Forgive me, I would not have sought this place out if I—if we—had somewhere else to go."

The woman tilts her head.

"Do you know where you are?" she asks.

Marjan nods. She waits, because deference is the only way with a stern matriarch, and she can already sense she is in the presence of one.

"Why have you come?"

Marjan lowers her gaze. She has rehearsed this story in her mind and hopes she gets it right.

"My daughter and I lived alone in Kabul. My husband was a soldier. He was killed serving in the army and now his family wants to claim us."

The woman is silent for a beat. Marjan thinks she sees her left eyelid twitch. Are they standing outside her home? She wishes she'd asked Ingrid for more details about this place.

"And why not let them take you in?"

Marjan meets the woman's gaze.

"It is not a kind home."

The woman nods. Marjan has spoken in the covert language of mothers.

"And your family?"

Marjan tells her that her parents are deceased and her relatives live in a distant province. She does not have the resources to travel that far, and they are too impoverished to help her.

"We are hoping to get on a flight to leave the country and only need a place to stay until we can get through the airport."

At the mention of a flight, the woman scoffs. From this hill, she has watched the planes traverse the sky, contrails cutting across the blue like cracks in glass. One day last week her son counted over forty flights. There were maybe ten yesterday.

"Your husband was a soldier. Why do you think you'll get on a plane?" The woman's eyes are narrowed now. Marjan would be more impressed with her interrogation skills if she weren't the subject of her questions.

"I don't know if I will. But we have to try."

The woman looks doubtful.

"And how did you hear about this place?"

"My neighbor, a foreigner. She worked on programs to help women and told me there might be a place for us here. She knew I was a widow. I know I am a stranger coming to you but I can promise, we won't be any trouble. We just need to be off the streets."

The woman lets out a long breath. She shakes her head. Marjan wonders if she's made a mistake, if she should have presented herself differently.

"Do you know how many women need a safe place to be? This city is full of them." She shifts her weight from one foot to the other.

"Please. For just one night or two. We don't have much but I will help with whatever you need. My daughter is bright and . . . and she can be helpful with other children."

The lavender sky has deepened. Being turned away would mean wandering Kabul at night and retreating to their marked apartment to await the return of the Talibs. If anything happens to Hawa, Marjan will not survive it.

"We cannot abide any trouble here. I won't hesitate to remove you," the woman warns Marjan, who nods in emphatic agreement. The woman casts her eyes behind her into her apartment, a subtle signal for Marjan and Hawa to follow her through the red doorframe. In the hollow of her home, surrounded by wide-eyed children, she stretches her arms out and smiles grimly at her unbidden guests.

"Welcome to the City of Widows," she says.

38

2014

Marjan's first call on the phone that Saboor left for her was not to Saboor. She had been desperate to call Hawa without Zargul breathing down her neck. She had called the day after each of her three visits to the orphanage to confirm that Hawa had not spiraled any further, that her waters had stilled, and that she was once again drawing pictures of sunny skies and oversize flowers.

Marjan dialed the orphanage's number. Her fingers were so shaky she had to delete what she'd entered and start over twice.

Atefa answered the phone. She recognized Marjan's voice immediately, as if she'd been expecting her call.

"She's doing well. Very strong results on her math exam yesterday. And the girls had a poetry class too. I'll have to find what she wrote. It was quite good."

"I'm glad to hear it," Marjan said.

"She's remarkable. I have worked with many girls of her age but never seen one so articulate and aware. She is a sponge in her classes as well. One of the teachers here has already promised that she'll stay on for another year so long as Hawa is in her classroom," she said, and laughed.

Tears sprang from Marjan's eyes. She was so resentful that Farrah and Wana took Hawa to an orphanage, but she is deeply grateful now that Hawa is in this gentle nest, that she has access to private school. This kind of life has been so far out of reach.

"Do you think . . . do you think I could speak with her?" Marjan asked.

"Speak with her? Oh, well, the girls are playing hide-and-seek outside right now and it might be challenging to find her. She's very good at the game," Atefa said, her laugh light.

"I don't want her to feel I've abandoned her completely."

"Yes, of course," Atefa said. "I understand that. But maybe we could give her a little more time before you reach out again. I could tell her you called. It's important for these girls to feel loved by their families while they're here, believe me. But I've learned over the years that for some girls, having contact with their families rocks them a bit too hard and it takes much effort for us to steady them again. Hawa-jan seems to be one of those girls."

"And what happened with those girls? Did they adjust?" Marjan asked. She didn't try to hide the desperation in her voice.

"They did. It takes time, and a regular schedule is helpful, like visits once a month. The girls respond to rhythm. We all do. The cycles of the moon. The patterns in a rug. The sun rising and setting. It lets us spend our energies on things other than anticipation."

When Marjan did not speak, Atefa went on.

"I can tell you are doing your best and you have raised a wonderful child under difficult circumstances. Be gentle on yourself. Every child, even under the best circumstances, has struggles on the way to growing up."

Marjan felt her lip quiver. She pulled her knees to her chest and nodded.

"Please . . . please tell her I called," she said.

"I most certainly will," Atefa promised.

Marjan hung up the phone, and a tight wail escaped her throat, the whistle of a pressure cooker. She stared at the walls, at the divots and chips that had become familiar to her. At the small fissures that threatened the integrity of the ceiling. At the place where a hole had been patched haphazardly, yellow strokes across pale green.

She missed her daughter. She woke nearly every night to the empty space beside her and felt freshly gutted. She had stopped crying, but the sadness lingered.

Marjan was glad for the small space and the seclusion. She needed to be alone with her thoughts. She was devastated mostly by the relief she felt. Atefa had given her permission to submit to the fatigue of being a mother. She was not wholly responsible for Hawa. She did not have to buy food for her or make sure she was warm enough or teach her to write a sentence or worry that she'd go deaf because Marjan couldn't afford the care she needed.

The thoughts in her head were too many and too loud and too insistent. Marjan needed to hear someone other than herself. She picked up the phone to call Soraya but couldn't recall her number. She reached into her bag for the small notebook she kept and flipped to the page where she'd had Soraya write it down. She was about to dial when the phone pinged.

It was a message from Saboor.

I was hoping you would have called by now. Maybe I'm not as patient as I made myself out to be.

The words were followed by a grinning yellow face.

Marjan closed her eyes. What did he want from her? He was a man, she reminded herself. It shouldn't be too hard to guess. She did not want to upset this man who had brought her a phone, this man who came to sit with her employer. She would be polite, she decided. Nothing more.

Thank you for the phone, she wrote. *I used it to call my daughter.*

Where is your daughter? How old is she?

Marjan answered. She explained that she was a widow, because she did not want him to think of her as a divorcée or worse. She started to type a farewell but a new message appeared. Her answers seemed to prompt more questions.

You must miss her terribly. I was away from my mother for a year when I was young. To this day, she says it was the most painful year of her life. I wish I understood then that my mother had no control over it. And it wasn't so bad being away.

This caught Marjan's attention.

Why were you away from your mother? Marjan asked.

Saboor explained that his father had been responsible for overseeing a construction project. He had to relocate for months to a city ten hours away by car. His mother had been unwell at the time, and his parents felt the change of scenery would benefit him. He was enrolled in a local private school, where he had excelled.

When I first saw you, I felt like you looked familiar. As if we'd met before, though I know we haven't. Maybe I recognized a feeling in you, the same my mother felt. If it helps any, your daughter will be fine. She knows you are nearby. And wealthy families spend so much to give their children these same opportunities.

Marjan reread his message. She did not reply.

If I've said something that upset you, I'm sorry.

She touched her face and wondered how to respond. She wanted to believe Saboor, wanted to trust his logic. She set the phone down, reminding herself that she was already walking a tightrope in the Rasuli home. She did not know this man. She could not know this man, and more important, he could not know her.

And yet somehow, he did.

Marjan, are you there?

What an unanswerable question.

39

AUGUST 24, 2021

Marjan is up at first light. She guesses she only slept twenty or thirty minutes at a time last night, waking up frequently to make sure Hawa was still between her and the wall and to watch the sleeping forms of her host and her children. Kobra has three girls and two boys. Her youngest is seven years old and her eldest, a boy, is fourteen. The arrangement is uncomfortable for Marjan, because she is acutely aware that she's placing Hawa in extremely close quarters with a teenage boy. He was very polite last night, offered them water without so much as a nod from Kobra, but a cup of water is not a reason to be less vigilant.

Kobra's home is a one-room structure. Facing the path where Kobra had stopped Marjan is one framed window. Long, thin mattresses placed against the walls leave very little bare floor to cover, so a small, heavily worn carpet in the middle of the room does the job. There are three throw pillows with satin covers in pastel green and embroidery that Marjan can tell even in the dim light are machine sewn. They clash with the burgundy covers of the mattresses but fit in with the haphazardness of the space. In the center of the room is an old metal stove with an exhaust pipe that drives straight up through the ceiling, directing smoke into the open air. Across from the door Marjan and Hawa had entered is a smaller back door that leads to the cooking area, a single gas burner and small fuel tank outside. A jug of cooking oil, a sack of rice, a bag of dry lentils, and two onions sit near the tank.

Marjan slips her dead phone out of her pocket and feels her anxiety soar. What if Jenna and the others have sent urgent instructions? And Soraya must be so worried, having not heard from them since they were outside the shelter. Then there's the chance she's received an update about Abdul Khaliq's whereabouts. Marjan sits up. There will be no more sleeping now. She moves across the room and out the door as quietly as she can, trying not to wake anyone.

Outside, she is greeted by a blushing sky, birdsong, and the faint rumble of cars. She fills her lungs with the air of this new day and looks around, wondering how she will charge her phone. When she had asked Kobra if there was anywhere she could charge her phone last night, Kobra had scoffed. The power in Kabul was unreliable. The power in the City of Widows was unlikely.

"Electricity is like romance. If you long for it, it will never come," Kobra says coyly. She has followed her guest outside, maybe more to keep an eye on her than to offer advice.

Marjan does not laugh.

"It's important I check my messages," she says.

Kobra brushes her hair out of her face, smooths it down with her henna-stained fingertips, the same color as the dress her youngest daughter wears. It hangs loose on her, a premature hand-me-down.

"Then swear you have no use for electricity," she replies. "And watch it surge through the wires."

She points to the corrugated roof of her home, and Marjan sees an orange extension cord running along the ground. It goes on past the tarp. "There. Sometimes the people at the base of the hill let us hook into their electricity, but I don't have to tell you not everywhere in Kabul gets the same power. They fix wires in some parts and leave others in the dark. The unjust economy of light. Anyway, we have a generator that we share here. It's a bit early to wake up the neighborhood, but this morning we should have enough fuel to run it and then you can charge your phone."

"Thank you," Marjan says, feeling relieved that there is a way to reconnect with Soraya and her American friends. "For everything, I mean.

You did not have to open your home to us. I know we are strangers to you. I'm very grateful."

Kobra nods in acknowledgment, then moves the conversation along. She's too practical for sentimentality and will not squander time in this way, with one woman humbling herself before another for doing the right thing.

"Let me show you the rest of our hill," Kobra says instead, and starts to walk up the narrowing path. "My home is the first. My mother—may her spirit be at peace—stacked the clay bricks herself so many years ago, when she first came here and started this community. I lived here as a child and then left when I married. But three years ago, my husband died of a heart attack and I decided to come back. This is where I feel most at home."

"I'm sorry you lost your husband. How many live here?" Marjan asks.

"I don't know. I'm not a bookkeeper or a landlord," Kobra replies, her tone implying that Marjan should ask better questions.

"Even the women who could afford the rent of a home in town cannot find a landlord willing to take a risk on a widow. They think a woman without a husband has only one way to support her family," she says, then sighs heavily. Marjan thinks of the many names she and Soraya have been called on the bus. She thinks of how many landlords turned her down before she was able to secure the apartment they've left behind.

They climb a set of steep steps. On her right, the wall appears as if it might crumble any moment now. They have reached a cluster of homes, a dozen small structures built of clay bricks on either side of the path. Most have a window similar to the one on the front side of Kobra's home. Some have actual doors with wooden frames. Others have tarps bearing the logo of a United Nations aid organization covering the doorways. They are well constructed, if not professionally built. The bricks are uniform and lined up evenly, sealed between the window frames and walls. The path between the homes is strewn with signs of life—a small soccer ball, a doll missing a leg, dirty jugs for carrying water, and small piles of shoes just outside the doors of the homes. A splintering wooden table sits in the center, a gas tank tucked underneath it. In the corner is a rusted steel drum set out to collect rainwater.

From inside one of the homes, Marjan hears the cry of an infant. It quickly melts from a wail to a whimper, maybe comforted by a breast.

"Did the government commission these homes?" Marjan asks.

Kobra frowns. "Did your colleague not tell you the history of this place?"

Marjan notes Kobra's ability to pick up on holes in her story. She'll have to be very careful. Hawa will need to be reminded as well.

"I worked more on other programs with their NGO, so I heard very little about this place. Only that no men live here," Marjan explains.

"Yes, and the fact that there are no men here makes it very undesirable to some and perfect for others," Kobra adds. "Like you and your daughter. Let me tell you about this place, then. All stories start with a mother. This story starts twenty years ago with my mother, Bibikoh. The women who followed her here gave her that name: Mother of the Mountain."

Bibikoh left behind five children when she passed. Kobra's siblings are scattered across Kabul, Pakistan, and Iran, chasing work and possibilities.

"My father was a good man but had a poor constitution. He died of a lung infection, leaving my mother with all of us to raise alone. And she would have done that, but the family wanted to marry her to my father's brother. You know how these things go. She was an unusual woman, especially for her time, so she decided she would leave instead and make her own way. She was the most skilled seamstress and that was how she kept us fed, but rent was steep everywhere. She talked to a couple of other widows in town—how many are there in Afghanistan? More than two million, I think. Anyway, this land was cheap at the time, when Kabul hadn't yet spilled over into these areas. They came here together because they were safer as a collective."

More widows followed, with sad stories and sad children in tow. Kobra's mother watched their numbers grow and decided shelter alone wasn't going to help them survive. She began teaching the illiterate women how to read. A few times a week, she would bang a spoon on the backside of a pot and summon the women who wanted to learn from her how to sew. Sometimes an organization would come along and deliver bags of food to keep the women and children fed, especially through the brutal Kabul winters.

"But the police were not happy with their presence. Or maybe they just saw another opportunity. We would hike up our pant legs to our knees, tie a cloth around our heads, and get to work gathering mud, shaping it into clay bricks to bake in the sun. We would build, layering rows of bricks to construct the walls of our homes. The police would wait until the walls were about shoulder high and then they would come and tear them down. We would hide from them, and once they left, we would get back to work rebuilding. They destroyed the house my mother built eight times before my mother finally found a way to get rid of them."

"How did she do that?" Marjan asks.

"How do you make anyone in Kabul do anything? Money, money, money."

How sad, Marjan thinks, that in addition to food, clothing, rent, medicine, and charity, people must include bribes in their household budgets.

"The women built all these homes," Marjan marvels out loud.

"You sound surprised," Kobra observes. Her shoulders pull back by degrees, and her head cocks to the side again as she assumes the same guarded posture she had when she first met Marjan last night.

"You think we would not be capable? Because we are women?"

Marjan shakes her head.

"Sorry, that wasn't what I meant," she says but that's not entirely true. She is ashamed to admit she sometimes harbors the same biases she despises.

Kobra is appeased.

"This place is called Zanabad, city of women. But we've had maybe five hundred widows call this place home," she says. "So we've become the City of Widows. With a safe place to stay, the women could spend their energies on finding whatever income they could—doing the washing or cooking for other homes or sewing clothing or linens. It is hard to make ends meet and many have no choice but to send their children to beg in the markets. Some of the women slip on a burqa and take up begging as well."

Marjan wonders if she has walked past any of these women. Kabul tolerates them, these figures hidden under the drape of a blue burqa. Sometimes they are shooed from busy corners by people who would rather not be reminded that mothers and babies are starving in such close proximity to their lives.

A door opens and a small boy, the one Hawa noticed yesterday, peeks out into the clearing.

"Salaam!" he announces when he sees Kobra. He eyes Marjan suspiciously, keeping half his body hidden behind the door.

"Wa'alaikum, bacha-jan," Kobra replies. "You're up early. For prayers, I'm sure. Go on inside and get to it, then."

He smiles bashfully but does not retreat.

"Who are they, Khala?" he asks Kobra, cutting his eyes only briefly at Marjan.

"A mother and daughter. That's all you need to know."

"Will they live here?"

Kobra raises her brows.

"Do I look like a fortune teller? Now hush before you wake the baby. And go outside to find your friends. We will all get to know each other better later."

The little boy obeys, and Marjan sees Kobra for what she is, a unadorned matriarch who doesn't need to be stationed at the top of the hill to mark her status, someone who knows that a home of her own is a woman's palace.

40

2014

Soraya, unsurprisingly, hadn't picked up the phone when Marjan called. One could never know who might be on the other end of an unknown number. Marjan sent a text message to let Soraya know it was her calling, and her phone rang within seconds.

"You have a phone!" Soraya cried. "Where did you buy it? I hope you didn't pay too much. I've been asking around for a place that won't rip you off."

"I didn't purchase it. It was given to me," Marjan admitted. She needed to tell Soraya about this peculiar situation.

"What does he look like?" Soraya asked.

"What does he look like? He looks like . . . like a man," Marjan said, flustered.

"Marjan, come on. It's a rainy day and I have cramps. I insist you do better than that."

"I don't know. He's maybe in his early thirties. Brown hair and light brown eyes. He's well-dressed and very polite."

"I could get a better description from a blind person. Do his teeth show when he smiles? Is his voice deep? Did he say anything flirty?"

He had a dimple, Marjan recalled. He was witty, and his eyes weren't just brown. They had flecks of honey in them that shone when he smiled. He'd tilted his head just a bit when she'd been speaking with him, as if readjusting himself to her frequency, and she realized no man had ever done that before.

And as for flirty talk, Marjan wasn't sure. He hadn't said anything lewd or suggestive. Saboor was not like that. He was mellow and kind.

"I don't think it's anything. He probably just took pity on me. A sad-looking housemaid with a daughter she can't take care of."

"First of all, he didn't know that when he first spoke with you. And now that he knows, has he stopped talking to you? Did he come back to reclaim the phone?"

"No." Marjan sighed. They had exchanged dozens of messages late into the night. He was the youngest of five, the only one of his siblings who was unmarried. He had a niece and a nephew the same age as Hawa. He asked thoughtful questions about her, as if he had real interest. Had it been hard raising Hawa alone? Did Hawa like the children's show with the puppets? How did she get along with the other children at the school?

Marjan noticed also the questions he did not ask. He didn't ask about Hawa's father or his family. He did not ask her why she didn't have ties to her own family. These were the first questions people usually asked, the ones they blurted out without thinking.

"He sounds like an educated fella. What did he study in college?" Soraya wanted to know.

"His family wanted him to become an engineer. They have three in the family already. He decided to study literature. He writes short stories and poems."

"A poet! Oh, Marjan. This is so utterly, perfectly romantic . . . but only if you tell me he has a real job during the day."

Marjan laughed. "He's the manager of the Yellow Tulip restaurant," she explained, and told Soraya about Agha Rasuli wanting to recruit him for his Dubai hotel.

"That place where dinner costs a month's salary? No wonder he's well-dressed. Oh, this is exciting, Marjan. More exciting than anything in my world. It's been one week since I've started working in this tech company, and I am losing my mind with boredom. If I never have to write up another invoice in my life, I'll die a happy woman."

"It's got to be better than being a housemaid to two people obsessed with their status. Leeda is the sweetest little lamb, but if it weren't for her . . ."

"You deserve better. The both of us should have jobs that are exciting and meaningful. I'd like to be a movie star. Or Minister of the Interior. Or a pilot."

"You're such a dreamer," Marjan said, but she liked that Soraya dreamed. She wished she could; surely she hadn't escaped Abdul Khaliq just to spend her life scrubbing the grease off people's dishes. She knew she was capable of so much more, if she just had a chance.

"If you don't have a head full of dreams, you'll leave too much room for nightmares," Soraya insisted. "Now, what's going to happen next with your poet?"

In the days that followed, Marjan and Saboor exchanged messages more often. His first text came before she was even awake, wishing her a good morning. One night, around nine o'clock at night, he made a request.

Can I call you? he'd asked.

In the quiet dark, Marjan considered how to reply.

Can I really tell you not to call your own phone?

The moment I left the phone at your door, it was no longer mine. You have no obligation to reply to any of my messages.

Marjan tried not to react too quickly. Was he saying what she wanted to hear or was he that thoughtful? She did not know but wanted to find out. They spoke for nearly an hour that night. He told her about a group of businessmen who had come into the restaurant for the first time and hadn't known what to order. Saboor asked permission to order on their behalf, promising that they'd be satisfied. They agreed, and he had the waiter bring out an array of mouthwatering, perfectly seasoned chicken and lamb kebabs served on a ship made of bamboo. The men had never seen food served on a boat before, one that took up half the table with its tall masts, a flag at the bow, and two bowls of dip at the stern.

"A boat? The restaurant I worked at had nothing of the sort."

He told her about the three levels, the chandeliers as wide as his arm span, the lattice panels, the ornate arches, the gilded frames.

"It sounds like a palace," she said. She liked the way he described things, the way he drew out words to convey stature, and that he sounded awed by the architecture, not arrogant about it.

"Maybe one day you can be my guest there," he said. "I know the best tables."

He did not linger on this comment. She pretended he had not sent her head spinning, imagining sitting across from him at a table, carnations between them. Choosing conversation over food.

"I want to tell you something else," he said. "I was married once. Very briefly."

Marjan braced herself.

"What happened?" she asked.

"We were very different people. She was far more devout than I am. She didn't like that I don't pray five times a day, and she really didn't like that she couldn't change that about me."

"My aunt always said judgment was for God alone," Marjan said, and Saboor agreed. He loved the devotion of the Sufis anyway, a transcendent connection to Allah.

The next day, she woke to a short poem.

I do not know the place I spent last night
Ecstatic dance all around me, the place I spent last night
There was a beauty, fairy-faced and cypress-statured and tulip-cheeked,
A ravisher of hearts, in the place I spent last night.

She smiled to herself.

Did you write this? she asked.

You flatter me. It's Khusrau. I'm not brave enough to show you my poems yet.

He became a buoy for her spirits. Three weeks later, Marjan could not imagine going a full day without speaking to Saboor. She told him about playful moments with Leeda, and he told her about lavish wedding events hosted on the top floor of the restaurant. Their worlds expanded; they were bearing witness to each other's days. It was only natural that they meet in person.

Would you join me for a walk in the park? The weather is beautiful, he texted.

Marjan held the phone at arm's length, certain he could hear her heart pounding.

I don't think that's a good idea, she wrote back.

Why not?

She was silent. She took a moment to gather her courage.

I need to ask you something, she wrote.

Please do.

What is this? These conversations we're having. I'm not sure what to think about it. I am not the type to . . . I mean, I hope you don't have the wrong idea.

It was his turn to gather his thoughts.

I assure you, I have great respect for you. I hope I've not said anything to make you think otherwise. When we spoke that first day, I didn't want you to stop talking. I felt like I had just started reading a most intriguing story and I want to hear more.

She agreed to meet him at seven o'clock, at the southern entrance to the park. She didn't have much to choose from but still fussed over what to wear, settling for black slacks and a mauve tunic over her slim figure. She pinched her cheeks to add color. Her dark hair reached the middle of her back, mostly because she hadn't bothered to trim it. Had she inherited these waves from her mother? She couldn't know. Her mother had always tied her hair up, she thought. Her memories grew fuzzier by the day.

She looked more like a woman than a child these days, an oval face with a prim chin. There were flecks of green in her brown eyes. Her brows were full and delicately arched, without much shaping on her part. She tried on a smile, batted her eyelashes. Tempted, she swiped lip gloss across her lips, looked in her mirror, and then wiped it off with the back of her hand.

Soraya invited her for an evening meetup as well, and Marjan turned her down with an explanation. Soraya cooed and celebrated as if Marjan had just announced she and Saboor were engaged. Marjan promised to call her when she returned to her room.

They met at the southeast corner of the park. Saboor's expression brightened at the sight of her.

"You came," he said.

"Was I not supposed to?" Marjan asked. She'd not meant to sound as coy as she did.

He laughed. "When I was a child, every time I made a wish on a fallen eyelash, my wish would come true. I confess, I thought about pulling out an eyelash for this occasion."

"Oh no! I don't think it works if you pull out the eyelash," Marjan replied, embarrassed.

"I think you're right. Some things we have to leave to naseeb," he said, then extended his arm in the direction of the concrete path as an invitation. Marjan followed him, trying not to feel too enchanted by his reference to destiny. Her aunt had taught her that only her will and deeds would shape her fate, and she'd always believed this to be true. But today, the allure of naseeb threatened her balance. She felt it in her stomach, like she was standing on a high cliff with her toes over the edge.

They followed the tree-lined walkway as it cut through grassy fields and saw small groups of men and women sitting on blankets spread on the ground, their glossy thermoses visible from a distance. Two boys carrying wooden trays of dried fruits offered them packets of almonds and raisins. Saboor asked how much as he reached for his wallet. Marjan looked away while he paid them. Though they were young and had no idea that Saboor and Marjan were unmarried, she worried what they might think of her.

But the boys ran off in search of more customers. Saboor and Marjan continued walking. Their conversation meandered just as they did. Saboor asked if she followed politics. Marjan shook her head. Thinking of the twisted voting she had witnessed in Parliament, she made a vague comment about the widespread corruption.

"I totally agree. So much that I am convinced a corruption of the soul is a prerequisite for anyone in public office," he said. "And I'm not surprised you can't stomach it. You seem to me a most honest spirit despite this . . . this . . . this world we've been born into. It takes real strength to maintain one's character."

"Are you corruptible?" Marjan asked.

"I'm here, aren't I?" he teased, then grew serious. "Sometimes I think that I'd be a better writer if I hadn't taken this job in the restaurant. An artist shouldn't be chasing paychecks, don't you think? I'm a romantic, but I'm also quite fond of a comfortable life."

"It's impractical not to think about a salary," she said. "I think we have to be practical always, even when we're dreaming."

Saboor stopped in his tracks. Marjan took two steps before realizing he was no longer beside her.

"What do you dream of? I mean, what kind of life do you imagine?" he asked.

Marjan finds it hard to believe she is speaking with a man who would ask her these kinds of questions.

"I want my daughter to have all she needs. I want her to wake up and know her mother loves her more than anything. I want to have her by my side and I want her to know a peaceful life," she said, picturing Hawa's face the last time she'd walked away from her at the orphanage.

"Hawa is fortunate to have a mother who's willing to sacrifice so much for her. But what about for you?"

"What do you mean?" Marjan asked.

"You are a mother, certainly," Saboor said. "But who were you before you became a mother? Who will you be even as your child, this precious arrow shot from your bow, soars across the sky? You are still someone, Marjan. What do you want for your life?"

Leaves rustled overhead, and two birds flitted from the outstretched branch of a nearby tree. She was not yet able to articulate what she wanted from this life, but she hoped Saboor would keep asking.

41

AUGUST 24, 2021

Dawn's aura has bloomed into daylight, and the hill is a flurry of activity and speculation. On top of their routines—feeding children and deciding which chores take priority—the women are buzzing with questions and assumptions and descriptions of the new arrivals.

She's very skinny. Her chin is pointy and her eyes have a little green in them, like polished jade.

Polished jade. When did you start talking so fancy?

How long ago did her husband die?

Her daughter is fourteen years old.

No, she's about my height. She must be six or seven.

Is she a troublemaker? The mother, I mean.

They have three suitcases with them. Her clothes look expensive.

Hmph. Maybe her eyes really are made of polished jade, then.

She told Kobra she wants to make a home here.

Where are her other children?

Maybe she had to leave some behind. She was crying to Khanum Kobra last night and that's why she let her stay.

Marjan is not excited to meet the other women. The fewer people she meets at this time, the better. The only reason she steps outside is to charge her phone. They were going to get the generator going this morning, but since the Taliban had stormed into town, the residents of this hill had chosen not to venture past the tarp that divided them from the rest of Kabul. Like everyone else, they kept their children at home instead of sending them to school. A year ago, a plague had crept through town, making people cough and gasp for air, turning bodies hot then cold. Isolation spared the women on the hill then, and they hoped their isolation would spare them now.

The women of this aloof city had made a painful but necessary choice. They claimed for themselves this island, this high sanctuary, in hopes that no one would go to the trouble of coming after them. They needed to know more about Marjan and Hawa before they decided if they could let down their guard. So when Kobra brings Marjan back to the generator, which sits where the path becomes a cul-de-sac, the women stand in their doorways or step into the clearing to get a closer look.

Kobra stands in the center and addresses the gathered women in a commanding voice.

"Ladies, this is Marjan. She is a widow like us. Her daughter's name is Hawa. They are not here to stay but are in need of shelter for a time. We can all understand that," she says. "We do not have an empty home right now, so she will stay with me and my children. Carry on as usual."

"Where did you live before?" one woman asks. She stands to Marjan's right, close enough that she can see that the rumor about her eyes being the color of jade was foolery.

"Not too far from here. In the apartment complex east of the German high school," she replies.

"In the apartments?" someone exclaims, as if Marjan has just announced that she had a private servant and driver. "And you have no other family to take you in?"

Marjan shakes her head. The less she speaks, the better.

A young boy pulls the string on the generator, and the machine sputters and coughs. He widens his stance and prepares to pull again, harder this time. The machine makes a weak gurgling sound. A little girl calls out that he should check the fuel, so he undoes the cap and gives the machine a light jostle. He confirms the tank is empty.

Kobra summons her son and another boy his age. Their new arrival will have to practice some patience while the boys fetch a couple of liters of fuel for the generator. Being matriarch of the hill was not Kobra's only job. Until nine days ago, Kobra also worked in the kitchen of the presidential palace. She chopped vegetables, washed pots, trimmed meat, and sometimes even served during meals. Her job vanished on August 15. Now that she's heard the president has fled the country with trunks of cash, she does not expect that she'll ever see any of the pay that was due to her.

Hawa stands at the periphery, almost out of view. She is nervous that she will say the wrong thing. Away from home, away from Ingrid and Khala Soraya, away from her school—it feels like their situation could not get any worse, and yet she knows that it can if she misspeaks. She chooses to stay tight-lipped.

"Do you want some?"

Hawa looks to her left. A little girl of perhaps four or five years holds out a square of bread. Her tawny complexion and the dirt under her fingernails tell Hawa she spends much of her time outside. She wears a loose-fitting green dress with yellow flowers. The collar is frayed, the cuffs darkened.

Hawa accepts the bread and thanks the little girl. She shifts her weight, holds the bread awkwardly for a beat but then realizes how hungry she has become and takes a bite. It softens in her mouth and tastes better than any bread she's ever had.

"My brother bought it. He's the one with the green shirt over there. And the one next to him is my mother," the little girl says, pointing to a woman sitting on a plastic chair. She has an elbow on one of the armrests and her chin in her cupped hand.

"Oh," says Hawa. "You and your brother live here?"

"Yes. And my two sisters. Well, one sister left for a month but now she's here again," she explains, her volume dropping on the last sentence. "My mother agreed to give her in marriage but then her husband brought her back. I think he changed his mind about her."

Marriage is more of a concept, an abstraction to Hawa, since she has never seen one up close. Her mother doesn't speak about her own marriage. Her music instructors are all married, but they did not bring their wives or husbands to school. Hawa once asked Ingrid if she was married. Ingrid had laughed and replied that she was married to her job, just like Hawa's mother. Hawa didn't quite understand what that meant, but Ingrid sometimes said things she didn't understand.

"How old is your sister?" Hawa asks.

"Fourteen, much older than me," she replies, and sees Hawa's eyes grow wide. The girl feels vindicated by her reaction. She's known all along her sister's marriage didn't seem right, but every time she brings it up, her mother tells her it's none of her concern. "And the groom is forty-two years old. Or so they say. His beard has bits of gray in it and his belly is this big."

She arches her back and rubs her hands over an imaginary stomach.

Hawa's gaze moves back to the mother sitting in the plastic chair. She studies her face, tries to understand why this woman would give her daughter to a man nearly three times her age.

"My sister stays inside most of the time. She doesn't talk or eat much. My mother says it's best if we just leave her alone for now."

Hawa thinks of the square of bread this little girl just gave her and the lingering taste of sesame seeds in her mouth. She realizes how this bite of food came to her. Was this the way the world worked? Did one girl have to go hungry so another could eat?

She wishes she had something to share too, then remembers what she has stuffed into her bag.

"Do you like music?" she asks the little girl.

Kobra squints against the sun. There is a light breeze coming from the west today, a change in direction. Kabul is changing direction too. All the ambition that had flooded Kabul is gone, replaced by a different zeal. This is why Kobra never trusted any of the foreign organizations. They came to this hill and saw the needs, then flipped through papers and left. Something about criteria. She looks at Marjan, petite and rather quiet. Still, something simmers behind those eyes; Kobra can sense it. Maybe this woman's colleagues can work some magic and get her out of here. If

Kobra had a connection like that, if she had a chance to take her children out of this country, would she try to?

She probably would.

She enlists Marjan's help lugging jugs of water up the hill. She expected Marjan to struggle with the weight of the jugs more but is pleasantly surprised to see she is barely slowed by the load. She is not wheezing or taking frequent breaks the way Zakia did her first week here. This is good. Because though Marjan promised they would not stay long, and though Kobra told her they had no more room for anyone on the hill, she also knows she would not throw this mother and daughter back into the wild, and certainly not while the wolves are roaming.

It is noon by the time they have the generator up and running again. Marjan is allowed to charge her phone to thirty-five percent before someone complains. Fuel is a precious resource.

Marjan powers the phone on, her foot tapping impatiently as she waits for the apps to load. Her messaging icon shows new notifications. She clicks and sees Jenna has posted several messages, some to the group and some to her privately.

Marjan, please reply. We're worried about you.

Marjan reads quickly, but then has to go back and read again, because in her eagerness to know what she's missed, she's skipping lines of text.

Yesterday, two FTPs made it through the gates. They managed to get their names on a manifest and will be boarding a plane this afternoon. The news gives Marjan a surge of hope. She tries not to envy them. They must have endured much shoving, pushing, and climbing to make it through.

The marine we've been in touch with says to wear something green. It's hard for them to hear anything at the gate but if you wave and point to your clothing, it will help them spot you in the crowd.

Please confirm if you understand.

Three FTPs reply that they understand. Marjan does as well, though she doesn't have a single green article of clothing in her small bag. She'll have to figure this out too.

We're each pushing the issue up the chain with our members of Congress too. We're not getting any direct instruction back from them and I'm not going to hold my breath. I think our best chance is to rely on the marines on the ground there.

Working with Jenna and the others, Marjan has learned that Americans don't have faith in politicians either.

Soraya has also sent multiple messages—one to the group and one privately to Marjan.

Please let me know where you are. My mother's blood pressure is high. She says she's fine but I want to be sure she's okay but then I'll go to the airport. I cannot stay here any longer and I'm scared we're running out of time. You're not responding to any messages. Are you okay?

Marjan hurries to reply, feeling terribly that Jenna and Soraya have been left to wonder about her and Hawa.

She calls Soraya's number, waits for her friend's full-volume chastising for zipping around town with a half-dead phone, but Soraya does not answer. She hangs up and tries once more but still no luck. She will have to settle for a text and decides to message both Soraya and Jenna together.

We are in Zanabad, she types. *A place where widows live on a hill. It seems safe. They gave us a place to stay last night. I will meet you tomorrow at the airport. Maybe tomorrow will be our day.*

Jenna replies almost immediately, relieved and encouraging. Marjan checks for a reply from Soraya so many times that she nearly drains her battery back to zero. She will offer Kobra some money in exchange for help using the generator once more. She tries calling again but still Soraya doesn't answer.

Marjan is desperate to know where Abdul Khaliq is, what he's up to. It feels like he's just over her shoulder. Hands trembling, she texts the number she has memorized, the contact that is still nameless in her phone.

Can you talk?

Dots appear on the screen, an incoming message.

You should not be speaking with my mother.

Marjan nearly drops the phone. She's been exposed, a lifeline taken from her. How much has been revealed to Abdul Khaliq? Everything, she has to assume. He will come for their daughter, if only to punish her.

That night, Hawa wakes often, stirred by her mother's movements and the blue-white glow of the phone on her restless face. How has the phone's battery persisted this long? She rolls over, faces the wall, and wishes away this false moon.

42

2014

Marjan thought every day about ending her conversations with Saboor, not because of anything he'd said or done, but because in her lucid moments she knew nothing could come of this relationship. How could a perfectly reasonable man like him be even remotely interested in a woman with a child and a troubled past? None of it made sense.

But Marjan, in her practicality, also needed a good reason to put a stop to this relationship. She found none. In fact, she found herself drawn to another hard truth. It was incredibly difficult to be an unattached woman in this world that required women to be claimed by a father, a husband, a son.

Life would be so much easier with a man.

She wanted to be a strong woman, like her beloved aunt and Samia from the shelter and her ancestor and the women she saw crisscrossing Kabul's streets with round sunglasses shielding them from the sun and shoulders back as if marching into a great battle. And like Elizabeth from *Pride and Prejudice*, self-confident and independent. How did they do it?

Marjan was often exhausted not by the work her body endured but by the load her mind carried—the strategizing and planning and counting and justifying and debating. She fell into sleep feeling like she'd spent all day dragging the sun across the sky, knowing tomorrow she'd have to do it all again.

So she found herself slipping further into a surprisingly comfortable place with Saboor and wondered if maybe some women could be strong because they didn't have to worry about everything alone. Knowing the night would end with a long, thoughtful phone call made the day's work tolerable. Saboor wanted to share things with her. He was interested in her opinions. During their walks through the city, he reassured her that she was not doing irreparable harm to her daughter, that Hawa was fortunate to be in a place where her intellect could be stimulated and she had other girls to play with.

"I did something today," Saboor told her on the phone one night. In the dark, it almost felt like he was curled up beside her, speaking into her ear. "I bought a bunch of children's books from the shop today and dropped them off at the orphanage. They won't allow a perfect stranger to enter, of course, but a very kind teacher took them from me at the gate. You told me the other day that she's read through all their books and I thought maybe she could use some more stories."

"You went all the way out there?" Marjan pictured Hawa holding a new book, reading a story she'd been gifted by a man who knew her only through Marjan's stories.

"I did. Ramadan is around the corner. It doesn't hurt to have a few good deeds to my name."

"I don't know what to say. That was very kind of you," Marjan said.

"Meh. Don't flatter me too much. On Friday, my sister asked me if I could tell she'd lost weight and God help me I lied to save my life. Pray for my soul, Marjan."

"You did the right thing. God is always merciful, but women are not," Marjan replied with a laugh.

"Ameen! Oh, Marjan," Saboor said, and Marjan felt her spine tingle to hear him speak her name this way, a quiet act of intimacy. "Marjan, I have to confess something to you."

"Another sin? You've been busy," she said, trying to hide her nerves.

"No, nothing like that. It's just that . . . I realized I can't imagine going through the day without speaking to you. I was thinking to myself, what does that mean? What is a man to do with this feeling? It's insanely simple, of course. But it occurred to me that I should ask you what you feel."

Marjan brushed her hair away from her face. What was he saying? She tried to focus, to capture every word.

"Marjan, when I speak to you after a long day, it feels like I'm breaking a fast. I've never felt this way before. I want more than this. I want more with you."

"Saboor, I . . . I . . ." Marjan stammered. She genuinely didn't know what to say. She was unprepared for anything like this. "I'm a complicated person. You know that."

"I know that. But what you have endured, your husband's death and escaping a family that would have transferred you to his brother as if you were chattel, that tells me how strong you are. To want to raise your daughter on your own terms, that's true courage."

Marjan found it hard to breathe past the lump in her throat. It felt unreal to hear these words from a man, from Saboor. She wished she could share more of her story with him but was nervous she would scare him away.

"Let's meet tomorrow night," he said. "Tell me you'll meet me."

There was that tingle again. She promised, then barely managed to get any sleep that night. They met at the park again. Marjan stuffed her hands in her pockets to keep from wringing them. They walked together, their shoulders occasionally touching and setting off sparks in Marjan's belly.

"Look at that," Saboor said, pointing to three boys playing soccer. "Imagine me at this age, still tempted to join them."

"Why don't you?" Marjan asked.

"Because they would run circles around me and I prefer not to embarrass myself in front of you," he said.

Marjan watched the boys, felt transported to that time in her life when she kicked a soccer ball in the dusty alleys of her neighborhood dressed as a boy. Saboor had been so open with her, telling her about the way his uncle had cheated his father in a business deal and his self-doubt as he struggled with poetry. What if she shared this small truth with Saboor as a test?

"I used to love playing soccer when I was a child," she said.

"Really? I wouldn't have guessed." He laughed. "Did your sisters also play?"

"Not exactly," she replied slowly. "I was very young and played with the boys in the neighborhood."

Saboor raised a brow. "That must have been quite a sight. A little girl playing with boys!"

"It wasn't much of a sight, actually. I was a bacha posh when I was a child."

This stopped Saboor in his tracks.

"Were you? Until what age?" he asked, and Marjan wondered what it meant that they'd stopped walking.

"Until I was thirteen," she said, watching his face. He seemed amused.

"Were you good?"

"As a bacha posh?"

"As a soccer player."

Marjan nodded.

"I was pretty good."

"I bet you were hard to catch. I would have tried, though."

Marjan looked at the ground to hide the flush creeping up her neck.

"Hey," Saboor said. He looked around. There was no one nearby in the park, a rare moment of solitude under the tall pines. He looked at her for a long moment and then smiled slyly before kissing her. His lips only grazed hers, which made the contact between them all the more electrifying. It was gentle and shocking. Tender and illicit. Marjan felt her body submit to his touch, she felt her own complicity in this rebellious act. He pulled away, righted himself, and covered his face with a hand. "Forgive me. I could not resist."

"Saboor, I . . ." Marjan faltered. What had she allowed? What had she invited? Marjan had never desired a man's touch before, but Saboor was unlike any man she'd ever met. She recognized a new kind of danger. She could not go on in this way, this impossible romance. "I . . . This isn't proper. I'm terrified Agha Rasuli will find out. Or someone will talk . . ."

"I'm sorry, my sweet. I didn't mean to make you feel you're doing something wrong. And I agree with you. We cannot go on this way," he said. He took a deep breath and held her hands in his. "You and I are adults and we can discuss this maturely. I would like for us to be married. I don't want to have to steal you away for a few moments here and there."

Marjan's hands would have flown to her face if he weren't gripping them so tightly. She looked away to hide her smile, this fizzy feeling inside. She feared her elation would attract God's attention.

"Be serious, Saboor."

"I could not be more serious, my love," he insisted. "Do you not enjoy my company?"

"You know I do," she said. She wanted more than his company. She wanted to touch his face with her hands, to lean her head on his shoulder. She thought of the way Zargul greeted her husband, the way she threw her arms around her husband's neck and pressed her body against his. Marjan felt that same impulse now. "But I was married before. I have a daughter. What will your family say?"

"Remember, I was married before as well." But they both knew it was not the same.

She turned away from him, looked at the small family walking toward them, two small children running ahead of a woman talking to her husband as she pushed a stroller. It felt like a rendering of something she never could have imagined.

Saboor touched her cheek. She turned ever so slightly to let her face fall into his hand, to let her body crave even more. To let dreams drive away nightmares.

"What do you say, Marjan?" he asked.

43

AUGUST 26, 2021

"The sun will be merciless today," Kobra says as Marjan zips her bag and checks her phone once more. "I've asked the boys to fill water bottles for you."

"You've been so kind," Marjan says. She has thanked Kobra often. She cannot thank Kobra enough.

Kobra shakes her head. She is uncomfortable with Marjan's gratitude, maybe more uncomfortable than Marjan herself. Samira, who has lived on this hill longer than Kobra, pulled her aside last night to express her concern.

She won't be the only one to come up here. We always try to make room, but what if she tells others and then two more women come? And then another ten? Before you know it, half of Kabul will be climbing this hill. What will we do then?

Kobra had learned so much from her mother, including a foolproof way to end any debate.

God is merciful, she said, and watched Samira sigh, because this was not a statement she dared refute, even if it felt a bit evasive.

"And you, Hawa-jan," Kobra says. "You do know how to win over an audience."

Hawa looks at her feet, hiding a coy smile. She loved the way the younger children had clamored over one another to get closer to her, to watch her blow a few clumsy notes out of the recorder. For some, it might have been their first time seeing someone play an instrument. She remembers gawking at the rubabs, the sitars, the tablas, and the harmoniums at the music school during her first week there, how excited she had felt to pluck a string, to press her lips around a reed, to tap her finger against a skin pulled taut. Those early notes were the beginnings of a conversation.

To Marjan's surprise, Hawa picks up the recorder from the corner of the room and places it into the hands of Kobra's daughter. The little girl's eyes flit from the instrument to Hawa's face.

"I can't play like you," she says.

"It takes a bit of practice," Hawa says. "But start with something simple."

"Like what?" the little girl asks.

"Like . . . like birdsong," Hawa offers, recalling one of the early classroom musings of her teacher. "Try to copy their melodies. They're short and simple and a good place to start."

Ustad Rafiqi had told them that humans found sitting in nature relaxing because birds only sang when they detected no danger around them.

Hear a bird sing and then you'll know you can rest your head in the grass. Close your eyes and let the sun put you to sleep for a stitch of time, he had wistfully explained.

"If you're going to copy birdsong, mimic the doves and not the roosters," Kobra warns. Her daughter buries her face into her mother's shoulder to hide her smile.

Marjan and Hawa say a few more farewells before heading down the hill. They do not know the women well and still they can sense they're being sent off lovingly, with whispered prayers carried on the breeze. They are not alone as Marjan lifts the tarp, as she and Hawa leave Zanabad.

We're on our way to the airport, Marjan types to the group.

Good. Keep us posted as you get closer. Jenna will share more instructions once we hear from our guy, Krista responds.

Marjan sends a separate message to Soraya.

Please come today. You are right. We are running out of time.

She waits for a reply, but nothing comes. She doesn't blame Soraya for wanting one more day with her mother. She might do the same were her mother still alive, but this is not the day to think about the family she has lost. She must quiet those thoughts.

"Do you think you would have learned to play without lessons?" Marjan asks her daughter. "If you had just a flute and a . . . a canary?"

Hawa bites her lip.

"I don't think so. But I didn't want her to feel discouraged."

"You would be a good music teacher, just like your ustads. Wasn't one of them a shepherd?"

Hawa nods. Ustad Rafiqi had many lives before music drew him in. He learned by walking through tall grasses, pressing his lips to the hollowed wood and testing out one note, then another. Even in the absence of instruction or an audience, the music surfaced.

"Music is an insistent creature. It wants to live. I didn't know this before," Marjan says. "But I've learned this from you. When I came to your concert, the songs you played were in my head for a week like a recording."

"They were?" Hawa seems taken by the idea she could have such a presence in her mother's thoughts.

They walk until they meet the main road. Marjan watches for a passing taxi, raises her hand and tries to summon one. When the fifth one passes her, she wonders if they'll have to take buses and walk to get to the airport but is relieved when a cab finally stops for them.

She tells the driver they want to go to the airport.

"The airport," he grouses. "People are killing themselves to get on a plane. It's an embarrassment, this mess they've left after twenty years. Sister, are you sure you want to go there?"

Marjan doesn't flinch at his resentment. She is unsure what to make of the last two decades but can say with certainty her life is better because of them.

Marjan had loved the clarity and structure of a mission.

She was given every detail in a briefing. By the time she climbed into a Chinook, she didn't need to look left or right to know who was sitting beside her. She knew the coordinates of their drop-off, the layout of the village, the name of the target, and how to hand off a prisoner. Hell, she knew the flavor of the candies they would be handing out to the children.

But she realizes now that while the plan for the night might have been clear, the plan for the following month was less so. And beyond that, the vision of the generals and people above them had become even more obscured, as if they were flying through a blanket of clouds.

It should be no surprise, Marjan thinks, that they've vowed to be gone by the end of the month. Their embassy is already closed, their staff evacuated. The only remaining troops are the ones at the airport. Five days from now, there will be no American presence in Kabul, and Marjan will have no chance of getting out with Hawa.

"You're right. But I have to try for my daughter's sake," Marjan replies, trying not to think about the horrific scenes she'd heard about at the airport. People had overwhelmed the gates, flooded the runway, and grabbed onto a plane even as it took off and gained altitude. Who would ever forget the image of people falling from the sky like wounded birds?

Marjan's phone lights up again. She expects it to be Soraya, but it's Jenna. This morning Marjan saw that Soraya had last been online around three in the morning. Maybe she hadn't texted because she didn't want to wake anyone with a ping at that hour. She should know no one is sleeping through these nights.

Ladies, roll call. Where are you? Jenna asks the group.

On our way, Marjan replies.

Okay. We're still seeing warnings that there may be an insurgent targeting the airport. Stay alert.

Maybe they make these warnings because they do not want us to leave, another FTP muses. *But we cannot stay here. I burned my papers. I am nothing.*

We're going to get you through. Do you have the signs with you?

There are small fires all over Kabul as people race to eliminate the evidence of their involvement with the Americans or other Westerners. Hard-earned diplomas, certificates, recommendation letters, and precious photographs—anything incriminating is turned to ash.

As they approach a checkpoint, Marjan takes Hawa's hand. She opens her phone and deletes the messages with Jenna and the others in case they check her device. The Taliban are guarding the outer perimeter of the airport while the Americans and Afghan soldiers manage the land inside.

Two Talibs stand on the dirt road; one has the end of his lungi pulled across his mouth, a screen against the dust. The rifle he's carrying is thankfully pointed at the ground. He peers into the taxi, looks Marjan and Hawa over, and asks for their documents.

"I have none," Marjan says meekly. "My husband is holding everything for us. He is already inside the airport."

The Talib turns his head and fires a wad of saliva onto the ground.

"Open your handbag," he barks.

Marjan sees Hawa go perfectly still. She obliges, unzips her bag, and holds the mouth open so he can see it contains nothing but a pen, a folded piece of paper, a few bills held together by a metal clasp, and two bottles of water.

"What is that?" he asks. "What's the paper?"

Marjan's pulse drums in her ears. The proximity to the enemy unnerves her. But the Taliban soldiers are all around them, within striking distance and utterly untouchable.

"Just a note from my elderly mother, a prayer for a safe journey," she says. She can feel Hawa's eyes on her.

The Talib conferences with the man beside him. From somewhere in the line of cars behind them, they hear the bleat of a car horn. One Talib leaves to investigate the noise. He raises a whip and lashes at the back of a man who tries to duck the blows, covering his head with his hands. There are shouts and horns and the occasional rat-a-tat of warning shots fired into the air.

Marjan takes stock of the surroundings. The airport perimeter is teeming with people. Tactically, it's nearly impossible to secure the area. They need to push through today, to get close enough that the marines can spot her and the sign she's been told to carry.

The Talib waves them through. She thanks the taxi driver, who shakes his head and warns her to be careful.

Marjan nods. With Hawa's hand in hers, she pulls out her phone and updates the group that she's arrived and will start making her way to Abbey Gate.

Good, Jenna replies. *Keep me posted.*

She spots a tall tower and sees two soldiers, Americans, it appears, standing atop a concrete wall topped with coiled wires. Behind the soldiers is the leaf-shaped airport. Military structures sit on the north side and passenger terminals are to the south. A single runway cuts through the center, a paved spine.

Progress is slow and painstaking. The sun ascends in the sky; the heat seems to be coming at them from all directions, even radiating from the ground beneath their feet. Marjan hears a child crying and turns to look at Hawa, afraid she's been hurt. But it's not Hawa crying; it's someone else's daughter. Hawa's cheeks are hot and pink thanks to the mighty summer sun.

When you get close, take out your sign but make sure you're close enough that someone can see it.

Marjan scans the crowd. There are two other FTPs here to try their luck today, but they are in different locations, too far apart to see one another, but they're hoping to converge at Abbey Gate. Three signs will be easier to see than one. Marjan is looking for Soraya, expects to hear her friend call her name or grab her by the elbow. Even in a mass of people this dense, she is confident they will find each other. That's the type of connection they have had since they first met.

"Stay close to me," Marjan tells Hawa. "Don't let go, no matter what."

Hawa squeezes tighter. Marjan feels it in her heart more than her hand.

They are near a hotel, just outside the airport's perimeter. A black office chair on wheels sits on top of a shipping container. One Talib sits in the chair, surveying the masses. Two others, dressed in uniforms of olive camouflage, stand beside him, foot soldiers. One wears a camouflage cap, the other a fuchsia bandana. Their weapons hang at their sides. People sit by the shipping container, trying to catch a sliver of shade. They are mindful of the Taliban patrolling the area, quickly learning how to coexist with them.

Marjan keeps her head low, her movements subtle. She records in her mind where the Taliban soldiers are standing. She and Hawa climb over a barrier. The airport wall is within view, on the other side of a canal of murky water. The moat of sewage is hardly a deterrent. It is full of people standing knee-deep in foul-smelling waste. Crumpled plastic bottles, scraps of fabric, and plastic bags float along the surface; some trash is caught in the loops of wire inside the canal.

On the other side of the sewage is a wall guarded by American marines. They are indistinguishable from one another in their khaki uniforms, heavy helmets, loaded vests, and dark sunglasses. They scan the crowd, trying to discern the signal from the noise, to find the person waving the right documents in a desperate mass but there are so many papers waving in the sun, a sea of white flags.

Marjan decides she wants to be closer before taking out her paper.

The woman beside her slides to the ground.

"Make room, make room! She's fainted!" someone shouts. A child wails.

The smell is overwhelming. Sweat, fear, waste. Some have been here for two days.

They look for openings in the crowd. They are petite and can fit through small spaces. There are men here alone or with friends. There are families with four or five children in tow, babies and toddlers in the arms of their parents. This is no place for the elderly. Marjan hears the gray-haired man beside her tell his son that he will not go any further.

"Not at my age," he says. His son pleads with him, even while his father kisses the top of his head and then does the same with each of his grandchildren. "God be with all of you."

It is a long walk to the road, but people step aside for the man, whose departure brings them one person closer to the gate.

Marjan checks her phone.

They'll be looking for your signs. Wave it and try to get their attention.

Marjan wipes the sweat from her forehead. She warns her body that fainting is not an option. She sets her duffel on the ground between her feet and extracts the folded sign from her handbag. With a pen she borrowed from Kobra, she wrote the name of a fallen marine, bleeding the pen dry to make the letters as thick and visible as possible.

Chesty Puller.

What does it mean? Marjan had asked the American women in their chat group.

He was a soldier. The marines will know his name was all the explanation she received. She guessed he must have been a good soldier. She did not know he was a legend among marines, a highly decorated veteran who had demonstrated exceptional leadership in World War II and Korea.

She holds the paper up by two corners, trying to position it so it will be visible to the soldiers on the wall, concertina wire to their backs. Just beyond them is the airfield, and every once in a while, they plucked a document from the crowd, examined it, and either turned the person away or helped get them over the wall.

"Hello! Please! Look here!" Marjan calls out. She shouts out the name written on her paper, hoping that will catch their ear, but it does not.

Another hour goes by. More people fall limp. The crowds side-step their bodies as their families try to revive them with small sips of water, but there is not enough to go around. Marjan makes Hawa drink from her bag, keeping her bottles out of view. Under these circumstances, there is little room for charity.

"Hawa, we are going to have to cross this water to get closer," Marjan tells her daughter, even as she questions this decision. Hawa nods. She either lacks the energy to protest or understands that their only option is to walk through human waste. They climb over a barrier. Marjan lowers herself in first, stepping with one foot and then the other. She hoists her duffel bag over her shoulder, tries to keep it from dipping into the water. Then she reaches for Hawa with both arms to help her come down into the canal.

It is hard to breathe. The sewage comes up to Marjan's knees and even higher on Hawa, who is covering her mouth and nose with the flap of her headscarf.

"Please!" Marjan shouts, trying to catch the attention of the marines above her from the canal. They are mere meters from the soldiers, as close as she can get. She tries to shout the name from the sign. "Chess . . . Chess . . ."

She falters. The heat is getting to her, and she has to look at the sign to make sure she's getting the name right. Her phone buzzes, and she pulls it out to read the update.

Ladies, might be wise to clear out of the area and wait for another day, one of the CSTs advises. *State Department just issued another alert. Looks serious.*

Marjan groans. Getting into the canal was not easy. Getting out will be even harder, especially with half their bodies soiled by waste. She looks left and right, wonders if she would be able to detect someone suspicious under these circumstances. Everyone around her looks too busy trying to get over the next wall to be thinking about setting off a bomb. She decides they will linger a little longer.

Another hour passes and then her phone alerts again. The Germans have had a bus full of people stuck at a checkpoint for the past two hours. At least she and Hawa made it through that obstacle. One of the FTPs responds with a picture of herself, signaling victory with two fingers.

We are inside!

Marjan's eyes well with tears. Her fellow soldiers are on the airfield, on the right side of this concrete wall. She is so happy for them, she could burst. She's also buoyed by their success.

"Look!" She shows Hawa the picture. "My friends did it. It's possible to get through. We just have to get their attention."

Hawa nods, hopeful despite the conditions. Marjan swipes her sleeve across her daughter's forehead to dry her sweat. She shouts louder; the man beside her looks over with annoyance. He has a toddler hoisted on his shoulders. With one hand, he waves a document sheathed in plastic at the marines, while the other hand holds the leg of his toddler. He is about six inches taller than Marjan, which makes a world of difference as they compete for the eyes and ears of the marines. Can they even hear anything above the drone of voices?

Marjan's phone battery is draining quickly. She's checking it often, looking for instructions and providing updates. The dark screen seems to draw the sun's heat and the device feels like a hot coal in her palm. She looks at Hawa and knows the day is having the same effect on her daughter. She opens her bag to offer her a piece of bread. Hawa turns her head away in refusal. The stench has killed her appetite.

More time goes by. Marjan sets her sunglasses on her head and holds her paper as high as her arms will reach. The sun threatens to blind her. Soraya should be here. She keeps looking over her shoulder, expecting her friend to appear. Soraya, with her striking looks, her commanding presence, she would have caught someone's attention.

"Please! Look here!" she cries. "I am FTP! We work with American CST!"

A man beside her looks at her with tepid curiosity. Another reminder comes in for everyone to be careful. *High alert.* Of course it's a high-alert situation. All the players are here—the American military, the last remaining Afghan special forces soldiers, and the Taliban.

Marjan does a practiced, quick scan and notes that the man wears only a thin tunic, too thin to conceal bundled explosives of ammonium nitrate. She thinks of the mission, one of their most treacherous, on which they found a stash of what looked like rice sacks. They were bags of fertilizer marked with a cheery logo from a plant based in Pakistan—a blue triangle with two green leaves.

Fertilizer. The irony rattled Marjan. What was meant to enrich the earth, to grow life, was instead being turned into explosives to kill unsuspecting civilians, target Afghan and American soldiers, and massacre minorities where they worshipped or where their daughters went to school.

She feels the tightness in her chest again. She checks her surroundings for suspicious individuals, anyone with an unusually intense expression, lumpy clothing, a heavy belt. It's nearly impossible to see through the dam of people.

Marjan, what are you wearing? The guy I know is going to be covering the gate near you.

Marjan takes a picture of herself and Hawa. She tries to send it, but the app is slow to upload and transmit the image.

"Madar? How can we make him see us?"

Marjan tries to think strategically. She relays that she's wearing a black scarf and a green shirt, a swap with one of the women on the hill. Her fingers are trembling. She cannot see the face of the marine. Her neck aches from looking up.

"I'm trying. I'm trying and our friends are trying too," Marjan says, even as she wonders if she should decide now when to call it quits. Will it be easier to get through the gate after nightfall? Families have been renting mattresses from shop owners near the airport. The area has turned into a refugee camp.

The afternoon has blurred into early evening. It is 5:33 p.m. but still light out. No one notices the man, cheeks sallow from spending the past four years in a high-security prison for plotting a bombing, make his way through the crowd. He has been out of prison for eleven days but still does not feel free. No one realizes he is twenty-five pounds heavier because of the vest he wears, the vest that will give purpose to this lowly life, the vest that will make him a most exalted warrior for God.

Another minute goes by.

Hawa wants to lie down. She hates that her legs are wet with sewage, the constant shouting around them. There is so much noise, such disorganized sound. She wants to feel the calm of birdsong.

Hawa looks up. She looks at the trees in the distance, at the swatches of blue sky with frayed edges.

There are no birds. Where have all the birds gone?

Hawa's question is answered by a thunderous boom and then a stunned silence. She cannot hear the shouting. She cannot hear the birds. She cannot hear her mother shrieking her name.

44

2014

Marjan sat with her back against the wall, her feet stretched out before her. She had called Soraya immediately upon returning from the park.

"This is incredible. Marjan, are you thrilled or should I be thrilled for you?"

"I'm a little nervous about the Rasulis. They might not like that we met at their home. I don't want them to think I was forward with him," Marjan said, fidgeting with the ends of her sleeves.

Soraya dismissed her concerns.

"Once they realize this is love, they'll pat themselves on the back for bringing two souls together. Matchmaking must have some sawab, does it not? What better way to secure blessings than by arranging a marriage! Has he already discussed this with his family?"

Marriage. After what Marjan had seen of marriage, she never thought she'd even consider it in her lifetime. Soraya did not share her hesitation, or even fully understand it. But Marjan knew that this feeling she had for Saboor, whatever it was, could not exist without a structure. Not in this world.

"And I don't mean to sound too forward," Soraya continued. "But I think he should ask me for your hand in marriage. I consider you a sister and it's only right that he begs for my agreement. And remember, tradition states the bride's family should be showered with gifts. Be sure to tell him my best colors are burgundy and navy, I favor flowy dresses, and I'm not picky about jewelry at all."

"This isn't a very traditional situation," Marjan reminded her friend. She was so deeply grateful for Soraya, for having someone she could share this moment with. Sometimes Marjan would read Saboor's messages to Soraya, needing her to confirm that she wasn't inventing him or this relationship.

"All the more reason to honor tradition," Soraya insisted. "But, Marjan, can I ask you something?"

Marjan knew what was coming. Any best friend would ask.

"How do you really feel about him?"

For all the hours Marjan had spent pondering this very question, she should have had a ready and definitive answer for Soraya. She did not.

"If you're asking about love, I'm not sure I even know what that means," Marjan admitted. That electricity, that flutter inside, was that love's signal? She listened to song lyrics these days with an analytical ear, tried to measure the lyrics against her own feelings. Did she feel lost in his eyes? Had she even noticed the shape of his lips?

"Of course I'm not asking about love. How can a woman really love a man before she marries him? Before she knows what kind of man he is when he's been fasting all day and the electricity has just gone out and his wife is busy nursing their second daughter? Love is earned and no one gets a salary before doing the job."

"For heaven's sake, Soraya. You turn everything into a rant. Then what do you mean?"

"I mean, do you think you can trust him? That's the only question you need to answer now, I think. Can you trust that he will treat you well? That he will be decent?"

"Soraya, you speak as if I have the luxury of options."

"Marjan, you speak as if you have none."

Marjan groaned.

"I love you as a sister. I will celebrate this moment with you so long as it's your decision and you are confident in this man. And so long as you are not entering into this because you think you cannot expect anything else out of this life."

"Soraya, this is me doing the very best I can for myself and my daughter. He's been nothing but kind to me. Whatever comes, I will make the best of it."

After her years with Abdul Khaliq, Marjan could not believe she was even considering the possibility. Saboor had unlocked something in her with his patience, his tenderness.

"Very well then," Soraya said. "When should I expect to meet this poet suitor of yours?"

Saboor needed a day or two to sit down with his mother and sisters. He was excited to share the news with them, to tell them his divorce would no longer hang over his head. He would be a married man after all, and he'd found his match on his own.

Two days passed, then three.

In every conversation, Marjan waited to hear about Saboor's mother's reaction. But the conversation was delayed first by his niece coming down with a fever so high that he had taken her to the clinic. Two days later, the girl was much better, but one of his father's oldest friends had passed and Saboor was going to attend the fateha.

"Well? What's the latest?" Soraya asked at the end of the week.

"He messaged me this morning and said he's going to talk to his mother this afternoon," Marjan reported. She was growing impatient as well. She could not wait for her new life to be realized, to have a home with Saboor, a home where she could be with Hawa and walk her to school every day, a home in which she wouldn't have to be the only breadwinner.

"Ah, on a Friday! Maybe this was an auspicious decision to wait for the holy day," Soraya speculated.

Marjan spent the afternoon handwashing Zargul's delicates and hanging them from the hooks installed above the laundry machine. Elbow deep in a bin of soapy water, she listened for the ping of her phone. Several times, she thought she heard something and towel-dried her arms only to find her ears had deceived her.

Afternoon turned into evening.

How are you doing? Marjan texted Saboor.

His reply came nearly an hour later.

Forgive me, darling. It's been a busy afternoon. Restaurant is packed but I was able to speak with my mother. She was so surprised. She has been worried I would be forever single, of course.

Saboor punctuated his message with a flower and a smiley face. Marjan felt her shoulders relax.

Call me when you can, she wrote back.

Marjan could not sit still. She'd done her best to work out her nervous energies in the Rasuli home, but it had not been enough. She stepped out of her room and filled her lungs with the night air, the faint scent of jasmine from the Rasuli garden, and heard the sounds of life from over the estate's walls.

Marjan missed Hawa terribly, even more now that it felt she was closer to being reunited with her daughter. She checked the hour. It was late, but surely the girls at the orphanage were still awake. She called, telling herself she would only ask after Hawa as she had been doing, but when a woman answered the phone, Marjan found herself asking to speak with her daughter.

"It is quite late and not your usual day to call. Would it not be better to call in the morning, at least?" she asked.

"Please. I don't mean to trouble you. It's just rather important that I speak to her," Marjan pleaded. She heard a sigh and then a request to hold. She steadied her breathing, thought about what she would say to her daughter. She hadn't yet gathered her thoughts when she heard Hawa's voice on the line.

"Hello?" Hawa said, and Marjan pressed her hand to the wall, steadied herself.

"My love? It's me," Marjan said, her voice trembling. "I'm so sorry it's been this long. How are you, janem?"

"I'm fine," Hawa said, her voice quiet and measured.

"Are you? I've missed you so much. I call all the time and get updates from Khanum Atefa. I'm so proud of you! She even sent me a picture of the cat you drew. Such long whiskers!" she gushed.

"You saw the cat drawing?" Hawa asked.

"I certainly did. And more. She knows how much it means to me to see your work." Marjan waited for Hawa to speak.

"Oh. Why are you calling so late at night?" she asked, a hint of melancholy in her voice.

"It is late. I just wanted to tell you that I've been working so hard so that we can be together forever, not just for a visit." Marjan didn't want to say anything more, but she wanted to brighten her mood too. "Hawa-jan, soon, though. Soon I'll be able to pick you up and we can live together again. Just like we used to."

"That was a long time ago," Hawa replied.

"It wasn't that long ago. But no, you're right. It was too long ago," Marjan said. "I think things will be easier for us. I've been working very hard and saving up and I . . . I hope I'll have good news to share with you soon. Good news for both of us."

"What's the good news?" Hawa asked, curious.

She couldn't tell Hawa about Saboor over the phone. She wanted to have this conversation in person. This would require so much care, so much preparation.

"I can't tell you just yet, but I'm hoping we will have a new home soon. I really want to come and visit you. Would you like that?"

"Yes! Why don't you come today?"

"I wish I could but it's late tonight, my love. I'll do my very best to come tomorrow. Is that all right?"

"You won't forget?" Hawa asked, and Marjan felt her heart being torn apart at the seams.

"I will not forget. I could never forget," she swore.

The next day, Saboor insisted on traveling with her to the orphanage. They shared a taxi, Marjan feeling very conscious of the driver, as if everyone in the world could tell they were unmarried by looking at them. Saboor was unfazed. He reached for Marjan's hand across the seat of the taxi. She pulled her hand into her lap and widened her eyes to silently chide him, but he, true to his spirit, laughed and responded with a poem.

Today, I am in your hands
Be loving, do not forget.
Tomorrow when I become dust,
What use are tears of regret?

"Have you memorized all of Mawlana's verses?" Marjan asked. She admired him for it, the sacred space he'd created in his soul where poetry lived and his ability to recite it at the drop of a hat.

"Those are not Rumi's words. Those belong to Hafiz," he corrected. "He wrote for the lovesick."

Marjan shook her head, looked away. She felt like a teenager, her youth restored by the flirting and these daylight transgressions. She was righted by the sight of a burqa-clad woman sitting on the sidewalk, an infant in the crook of one arm and her other arm stretched out begging for charity. Marjan saw women like this often and knew that even a half step in the wrong direction could put her in that same predicament.

"I told my sisters as well," Saboor said. Marjan turned and looked at him.

"You did?"

Saboor nodded.

"Do they know about today?" Marjan asked, choosing her words carefully so as not to give too much of her story away to the driver. "Do they know about Hawa?"

"Yes," he said.

"And?"

"And they have concerns, of course. That's understandable. But they are mothers and I believe their hearts will warm to the situation. That's why I think the sooner we proceed, the better," he said, reaching over to give Marjan's hand a quick squeeze.

Marjan wasn't surprised they had reservations, and Saboor's reassurances soothed her. He knew his family, and they had told him repeatedly that he deserved happiness after what he went through in his first marriage.

Saboor started to hum. He was terribly off-key and turned the melody into an unrecognizable thing. He did this sometimes, having realized that his warbling disarmed Marjan. She covered her face to hide her laughter. By the time they arrived at the orphanage, she'd forgotten about his sisters and felt the nervous excitement of finally seeing her daughter again.

Saboor waited outside. They'd both agreed that he should not yet meet Hawa. He went for a stroll while Marjan went through the gate and entered the familiar yard. The sunflowers were growing in height, as tall as the girls who lived inside.

Hawa ran into her arms, and Marjan held her tight. She missed the scent of her daughter's head, the softness of her neatly combed hair, parted down the middle and tied into two ponytails. Was she taller? She looked taller. They spent the hour connected, Hawa's hand in her mother's. Marjan touching her daughter's shoulders and face. Their eyes locked on each other. Marjan kissing Hawa's forehead, her shoulder.

Hawa told her about the songs she had learned that week and the new girl who had arrived only a week ago. She told her about the games they played in the yard and showed her the schoolwork she'd completed, red stars drawn on the tops of thin worksheets.

When the time came to depart, Hawa did not scream or shout or throw herself on the ground.

"You told me on the phone that you had good news," she said.

"I do. I think I have found a home for the two of us together," Marjan said, her voice softly effervescent. "It shouldn't be much longer now."

"But you said that so long ago," Hawa insisted. "And you didn't come for so long. I told the other girls that you would take me with you today."

Marjan cursed herself for whatever she might have said to give Hawa this idea. Her mind raced. What if she pulled her daughter out of this school today? What if she hid her in her room behind the Rasuli home? What if she told Saboor they should do a nikah right now? Being married before God was all she needed so that she and Hawa could live with him.

"We need to be patient, my love," Marjan said.

Hawa began to sob.

"Hawa. Hawa, janem," Marjan said, trying to break through the storm. She took her hands into her own, tried to ground her with her touch.

"Just go. Just go just go just go," Hawa moaned.

So she did. Once more, she ran out of the building and into the street where Saboor stood waiting for her. She stumbled into his arms, her fingers cold and her face wet with tears. He cupped her face in his hands, brushed the tears away with his thumbs. She was too devastated to care about people on the street witnessing this untamed moment, this public breach.

"Shh, my love," Saboor said, guiding her back to the main road so that they could find a taxi. The sun had dipped behind the mountain in a glorious sunset, an actor exiting the stage in a flourish. The sky was the color of faded ink, of secrets and solitude. Of course Saboor would speak the words Marjan needed to hear most at that very moment. "All will be well soon enough. We just need to bring her home."

45

AUGUST 26, 2021

The world has gone dull and dark, the air heavy with dust and a sharp-smelling smoke. Hawa wipes the slick, the sweat and grime, from her face. She is standing but pressed to the wall of the canal. She hears a distant rattling, drumbeats without a rhythm. Something is on her face. These are her mother's hands over her face, she realizes. Her mother is beside her, shielding Hawa's body with her own.

A bomb, Hawa realizes. She has never been this close. Her hearing returns, and she starts to detect the screaming, the wailing. The rattling is not a rattle. It is bursts of gunfire, the discharge of automatic weapons. She looks up, through the triangle between her mother's chin and her shoulder and sees two marines lifting a woman off the ground, her pants red with blood. Another burst of gunfire. Hawa flinches; she presses her forehead against the wall.

"Don't move! Don't move!" Her mother's voice breaks through the chaos. "I'm right here. Don't move."

A mother begs someone to help her infant, a limp body in her arms. She rips off her headscarf and wraps it around the bright blood on her baby's head.

Every corruption of the day is more egregious than the last. The chaos will not end. Every shot startles Hawa, sends shocks through her body.

And then it is over.

"It's bad. Hold pressure over it. Let's get him out of here!" she hears an American shout.

Marjan looks over the edge of the wall. People have scattered. Some are crawling. A man lies on the ground facedown. His wound is not visible, but there's no doubt he's breathed his last. The Americans are carrying some of the casualties in through the gates. A teenage boy is on his knees beside his mother's body. Above her ear is a gaping wound. He has her wrist in his hands and his ear to her chest. He looks up at the marine standing above him, scanning the crowd for new danger and trying to salvage what he can from this mess.

"She's alive!" the boy cries in Dari. He points to his mother's chest, insists that there's a sound worth hearing inside her rib cage. "Please help my mother!"

The word for "mother" transcends languages, as does the boy's desperation. The marine crouches down, feels her neck for a pulse, then signals another marine to join him. They carry her through the gates too.

Hawa feels her mother pull away. The smoke stings her airways all the way down. She can feel the dust in her mouth, her lungs. Her mother's hands are on her now, touching her head and shoulders. Marjan turns her around, looks at her face, her chest, her legs.

I'm okay, she wants to tell her mother, but she is coughing now. She can't get the words out.

"Hawa! Oh, God, Hawa. You're okay, thank God."

But it's too soon to be relieved. They're not safe just yet. Marjan pulls herself and then her daughter out of the canal. They crouch on the ground to catch their breath. The Americans have soldiers outside the gate, more than the few Marjan could see before the explosion. They are gathering their casualties, the limbs limp, moving quickly. One marine stumbles, shouts as he runs toward a figure lying on the ground.

Marjan's ears ring. She feels her nose running, touches the back of her hand to her face and sees it come away smeared with blood.

It's just a nosebleed, she tells herself. Every part of her aches, as if she'd been picked up by the meaty hand of a giant and thrown to the ground. But she detects no wounds, no bullet holes, no blooms of blood. There is debris in her hair, and her mouth is so dry it's hard to talk.

Marjan uses her headscarf to wipe her face. She looks around again, sees people moving in all directions. Is it over? That is her primary concern. Some attacks are phased. There is an initial explosion, maybe a roadside IED that takes out one group of people. Then a second assault is launched on the people who rush toward the scene, the colleagues, the first responders, the neighbors.

It is pointless, she knows, to even debate how long she must wait before she can be sure the attacker or attackers don't have something else up their sleeve. She is focused now on the marines carrying people through the gates.

"Help me, please!" Marjan cries out when she sees a marine run past. This could be the opening she needs. She tightens her grip on Hawa's arm, terrified that they'll be separated.

"Please, you see my daughter. Please let us go inside," Marjan pleads. "I am FTP!"

The marine rushing past them pauses to look at Marjan. Maybe the blood on her face caught his attention. She has Hawa out of the sewage now. They are on the wrong side of the ditch, but she is willing to jump back into the filth if it means they get a chance at escaping.

"Are you hurt?" the marine asks Hawa.

Hawa is a bit stunned by the blast, Marjan can see it on her face. She shakes her head and Marjan's heart breaks. She's never been a complainer.

"I have a message from my American friends. They are soldiers. Please, look!" Marjan looks around for the paper she had been carrying, but it is gone. Maybe swallowed by the murky waters of the canal. She tries to say the name she had so carefully written, but she fumbles on the hero's name.

But even to her own ears, her words are hard to understand coming out of her sandpaper throat. She tries to get closer to the marine, but he is already looking in another direction, summoned by another soldier in uniform.

Marjan wonders if there might be another way in, another gate. With Hawa in tow, she tries to wind around the airport perimeter. Bodies are strewn on the ground. Three people carry a wailing woman into a vehicle. When she sees Hawa's eyes linger on the injured, she tries to turn her in another direction.

"Please," Marjan calls to a soldier passing by. She just needs a moment to explain, to show him the messages on her phone from her sisters in arms. And if he's the one Jenna's been in touch with, she won't have to explain much.

But he doesn't give her a chance.

"Back off! I need you to back off!" he shouts, and Marjan's hands go up, declaring her obedience, because she sees something familiar in his eyes. He's on guard, his defenses activated by the assault. She's felt the same way on a couple of missions when things went from routine to tense to utterly sideways.

And then he is gone too.

They circle the area, but Marjan cannot find a way in. The dust starts to clear, and Hawa is falling behind. The gates that had allowed some people in are now sealed shut. The badly wounded have been taken in; everyone else has been left on the outside.

Marjan looks at her phone. There are so many new messages. She scrolls through quickly but finds nothing that gives her direction. There is one text from the number she has not saved as a contact.

Sister, we've just seen the news about the bombing. Please let me know you are all right.

Marjan's fingers shake as she types out a brief response.

We are still here.

"Hawa?"

Hawa's hand is not in hers. She looks left and right. She let go for only a second, just to tap out four words. How could she have vanished?

As she swivels, a man jostles past her and in his panic knocks her to the ground. Marjan looks up and sees him holding his arm, blood dripping from his elbow. She tries to push herself up to standing. She lifts her head and catches a flash of color, the blue of Hawa's shirt.

Hawa is crouched on the ground, only a few feet away, beside the fanned chadori of a woman kneeling with her head to the ground as if in prayer.

"Hawa!" She crawls to her daughter, gets close enough to see the woman lift her head. On all fours, she turns her face to the sky and lets out a moan that Marjan knows all too well.

Hawa is on the ground, holding the hand of a little girl whose face is perfectly still and intact. Brown curls cling to her forehead. Her hair is spread on the earth. Her eyes are open and her lips parted as if she's been caught by surprise. She has been struck on her left flank, her clothing torn and wet with blood. There is no question of survival.

"Hawa!"

Marjan pulls her daughter up by her shoulders. She picks up Hawa's bag too. She wants to say something to this mother, but her face is buried in her hands. A man, probably her husband, has joined her with a young boy close to Hawa's age. The father lifts the child off the ground. His knees nearly buckle as he rises. He leaves a trail of her blood as he walks away.

Marjan touches the mother's shoulders.

Her mother tongue has so many ways to issue condolences, an invention of necessity.

God rest her soul. May the heavens await her. God forgive her any sins. Her fate is our fate. May her spirit be bright.

Marjan cannot bring herself to say any of them. They are useless. Insulting, almost, in how dismissive they are of the suffering. The mother grabs at the earth wet with her daughter's life, bewildered. Marjan helps her to her feet, puts the stunned boy's hand in his mother's. He reminds her, as every boy does, of her own lost son.

"It is no use to linger here," Marjan says. She can see the mother desperate to stay at this spot where just a few moments ago her daughter's eyes still lit up at the sight of her. The body carried away cannot be her child. Her child must be here somewhere.

Her husband looks back over his shoulder, pleads for them to follow. She and Hawa guide her back to the road, where another relative takes her by the arm. The boy's face is tear-streaked and pale.

Marjan and Hawa walk among throngs of stricken souls. They go two miles before they find a taxi that will take them back to Zanabad. Marjan's monies are nearly depleted. Hawa has been silent all this time, stoic. Should she ask her why she went to the little girl? She decides against bringing it up again. She doesn't want to make Hawa think about her.

She lifts the tarp and watches Hawa duck under and start climbing up the dirt path.

"Madar! Madar!" a child calls. "They are back!"

Kobra emerges, stands before them on the path well before they reach her door.

"Dear God," she whispers. They are quite a sight. Their skin is darkened by smoke and dust. The blood on Marjan's face has turned maroon and flaky. Then there's the shock of their sewage-soaked clothing. The sun has dried their pants, but they reek still. Kobra shakes her head. This world is determined to leave them no dignity. She calls out to her son. They will need water and something to eat.

Her son looks at the figures making the slow climb up the path. Because he is his mother's son, he sees what she sees and knows what needs to be done. He runs off to fetch a jug for water, enough for two people to bathe.

Marjan lets Kobra's daughter take the duffel from her shoulder. Kobra offers her a cup of water, and Marjan hands it to Hawa for her to drink first. Only once Marjan and Hawa have had a chance to wash the day off their bodies, when Hawa has been led away by Kobra's daughter to have her hair brushed and braided by a woman living further up the hill, only then does Kobra join Marjan on the floor of her home. She hands Marjan a pillow to place behind her back.

"I took my daughter to the most dangerous place in Kabul. She will never be the same after what she's seen. So many lost their lives today," Marjan says.

"But not you," Kobra responds.

"It could have been us," Marjan mumbles. "And it was all for nothing. We're still here. All I've done is fill her lungs with smoke and her head with death."

"You could not have known."

"There were warnings," Marjan insists. The full weight of the day is bearing down on her and threatens to collapse her from the inside out. "I'm supposed to keep her safe. I don't deserve her."

"God, you're impossible," Kobra says with a sigh. "What does a warning mean in this city? You were doing what half of Kabul was doing—trying to get your daughter to safety. When was the last time a mother let a little fear stop her from doing that? She is with you and that's all that matters."

Marjan does not have an answer, but she's also not feeling absolved by Kobra's reasoning. She is sure she could have done things differently. When night falls, she and Hawa curl up again on the borrowed space in Kobra's home. She listens to her daughter moan softly as she sleeps, and thinks about what Kobra said.

She is with you and that's all that matters.

She wonders what Kobra would think if she knew about those years when Marjan chose to leave Hawa at the orphanage. She might be less inclined to forgive Marjan if she were to hear about that time in their lives. Marjan's head spins with old and new regrets, their imprints on her heart like boot prints in soaked earth.

46

2014

Marjan envied Saboor's ease of mind, the confidence with which he believed every challenge was, in fact, not a challenge at all. He promised Marjan he would break the news to the Rasulis that they were to be married and that Marjan would no longer work for them in their household. He had described his family home to Marjan in such detail that she could already picture the room they would share until they could, one day, secure a small home for themselves.

He was arranging for the nikah to happen the following week, in six days. The day after, they would go together to the orphanage to bring Hawa home. Saboor had already picked out a private school for Hawa to attend. His niece had graduated from the elementary grades there, and his sister raved about the teachers.

Soraya's life was running in the opposite direction to Marjan's these days. At Soraya's insistence, her mother had rejected a suitor. The young man's mother had been quite persistent—seven visits over a two-month period. Soraya had seen the man, an accountant and in-law to one of her relatives, a few times at family gatherings. But Soraya noted that his sisters had not gone to college, and her sleuthing had revealed that his family had deemed it an unnecessary commitment of time and energy for a woman.

"My aunt, the one who works as a journalist, she's the only one who defends me. My mother says the man I'm dreaming of does not exist, but I think she's wrong. I just think the good ones are harder to find. I don't want much. I just want to be able to choose how I live and work and dress. I want to count for something. Is that really too much to ask for?"

"It isn't much at all," Marjan agreed. "But it's also everything. Saboor told me I wouldn't have to work after we are married but I want to. I want to go to school too. He promises that he's fine with both. His first wife worked as well."

"Tell me again. Why did they divorce?"

"He wasn't as devout as she was. And he says she hated that he wrote poetry. Told him he was too much of a dreamer."

"She hated him for his poetry? Wow. Has he shared any of it with you? What if it is really bad? What if . . . what if his poems don't even rhyme?"

Marjan chuckled. "He has shared some with me and I like it. He's shy about sharing it with others, so I don't know if he'll ever even try to make a living out of it. Does anyone? Did Rumi have a day job? Maybe Hafiz was a carpenter who wrote on the side."

"There's nothing wrong with that. I rather like the idea that they went home sweaty and tired and sore and then wrote their reflections. Gives those of us counting receipts all day hope that there could be greatness in us too."

Soraya's mother had fallen ill, and she'd needed to put her studies on hold for now so that she could help manage the family's expenses. If her father were still alive, she would have graduated by now.

"There has to be more than this, Soraya."

"There is. I can feel it."

Sometimes they believed together. Sometimes one had to do a touch more believing to make up for the other. Marjan had come to understand friendship was this vital act, keeping each other from being pulled down by the undercurrents.

Two days before the nikah, Soraya met up with Marjan at their usual café. She walked in with a silver gift bag, which she placed on the table before she slid into a wooden chair. Marjan had already ordered them green tea and a pastry to share.

"Believe me, I wanted to get you something better," Soraya said.

"Stop that. You didn't need to get me anything," Marjan chided. She reached into the bag and pulled out the contents—a plum-colored lipstick, a brown eyeliner pencil, and a compact with coral-colored blush.

"You can be as plain as you want every other day, but a woman should glitter on her wedding day," Soraya explained. "And for the photos, especially!"

"Thank you," Marjan said, twisting up the lipstick in amusement. "I am certain I have never before glittered."

Marjan's phone pinged, as if on cue. She looked at it and saw a message from Saboor.

Whose idea was it to put Fridays all the way at the end of the week? The wait is too much.

She blushed, then showed her screen to an expectant Soraya, who made theatrical, lovesick sighing sounds. She only stopped when she realized she'd caught the attention of the three women sitting a table away.

"Forgive me, we just watched a Bollywood movie," she explained, and then straightened her back and wrapped both hands primly around her mug. "I still can't believe I've not met him, though. How can any of this be legitimate without my blessing?"

"I know. He's wanted to meet you as well, but he's been so busy with work. It's rare for him to be off for an evening."

"I know, I know. And I've been working my fair share as well. That's fine. I'm rather happy having a grudge to hold on to for eternity. Tell me about Hawa."

"She's doing well. There's some kind of music program and she's shown interest."

"In music? Oh, I like that. She and your poet will make a good pair, won't they? He can write the lyrics. She'll compose the melodies."

"And where does that leave me?"

"Singing, my love. That leaves you singing!"

Marjan laughed, her head thrown back and her smile bright. This was as close as she'd ever come to a song.

The next day, Marjan went to see Hawa. She had already discussed her plans to pull Hawa out of the orphanage with Atefa over the phone. She hadn't wanted to say anything to Hawa too far in advance, but she also didn't want to shock her daughter, and the nikah was nearly upon them.

She sat with Hawa on a rug in an empty classroom, a bookshelf beside them.

"You look smarter every time I see you! I hear you've been learning a bit about music lately too?"

Hawa nodded. "I like it. Someone brought instruments and we got to play with them. A tabla, a sitar, a flute, and . . . I can't remember what else."

"Was there a harmonium? I love the sound of a harmonium," Marjan said.

"Yes! That's the one I forgot," Hawa replied.

"Hawa, janem. Remember I told you I have some news to share with you?" Marjan asked. Hawa looked at her mother askance, hesitant. Marjan took a deep breath and began to tell her daughter that she would finally be able to pull her from the orphanage in less than a week. She told her about the private school and the incredible teachers there. She told her that they would be moving into a nice neighborhood of Kabul, nicer than anywhere they'd lived before. She told her that she'd been working so hard and had managed to save up a bit of money.

"And we will be living with someone, Hawa, janem. He's a very nice man."

"A man?" Hawa's brows knitted together.

"Yes, a man. He's very kind and I've agreed . . . I've agreed to marry him," she said, though truthfully, it sounded like a confession. She felt the flush in her cheeks, the eager heat of shame. She had no reason to be embarrassed by any of this, but she was, especially as she spoke the words to her daughter. Hawa looked at her in bewilderment.

"You're going to get married?" she said.

Marjan tried not to feel upset. She reminded herself that Hawa was a child and could not possibly fathom what Marjan had to worry about in a day, how perfectly impossible it was to build a real life out of sticks and feathers.

Marjan kept talking. It was all she could do.

"The school is only ten minutes away from the home. I'll walk you there in the mornings and I'll come to pick you up in the afternoons. I know you'll miss these teachers, but Khanum Atefa said you've been so brilliant here and that you'll fit right in at any of the top schools in the city."

Hawa threw her arms around her mother's neck and sobbed into her chest. Marjan rocked Hawa as if she were once again a baby. As if they were going to rewind time and live these years all over again.

By the time she left the orphanage, she was feeling as hopeful about her future as she had ever felt. It was already dark when she returned to the Rasuli home. The kitchen light was on, Zargul's silhouette backlit. She wouldn't have to answer to her for much longer, wouldn't have to explain her whereabouts or let Khanum Zargul or Agha Rasuli know ahead of time that she would leave for the evening. She wouldn't have to ask her employer for her weekly pay, as if he were giving her charity instead of earned wages.

She always had trouble sleeping, but on this night she lay awake imagining what their nikah might be like, how it would feel to don a green veil and commit herself to Saboor before Allah and witnesses. Saboor had asked her if she wanted someone to represent her. Normally, a father or brother or uncle would speak on the bride's behalf, voice her agreement. But Marjan had no one, and Saboor suggested she could speak for herself, which had impressed Soraya as well.

It was impossible to think of her upcoming nikah without recalling her first nikah, the day she, a thirteen-year-old girl, had been given to a man with three other wives, with children her age, with not an ounce of empathy for her. Should she have run away then? How far would she have gotten? Could she have done anything to save Parwin from a most intolerable life? Could she have saved Shahla from becoming a mother while she was still a child?

There was no going back. There was only the path ahead, a future with Saboor.

She was thinking of him when her phone lit up, a message from Saboor.

Are you awake?

You'll have a long life, she wrote back. Superstitions were a universal language. He would know this meant she'd been thinking about him when his message came through.

Marjan, I'm so sorry.

What for? Marjan typed, but then she erased the question, because in the time it had taken to write those two words, she understood.

47

AUGUST 27, 2021

Marjan sits with her back to the wall as a soft light slips through the window. The night had been another restless one. Scenes from the airport replayed in her mind, no matter which direction she faced, no matter how tightly she closed her eyes. Hawa had whimpered in her sleep, and Marjan rubbed her back, kissed her head, and whispered in her ear that they were safe in Khala Kobra's home. She could think of no other way to soothe her daughter.

Her phone lights up.

I hear there will be more flights today. Maybe it won't be as crowded after what happened yesterday.

Marjan knows the bombing won't keep people away. If anything, it will drive more people to rush to this temporary portal.

Has anyone heard from Soraya? I have sent so many messages.

In come a string of replies in the negative, and then a haunting question.

Could she have been at the airport?

There is a flash of panic. Was Soraya among those left on that field of death? Did Marjan and Hawa walk right past her?

And then her reason returns.

Impossible, Marjan thinks. She would have told Marjan if she were coming. And if she'd been at the airport, she would have tried to meet up with her and the other platoon members. And then there's the undeniable truth that Soraya would have been searching for Marjan and Hawa. She would have been desperate to make sure they were safe after the blast and gunfire.

No, she writes back. *Her mother wasn't well and she needed to get her medications before she left. She needed another day.*

But even this doesn't explain why Soraya isn't answering her messages. Maybe she's feeling too guilty to leave her ailing mother. Maybe she's putting her family before herself, as she has so often.

I will go to her home this morning, Marjan writes, then turns her dimmed screen off to stretch the life of the battery. There is enough light in the room that she can now see the dirt under her fingernails, trace reminders of yesterday's ordeal. She hopes she was able to get the stench of yesterday off the clothes she and Hawa were wearing, the clothes that now hang on the line outside Kobra's home.

Kobra's home. She has already stayed here far longer than she intended to and far longer than Kobra expected her to. But what now? When will the flights leaving Kabul resume? She flips through the choices she has, all terrible. She could try to find a smuggler to get them across the border into Iran or Pakistan or Tajikistan. But the long stretches of road and night travel involve another catalog of dangers. She cannot subject her daughter to those. The Americans had already stated that they would be out by the end of the month. Marjan had another four days to try to get onto a flight, and if that failed, then she would be forced to consider her alternatives.

Hawa lets out a heavy sigh and then her eyes flip open, as if she'd been awakened by an alarm. Marjan rubs her shoulder, her back. She tucks Hawa's hair behind her ear and lets her thumb graze her daughter's temple. Hawa stares at her mother's face, and Marjan knows she is trying to read her expression. She forces a smile.

"Are we going back there?" Hawa asks.

Marjan swallows hard, then raises one finger over her lips and nods at the other still-sleeping forms in Kobra's home. She needs a little more time to answer that question. She mimes for Hawa to close her eyes and get some more sleep. She slowly stands and slips out the door, fills her lungs with the warm air of a new day.

Marjan needs to go to Soraya's home early, because she does not know what the rest of the day might bring. She will check the clothes on the line first, then go inside to wake up Hawa. Marjan rolls up a sleeve of her top and realizes her hands are trembling.

It is just hunger, she tells herself.

She hears a cough and realizes she is not alone. Whirling around, she sees a teenage boy sitting on an upturned pail, the gangly son of one of the widows who lives further up the hill. He's wearing an Adidas T-shirt and pants that do not reach his ankles. He is probably no more than fourteen years old, nearly a man.

"Good morning," he says.

"Good morning," Marjan replies. "What are you doing up so early?"

The boy looks surprised by her question. "I always get up early. I have chores to do and it's best to get them done before the sun gets too strong."

"What a good son you are," she says.

He shrugs and looks at the ground.

"Will you go back to the airport today?" he asks, squinting at her.

"I . . . I am not sure," Marjan replies. "I do need to go into town this morning and pay a friend a visit. I'm not sure how that will go."

"Are you afraid of the Taliban?" he asks.

Marjan does not want to admit just how afraid she is. Nor does she want to admit that she has extra reason to be fearful of them.

"The whole city is nervous," she says.

He nods, as if this is what he was thinking as well.

"I was in town two days ago to see what's happening. I even went to the zoo," he says, stretching his legs out and rubbing at the back of his neck. "I saw a bunch of them there, shouting at the bear and pointing their guns at the jaguars. They were climbing the cages, laughing. Looked like they were having the best time."

Marjan can imagine their hands gripping the green fencing of the enclosures, standing atop the low concrete walls painted with spots of burgundy, blue, and green. She has taken Hawa there a few times, walked her past the statue of the memorialized lion at the entrance without telling her that this false jungle had, at a most precarious moment in her life, pressed her to hang on. She hated to think of the Taliban there, in one of the few places in Kabul that inspired awe in children. She has seen the footage from other cities, the Taliban fighters riding a merry-go-round, or paddling swan-shaped boats across a lake, or driving bumper cars at an amusement park. Despite their heavy beards and weathered faces and shouldered weapons, there was something childlike in their expressions. As if they were men on the outside only, and misguided children on the inside. Most of them probably were.

"Did they say anything to you?" Marjan asks.

"No, those idiots were too busy taunting the lion," the boy says, shaking his head. "Can you believe that? Don't they know what a lion can do?"

48

2014

"They were opposed to the idea of me from the very beginning," Marjan revealed. They were back in the café, the television in the corner playing an evening news program. Two anchors sat straight-backed behind a long desk.

"And he hid this from you? Oh, Marjan. I'm so sorry," Soraya said.

Marjan couldn't bring herself to repeat everything Saboor had said in that middle-of-the-night phone call. She shouldn't have picked up. She shouldn't have allowed Saboor to go on as long as he had, to deliver to her every painful thing his mother and sisters had said about her before they'd even had a chance to meet her.

They think I should marry a girl, an untouched girl. I can't believe how regressive they are, how backward. And how hypocritical. They think because you were married before and because you're estranged from your family that you are of poor character. What about me? I was married before too. Am I used, unclean, and sullied? Am I tainted as well?

Used. Unclean. Sullied. Tainted.

Marjan was thrown back in time. She was once again a thirteen-year-old child, hands shaking as she tried to clean the blood from between her thighs. She was grateful for the small grace that was hearing these words alone and blanketed in darkness.

Used. Unclean. Sullied. Tainted.

Marjan pressed her knees together.

I have argued with them but they are unrelenting. You know me, Marjan. You know that I was never bothered by your previous marriage. Your darling Hawa. I was not bothered in the least. I am a man of modern sensibilities. I am not so callous as to blame you for what fate doled out. It wasn't your fault. It's not as if you left your husband. He died. You are . . . you are an innocent character in this tragic story.

Marjan realized that the tenderness she saw in Saboor was not tenderness at all. It had been weakness. Had he ever really loved her or had he fallen for her tragic story?

She begged him to stop talking

They're so eager to control my life. They don't want to see me married at all, that's what I think. They don't care how I feel.

Saboor, shut up. The acid in Marjan's voice interrupted his monologue. She wanted to call him weak. She wanted to point out his hypocrisies. She wanted to break this phone that he had purchased for her but instead made one final request. *Please stop talking. I don't want to hear another word.*

"And then you hung up?"

"And then I hung up."

"Oh, that's good! What a shitty poet," Soraya said.

"His poems didn't even rhyme," Marjan confirmed, and Soraya snorted.

"Consider yourself spared, Marjan. I know you've been betrayed and hurt but you were managing before him. He would have added heartache to your life. And what a blessing that Hawa never had to see his miserable face."

"I wish I hadn't told her about him. What is she going to think of her mother? How can I explain to her why I wasn't good enough for him?"

Soraya was silent on this.

"It's my own fault," Marjan admitted. "I thought he could make all my troubles go away."

"Let's make a promise. Let's promise to stand on our two feet before we entertain the possibility of any man."

Marjan nodded, stirred her tea into a small tempest, then watched it settle. She tapped her spoon on the lip of the mug and set it down on her napkin.

"But how are we going to do that?" she asked.

"I don't know. But we'll find a way," Soraya assured her. "Together."

The news anchors cut to a journalist on the scene of a political meeting. She straightened her headscarf, raised her microphone, and began to speak.

"We're here at a two-day dialogue hosted in Kabul, a chance for the presidential candidates to speak directly with women leaders from across the country . . ."

Soraya spun around in her chair.

"Khala Mina! That's my aunt," she pronounced with a smile.

Marjan had such respect for Mina, for any woman who was brave enough to look into the camera and speak exactly what was on her mind. She'd been awed to learn Mina and Soraya were related. She tried to hear what Mina was saying.

Over two hundred women from all thirty-four provinces eager to hear eight candidates or their vice-president running mates present their plans for the advancement of women . . .

"Look at that, Marjan. Things are changing. These men know they can't run this country on their own. There are possibilities now that didn't exist for our mothers. Just imagine what the future might be like for Hawa."

Marjan thought of her days sitting in the parliamentary building, men and women as colleagues, even as they debated and shook their fists at one another. How much had changed because of those women?

"You must be so proud of your aunt," Marjan said.

"I am. I wish I got to see her more." She sighed.

Marjan's eyes lingered on the screen.

Tomorrow's discussions will focus on fraud and corruption. Stay tuned for our reports on the subject. In the coming weeks, I'll be taking a closer look at the lucrative contracts signed between Americans and warlords with dismal records of human rights abuses.

Marjan froze. On the screen were three pictures of men in various poses—one looked like the type of picture taken for a passport, the second was a grainy colored photo of a man standing in front of a jeep, and the third was of a grim-faced man looking over his shoulder. Marjan's heart pounded so hard, she thought she might fall out of her chair.

The third man, the one looking over his shoulder, was the husband she had escaped, Abdul Khaliq.

Soraya shook her head.

"She's received so many threats for her reporting on these kinds of people. Voicemails. Messages online. The family loved her until she became a little too known. Then it was like she was afflicted with leprosy."

Marjan had never known too much about how Abdul Khaliq had ruled over their village and the surrounding areas, but she knew all too well that he'd ruled over their home with an iron fist. She'd heard about his contracts with the Americans, an approbation of a higher order. Marjan realized her hands were shaking. She tucked them under the table so Soraya wouldn't notice.

"But Khala Mina doesn't care. She lives for her work and that's what I want to do. I don't mean that I want to be a journalist. That's too much writing for me. I mean, I want to feel fired up about my job. Don't you think it's possible, Marjan?"

At the sound of her name, Marjan was brought back to the present conversation.

"Hm? Yes, it's possible," she said, turning her attention back to the television. The cameras were back on the anchors sitting in the news station. There were floods in the north. Conservative lawmakers were calling for the elimination of a minimum marriage age for girls, abolition of shelters, and ending criminal penalties for rape. A new law proposed to prohibit authorities from questioning relatives of criminal defendants.

Marjan shook her head. In theory, the laws would have punished Abdul Khaliq for what he had done to her. Rape. Underage marriage. Domestic violence. The only witnesses to her abuse had been his relatives, and if they could not be questioned, that would have left her testimony alone. How far would a girl's accusations go?

She was still reeling from the sight of Abdul Khaliq.

"That was him," she whispered to Soraya.

"Who?" Soraya asked, confused.

Marjan pointed to the television screen and offered the briefest explanation.

Soraya's mouth dropped open. She reminded Marjan she was safe, far away from the warlord and his influence.

"Never tell your aunt," Marjan warned. "I don't want anyone to know."

"I would never," Soraya swore. Marjan nodded, wanting to believe her friend.

"I don't know. Maybe I should just accept what I have. It hurts too much to hope for something much better than this."

"Marjan," Soraya said, leaning across the table. She reached out for Marjan's hands. "You can't think that way!"

Marjan's hands came up from under the table but only to hide her tears from the other people sitting in the café.

"How can I not?" she asked.

"Marjan, is this really what you want to tell Hawa? *My daughter, be prepared for the worst. Don't bother studying. There's no hope for you, my brilliant child. Now come, let's braid your hair.* Is that really what you want to tell her?"

"Of course not," Marjan said, her exhaustion evident in her voice. "But it's like I'm in a hole and the bottom keeps sinking under my feet. It's really hard to get up every day and fight. I'm not a soldier, Soraya. I don't know . . . I don't know how much more I can do."

Marjan thought of her sister Parwin slowly picking up a canister of fuel and pouring it over her head like a ritual ablution. For the first time in her life, Marjan understood the resignation, the relief she must have felt just before she struck the match and set herself ablaze. That window into her sister's desperation terrified her.

Soraya bit her lip.

"We'll find a way," she said, her palms still resting on the table, open and ready to receive her friend. Marjan felt her breathing slow, the settling of a tempest. She slipped her hands into Soraya's and held on tightly.

49

AUGUST 27, 2021

Every time Marjan checks her phone, the death toll from the airport bombing climbs. By the time the estimate reaches one hundred, Marjan is nearly sick to her stomach thinking how narrowly she and Hawa escaped injury or death.

"Madar, will Khala Soraya come with us to the airport today?" Hawa asks. Her bag is beside her on the seat of the taxi. Marjan looks at the rearview mirror to check if the driver is paying attention to their conversation. She wishes they could travel by foot and conserve the little cash they have, but she does not want to be so exposed in the city. Maybe she can try the banks again today to see if they will allow anyone to withdraw money.

"I hope so," she says. "God willing, her mother is feeling better."

Marjan knows just how hard it is to run toward a future when it means leaving behind loved ones. She pictures her own mother, her sisters, her aunt. Even her father. There was a time, before the opium and before the hunger, when he would carry her around like a trophy. When he would put an arm around her as he listened to the news on his radio. Marjan stops her thoughts. She cannot risk the melancholy that comes with remembering.

"What will happen to everyone on the hill?" Hawa asks softly. Her mother looks discomfited by her question.

"I don't know," she confesses. When Marjan had shouldered her bag and faced Kobra this morning, Kobra had squeezed her hands tightly.

Inshallah, you will be successful today and not come back, she'd whispered.

"But I do know that those women are some of the toughest women in the city."

"Resilient," Hawa says. That was the word Ingrid had used with deep admiration. *Afghan women are so resilient.*

It was a dangerous myth, this idea that just being Afghan gave a woman some survival superpower, the ability to withstand such brutal oppression. It gave the world permission to turn its back. Afghan women were *resilient* because people saw only the ones who survived. No one paid attention to the ones who didn't.

Marjan keeps her headscarf pulled low over her forehead and her sunglasses on so that she can scan the streets for overzealous Taliban patrols or familiar faces.

Marjan realizes Hawa is singing softly, probably to mute the noise in her head.

The taxi driver steals a glance in his rearview, peers at Hawa with curiosity.

"A little singer," he notes. "Is her father a singer?"

Marjan, whose eyes have been scouring the streets for her husband's likeness, feels her stomach flip.

"My father is dead," Hawa says sharply.

The taxi driver clucks his tongue in measured sympathy.

"May God forgive his sins," he says.

The rest of the drive to Soraya's home passes in silence. The Taliban are roving about, but they are not stopping every pedestrian or every car. They are still celebrating that for all his bluster and finger wagging and flag-waving, the president has abandoned his people, his nation, and his presidency.

"Here you are," the taxi driver says. "And I said I will wait but not more than a couple of minutes. I hope your friend knows this."

"We will be quick," Marjan promises again. She's negotiated this two-part journey with him with the hope that Soraya will be ready to go. She should be. It's the long hand of the clock they watch most these days; every minute matters.

Marjan nods for Hawa to get out of the taxi. She has been to Soraya's home only a few times, and each visit was brief and purposeful. She first visited when Soraya's uncle passed away and after that to pay her respects on the Eid holidays. Soraya's family seemed nice enough, but she didn't want to linger long enough to invite conversation or speculation. She also had no desire to bump into Soraya's very judgmental cousin, the one who had felt duty bound to check on them often since Soraya's father died.

As if I'm not an adult. And as if I don't have a mother still, Soraya would scoff.

Marjan knocks three times on the outer door then steps back, looks up and down the quiet side street. Hawa is at her side. She pulls her sunglasses off just as the metal door swings open. A young boy stands before her, a bit older than Hawa. This must be one of her younger cousins.

"Salaam," he says solemnly.

Marjan returns the reply, smiling briefly at the child.

"I'm here for Soraya-jan," she says.

The boy stares at her for a beat, as if it's taking some time for her words to register. Then he nods, steps back, and opens the door wider so that they can enter.

"Everyone is in there," he says.

"Everyone? Is Khala-jan okay?" Marjan asks, suddenly concerned that something's happened to Soraya's mother.

He shrugs.

Marjan and Hawa step into the courtyard of the house. It is a narrow alley with a bicycle leaning against the stone wall. The main door to the home is a few meters away, just past a small rosebush and two tomato plants. Soft murmurings come from inside the home. Has something happened to Soraya's mother? Do they have family over? Maybe this is why Soraya has not been answering her phone. Marjan pauses at the door, sees about a dozen pairs of women's shoes, and thinks of the impatient taxi driver waiting on her outside.

"Sweet boy, I don't want to disturb the family," she says quietly to the child. It is a private moment, and she feels like she's intruding. Hawa peers through the window.

"It's okay. There is room for you both," he says. He is a perfectly obedient child with eyes the color of burnt sugar, just like Soraya. Marjan realizes she's looking at Soraya's nephew. Soraya had her arms around him in a picture from last Eid.

"Are you Jawad-jan?" she asks, and the boy nods. "I thought so. Your khala Soraya talks about you very much. She tells me you have the best grades in your class and that your paper airplanes rival some of the military planes."

Jawad's gaze drops to the earth.

"Madar," Hawa says, still staring through the window. Marjan tries to pull her away, doesn't want her looking like she's snooping.

"Jawad-jan, do you think you could tell her that Marjan is here?"

"Who should I tell?" he asks.

"Go on and tell your khala Soraya, of course," Marjan says.

"Madar." Hawa's voice trembles. Her face is pressed against the glass.

Marjan becomes suddenly aware of the absence of sound and movement in this cramped courtyard. There is not even the slightest breeze, not a whisper of air. It's as if everyone has stopped breathing.

She goes to the window, but she can't see through the glass. Is it foggy or has her vision blurred? She kicks off her shoes and steps into Soraya's home, her entrance observed by a dozen pairs of forlorn eyes. She spots Soraya's mother seated on the floor, her back to the wall and her face hidden behind her splayed hand. A woman sitting next to her has an arm around her shoulders, a crumpled tissue in her other hand.

And against one bare wall sits a rectangular wooden box, an assembly of planks.

"Dear God," Marjan whispers. She is compelled forward. There, wrapped in a white sheet, is a face Marjan can hardly recognize. Soraya, or this impossible likeness of her, has been drained of color but for a dusty lavender bloom across her left cheek and under her right eye. A strip of cloth wrapped around Soraya's face and knotted at the top of her head keeps her jaw shut. She has been forever silenced.

Marjan falls to her knees, her head gripping the roughly planed edge of her best friend's coffin. She cannot breathe. Her barefaced grief triggers a fresh wave of sniffles in the room. Tissues are plucked from paper boxes. Hawa's hands touch hers, and Marjan realizes her daughter is standing beside her, staring at the woman who has showered her with affection. Marjan does not have the liberty to lose herself here. She forces herself to her feet, pulls Hawa away from the coffin.

She turns and kneels again, this time in front of Soraya's mother, whose eyes are puffy and pink.

"May Allah," she says, choking on her words. She takes Soraya's mother's hands in her own. "May Allah grant you patience."

Her head is reeling. She thinks of her last conversation with her friend, how anxious she'd sounded. Soraya's face bears the stigmata of a special type of violence.

"Who did this to her?" Marjan asks, shaking with outrage. Behind her, tongues cluck and sighs slip from reticent lips.

Soraya's mother moans softly, then pulls her hands away from Marjan and wipes her tears with the corner of the shawl draped across her lap.

"You came here. You saw her. Now you can take your daughter and leave," she whispers.

"I'm sorry, I did not know. She wasn't replying to me. I came to check on her," Marjan says, weeping.

"Dear God, I wish you hadn't," Soraya's mother says, louder this time. Loud enough for the room to shift with discomfort. Marjan stiffens. She is not welcome here. She rises slowly, reaches for Hawa's hand, but her daughter is not at her side.

Hawa stands by the open coffin, staring at Soraya's face as if she is a puzzle Hawa is trying to solve. Her face is slick with tears.

Marjan takes one last look at Soraya's still form before retreating from the room. Outside, Soraya's nephew remains in the courtyard, leaning against a wall. He digs into the ground with the toe of his sneaker, makes a shallow grave.

"Who did this to her?" Marjan asks Jawad, but the boy only shrugs. She needs to know who to blame because a voice in her head screams that this is all her fault. If it weren't for Marjan, Soraya wouldn't have become a soldier. She curses herself.

"Your khala loved you deeply," she says. "Somebody hurt her and—"

"Jawad, go and fetch some water so I can make another pot of tea," comes a voice from behind Marjan. Marjan spins around and sees a woman in a black dress has emerged from the house. She takes two steps toward Marjan. She looks familiar, and Marjan wonders if she has met her before. Or maybe she saw her when Soraya showed her photos from family gatherings on her phone.

Marjan wipes her tears with the back of her hand.

"You have questions no one wants to answer," the woman says to her. "But I believe Soraya would want you to know the truth. Allah took Soraya's father too early and left her only with brothers who could not stand up for her."

"Who did this?" Marjan asks.

The woman closes her eyes for a moment, then quietly reveals the truth.

"Soraya's cousin could not make it through high school. He envied her paychecks. Her self-reliance. Her bravery. He claimed she had brought shame to the entire family. Yesterday, he came to this home unannounced. Her brothers were not here and her mother was powerless against him."

Marjan has heard of this cousin. Soraya had dismissed him as a nuisance, a closed-minded idiot of unremarkable consequence, because, after all, didn't every family have one or two? But the arrival of the Taliban had spun the city, the country, into a frenzy. While most were seeking cover, there were others who saw in the stark white flag a reclaimed homeland, a symbol of vindication.

"Soraya actually pitied him," Marjan laments. "She said losing his mother so young scarred him."

The woman sighs.

"Soraya was generous," she says, then turns her attention to Hawa. "What a terrible sight you've seen. I think I've heard about you. You're a musician, aren't you?"

Tears run freely down Hawa's cheeks. She nods at the woman.

"The rubab is a wise choice," she says solemnly. "It gets to the very soul of the listener."

"Soraya was going to achieve so much. And not just for herself. She is my very best friend in the world. My only friend! And there will be no justice for her," Marjan says angrily, speaking of Soraya as both here and gone because she is in disbelief still.

The woman considers this. Even if Soraya's mother or brothers were to call the police to report this murder, who would appear? The Taliban would likely reward his vigilantism. An eager foot soldier will always find an army to take him in.

"Not anytime soon. But one day, maybe," she says, which is as close as she can come to the truth. She adjusts her headscarf and prepares to return to the house. "May God be with you."

Hawa's ears perk at the familiar timbre of the voice, at the unique sign-off she would overhear when her mother tuned into the program.

May God be with you all and, inshallah, may I come to you tomorrow as the bearer of brighter news.

"You are the one from the television," Hawa says. "You report the news."

Marjan stares at the familiar face and suddenly understands she's been speaking to Mina Noori, Soraya's aunt. She is without her usual makeup, and there are dark circles under her eyes.

"Forgive me," Marjan begs. "Soraya loved and admired you so. So many of us do."

Mina looks away and inhales deeply, maintains her composure.

"Do you have a safe place to be with your daughter?" Mina asks. "They are searching homes and looking for certain people with particular interest."

"They already searched our home," Hawa says, then looks to her mother as if to ask if she's said too much.

But Marjan does not chide her daughter. She trusts Mina. It's as if Soraya is standing between them, joining their hands together.

"There are flights for only a day or two more, if we're to believe what we're told," Mina adds.

"Yes, there is not much time," Marjan affirms. "What about you. Will you try to leave?"

Mina sighs. "My heart tells me to stay. I don't want to abandon my work, my family, my homeland."

"And your head? What does your head tell you?"

Mina huffs, shakes her head. "My head tells me I cannot stop rain from falling."

Marjan pulls her phone out of her pocket. She asks Mina for her number, just in case. Mina reads it to her, watching to make sure Marjan records the digits correctly. Then she watches the mother and daughter slip out of the gate, leaving her to rejoin the hushed mourners, the circle of women with hands cupped in prayer, watching Soraya's mother moan and rock and sway as if she is again a young mother lulling her precious daughter to sleep.

50

2014

Every sound grated on Marjan's nerves. The whistle of the tea kettle. Slippered footsteps across the tile floor. Zargul clearing her throat. The blurred bleating of car horns.

But even worse than the noise was the quiet. When she was alone in her room, contained by the four walls, she could almost hear herself coming apart at the seams. She silenced her phone's ringer, which Soraya did not appreciate.

I need to know you're okay, she'd insisted in a text message.

I'm fine. I just don't feel like talking, Marjan had replied.

Pretending that nothing was awry during the day drained her. She scrubbed, wiped, sliced, scoured, soaked, chopped, swept, and more without thinking, her limbs moving out of habit, her body accepting of the strain. Almost grateful for it. It made sense to hurt.

Khanum Zargul and Agha Rasuli hardly paid attention to her, but Leeda seemed to notice something was different about Marjan. While Marjan fed her a bottle, her small hands batted at Marjan's face. She watched Marjan even as her small mouth worked the nipple and drained the formula from her bottle. Marjan stroked her forehead, brushed the silky, chestnut hairs to the side, and tried to imagine what she would look like in a few years, what kind of girl she would be. Had Marjan's mother once held her like this? Had she wondered what the future held in store for her daughter?

Maybe she had always known. Maybe that was why she'd reached for the opium.

Marjan's pain was acute and angry. Steel wool grinding at the cavity in her chest. If she could have reached for something to numb it, she would have.

It was the light of the phone that alerted her to the call. Marjan saw his name on the screen. He had texted her three times already. He wanted to talk. This was his third call.

She answered the call but didn't say a word.

"Hello? Marjan? Marjan, are you there?"

"What do you want?"

"Oh, there you are," he said wistfully. Sweetly. "Marjan, oh, I've been thinking about you all day."

"What do you want?" she repeated, her voice flat.

"To talk to you. To hear your voice. Marjan, for so long you've been the first person I reach out to every day, in the morning, when I get back from the restaurant . . . and to not speak at all now, that feels like cruelty. Doesn't it feel that way to you?"

"Cruelty?" Marjan echoed. Saboor was buoyed by this response.

"Yes, cruelty! I don't want to let go of you," he continued. Marjan closed her eyes, hating that she'd been hoping he would say this, hoping she could continue to feel wanted, yearned for.

"But you did," she said.

"I'm not ready to give up, Marjan. I think it may just take some time. My family will come around. And in the meantime, there's no reason we should deprive ourselves of conversations, of precious time together," he said. "All the great love stories are stories of patience and persistence, Marjan. Layla and Majnoon. Romeo and Juliet. Yusuf and Zulaikha. You've heard of them, haven't you?"

"Yes, but—"

"Meet me in the park tomorrow night, my love. Let's discuss this in person. I'll be waiting for you at seven. Until then, sweet dreams."

Marjan hung up the phone without responding to his invitation. His voice, deep and soothing, lingered in her ear, as it always did after they spoke. He was right. Every great love story required a struggle. She thought of Elizabeth and Mr. Darcy. Was she being too hasty?

Marjan didn't want to think about it anymore. She tapped on an app for videos and clicked on a song. The first one that came up was a pop song; a young man in a white suit wearing sunglasses nodded his head as strobe lights pulsed around him. Marjan thumbed through the videos and landed on something slower, a ballad.

My lips on your soft lips . . .

She could not stomach the lyrics.

Marjan flipped to a streaming news channel.

The Afghan National Army is recruiting women for a unique and newly created military position. Recruits must meet requirements but no experience is necessary. Training will be rigorous. The service to our country will be rewarding. Those interested can contact—

Marjan turned the phone off. This could mean only that there was no end in sight to the fight for the country. She laid her head down and closed her eyes. There had to be someplace between war and love, somewhere a woman scorned could close her eyes and rest her head.

The next morning, Marjan rose for her duties. Now more than ever, she needed this salary. If she worked hard enough, she might eventually be able to rent a place for herself and Hawa. She entered the Rasuli home and saw that the entertaining room was again a mess of dirty teacups, glasses, and plates. There were empty cans of triple-caffeinated beverages, oversize lettering on red aluminum. Before she could get started in the kitchen, Zargul handed her a list of groceries and a few bills and sent her to the market. Marjan went from shop to shop, gathering the meat and vegetables, the bread and the specific brand of chips that Zargul craved in the afternoon.

She returned to the house, arms heavy with bags, and unloaded the purchases onto the kitchen counter. Marjan was to prepare rice and beef stew with potatoes. She checked on Leeda first and, finding her asleep in Zargul's arms, returned to the kitchen and started to chop two onions.

Tears sprang from her eyes, and she wiped them away with the sleeve of her dress.

As she chopped, she wondered if she should consider meeting Saboor in the park at seven. He had painted so vivid a picture of their future together that she could see it too, like they'd watched it sitting side by side in a movie theater. Maybe talking face-to-face would help her decide what to do.

Her eyes burning and her hands shaky, she decided to leave the onions and gather the used dishes from the room downstairs.

"Marjan!"

At the sound of Zargul's shrill voice, Marjan's arms jerked and two teacups fell from the tray she was carrying up the stairs. She shouldn't have been so easily startled, but she hadn't gotten much sleep the last few days.

"Why did you do that?" Zargul demanded from the top of the stairs.

"Sorry, when you shouted—"

"I didn't shout. I was calling your name only to ask if you'd heated up Leeda's evening bottle," Zargul replied, her hands on her hips as if she were a threatened bird puffing its feathers.

"I'm sorry. The milk is on the counter," Marjan replied. "I'll get the broom."

"The broom won't get it all. You've just created more work," Zargul made sure to mutter loud enough for Marjan to hear her.

Marjan stepped gingerly around the shards of glass, careful not to let the two surviving cups roll off the tray as well. She was grateful to make it to the kitchen without slicing her foot open. With the broom and dustpan in hand, she returned to the scene of her crime and began to sweep up the debris. Because she'd been so close to the top, there was glass on almost every step. When she'd swept everything up, she returned with a wet rag to pick up the glass dust left behind. If Zargul felt so much as a grain of sand under her foot, she would hear about it.

Agha Rasuli walked through the door to find her crouched at the bottom step. She stood quickly and straightened her headscarf.

"Salaam, good evening. Let me get out of your way," she said, certain Zargul was waiting upstairs to report the broken cups to him. Because he'd hired Marjan, every one of her mistakes was weaponized by his wife. Sometimes there was so much friction between the couple; it was a wonder the house hadn't yet caught fire.

Marjan realized Agha Rasuli wasn't stepping past her to go up the stairs, nor had he said anything yet.

"I didn't expect something like this from you," Agha Rasuli said. "But clearly I should have."

Of course, she thought. Zargul must have texted him already.

"I'm sorry. I'll be more careful next time," she said.

"Next time? Who else do you have your eyes on?" he asked, stunned by her response.

Marjan's insides knotted up.

"I should have worried about having guests over in your presence. How did you even . . . You must have gone to great lengths to get his attention!"

Please, no. Saboor wouldn't have told Agha Rasuli about their relationship, would he?

"How long was this going on? Not that it even matters. Were you trying to turn my house into some kind of . . . some kind of . . . brothel? How many of my guests did you entertain?"

Marjan struggled to breathe.

"Agha Rasuli, please. I've done nothing of the sort. I would never," she swore, her voice quavering.

"I felt pity for you. That nurse made it seem like you were some noble person, practically a hero or something. What noble woman throws herself at strange men?"

"I swear to God I did not—"

"And with my wife and infant daughter in this home! Are you trying to ruin all our names?"

Agha Rasuli's accusations grew loud enough to summon Zargul.

"What's going on here?" she demanded. "I've just gotten Leeda to sleep and we've had enough chaos here today."

"What chaos?" Agha Rasuli demanded.

"She broke teacups on the stairs. Careful where you step," she said sharply. "What are you yelling about anyway?"

Marjan took short, deliberate breaths. She needed to speak clearly, and she needed them to believe her.

"After all we've done for her, it turns out this woman has been having relations with some of my guests. I'm trying to build a business and she's flirting and doing God knows what else to ruin our good name!"

"My God," Zargul cried. Her hand flew to her mouth. "How did you find out?"

"Please. This is not true!" Marjan's protest went unnoticed. Her fingers tingled with nervous energy.

"One of my friends asked me if I knew about Marjan and Saboor. Apparently, she's been having some kind of affair with him. Can you imagine that?"

Some kind of affair.

The lights flickered.

"It was not like that. He wanted to marry me and I had agreed to marry him. We were supposed to be married Friday."

"So you're marrying him?" Zargul asked incredulously. She would have sounded less shocked if Marjan had announced she'd been hiding a third leg. Marjan balled her hands into tight fists as she tried to hold on to herself.

"No. No, that's not what's happened," she said, her voice steeled.

"Are you pregnant?" Zargul asked.

"No! It was nothing like that!" Marjan cried.

"This is so shameful," Zargul declared. She turned her attention to her husband then. "I told you this wasn't a good idea but you insisted."

"Don't you dare blame me for her actions. I brought her to help you, since you're too spoiled to live without help," Agha Rasuli shouted at her. "God, do women know how to ruin a man!"

Zargul gasped at this accusation. She blinked rapidly, her eyes wide.

"I can't believe you would say such a thing to the mother of your child.

We're talking about what she's done to our household right now. I can't have people thinking this is the kind of home we have."

"We gave you shelter, food, and on top of all of that, we even gave you a salary," he said to Marjan. "This is how you repay our charity? You need to leave."

"It was not charity. I worked for that salary."

"Yes, yes. You did all kinds of work here, didn't you? Marjan, we won't have you here another moment. Get your things and leave."

"I did nothing wrong. I did all the work you asked of me and then some. I cared for your daughter as if she were my own."

Zargul scoffed at this.

"Your own? She's lucky she's not your daughter. And your daughter is lucky she's at the orphanage," she said. Every word was a blade. The lights flickered again, the circuit overloaded somewhere behind the painted walls.

"I pray your daughter never knows how cruel her parents are," Marjan fired back.

Agha Rasuli was suddenly inches from her face, close enough that she could smell the liquor on his breath and see the flecks of gray in his stubble.

"Get out!" he roared, pointing at the door. Marjan wanted nothing more than to oblige. She walked underneath his raised arm and slammed the door on her way out.

"Why did the lights go out? Did she do that?" Zargul yelled at her husband on the other side of the door.

Marjan went to gather her belongings. She shoved her clothing back into the bags her roommates had brought to her in the hospital. The entirety of her life fit into two bags, and this was fine because she could not carry any more.

Stepping into the night with a bag on each arm, she understood just how precarious her situation was. She walked to the park, the path familiar at every turn, and still she felt unsure of each step. As if the city might have rearranged itself. As if the streets and buildings were conspiring to disorient her.

She stood across the street from the corner of the park. People walked around her on the sidewalk, men mostly. The smell of kebabs smoking on a charcoal grill competed with the bitter exhaust of a generator. Storefronts glowed with pink or green lights. Headlights of passing cars took turns illuminating the modest curbside trees. The city was alive.

She recognized the shape of him, standing beneath a pine tree. His eyes on his phone.

Marjan took two steps into the street. She considered turning around. She took one more step toward Saboor, when a hatchback came around the bend and nearly clipped her.

She stumbled backward, caught her breath.

"Hey, what's wrong with you? Watch where you're going!" someone shouted.

Where was she going? There was no floating haven between love and war for her. It was time to choose a side.

Marjan crossed the street.

His face melted into a smile, boyish and sweet, at the sight of her. She couldn't remember anyone ever looking at her in that way. She hadn't thought it possible.

"And then she appeared," he said, and Marjan let out a soft whimper. He reached for her hand, his eyes going soft with concern when she did not take his.

"Janem, you're upset. Tell me what's happened. Talk to me," he coaxed.

She had fallen for him, stumbled headfirst, and in the tumble she'd lost her direction.

"They fired me. And kicked me out of the home. All because of you!"

She was close enough to feel his body heat, to remember the tingle she felt when he caressed her face.

"What spiteful people! Let me think," Saboor said. "My love, I have some money. We can find a room for you somewhere. You are bright and hardworking. You'll be back on your feet in no time."

He took her hand. Marjan needed to be held.

"They accused me of . . . of . . ." Marjan couldn't bring herself to repeat the accusations.

"Remember, fate has always tested the patience of the most lovestruck hearts," he whispered.

A gust of wind tumbled down the Hindu Kush, swept into the valley, and brushed against Marjan's cheek like an ancestral whisper.

Saboor was a man who believed himself a poet, but the poems he'd shown her had been years old. He was adamantly against sharing his work with others, so he'd never published a thing. And when Saboor's family called her a used and polluted woman, he'd made pitiful excuses for them. How would they treat Hawa, if they spoke of her in such a way? Saboor wasn't simply private, or a dreamer. He was afraid. Saboor had not an ounce of fight in him and love demanded great courage.

"Marjan, we can figure this out," he said. "Marjan!"

But Marjan was already gone.

51

AUGUST 29, 2021

METRA MEDIA

Mina shuffles the papers in front of her while she waits for the cameraman to show up. She checks her phone again. He is late even by his lax standards. It will be just the two of them today. He probably knows this. The producer must have messaged him as well.

She clicks on her messaging app and sees the missive her producer sent her last night.

Forgive me but I cannot bear the thought of my wife and children paying a price for my work. If I am killed or imprisoned, what will become of my family? I beg you, look after yourself. They will not take lightly that you broadcast your criticism of them. I say this with deep respect.

She wonders how far he has made it by now. Perhaps they are in Mazar already. Mina can hardly blame him for fleeing. On the contrary, she's glad for him. She will feel relief when her phone pings with an update that he and his family are out of the country and tells him as much in her reply.

But where does that leave her? She did not burden him with this question. Nor did she tell him that last night, when she received his message, she'd been sitting on the small bench by her door, her shoes in her hand. She'd been staring at the cemetery dirt caked onto the soles.

She wishes that the sound of Soraya's laughter weren't so clear in her ears. Then again, maybe if she'd been around the family more, she would have realized just how dangerous that hotheaded boy had gotten. Maybe she could have saved Soraya somehow.

A new message pings.

I'm sorry I'm not there. I've been thinking. Let's not record a program today, the cameraman writes. *It's not safe. It's especially not safe for you.*

Mina puts her phone facedown and rubs her eyes, still puffy and pink. Of course it's not safe. She didn't choose to become a journalist for safety. They could each name a handful of media figures they knew personally who had been killed in the past ten years. But journalism had summoned Mina as clearly as the azaan that reverberated through the streets five times a day. Truth telling was her calling; it stirred her from her repose.

A small voice sings for her the song lyrics that once resonated so deeply within her spirit. It is Ahmad Zahir's voice, the crooner of the seventies who left a nation lovesick and swaying. A half century later, still no singer is as beloved as he.

Life is an onward march to an end
Spend not this vanishing moment enslaved
For a life that is lived in shackles
Is a life that is lived in vain

Like Mina, Soraya had lived by this verse and look where it got her. The last lines repeat in Mina's head, a broken record.

For a life that is lived in shackles is a life that is lived in vain.

Those lines alone are a complete ballad.

Mina pulls a splinter from her finger. The wooden coffin she purchased for Soraya hadn't been easy to find. The coffin makers were swamped with demands after the airport bombing, but a year ago she had interviewed two brothers, Qadir and Kareem, who had stumbled onto the fact that coffin making was a solid livelihood. Their craftsmanship was simple, for these were not luxury purchases. Many people followed tradition and buried their dead wearing only a shroud. But victims of detonated IEDs or suicide bombers were reduced to pieces. Families claimed whatever body parts they could identify. Other bodies were too charred or deformed to look at. Those families wanted coffins. The younger brother, Kareem, was more sensitive than his older sibling. He always had been. When a request for a child-size coffin came in, Kareem would get to work without telling his brother. Alone, he would cut the short planks that would house a truncated life. It was Kareem who answered the phone when Mina called; Kareem who heard the grief in her voice and toiled late into the night to make Soraya's coffin.

Mina clears her throat, mostly because the room has been too silent for too long. She tries to reread the script she has written for herself, about the new disaster that has rocked Kabul.

Americans carried out a deadly drone attack today, killing ten members of a family in their home. While the American military claims this was a "righteous" kill, information we have received locally differs. Relatives of the victims tell us that Zemari Ahmadi, the target, worked for a U.S.-based humanitarian organization that provided nutrition and education to those in need. What were thought to be jugs of explosive materials were, in fact, containers of water. Relatives relayed that several of the family members worked for international organizations and some even had visas to travel to the United States. Seven children were killed, the youngest a two-year-old girl named Sumaya and a two-year-old boy, Ayat. The others include Faisal, age sixteen; Farzad, ten; Malika, six; Arwin, seven; and Benyamen, six.

No one ever wants to read the names of dead children, but to Mina it is of the utmost importance. She wishes she could sit the American generals down, make them stare at pictures of these precious faces, and read these names to them until their ears bleed. *Sumaya. Ayat. Faisal. Farzad. Malika. Arwin. Benyamen.*

She turns the paper over and huffs. Who will say Soraya's name?

She has gone over this a thousand times. It may not have been the Taliban who killed Soraya, but it is their new presence, their looming authority, that emboldened Soraya's cousin. The Taliban will likely clap her murderer on the back, grateful. How many more women will be killed with impunity going forward?

Mina also knows that speaking about Soraya publicly will only bring more attention to her mother and brothers, brothers who only now regret that they hadn't pushed back harder against their cousin's vitriol. If their family's shame were to become public, Soraya's mother would suffer a stroke, and Mina doesn't want to be responsible for that. But the real reason Mina won't talk publicly about Soraya's murder is because she can already imagine the way her niece's name will be desecrated online. Salacious lies will be told to turn her into the villain and her killer into a hero.

So Mina buries the story, just as they buried Soraya's body. The omission makes her complicit. Diminishes her as a journalist, as an aunt, as a woman. She shoves the papers off the desk, discards everything she'd been planning on reporting to her viewers. They drift to the floor like autumn leaves. Silent. Weightless. Inconsequential. Mina releases a wail from the depths of her soul.

52

2014

"What did you decide to tell your mother?" Marjan asked. The bus driver swerved to avoid something in the road, and Marjan, holding on to a pole, nearly lost her balance.

"Nothing just yet. She thinks I'm going to my regular job," Soraya said. "But if this works out, I have a plan on how to break the news to her. I'm going to first tell her that I'm becoming a taxi driver. Then I'll tell her I'm going to try out for the men's cricket team. And finally, I'll tell her I'm auditioning for a part in a Bollywood movie. She'll be so horrified that she'll be relieved to hear I've enlisted in the army."

Marjan hid a smile. She could hardly believe she'd signed up for this. The advertisement hadn't provided much description of the role other than to say the military was looking for women to be part of a special unit. Marjan had never held a firearm. When she imagined herself holding one, she was surprised at the rush she felt. Her shoulders pulled back instinctively. She and Soraya were on their way to Camp Scorpion for a weeklong selection process.

"Why do you insist on torturing your mother?"

"It keeps her mind off her arthritis. I'm such a thoughtful daughter."

"Putting your brothers to shame," Marjan adds.

Eyes followed them as they got off the bus. Whispers as people wondered what two women were doing at a military stop.

They stepped off the bus and stood on the side of the road for a moment.

“So, we’re really going to do this?” Soraya asked, her confidence dimmed now that they were standing outside the training camp. But Marjan wasn’t having second thoughts.

“I have this feeling . . . I don’t know how to describe it . . .”

“Indigestion? That was a lot of green onions on your lunch.”

“Not indigestion. I feel like . . . like maybe this is where I’m meant to be. And I can’t remember the last time I felt this way.”

“Well, maybe thank Saboor. We wouldn’t be here without that cowardly poet,” Soraya says with a shrug.

Marjan, with Soraya’s help, had managed to rent a room in the cheapest hotel they could find for a few days. She found a job in another restaurant, offering to work as much as they needed and more. She cleaned the owner’s home when she wasn’t at the restaurant. She found a room, nothing more than four walls and a door, that cost less than the hotel. It didn’t matter.

I’ll have to fight for myself, Marjan had realized. Maybe going to battle for oneself was a great love story too. She remembered the advertisement she’d heard about women soldiers. She had nothing to lose. There was no way she could work and care for Hawa with these temporary jobs that offered her a fraction of what she needed to survive. She needed a reliable way to support herself and provide for her daughter. And perhaps she could do a small part to make this country safer for Hawa.

Marjan had been fighting almost all her life. At least she’d finally get paid for it.

Marjan didn’t ask Soraya to join her in interviewing for the military position. But Soraya had been frustrated by the utterly unexciting job she had, the constant pressure to be a good girl and get married. She’d been intrigued by the advertisement Marjan had described.

I would wear a uniform and carry a gun? I’m in, Soraya said, already delighting at the vision of herself wearing camouflage.

The Ministry of Defense’s television advertisement hadn’t really prepared them for the selection or training process. They had understood there would be travel and physical activity involved, tests to pass. But it was impossible to understand what that looked or felt like.

Step one was proving to the Ministry of the Interior that they had their family's permission to apply. Soraya had taken her younger brother with her to the ministry's office so that he could sign a form. He'd grumbled about it but finally agreed when she'd threatened to stop washing his clothes and cooking for him. Marjan, as a widow, had been allowed to grant herself permission. Anyone thought to have connections to insurgents, who might be trying to infiltrate the platoon for nefarious reasons, was removed from the process.

They sat at desks and circled answers on a bizarre test of shapes and logic to confirm that they met the intelligence requirements. Then came the questions Marjan really hadn't anticipated. *Can you maintain a cover story? Do you cry often? Have you ever tried to harm yourself? Do you have any repeated, disturbing dreams of past stressful events?*

Marjan had all the wrong answers. But she kept those to herself and gave them the answers they wanted to hear.

Their heights and weights were recorded. A doctor listened to their heartbeats and asked about their medical histories. They urinated into cups. They were introduced to burpees and ordered to do pushups. They trekked twenty kilometers over rough terrain, carrying a full load of gear to prove they had the physical strength to undergo the next phase—basic training.

There was no time to celebrate passing any of these tests. They woke early and started with weapons training, loading and cleaning weapons, learning the proper positions from which to fire a gun. From eight to nine o'clock in the morning, they ran a rigorous course around the base. From ten to noon, they underwent more skills and endurance training. They would pick up weapons from large, numbered metal containers with rusted hinges then ride tan jeeps to the practice area where they would shoot from crouched and standing positions. Weekly hikes across mountainous terrain carrying thirty-five pounds of gear in blazing heat. Climbing, hiking, fast roping, securing a building for entry. Lunch was a time to recharge, fill their stomachs. There was more physical and tactical training in the afternoons, sessions diagramming their roles in the missions ahead and learning why they were needed for missions in the first place. And if they stumbled in their training, Elaha would have them run holding their rifles over their heads.

The Americans had realized that their soldiers entering villages faced barriers. They couldn't talk to Afghan women, which meant they were gathering only half the intel they could be, establishing half the relationships. That was how the Cultural Support Team came to be, a small and exclusive unit of extraordinarily capable women soldiers who would support the military's special operations combat forces. Jenna, Krista, and the others could engage Afghan women without crossing cultural redlines. They could go where men couldn't to build rapport and ask questions.

But there were still language and cultural barriers, and so they needed an Afghan counterpart to the CST. The Afghan military leaders began recruiting for the Female Tactical Platoon, a combat unit of specially trained women who would work alongside the Americans to conduct night missions, gather intel on local insurgent activity, and track down targets. They learned what to look for in a search—guns, munitions, passports, SIM cards, memory drives, ID cards.

Marjan and Soraya were the latest additions to the FTP.

Most of the women stayed on the base four days out of the week. Some came and went, which was fine by the higher-ups so long as they were on time. Tardiness was not tolerated. Marjan nervously asked their commander, Elaha, for permission to stay on the base without home breaks. She explained that her relatives were in the provinces, that her daughter was in an orphanage, and that she could not afford to rent a room for herself just yet.

Elaha managed to get her approval to stay on the base.

"Use your time wisely," she advised, and Marjan promised that she would. Every day she jogged, lifted weights, and, after a couple of weeks of leg-flailing exertions, she managed to do a pull-up. She woke up stiff and sore, but it wasn't pain that she felt. It was a satisfying ache, an awakening of her body, and a realization that she was capable of far more than she'd ever known. She felt new tightness in her arms and legs, a solidity of her form even when she was going from sitting to standing and a vigor in her steps that was entirely new.

She didn't spend all her time in the gym, though. She ventured into the city to browse at a bookstore she'd discovered, to flip through the pages of books she couldn't afford. She recognized faces and names and covers, realized how much she had absorbed while she sat in Parliament, even in her precarious state. There were books about world leaders: Barack Obama, Saddam Hussein, Hillary Clinton. There were books on English grammar and Afghan history and guides to help pass tests Marjan had never heard of. There was a book about a girl named Malala, a Pakistani girl who had been shot in the face by the Taliban simply because she wanted to go to school.

Back at the base, Marjan sometimes picked up her worn copy of *Pride and Prejudice*, but she was too restless to get through more than a few pages at a time. The language could be exhausting and required so much attention. But there were also concise, powerful sentences, and those Marjan underlined with a blue pen. *The distance is nothing when one has a motive.* Her English was improving at a rapid clip, thanks to all the time they were spending with their American counterparts.

Marjan was gearing up for her first mission two months later.

By this time, her initial impressions of the American women had evolved. They'd struck her, at first, as intimidating. Friendly but rigid. Before Marjan and Soraya threw themselves into training, they wondered if these American women were built of some other substance. They were rugged and strong, both physically and in the way they spoke. As they spent more time together, Marjan came to know them as individuals, to understand that they had hard stories too.

Krista, because of her mother's drug addiction, had been raised by her grandparents. Jenna came from a military family and was eager to prove she was just as capable as her brothers. In fact, all the women were working hard to prove themselves, Marjan realized. Over two hundred women had applied to become CSTs. Only half were invited to make it through one hundred hours of hell, tests of their physical and mental endurance. And only twenty were selected to join an elite team from the military's top-tier combat regiments.

You think our guys want us here? Jenna had said during a training hike. *Not at all. We work as hard as we do because we don't want to give them the smallest reason to kick us out. If the mission fails, they'll be so quick to blame us.*

People ask my husband why he allowed *me to sign up for this,* Georgia added, overhearing their conversation.

Ha! People asked my hubs the same, Krista shouted.

It struck Marjan that Americans talked so much about women's equality because they were still trying to figure it out themselves.

Before their first mission, Jenna reviewed with them the plan for that night. They would be dropping into a village to locate a high-value asset, a man thought to have information on where the local Taliban group was engineering improvised explosive devices, IEDs, that would be used against them.

"First-mission nerves can be bad," Jenna warned. "Remember your training and take a deep breath before you grab that rope. You're ready."

Soraya had shown up, as she always did, wearing her signature shade on her lips and a blur of sable across her eyelids.

"Can I ask a question?" she asked Krista. They had paired off for some training exercises and had had plenty of long talks, but still Soraya seemed nervous to ask.

"Yeah, what's up?" Krista asked.

"Is it true that one American woman . . . on a mission . . . she is killed? Is this true?"

Krista nodded.

"Her name was Ashley," she said. And she told them the story of a CST she never had the chance to know. Ashley had signed up to serve God, family, and country, something that made sense to the Afghan women listening intently to her story. She was just over five feet tall. Her grit and spirit earned her nicknames and instilled confidence in her team. But Ashley's strength was no match for the daisy chain of IEDs she stepped on when a mission took her unit to a booby-trapped compound.

The room grew still. They could see it in their minds, the devastation caused by one wrong step. Jenna bent over in her chair and retied her boot.

"Just remember your training," she said. "Look out for each other and never let your guard down."

The hour arrived. The helicopter blades cut through the silent night, whipped the air into a frenzy that mirrored Marjan's nerves. She looked over at Jenna, who steadied her with a nod.

You've got this, she could almost hear Jenna say, in that peculiar, abbreviated way the Americans communicated.

They descended into a village, approached the isolated home the Americans had identified as the target, and woke its sleeping inhabitants. Men, women, and children stepped out of their house, bewildered. A little girl rubbed her eyes, as if she might be dreaming the soldiers standing before her.

They kept the women and children in one area, promised them no male soldiers would be approaching them. Krista took off her helmet and wrapped a scarf around her head. The American women had taken to doing this so they would look less like soldiers.

"Line up here. We're going to be doing a search and then I'm going to ask you a few questions," Marjan said. An elderly woman spat on the ground near Marjan's feet.

Jenna signaled for Marjan to follow her. They went around to the side of the home, a secondary structure surrounded by signs of rural life. Chickens clucked with alarm at their approach. Troughs made of clay held hay for animal feeding. The musky smell of animal hides and waste intensified. A small goat brayed. Jenna tapped on the door and instructed anyone inside to come out. Marjan identified herself as military, repeated the instructions.

A moment later, the door slowly started to swing open. Marjan wished her night-vision goggles could help her see through the door. She tightened the grip on her weapon, recalled her training.

You need to be able to go from calm to kill in a flash.

She raised her weapon, aimed it at the widening gap as the door opened.

It was a woman, wisps of tangled hair peeking out from under her headscarf. Her clothes had taken up the pungent scent of the animals. She raised her downcast eyes and looked from Jenna to Marjan, then past them.

"What are you doing in there at this time of night?" Marjan asked her.

She did not respond.

"We're not here to harm you. But to keep us all safe, we're going to search you," Marjan said. "Do you have any weapons on or around you?"

The woman shook her head.

"Is there anyone else in there?"

She shook her head again. Marjan patted her down through her clothing, felt the truth of how thin the woman was, how dangerously close she stood to not existing.

"Why were you in there?" she asked again.

"That is where they tell me to stay," she said with a resignation that made Marjan think of her dead sister, Parwin. She recognized in this woman a life she had narrowly escaped.

Jenna looked at Marjan expectantly. She translated the situation.

"Shit," Jenna muttered. "Bring her around to join the others."

Marjan led her around to the home, where five women and six children had been gathered, some standing, some sitting. The woman from the barn kept her distance until one of the women, a middle-aged mother with a red scarf, motioned for her to come closer. She whispered in her ear, and the woman nodded. Two little children wrinkled their noses at the stench on her clothes.

The women and the premises were searched. Marjan put her training to good use, engaging each woman with tactical questions meant to slyly uncover identities and relationships, activities and alliances. The woman from the barn was the second wife to one of the men being questioned by their male counterparts on the other side of the house.

"Why was she with the animals?" she asked the other women.

"She has problems," one of the women said, pointing vaguely to her head. "Sometimes her husband loses his patience with her."

Marjan recalled how she had been treated by her husband's other wives, by his cruel mother. The memories turned her palms clammy. She owed her survival, in some part, to Jameela, the one wife who had showed her kindness. The one who had quietly taught her to avoid the matriarch's ire, helped her care for her newborn son, and made her feel less alone. Without Jameela, Marjan might have found herself sleeping among the livestock.

Communications came in from the other team. They had found their target and would take him in.

"Time for us to roll," Jenna said.

"What about . . ." Marjan started to ask but stopped. She knew nothing could be done about the woman made to sleep among the animals. Saving her wasn't part of the mission.

Soraya signaled to the women that they could return to their home. The elder woman, the one who had spat on the ground, was about to disappear through the doorway when Marjan put a hand on her shoulder.

"No woman deserves to be treated like an animal," Marjan said.

"Who are you to say . . ." she snapped, but Marjan closed the gap and thrust her gun between them. She saw her mother-in-law in this woman's eyes, and it unleashed something feral in her.

"If I come back here and find she's still being mistreated," Marjan warned in a harsh whisper, "you will pay."

"Psh," the old woman scoffed. "I doubt you idiots could find your way back here."

"The distance is nothing when one has a motive," she recited, and she saw the elder woman's brow furrow, the lines on her face deepen. Marjan smiled sweetly, then turned her back and retreated into the dark.

53

AUGUST 29, 2021

Oh my God, Jenna writes. *Are you sure? Did you confirm this?*

If Marjan hadn't seen Soraya's lifeless body, she would have doubted the news as well. She has spent the last couple of hours trying not to think of Soraya's final breaths, the fight she surely put up.

Yes, I saw her. She is gone, Marjan confirms. She and Hawa are standing just around the corner from a main road. She needs to regroup before they head to the airport for one more try.

Her cousin? WTF, Jenna says.

She was such a warrior. I'm so sorry, Krista writes.

Marjan sighs at this strange turn of phrase, this mixing of guilt and sympathy. It is fitting for her. She is sorry. She is so sorry. Fatigue is wearing her down. She is living in exile in her own homeland, a homeland for which she has risked her life.

She tells the group chat that she is heading to the airport now and asks if there are any instructions for which gate she should get to. Hawa watches the exchange of messages over her shoulder.

We need you to catch the attention of the marines at the gate. What color is your headscarf?

It is blue with gray stripes.

Do you have something brighter? Something that will stand out?

Marjan wants to scream. She has been doing all she can to avoid standing out. Why must she be all things at once? Invisible and obvious. Strong and gentle. Brave and cautious. Mother and father. She leans her head back against the concrete wall.

"Madar?" Hawa's voice is shaky. "Why did Khala Soraya's cousin kill her?"

Marjan is too depleted to be anything but truthful.

"Khala Soraya and I were part of a special military unit. We were soldiers. Her cousin did not like that she did this work. He accused her of shaming their family."

"But you always told me you were . . . You were soldiers? Real soldiers with guns?"

Marjan nods.

"And you were fighting the Taliban?" Hawa asks.

"Yes. That's why they're looking for us. We were responsible for sending many of them to prison. Now they want revenge."

In the end, the truth was so simple. So effortless.

"Have you ever killed anyone?" she asks.

Marjan hesitates. Hawa does not look away.

"I have not," she says. Hawa blinks quickly. Marjan had hoped that the day she finally revealed her story to her daughter, it would have been a careful excavation, not a crate tipped over, contents spilled.

"Is that the truth?" her daughter asks.

"I never needed to," Marjan replies honestly. But the truth buried in the truth is that she would have fired her weapon if she'd needed to; she would have taken a life to save her own, to save her sisters in uniform, to save her country.

"What about Khala Soraya?" she asks, unflinching.

"It was the same for her. Khala Soraya was a great soldier. We trained together and rode in helicopters and went on night missions. We worked with the American soldiers. That's why they're trying to help us get out now. But you mustn't say anything about this to anyone. Understand?"

Hawa nods.

"But you never told me about a helicopter. And all those nights you were gone."

Marjan can see Hawa trying to organize her questions. She presses her hands to her head and then turns to her mother with one question that must have risen above the others.

"Who is sending you those messages?"

"Those are American women. They are the soldiers we served with and they're trying to help."

"No," Hawa says. "Not the messages in English. The other messages, from someone who says you should save yourself and your daughter from him. Who is she talking about?"

Marjan's vision blurs. Her heart pounds in her chest. When did Hawa go looking through her messages? And why must she be confronted with this now? Here?

"She's a friend. She was just talking about the Taliban." Marjan has been consumed with thoughts of Shahla. Has she been punished for their secret communications? She can do nothing but pray.

"Which friend?" Hawa asks. "I've not heard you talking about another friend."

"You haven't met her. She's from a long time ago."

"How does she know you're in danger?"

Marjan is quiet for a moment. Hawa's life has been shaped by the story Marjan has told her, in the same way a body is shaped by the bones within it. What happens when those bones are broken and rearranged? Will Hawa come undone?

"I was given as a bride to a terrible man," she tells Hawa. "I told you that he died but that is not the truth. I ran away from him. And the person warning me is my sister. She is married to his cousin."

A Taliban police truck drives past them. Marjan turns her face away from them. They walk a couple of steps so that she can check the surroundings. She must remain vigilant.

"My father is alive?" Hawa asks, and her mother nods. One question gives way to ten more.

"Where is he? What does he know about me? What does he look like?"

Marjan hadn't imagined revealing to Hawa the truth about Abdul Khaliq on a street corner while he was lurking in the vicinity.

"He does not live in Kabul, but he is here," Marjan explains. She tells Hawa the briefest version of her encounter with Shahla. She tells her about Abdul Khaliq's alliances with the Taliban and the message from Shahla's son. Hawa's father surely knows about them now, is looking for them. She feels immense relief in unburdening herself of this secret, almost forgetting that Hawa is her child, not a confidante.

He was a terrible man, Hawa thinks, because she feels the familiar bloom of longing in the cavity of her chest. *But was he very, very terrible?*

Hawa senses she should not ask this question.

"I was so young. I was only thirteen when I was given to him, just a little older than you are now. And he was a grown man, a very powerful man who always got his way."

Hawa struggles to understand this. She is awfully close to thirteen and cannot imagine being given away to a man.

"I'm sorry I kept this all from you, but you were so young. I couldn't risk anyone finding out."

Her mother couldn't trust Hawa to keep her secrets. This strikes Hawa as almost funny, considering how many secrets she has kept from her mother. She never told her that she used to wet the bed at the orphanage, the shame she felt having to ball up the sheets before anyone could see. Pointless, of course. Her bare mattress told the whole story. She never told her mother about the girl who cut off a chunk of her hair. Khanum Atefa had to trim her hair short just to even it out. She'd never told her mother that she'd tried to endear herself to another girl's mother, a woman who came every week and showered her daughter with affection. True, Hawa squirmed out of Marjan's hugs but not because she hadn't wanted them. It felt good to see her mother's crestfallen expression, the hurt so plain on her face. It also felt terrible, and Hawa would cry after those visits, wishing for her mother to come back so that she could apologize and be held in her mother's embrace, a pearl tucked inside her steadfast shell.

But her mother knows none of this because Hawa is very, very good at keeping secrets.

"The airport is our only choice right now, Hawa, janem," she pleads, readying herself for her daughter's protests.

Hawa's eyes glisten.

"Okay, let's go," she tells her mother, watches her dry her tears with her sleeve and straighten her shoulders. Her mother reaches for her hand and Hawa gives it to her because she can see her mother needs it.

They turn the corner and join the bustle on the street. Uncertainty hangs in the hot Kabul air. A woman is trying to sell kitchen appliances to a skeptical restaurant owner. A fruit vendor counts the afghanis he has collected today and wonders if these bills will be worth more as kindling next week.

"Madar, wait!" Hawa says when they are halfway down the block. She points to a rack of fabrics hanging in a shop, a rectangle of space with its narrow walls covered in chadoris, long headscarves, and burqas. Toward the back of the store is a stack of brightly colored fabrics, each folded and contained in plastic sheaths. Marjan squeezes her daughter's soft hand. They take a step toward the store, take cover from the sun under its short awning.

"Agha, how much for one of those headscarves?" Marjan asks the shop owner, a bald man with a scruffy beard and generous belly.

The owner does a double take. There is a reason he has pushed those colorful scarves to the back of his little shop. It is the hijabs and burqas that are selling these days. Last month, he sold no more than five each day. Yesterday, he sold seventeen.

"These?" he asks, as if Marjan has made a mistake. "Sister, this will not cover much."

She points again to the back.

"That one," she repeats.

The store owner shrugs. He can't save everyone.

"Twelve hundred afghanis," he says.

"Twelve hundred?" she asks, incredulous. "That's three times what they usually cost!" But he insists it's a fair price and suggests she check any other store to see for herself.

Marjan checks her phone, then pulls her wallet out of her bag.

"Which color do you prefer?" he asks while she counts out the bills.

"Your least popular color," Marjan says. The man raises an eyebrow, takes a sip of tea from a paper cup, then pulls out an orange headscarf from the pile, and hands it to her unceremoniously. There is a woman behind her eyeing the hijabs. He can't afford to lose a customer.

Marjan and Hawa continue another hundred meters before they find an empty taxi. Will this be the last ride to the airport? This city is closing in on them.

Hawa has opened her bag on her lap. She touches the body of the tula, reassures herself of its presence. If she could, she would have packed music books and a rubab into her bag. Since she's dreaming of the impossible, why stop there? She would have packed the entire youth orchestra and her instructors, the founder of the music school and the brick building that witnessed her transformation from an orphan into a musician. She would have built an ark so she could save them all from this flood.

But she is just a girl with two hands and salt water lapping at her knees.

54

2016

The American women and Afghan women spent downtime together, learning about each other through observations and questions and discussing their latest crushes. Everyone, it seemed, was in love with someone or something. An impromptu henna party, Elaha's idea, had been an entire education. Zarifa had a tube of muddy paste and was making intricate patterns on the backs of the hands of her fellow soldiers. Jenna took a sniff of the paste and raised an eyebrow.

"And this stuff is good for hair too?" she asked.

Zarifa nodded.

"They do it on the boardwalk in Ocean City too," Misty added. She and her four younger siblings were raised by their grandmother. She doesn't talk about her mother or father at all, Marjan noted early on.

"Christmas came early, ladies. Look what I got!" Krista sang out as she entered the room. In her hands was an olive-colored funnel, flat in shape and with a very long stem.

"What is that?" Soraya asked.

"A genius invention," Krista said. She placed the funnel near the crotch of her pants to demonstrate. "You can use it to pee outside without having to drop your pants all the way."

Marjan stifled a laugh.

"Perfect stocking stuffer for a tomboy." Jenna laughed. It was late

November, and it was hard for the Americans not to think about the holidays they would miss because of this deployment.

"What is a tomboy?" Marjan asked.

"A tomboy," Jenna explained, "is a girl who likes to do things boys usually like to do. Like playing football or climbing trees. They don't want to wear skirts or makeup or play with dolls."

Marjan's mouth fell open. Was Jenna describing a bacha posh? Did Americans dress some of their daughters as sons as well?

"I . . . I liked to do those things when I was a kid."

"So you were a tomboy too? I think most of us were," she said, pointing to herself and meaning the American soldiers. "Actually, I thought only tomboys would want to be in the military. But it's different for you all. You're the most feminine soldiers I've ever seen."

Krista nodded. "Heck yeah. Can you imagine what would happen if we showed up to basic training with red lipstick and mascara? These Rangers already call us the 'bun brigade.' They can't stand us being here and think we're going to get them killed. We need them to see us as soldiers, and not *women* soldiers."

"That's why I curse hard and chew tobacco," an American woman joked from the back of the room before returning to her magazine.

Jenna stuck her tongue out in disgust.

"It's like we had to leave part of ourselves behind to show up for this job. But that's not the case for you all and especially not this one," Krista said, pointing at Soraya.

"I don't know what you're talking about," Soraya said, batting her eyelashes and pretending this was the first time her flair for makeup and fashion had been brought up.

Marjan thought of those years she spent as a bacha posh, the freedom she'd had to live as a boy. Without a son, her parents cowed to pressure to keep their daughters home instead of sending them to school. Marjan had gladly become the brother they needed. She'd loved the power she'd gained by masquerading as a boy, the authority and the confidence.

What a lie it had been.

A girl dressed as a boy was still a girl and would inevitably be treated like a girl.

"But this is the problem. So many Afghans think women cannot do this work. If we wear no makeup and sit like a man and talk like a man, then they will tell us we are trying to be a man. They have to see women doing this work to understand that a woman can do this work. Not just a woman acting like a man," Marjan explained.

"Yes, yes," Khatol, an FTP with a round face and kind eyes said, clapping her hands. Khatol was one of the few FTPs to have a father fully supportive of her military ambitions. She was engaged to a soldier she'd met while stationed in one of the provinces. "She is right. My uncle says if women work, they will be too tired to take care of their children. They will come home hungry and wanting to sleep."

"He is right," Soraya said, which drew looks. "I hear this happens to many men."

Marjan noticed that both the Afghans and the Americans laughed. The only person not laughing was Elaha, their commander. Elaha was soft-spoken, deceptively gentle in demeanor. But she was a commanding force as well and knew how to coax courage from her platoon.

"When I first had the idea to join the army, I didn't want to be anything like the women who marry and are surrounded by children and in-laws," she said. "I wanted to be different, the only one. But then I heard the story of the simurgh. It's from a book called *The Conference of the Birds*. Do you know it?"

No one moved. Khatol was the first to admit she hadn't read it. It was a centuries-old Persian poem and these women weren't exactly students of ancient literature.

"I'll tell you, then."

With the promise of a story, Elaha had their attention.

"Before us, in the times of warriors and winged creatures, a conference of birds gathered to choose from among their flock a leader. But a hoopoe announced that the ideal leader already existed and lived at the peak of the highest mountain in the lands. It was the simurgh, a bird of epic proportions. If it stretched its wings, it could hide a mountain behind its feathers. So, off the birds went to find this noble chieftain. On the way, they encountered seven challenges, and many abandoned the quest because they were distracted or fatigued or led astray by diversions. When they neared the mountain, they were reduced to a flock of only thirty. And how did he describe them? *Thirty exhausted, wretched, broken things / with hopeless hearts and trailing wings.* These thirty, the ones who persevered, flew to the peak of the mountain, but instead of finding a winged leader, they were rewarded with the realization that they, together, were the epic simurgh. Their unity and determination had helped them ascend to the highest peak."

"She's not making it up," Khatol said, holding up her phone. "I found it online. Shall I read you a verse?"

Khatol cleared her throat, closed her eyes as if she were in a cloud of smoke, and read in a breathy, operatic voice:

We've gone too far, we can't turn back
Bemoaned the Sorrow bird
One can't retreat on a circular path
Said the Hoopoe, undeterred
The Phoenix lived a thousand years
A wise creature without a herd
And when his final hour came
His nobility was stirred
He spread his wings, summoned flames
And from his ashes a new Phoenix emerged.

Marjan stared at her feet then, willing herself to remember every detail of this tale so that she could relay it to Hawa, to seed her with legends just as Khala Shaima had done for her.

"Commander, are you telling us that we are a bunch of birds?" Wahida asked.

"Didn't you say your father calls you his little canary?" Khatol teased Wahida.

"He calls me an eagle!" Wahida replied, flicking Khatol's shoulder. "He would call you a crow if he heard you singing along to the radio." She tilted her head back and cawed.

Khatol's mouth opened in feigned indignation.

Elaha sighed as an exhausted mother might.

"I've only shared the story with you. It is up to you what you will make of it."

Their time on the base was steeped in physical activity, in labor meant to strengthen their bodies. But there were also moments like these, unintentional and scattered, that strengthened their warrior spirits and their sisterhood.

Two days later, ahead of the morning training sessions, Elaha presented Marjan with a worn paperback copy of the *Shahnameh*, yet another centuries-old poem. The book had more pages than any Marjan had ever held.

"What is this for?" Marjan asked.

"You seemed to be intrigued by the classics," Elaha said. "You might like this as well."

Marjan thanked her, wished she had something equally thoughtful she could offer in return, but Elaha was already on her way to change into her uniform.

That evening, her body ached from another full day of training. Her hair was still wet from her shower. The other women played cards nearby, but Marjan had declined to join. She missed Hawa fiercely. It was harder than she imagined to be away from her for so long, and though the trainings kept her busy, she was left with plenty of time to second-guess every decision she'd ever made, especially those involving Hawa.

What had made her think she could be a soldier? Who was she trying to be?

Marjan picked up the book Elaha had given her. It was impossibly long, and she would never finish it. She decided to let naseeb guide her, fanning through the passages and reading a verse here and there in the epic poem about love and war.

Flipping through, she landed on a verse about a woman named Gordafarid. Daughter of a warrior, Gordafarid was standing in a fortress when she learned their commander had been taken by the enemy.

Shamed on her leader's behalf,
Her cheeks turned dark as night.
Into the armor and helmet she went
To ride fearless toward the fight.
She, a lion, roaring at enemy ranks:
Show me your men of might!

Marjan set the book down, thinking suddenly of her orphaned great-grandmother dressed in a man's guard uniform. She thinks of herself in a soldier's uniform. These lines were written thousands of years ago. Why did she feel as if they'd been waiting for her to turn the page and discover them? And why was she finding them now?

55

AUGUST 29, 2021

They approach the first Taliban checkpoint. Marjan averts her eyes. She whispers for Hawa to do the same. A bearded fighter with a turban, his once-white tunic gray with grime, sticks his head into the car window. The tip of his gun pokes out from behind his shoulder. The taxi driver announces that he is merely dropping his passengers off.

"What papers do you have?" the Talib demands. He cannot be more than twenty years old and has the eyes of a boy. Marjan almost pities him.

"Brother," Marjan pleads. "My father is at the airport now. He is very ill and needs me to care for him. I have no papers. I am here only with my daughter."

"Where is your father going if he's so ill?" he asks.

"His doctor told him he needs to go abroad to be cured of his illness," she tries. "He has no one but me. Please, be merciful."

"Was he a good father?" the Taliban asks. He seems genuinely curious.

"He taught me to pray," she says.

Hawa listens intently, notices that a long scar runs the length of the back of his hand and wonders what other wounds he has. The Talib looks off to the distance for a moment. Marjan, sensing indecision, rests her hand on the open window so that the foot soldier can see the colorful edges of the bills tucked into her hand.

The Talib takes a long drag on his cigarette, throws it onto the ground, and in one swift move snatches the money from Marjan's hand. He has pocketed more in the past two weeks than he has earned in four months of fighting.

"Go on! Go!" The Talib waves the car on gruffly.

They make it through the checkpoint. The driver is eager to unload his passengers and leave the chaos of the airport.

"Stay close to me," Marjan says to Hawa as they inch their way in the direction of the gate Jenna has directed them to, a gate away from the site of the bombing. An hour goes by, and they have made pitiful progress. In front of them is a human barricade. People are frustrated. They are not their best selves. There is little time, patience, and hope left. They either get out now or slink back to their homes and wait to find out what the country will look like tomorrow.

Maybe a different gate? she asks Jenna. Jenna says she will ask her contact. Marjan feels like a blindfolded crossing guard.

She looks at her daughter. Her cheeks are already flushed with heat. She hands Hawa the water bottle and encourages her to take a small sip. The sun is indeed brutal.

Another hour goes by. They continue to squirm and push their way toward the gate. If she could just get one American soldier to see her.

Marjan sends Jenna and the others an update.

It is hard to move, she writes. *Please tell your friend we are here. My headscarf is orange.*

She quickly swaps her headscarf for the orange one she's purchased. She snaps a picture of herself in the bright scarf and sends it to Jenna.

I'm sending it now. But try to get closer.

Shouts ripple through the crowd behind them. Hawa hears a pop. And then another.

"Madar!" she shouts, ducking her head.

"Keep your head down!" Marjan shouts, trying to position herself as a shield over her daughter's body.

Two Talibs are firing into the air just above people's heads, as they have been doing to control the crowds. Screams and shouts follow. People crouch, hands over their heads. Two marines stand on the wall nearby.

They're looking in the direction of the gunshots, hands on their triggers. Marjan looks around and sees a chance.

She whips the orange head scarf off her head and waves it in the air. She is on her toes, reaching for the sky.

"Here! Please, we are here!" she shouts. "Hello!"

She waves both arms around wildly, the scarf flapping like a bird caught in a net. The marines stand side by side. One points in her direction, and Marjan jumps.

"Here! Yes, yes, yes! We are here!"

She continues to wave her orange headscarf. The gunshots have quieted. The crowd is upright once more, people stepping and worming through openings.

"Madar!" Hawa shouts. "Is that man looking at you?"

This gives Marjan fresh energy. She can't tell if the marines are looking at her, but maybe Hawa is right. Her eyes are fixed on them, trying to decipher their posture, their movements. One turns and looks over his shoulder. Or maybe her shoulder. Marjan cannot tell from here.

"Madar!" Hawa pulls on her arm, and Marjan looks down at her daughter, follows her gaze a hundred yards to her left and realizes that indeed there is a man looking at her.

She would recognize his face anywhere.

At the sight of Abdul Khaliq, Marjan goes breathless. For an instant, she is a girl again, soft and small as a sparrow. Her muscles go slack.

Then she looks at Hawa.

"Get down!" Marjan orders her daughter. Hunched over, she leads her away from the father she's never met. Marjan balls up the orange headscarf as they duck and weave between people. She stuffs it into her bag and pulls out her black headscarf. She lets go of Hawa's hand for just long enough to put it on.

Along the way, Marjan spots a group of people gathered around a tree. She looks over her shoulder and doesn't see Abdul Khaliq. She wraps the orange headscarf around a low branch just behind the cluster of people. No one even notices.

"This way," she says, pulling Hawa toward the street. She looks left and right, desperate for a place to hide. Hawa follows, her bag slapping against her hip, her legs threatening to buckle. But she presses on because she cannot let her mother down.

"Madar, there!" Hawa shouts. She is pointing to a taxi unloading passengers, a family of five.

Before the last child exits, she shoves Hawa into the back of the car.

"Hey, hey! What are you doing?" the driver asks.

"Please!" Hawa cries to the driver. "We need to leave!"

Marjan promises to pay the fare.

"Change of heart?" he asks as he pulls away from the curb. "Good idea. People need to have some self-respect. Stop panicking, I told my wife. Stay in the homeland and you'll see. No one will bother us."

Marjan keeps Hawa low on the seat but looks back in time to see Abdul Khaliq standing by the roadside, her orange headscarf in his fist like a captured flag.

56

2017

"Are we on for tonight or what?" Jenna groaned. The women soldiers, Americans and Afghans, were killing time in the mess hall while they waited for final word on the plans for the evening. Winds were picking up, and a few dense clouds lingered near the horizon, like eager guests in a doorway.

Marjan shifted in her seat, pulled her elbows off the long table, and placed her hands on her lap. She had been restless, unnerved since the afternoon briefing on the mission. A red laser light pointed at the river they would cross and the three roads that connected the village with its neighbors. The laser bounced from the clearing where the helicopter would hover as they fast roped to the ground, then pointed to the path they would take to approach the village unseen. Then the red light made wild circles on the compound they would target, where two high-value targets linked to insurgent groups were thought to live.

Marjan wiped her palms on her government-issued pants. Her stomach felt ready to revolt. She took a sip of water. She could tell Elaha that she wasn't up for tonight's mission. She should have done it right after the briefing, but she had hesitated. Then came word that they might not fly, and she thought if she waited, she might not have to ask to be excused.

Since waking that morning, nothing seemed right. She'd wondered if she was getting her period or if the cash she'd withdrawn from the bank might have fallen out of her purse on the way home.

Marjan was always mildly worried. It was the soundtrack of her life, playing on an endless loop. What if, what if, what if.

It had been one year since she had reclaimed her daughter from the orphanage. They slept in one room now so that Marjan could watch Hawa, curled on her side with one cheek pressed against the mattress. Sometimes, in the middle of the night, Marjan would move closer to Hawa to hear the light whistle of her breaths moving between pursed lips.

What if I'd been able to convince the Rasulis to let her live with me? What if I had found another way?

She wished she were home now, sleeping beside her daughter instead of waiting for someone to announce that they would not be flying over that thin bend of river and into a clearing one mile away from the target compound.

"I can't sit still anymore," Jenna said as she pushed away from the table. She stood and raised her arms above her head in a long stretch.

"Weren't you saying you had a migraine earlier? It wouldn't be the end of the world if you got a night off," Gabby said. She'd been a cross-country star throughout high school and showed no signs of slowing down. But when anyone fell behind on their training runs at the base, Gabby slowed her pace just to encourage them.

"I said you were *giving* me a migraine," Jenna clarified. "And I didn't bust my ass to get into this unit so I could sit around on a base all day."

Grunts of agreement. They were, on a whole, an impatient bunch.

"Why did you want this?" Krista asked, mostly hoping a conversation would make the time go by faster.

"For the incredible work-life balance, of course," Jenna replied with her signature dry humor.

There was laughter at the table. Khatol hid her grin behind her hand. They might not know exactly what was meant by "work-life balance" or some of the other phrases the Americans used, but the sarcasm needed no translation. Marjan realized she had just pressed her lips together to stifle her own smile. Soraya threw her head back and laughed with her whole being. She and some of the other FTPs were more like the American women in that way, comfortable with their joy.

"For me, it's a family thing," Gabby said. "My dad served. My granddad served. It's in my blood. What about you?"

"The angel of death made me do it," Krista said, grinning.

"You taking orders from the devil?" Jenna asked with a raised brow.

"Satan's not the angel of death," Krista chided.

"She's right. It is not Shaitan. It is Azrael," Soraya explained, sitting up. "My father used to tell us about him just to scare us. When God has decided a person's time has finished, he sends Azrael to take the soul from the body. There is a story about this. They say God gave Azrael the name of a person whose time was finished. Azrael visited the man. He was so scared. When he saw Azrael, he knew his name was written on the list of souls and Azrael will return him to God. The man did not want to die, so he ran far, far away. He traveled for one week and did not tell anyone, not even his wife or children, where he was going. He covered his head so no one could recognize him and hid in a cave on the side of a mountain."

"It was not a mountain. You're telling the story wrong," Khatol protested in Dari. She could understand English very well but wasn't as comfortable speaking it.

"There are a hundred versions of every story, aren't there? This is the way the story was told to me," Soraya replied good-naturedly. "The man slept that night and thought himself very clever, but when he woke up in the morning, the angel Azrael was standing over him.

"'What are you doing here?' the man asked and Azrael explained. 'God instructed me to take your soul from your body at this location and on this date, and I have been thinking and thinking, How can I make you travel so far from your home and your family? But here you are, at this place and at this time just as it was written.'"

Jenna, Krista, and the other women chuckled. Soraya leaned back in her chair and looked over at Khatol for her approval. Khatol shrugged as if to say her telling had been acceptable.

"But that's not the angel of death I was talking about," Krista said.

"You're talking about the gunship," Gabby guessed. She was also the munitions expert of the troop, a recorder of minutiae, and a history buff.

"The AC-130. They fly that beast nice and low, and while the pilot's making a big loop around the targets, those guns are blazing off the side. The Gatling fires thousands of rounds per minute. They call it the crowd-pleaser."

"Crowd-pleaser? What does that mean?" Marjan asked. The only way to improve her English was to ask about every new word or phrase she heard, even if it meant revealing her ignorance.

"A crowd-pleaser is something that makes a lotta people happy," Gabby explained with a chuckle.

Marjan saw Khatol stiffen. They were all soldiers here. They had all signed up to fight. Still, they couldn't help but remember that AC-130s had mistaken more than one Afghan wedding party for militants.

"Closer, but that's not the angel of death I'm talking about either," Krista said. "There was a woman from my town who was in the Air Force—Colonel Allison Black. She was a navigator on an AC-130 gunship and she was on a combat flight supporting Special Forces on the ground. Green Berets, I think. She spots some suspicious-looking targets and tracks them back to a compound in the middle of nowhere, with a few cars and a couple dozen armed guys. She's on the radio reporting what she's seeing to the Special Forces and gets the green light to start firing. She lets it all rain down on them, one-oh-fives and forties, and in the meantime the friendlies on the ground have an Afghan warlord with them, some general. He's hearing her voice on the radio, and he can't believe a woman is running this mission. He says something like, America is so determined to beat the Taliban that they send their women over to kill them."

"Hell yeah," Jenna says with a laugh.

"So, these targets are just getting wiped out. The Afghan general gets on his radio and starts messing with the targets. He tells them they're getting killed by an American woman and even puts his radio on so they can hear Black's voice coming through. The general saw the laser pointer coming down from the sky and, hearing all the hellfire, he called her the Angel of Death. The nickname stuck and he even sent her an AK-47 as a gift."

"Oh, I know this woman! I heard about her," Elaha insisted.

"Did I miss anything?" Krista asked.

"I don't know too much, only that she killed a lot of Talibs that day, maybe fifteen years ago? I was too young, but some of my relatives heard General Dostum talking about her at an event. He was telling women they did not need to suffer in the dark the way they did under the Taliban. He talked about an American woman soldier and called her the Angel of Death. He said if we fight the Taliban, Afghan women can be strong and free like American women. This made me want to become a soldier too."

"Fifteen years, here we are," Jenna repeated. The span of time quieted the circle of women. A decade and a half of fighting the Taliban. How many more years would it take? How many more missions? Some nights were a total waste. Some were wins. But still, in the distant reaches of the country, Talibs still gathered in compounds just like the one the Angel of Death had ordered wiped out two decades ago.

"I am happy I became a soldier," Khatol declared. "I don't think I want to do anything else. And if I die, at least I die fighting for my country."

"Amen, sister," Krista echoed. "I don't know how you all do it, though. Signing up for this job when you have to hide what you do from just about everyone you know. And you still show up smiling."

"And made-up like you're about to walk a red carpet," Jenna added, shooting a pointed glance at Soraya for their running joke.

"If I die, I die pretty," Soraya reminded them, batting her eyelashes at Jenna.

Marjan stood up to stretch. She was finding it harder and harder to sit for more than a few minutes at a time these days. Her legs were restless. She had grown restless.

"If I die, I die fighting for my daughter," Marjan said. The room grew still again at the thought of girls like Hawa. Would they have the freedom to write music and climb trees and graduate from high school and choose if they wanted to marry? Would they live in peace or would they need to take up arms too?

How many angels of death did one country need?

"Heads up, soldiers. We're rolling out in thirty minutes," an officer announced from the doorway before disappearing again.

Marjan checked her phone. There was no message or missed call from Ingrid. What would her life be like if Ingrid hadn't decided she wanted to learn more about halfway houses that day? Marjan didn't want to think about it.

She started a text message to Ingrid.

Is everything good? Hawa is sleeping?

"Marjan! I need you outside," Elaha called out. Marjan nodded and shouldered her backpack. She glanced down at her phone and decided against sending the message. She felt an urgency to send some kind of message to her daughter before getting on the helicopter, though she couldn't think of what to say. She reread her message. If Ingrid was asleep, Marjan didn't want to wake her with such a meaningless note or one that would make her worry unnecessarily.

She deleted her message and followed her commander outside.

"Are you okay to fly tonight?" Elaha asked.

"Yes, of course," Marjan said, trying not to let her voice betray her. "Why?"

"Because ever since we were briefed on tonight's mission, you . . . you don't seem yourself. And if we're about to take off, we need everyone sharp and at their best. Is there anything I should know?"

This was Marjan's chance to say she wasn't feeling well. She could even tell her commander the real reason her palms were sweaty just thinking about descending into that village where her older sister, Shahla, had been taken to as a bride all those years ago. She had no way of knowing if Shahla still lived there. She certainly had no idea if the compound they had talked about in the briefing belonged to Shahla's husband.

But Shahla's husband was related to Abdul Khaliq. And if they were hunting nefarious figures in the area, there was a decent chance Abdul Khaliq and his family were somehow involved.

"I'm fine. I guess I'm like Jenna and I don't like waiting around," she said, trying to sound unruffled.

Elaha looked uncertain, but Marjan knew the hour was late and having a platoon member back out wouldn't reflect well.

"Mistakes cost lives," she warned.

"I won't let you down," Marjan promised.

Marjan adjusted her helmet and checked her gear for the tenth time, the whirling blades of the helicopter lifting them into inky skies. There was no running from Azrael and there was no running from this mission. Marjan closed her eyes and put her trust in the angels of fate.

57

2017

In the early weeks of Marjan's tactical training, she was introduced to fast roping. Under a high sun, Marjan, Soraya, and the other recruits gathered around a tall wooden platform about twenty-five feet off the ground. Two American soldiers climbed up a side ladder, stood atop the platform, and, at the nod of their superior, slid down the twin ropes with such ease that Marjan was eager to give it a try. She slipped through the other women and wrapped one hand on the wooden rung of the ladder. She waited for a signal to ascend, and Soraya watched, her expression a mixture of pride and nerves.

Then came the order.

Marjan climbed the ladder with ease, but the moment she had two feet at the platform edge and looked down, her enthusiasm dissipated. She wrapped her gloved hands around the rough rope, the material designed to protect her palms from friction.

Go!

Her limbs felt like clumsy appendages, the rope an untamable creature, and the height a brutal intimidation. Marjan gripped the rope tightly, and instead of sliding toward the ground as the other women had, she dangled in the air, her legs flailing beneath her.

Slide!

The word was just noise, though. Marjan was preoccupied with the distance between her body and the ground, and the not-so-distant memory of life in a cast. Elaha was on the second rope, descending while Marjan dangled. She could not loosen her grip on the rope.

Marjan, breathe!

Soraya's voice cut through the noise like lightning against an inky sky.

Loosen your grip! Let the rope slide!

Nothing about her first descent felt right. Neither did her second or her third. Each time she climbed the ladder, she was sure this go would be different, but then she would find herself dangling from the rope, legs flailing again. She landed with a thud on her side, on her behind, on her knees.

She understood what she needed to do, but how did she get from theory to practice?

Elaha, the captain of the unit, pulled her aside.

The rope will not save you. Don't cling to it. Use it. Trust your arms and legs.

Marjan looked down at her arms then, the arms that had climbed trees and protected her face from incoming blows and rocked her two babies to sleep and loaded a weapon and carried home bread and milk to a little girl who should never have to live through what her mother had survived.

Marjan climbed the ladder again, and this time came down the rope at a steady, deliberate pace. *I trust my arms and legs. I trust myself.*

The helicopter hovered over the drop site. Soraya signaled for Marjan to go ahead. She nodded and grabbed the thick rope, her left hand over her right with just the right amount of tension. Her feet came together around the tail of the rope, and she slid down in one smooth motion, landing on her feet and moving out of the way immediately so that Soraya and the others could descend after her.

"We're clear."

The helicopter lifted away as they started their trek to the village. Marjan could hear her own breathing, heavier than usual, and knew it was more than just the weight of her gear. They were stepping into unknown territory with every mission, and even the best of people did not take kindly to unannounced visitors. She needed to be on the alert for people who might spot them approaching in the dark.

Don't think about Shahla, she told herself. Missions were dangerous and full of surprises. Intel stuffed inside a mattress. An AK-47 buried under two fingers of dirt. Gunfire erupting in the dark. Pressure plates daisy-chained to maximize casualties.

But it wasn't just her sister who was on her mind. She would be entering the village where her husband's extended family lived. What if someone recognized her and told Abdul Khaliq? What if he was there? She told herself she was unrecognizable in this gear and tried to focus on her immediate surroundings, the location of her fellow soldiers, and the weapon in her hands. She scanned left and right, the dark world glowing green with the aid of her night-vision goggles.

"I think I spotted movement. Due east from where I'm standing about a hundred yards out."

"I'm close by. Looks like an animal. Maybe a dog? Or a goat?"

"Roger that."

They advanced slowly, cautiously.

At the perimeter of the village, Marjan looked to her right to confirm Soraya's presence. She hadn't told Soraya about Shahla and this village. She worried that her best friend would find a reason to talk her out of the mission. She couldn't risk it. Marjan had lost so much at such a young age. She'd been a sprig chopped off a tree. How many nights had she prayed to God that she might one day see her mother, her sisters, and her khala Shaima again? She even prayed she might see her drug-addled father, to tell him how much suffering he'd caused her. Maybe he regretted what he'd done to them. But there was no easy way to reach out to them without the risk that Abdul Khaliq would find her.

"Entering. On my count," a soldier directed.

When it was her turn, Marjan hesitated for a beat. No one but Soraya noticed. She looked over at Marjan with a tilt of her head, a silent question Marjan could hear loud and clear.

Are you all right?

Marjan nodded at her friend, grateful that she hadn't said anything the rest of the team would hear. She didn't want to alarm or distract anyone. She pulled her shoulders back and corrected her stance.

"We want to keep you and your children safe," Jenna shouted to the compound's residents. "We will make sure the soldiers do not come near you. To keep all of us safe, we will start by searching everyone. We are asking for your cooperation. Follow our instructions and we can do this safely and quickly. We need everyone to come outside, adults and children." Commands shouted in English were immediately repeated in the local language.

There were shouts inside, the sound of footsteps and a door slamming. Marjan and the other soldiers stood with their hands on their weapons, waiting to see if the people inside the compound would comply.

"All teenage boys and men over here!" a soldier yelled.

Slowly, a dozen people trickled out of the compound. Soraya and Jenna stood closest to the gate, pointing the women and children in one direction while the men were directed in another. This was why Marjan's platoon was so essential. Though they came in the middle of the night, armed and in uniform, they were also Afghan women. They could reassure the nervous wives and mothers that they meant no harm. They were not foreigners.

Marjan scanned the startled faces of the people jolted from sleep. What might Shahla herself be like now, seven years since she last saw her?

"We just have a few questions for you," Jenna told the gathering women. Soraya translated for her, projecting her voice to the dozen figures standing before them. "Is this everyone? We will be searching inside, and it is safest for everyone if we know. Surprises are not good for anyone. We need to know if the house is not yet cleared out. Is everyone outside now?"

"No, not yet," a teenage girl blurted out. A woman standing beside her, perhaps her mother, chided her for speaking out. The girl looked from her mother to the strange soldiers in front of her, unsure who to be more wary of.

"God damn you all," an older woman called out bitterly as she emerged from the doorway. Her gait stiff, she rested her hand on the clay wall of the home. "Shameless. Good that you are hiding your faces. You can all eat shit."

"I don't know what she said but I think I understand what she said," Krista muttered.

"She is not happy we are here," Marjan explained.

Krista nodded. "Yup. That's what I heard."

They approached the women and began the searches, patting them down to look for weapons or concealed items. They were thorough by necessity. Once, a platoon member discovered a rifle hidden under the bulky dress of a middle-aged mother. And another search had revealed identification cards in the folds of an infant's swaddling.

Soraya approached one of the women and asked again if everyone, including all the men, had exited the home. The woman nodded in confirmation.

Marjan looked over her shoulder, trying to see the other homes in the area. If Shahla did not live here, did she live somewhere nearby? Did any of these women know her?

"Let's get started," Krista said, and nudged Marjan.

Marjan blinked rapidly, brought herself back to the task. She was the lead during the interrogations. They'd all been trained in tactical questioning, but the platoon quickly learned that Marjan excelled at it, finding ways to build some semblance of trust and detect from body language when a woman had more to say. Sometimes it was a child who provided a key piece of information. Marjan let her weapon hang over her shoulder. The others held theirs pointed to the ground but in their grips, ready for any surprises.

"How old is your daughter?" Marjan asked a young woman cloaked in a long prayer shawl, a whimpering child in her arms.

The woman answered with a scowl. She turned away, shielding her daughter's face from view, and then looked to an older woman standing nearby. Marjan understood. She wanted to make sure the older woman had seen her scowling, that she was mirroring the group sentiment in facing these strangers.

The child looked to be about a year old, wriggling and fussing. Hawa had been the same at that age.

"She will be a strong girl. Clever like her mother," Marjan said, and saw the young mother's face soften, because she had said what every mother wanted to hear—that she carried something of her mother in her, something she would need to survive this harsh world.

It wasn't all performance for Marjan. She saw curiosity in the eyes of the little boys and girls even as they eyed her firearm and uniform, and in the toddlers who clung to fistfuls of their mothers' skirts while strangers entered their home. Even on those nights their sleep was interrupted, the children delighted at the cheap candy placed into their outstretched hands and tried to get as many pieces as they could. They understood that, like food and electricity and money, there simply wasn't enough childhood to go around.

"How close is the nearest hospital?" Marjan asked a middle-aged woman wearing a black dress with a faint floral pattern.

"It's not close at all," she replied.

"How far, then?"

She frowned, calculating in her head.

"Maybe two hours away," she said.

"By car?" Marjan asked.

The woman nodded.

"Have you ever been to the hospital?" she continued. The woman sighed heavily.

"I've not. But my husband took our son when he broke his arm."

"Brave boy to be in a small car so long and in pain. What type of car does your husband have?"

"He doesn't have a car. He had to borrow a jeep from his brother. Her husband," the woman said, nodding in the direction of the younger mother Marjan had been speaking with earlier.

Marjan nodded. She went down the line and asked a few more questions of the other women and girls. *Do any of the men here travel often? Have you seen any strangers in town?*

As she spoke to the women, she noticed that the baby in the young mother's arms was coughing. The sound was too familiar to ignore. She walked back to the woman.

"Maybe some steam will help clear her little chest," she suggested. "If you see she's breathing hard, you may need some medications for her."

"What do you know?" the woman snapped. "You're not a doctor. And you don't know anything about a sick child."

"Yes, I do," Marjan replied. "My daughter had the same cough when she was little."

"You have a daughter?" the woman asked, as if she might have heard wrong. Marjan nodded, though she wished she could take back what she'd just said. She wasn't supposed to reveal anything personal.

She and the other platoon members were accustomed to being met with surprise. When they descended upon homes in rural areas, into communities that knew little of what was happening in Kabul and cared even less, they were usually the first women anyone had ever seen in uniform, with weapons.

"Do they really allow you to do this?" the teenage girl who had spoken up about her grandmother called out. Her mother clucked her tongue to hush her.

"Who do you mean?" Marjan asked.

The girl chewed her lip, hesitant to say anything more.

"If you mean the government, yes. Many women serve in the army. And on police forces as well. And if you mean our families, yes." That last part was a lie, but it was true for other FTPs. Marjan saw no harm in throwing wildflower seeds into the wind.

The girl took in this revelation. Meanwhile, Marjan turned her attention back to the woman whose husband had a jeep.

"By any chance, is your husband's car white?"

"No," she answered, almost eagerly. "It's black."

"Ah, okay. Is his name Abdullah?"

"No, his name is Rahmat," she said.

Marjan nodded. In the morning briefing, they had been told the target was a man named Rahmat. Marjan wasn't privy to intelligence sources, but from what she had been told, surveillance had spotted this man traveling to and from hot spots where suspected insurgents had been gathering in a black jeep. They needed only to identify who was married to this young woman now and they would have their suspect.

"And do you know a man named Abdul Khaliq?" Marjan asked, trying to sound nonchalant.

Recognition flashed on the face of the older woman. Her lips tightened.

"Maybe a name close to that?" Marjan pressed. "His life may be in danger. We hear he's angered some very unsavory people."

"They've got him," Jenna announced. Marjan could picture the scene playing out just out of view. Rahmat was likely standing with Special Forces soldiers on either side of him, zip ties around his wrists.

"We're going to search the home now," Soraya announced. "You will all remain here while we go through."

Marjan and Soraya approached the open doorway with their rifles in their hands. Marjan nodded, and Soraya entered first, sweeping left and right. They entered the empty family room, then moved further in, clearing one small room at a time. Marjan took in the blankets and pillows, the brick-colored rugs with intricate patterns and fringe ends, the ceramic vase with long dried stems sitting atop a round wooden side table with chipped edges. The kitchen was a small space with an open cabinet. On the shelves were stainless steel bowls, a plastic colander, a jar of knives with their blades pointing down, two frying pans, and a large pot. A five-gallon yellow jug of cooking oil sat in the corner like a sentinel.

Marjan moved into the hall. There was one more room toward the rear.

"I'm behind you," Soraya said.

Marjan had been trained to expect the unexpected. She had, thus far, never had to pull the trigger her finger rested on, but she knew she could find herself in a situation where that was necessary at any moment. In training, they'd practiced moving through mazes meant to simulate the walls of a home, turning corners and taking aim at the hearts of cardboard targets.

So when Marjan stepped into that room and saw a cloaked figure crouched in the corner, she did not falter. She trained her weapon directly on this person who clung to the shadows.

"Hands up!" Marjan shouted. "Hands up now!"

Two hands went into the air, shaky and weak. The figure lifted her head, and the round beam from Soraya's flashlight fell on a pale face, exaggerating the dark shadows under eyes that Marjan would recognize even if a thousand years had passed.

Shahla.

58

AUGUST 29, 2021

Word of Marjan's return prompts the women of the hill to gather. They are invested in her story now, this young widow and her child.

"You gave up so soon?" Kobra asks. "You've been trying for days. But today you just throw your hands up and come all the way back here."

Marjan nods, stone-faced.

"I don't buy it," Kobra declares. There are murmurs of agreement from the gathered women, whispers that encourage Kobra to push harder, to demand answers on their behalf. "We've taken you and your daughter in. We've helped you. We deserve to know. What are you hiding?"

Marjan purses her lips. She wonders where Zarifa and Elaha are right now. Being welcomed into another country maybe? There's been little talk about what happens after boarding an evacuation airplane.

"I am . . . I was a soldier," Marjan says. "I served in the military, in a small unit of special forces."

"But you're a woman!" someone calls out, as if this is a revelation.

"The Taliban have our information. They've taken over all the ministries. They have our information, our files. They came to our apartment. We evaded them once, but we won't be able to trick them again. They are searching for people who worked against them. I am one of them."

"Make her leave!" a woman shouts. "We don't need those men trampling through our homes. What will happen to us?"

Concern ripples through the room. Kobra tries to still the waters, but it's more difficult because she herself is uneasy with Marjan's presence. She considers the mother and daughter before her, crosses her arms. No, it's not Marjan's presence that makes her uncomfortable. It's Marjan's reticence. Most of the women on the hill are eager for someone to hear of their suffering, to know what they have endured. Kobra, like a librarian, has spent her life surrounded by their stories. With Marjan, she feels she's opened a book only to find a chunk of pages torn out.

"Please take your daughter and go," someone pleads. Hawa turns to the women, searches for the voice, but the women are murmuring to each other.

"Hush! I have questions still," Kobra says sharply. Marjan lets out a heavy breath. She feels as if she's been dropped into a mission with no intel, no time to strategize. "You have seen hell at the airport already. Today, you are quite shaken. Why is that?"

"I haven't slept in days. If we don't get on a flight—"

Kobra takes another step toward Marjan, close enough to see the fine lines and purple shadows beneath her eyes.

"Who is he?" Kobra asks.

Marjan will not be tricked into answering a question that hasn't been asked.

"You are frightened of him, even in your sleep," she says. Marjan stiffens as Kobra takes a step closer. "I don't sleep well either. None of us do."

"I was a soldier. I'm entitled to nightmares," Marjan says.

Kobra shakes her head.

"It's not war that haunts your sleep. It's a man," Kobra says. "*Don't take her.* That's what I heard you say. Who were you talking about? Who are you running from?"

Marjan's lips press into a thin line.

Hawa looks to her mother. *M-A-D-A-R,* she thinks, though she does not know why the letters her mother traced onto her back with a fingertip have come to her now on the palm of her hand. Hawa is unnerved to see her mother this way. She looks directly at Kobra.

"My mother has made a lot of enemies in her life," Hawa says, her voice quavering. "But I'm the reason we are in danger."

"Hawa—" Marjan starts to object, but Kobra raises a hand.

"Explain what you mean," Kobra orders Hawa. Marjan is silent. She has succumbed to an understanding that this, too, is her naseeb, a fate of her own making though not of her own design.

"My mother ran away from my father years ago. He is not a good man but he is powerful and angry. We saw him today at the airport. He is looking for us. He's looking for me."

The room quiets.

"This changes nothing," one woman says. "We cannot have her among us. We have our own children to think about!"

"I'm sorry," Marjan says. "I thought we could hide safely among you. I never meant to put any of you or your children in danger. I think . . . I think it is best that we go."

"Where will you go? What will you do?" Kobra asks.

"I will find a way." Marjan's promise sounds more like a prayer.

She takes Hawa's hand and feels a small squeeze.

"We cannot cast you onto the street just yet," Kobra says.

Behind her, one woman clucks her tongue. Another curses her own terrible luck. And a third murmurs that God is merciful. There is no consensus, of course, but there is respect for Kobra, a deference she's earned over decades.

"You can think and plan here for now. You two," Kobra says, pointing at the women standing by the doorway. "See what we can offer them to eat."

"Why are we doing this?" a woman mutters. "She's not even a widow."

"And don't we all know that sometimes that is worse?" Kobra asks of her bereft neighbors. She is met with silence, a slow dispersal of women and children into the yard. Marjan's temples throb. She buckles, falls onto the cushion where she slept, where Kobra overheard her mumbling, pleading with her demons—*Don't take her.* She covers her face and sobs. She has never done this in front of Hawa, but she is capsized.

Hawa falls to her knees, touches her mother's shoulder. She's never seen her mother this way, unraveling. Hawa is unnerved by the sight, but she feels something else too, something she can't name. Like a hand has wiped the fog from the mirror she's been gazing into.

Don't take her, her mother had said in her sleep. Her mother wanted her. Her mother would not leave her. Her mother was fighting for her.

"Let your mother rest a bit. You, daughter of a soldier, can join the others outside," Kobra says, ushering Hawa out of the room. Hawa obeys, wanting to get some air. Outside, two little girls stand behind a timid sapling, hoping it isn't obvious they are eyeing her.

Hawa tucks her hair behind her ears, avoids their gaze. She sits on the ground outside Kobra's home and prepares to stay vigilant while her mother rests. It is, she imagines, what a soldier would do.

"Hey," a girl with long brown hair calls. "Is your mother really a soldier?"

Hawa nods. Two more children join, a shaggy-haired boy and a girl wearing a faded green dress with crepey sleeves and a panel of embroidery on her chest.

"I told you," the little girl whispers to him. They walk around the tree and sit cross-legged on either side of Hawa.

Four more children join. The circle widens.

"Is your mother the only one?"

"No," Hawa said, thinking of Khala Soraya. "There were others."

"Has she ridden in a tank?"

"Can she fly a jet?"

"Is she a sniper?"

"How many terrorists has she killed?"

Hawa has all these questions herself, and more. She has never seen her mother in this light, a woman to be admired. Even feared.

"I can't talk about it. It's all top secret," she says, because it feels good and is probably true. She hopes one day she'll know everything there is to know.

"Were you learning to be a soldier?"

"No, of course not. I was . . . I was learning to play the rubab."

"If I were going to play an instrument, I would have chosen the tabla," a boy declares. He points his elbows out to his sides and begins to wiggle his fingers across imagined drums.

"I like the sound of the harmonium," a girl says, grinning. "And I would pick the tambourine for my baby sister. She's good at clapping."

Hawa misses her rubab, misses the way it fills the hollow of her lap, the space she has carved out for it in the same way the mulberry tree is hollowed to make space for music. In the same way that silence makes space for sound and hurt makes way for healing.

Pick up your rubab, Ustad Rafiqi had once said to her. He repeated the instrument's name a second and third time, splitting it down its center and revealing its essence as if it were an exotic fruit. *Ru-bab. "Ruh" means soul. You know this. And in Arabic, "bab" means door. Watch your audience and you'll see that the notes from this instrument are indeed a gateway to the spirit.*

"I want to hear you play music," a small girl says, the one chosen for the tambourine. She falls into her older sister's lap.

Hawa does not have a rubab, but she does have the wooden flute in her bag, the bag that sits just outside Kobra's home. She retrieves the tula and returns to her audience. It is the simplest of instruments, one that they used to teach the basics of music to all students. She positions her fingers on the holes in the lacquered shaft, brings the tula to her lips. There is only one song she knows. It is a spare, doleful melody. The children's heads and trunks sway to the rhythm, as if they are once again in the arms of their mothers. As if they are sky-bound sunflowers in a summer breeze.

The children don't know the lyrics, but the women on the hill do. The music stops them in their tracks, penetrates their thoughts. Hawa sees the rapt faces of her audience and continues. They are unaccustomed to this proximity to music, this contact with its elemental form. It is the difference between looking at a picture of fire and feeling one's hands warmed by a flame.

The song could go on forever. How will she know when to stop?

Further down the hill, a woman lifts the corner of the tarp and considers the dirt path, the small trees, the railings. She is tired and has spent all day calling herself a fool, fighting the urge to turn around. She sees nothing beyond the tarp. Her headscarf clings to the sweat on her brow, and her breathing is heavy. She doesn't have the energy to go up this hill and can't imagine this is anywhere useful anyway. She drops the tarp and takes a step back toward the road but stops when she hears the sound of a lonely flute, the kind a shepherd would use to soothe his flock, and she follows the notes up the hill.

Hawa holds the last, low note then sets down her flute. The children follow her gaze to the approaching stranger, a woman with a familiar face. The woman drops her bag and lets her headscarf fall to her neck.

"Hawa. I can't believe I found you," she says.

59

2017

"I can't believe I found you." Marjan stared at her sister, at Shahla's arms trembling as she held them up and within view. She realized she still had her weapon trained at her sister's head and lowered it abruptly.

"What are you doing?" Soraya asked. "We have to search her."

"I'm not well. Have mercy," Shahla said weakly.

"Shahla, it's me," Marjan whispered, kneeling at her sister's side. She sensed Soraya's bewilderment, her controlled panic. She felt the presence of the rest of the team outside, the soldiers waiting on their signal that the premises had been fully cleared, every room searched.

"Who? What are you saying?" Shahla asked in disbelief. She tried to rise but faltered.

"I don't know what you think you're doing," Soraya snapped, shooting a glance over her shoulder.

Marjan touched Shahla's face, which, to her astonishment, now looked so much like their mother's. On the day the three sisters were given away as brides, Shahla had become wife to a man far more decent than his cousin Abdul Khaliq. Still, the years since had been hard, and it showed.

Shahla shook her head, as if she were tired of tricks.

"Shahla, it's me, your sister. I've missed you so much," Marjan said, her voice cracking. Behind her, Soraya communicated to the others that they had one woman who appeared to be ill, possibly contagious, still in the house. They were questioning her now and then would resume the search.

"Dear God, Rahima? Is it you? What are you . . . Where . . . Rahima?"

They embraced, and despite her gear and the layers between them, Marjan could feel the heat emanating from her sister's body.

"You're so warm."

"I think it's malaria," Shahla said, squeezing Marjan's hands. "The fevers come and go. I'll be all right."

"Your children? How are they?"

"Praise Allah. My sons and daughters are healthy and good to me. They are everything to me." Shahla smiled weakly, beads of sweat lining her upper lip.

"Searching now," Soraya communicated to the rest of the team. "Will be out in a minute."

Marjan's mind raced. She did not want to let anyone know that Shahla was her sister, just as she did not want anyone from this home to know who she was to Shahla. But she also did not want to lose her sister again.

"Are you really a soldier? They said that you ran away, but I thought maybe they had done something to you. I cried so much, little sister."

"Marjan . . ." Soraya said. It was a gentle warning that they could not stay in this room for much longer.

"I am as well as I can be. I've missed you more than you could ever know. Do you have word about our family?" Marjan asked, half afraid to hear the answer.

Shahla sighed deeply.

"God gives and takes," she said, and Marjan felt a heaviness grow in her chest. It was very much like Shahla to find a way, even in the throes of her own illness, to deliver the coming news gently.

"Our mother died just six months ago. Our father fell from a ladder three years ago. Our younger sisters are married. Rohila has three children and Sitara has two. You must have seen her. She is married to my brother-in-law and lives in this home with us."

Marjan's mind flashed to the way the young mother's eyes had caught her attention. How had she not recognized her own sister?

"That was Sitara?" Marjan asked. She wanted to run outside and throw her arms around her sister.

Shahla nodded; then her face grew serious.

"Say nothing to her, Rahima. She is young and petulant. She speaks without thinking. Our parents were shadows of themselves when they raised us, and even less present for her. I encouraged my brother-in-law to marry her so I could have her close."

"We're searching this room. You cover the first room," Soraya called out to one of their teammates. She began moving around the floor cushions and lifting the edges of the carpet. "Forgive me, but I must look through your space."

"And Khala Shaima?" Marjan asked, because she could not leave this room without knowing what had happened to the aunt who kept her alive with her stories, with her faith, with her courage. Without Khala Shaima, Marjan might not have had reason to believe she deserved more from this life. Her aunt had been unwell her whole life but was particularly weak at their last visit. Marjan had marveled at the strength it must have taken for her to make the trip to Abdul Khaliq's compound that day.

"Khala Shaima, who loved you more than anything, took her last breath not too long after your disappearance. She was the one who learned you were missing. She went to visit you and the family reported you had run off. I was devastated, but she told me not to grieve. A fighter, that's what she used to call you. 'There are brave girls everywhere but few like Rahima, a girl who has more strength in a fingernail than a warlord has in his whole body.'"

"Marjan! We have to move." Soraya was growing impatient.

"If I give you a phone number, will you be able to contact me?"

Shahla, one hand on her sister's arm, shook her head.

"I do not have a phone," she said. "Give me your number, sister."

Shahla pulled a pen from the corner, where a small metal cup held a splash of water. There was no scrap of paper in the room to use so Shahla lifted the hem of her dress and offered the white cotton lining. "Maybe one day I will find a way to use it."

Blinking back tears, Marjan nodded. She wrote her number on the cotton, the tip of the pen catching on the fabric. When she was finished, she flipped the hem over so no one would see what she had written.

"Come, let me kiss your face," Shahla insisted, reaching both hands out. Marjan felt like a child then, like a little girl returning to her mother. She kissed her sister's hand and wiped away her tears.

"I have a little girl," she said to Shahla. "I wish that she will meet you and her cousins one day."

"God is generous," Shahla said, her eyes flashing upward. But Marjan knew there would be no return mission here. She could never appear without alerting the family. Both sisters understood that this encounter had been a one-time gift. But there was no reason to sully the moment with reality.

"This room is clear!" Soraya called out as Marjan rose to her feet. "We're coming out."

Soraya had to tug on the sleeve of Marjan's olive uniform to get her to take the final step out of the small, dank room. They joined the others and searched the rest of the premises—lifting floor mattresses, checking inside of pots, sifting through clothing, inspecting the area behind the house. They found nothing on this particular visit, no sacks of fertilizer that might be used for explosives, no cache of weapons, no bags of money. Some missions did not yield incriminating evidence, but they would turn over their target and the government would take over the interrogation from there.

"Looks like we're almost finished clearing here. I'm going to go back outside and see if the women remember anything new."

Soraya looked directly at Marjan, the area dimly lit. *Don't do anything stupid,* her posture said.

Marjan stepped into the night air again, her chest a cage full of butterflies. She kept her gaze low, tried not to make immediate eye contact with anyone outside or appear flustered. She stood in front of the gathered women and children, trying to control her breathing.

There stood Sitara, shifting her child from one hip to the other. She was young but likely already feeling the strain of motherhood on her body. Marjan saw what she had missed in her face only moments ago. The playful eyes and pouty mouth. Shahla had been like a second mother to them all, but especially to the youngest sisters.

But Marjan also saw the edge that Shahla had warned her about. Sitara scowled, said something sharply to the woman standing beside her. When her eyes met Marjan's, she marched up to her.

"How long are you going to keep us out here? My children need to sleep."

Marjan wanted to pull her close, to kiss her face that she now realized looked so much like her own. She looked at her niece and nephew and hated that she had disturbed their sleep. She wondered which of these children belonged to Shahla. She had a thousand questions for Sitara, but she also knew there was no way to ask them.

"We're almost finished. Your children are precious. They're fortunate to have such a caring mother. Your family must be proud," she said.

Sitara recoiled, her brow furrowed. No one had ever said such words to her, much less a soldier working for what her husband said was a government corrupt to its core.

"You have no right to speak of my family," she snapped.

Marjan said nothing, and Sitara gloated, feeling triumphant that she had silenced this strange soldier.

"We've got our guy. Let's roll out," a voice called. Krista, Jenna, and Soraya thanked the women for their cooperation and told someone to make sure they looked after the woman in the back room. She needed some fresh drinking water and maybe a visit to a medical doctor.

On the Chinook's underbelly, a red light signaled its readiness. The helicopter lifted off, cutting through the rural silence with the staccato beat of its blades. Clouds of dust rose from the earth like dancing djinns, keepers of the night's secrets.

60

AUGUST 29, 2021

"Why have you come?" Marjan asks.

"Soraya told me you were coming here. She was worried about you. I didn't want to risk communicating by phone. God alone knows what they can and can't track with all the new equipment they've inherited from the Americans. Well, God and the Pentagon," Mina grouses.

Kobra recognized Mina and was happy to turn her home over to her and Marjan so they could talk. She likes Mina's penchant for justice, her no-nonsense questions. So many police officers fattened their wallets with money the widows gave so that the homes they built here would not be knocked down yet again, so that their city would not be turned to dust because of some archaic ordinance. Kobra is with the other women now, reassuring them that even though another woman has entered Zanabad, things are under control.

Kobra hopes this is true.

"I have never wanted to leave my homeland." Mina sighs. She rubs her left temple, wills away a blooming headache. "Look what they've done to us, these allies. People are watching us cling to the outside of airplanes and fall to our deaths. It's humiliating. Tragic. I wanted to stay and do the job I have been trained to do. The job I love doing. But I fear there's no place for me here. They'll make sure of that."

Marjan nods. She has seen what life is like in areas controlled by the Taliban. They will not stomach a woman reporting on their activities.

Even this progressive city—one that loved Mina's interjections of poetry, her scripture-supported feminism, her unflinching criticism of corrupt leaders—even the people of this city can turn quickly on a rogue woman. The Taliban are radioactive. Their proximity causes small but fatal mutations in men and women. There is nothing to see immediately, but before long, a cancerous cell will manifest and multiply. Lives will be cut short and there will be no bullet to trace, no wounds to see.

"I want to leave with you," Mina says.

Marjan nearly laughs. "I wish I could help you. I've tried and tried and failed each time. And this morning—"

Marjan stops abruptly.

Hawa shoots her a look, reminds her that the tie that binds them to this woman is Khala Soraya. Mina picks up on the glance.

"What happened this morning?" she asks.

"You know that Soraya-jan—I cannot bring myself to think of her gone—that Soraya-jan and I served together in the military. You know, of course, that for this we have targets on our backs."

Mina nods.

"But there's more," Marjan says. "You have reported on a warlord, one with a long history of dirty deeds."

"That describes many. Be more specific."

"Abdul Khaliq," Marjan says.

"Ruthless, that one," Mina recalls. "And clever. He pretended to be progressive and had manipulated an election to have his wife in Parliament for a while as his proxy."

Marjan takes a deep breath. "Badriya was one of his wives. I was another."

Mina drops her headscarf and stares at Marjan.

"Soraya made no mention of this," she says.

"I asked her not to. I couldn't let anyone know."

"I see," Mina says, her mind calculating implications and reassessing risks. She extends her legs and fans herself with a folded piece of paper she's fished out of her purse.

"I ran away before Hawa was born," Marjan explains. "He knows about her, though. I've secretly been in touch with my sister who is married to his relative. I think my nephew has betrayed us. And this morning, I spotted Abdul Khaliq at the airport. We escaped but he'll be on the lookout for us."

Mina knows enough about Abdul Khaliq to guess his intentions. Men like him don't tolerate disobedience, especially from women. Marjan will share Soraya's fate, but not Hawa. Hawa will become a servant in her father's household and live a life of penance for her mother's sins.

Mina has a full-blown headache now.

"We could try to cross a border," she says. "But that means driving, and who knows how many checkpoints they've set up. We would have to pay a smuggler, a driver. It's risky. Our best hope is still the airport, before the last flight takes off."

Marjan agrees with her assessment. "But how to get through?"

They talk about the various gates, the crowds, the heat, and the threat of another terrorist attack. Marjan recounts to her their previous attempts, the checkpoints down the road, the trench they waded through, the hordes camped out on the periphery. She tells her about the guidance from her American sister soldiers.

"We have to try something different," Mina says.

"Different how? It's the same airport. And now he knows I'm going to be there. He recognized me, after all this time. I waved that stupid orange scarf around and caught his attention."

"If he hadn't been there, that orange scarf might have gotten the attention of the right people. Do not blame yourself," Mina admonishes. Marjan's eyes brim with tears because it feels like Soraya's voice is coming through her aunt. Marjan wipes her tears brusquely.

"I don't know if I can slip past him," Marjan says.

"Probably best if he doesn't see either of us," Mina says, and sighs. "We could both throw on chadoris but that will keep you from signaling the Americans guarding the gates. We need them to let us through."

They meditate on this. In the background are the sounds of this city within a city. The *oomph* of a deflated ball met by a child's foot. The clanging of a metal spoon against an aluminum pot. The chirping of a child echoing her mother's orders to her younger siblings. A petty quarrel over a clothesline.

"You escaped him years ago. How did you do it then?" Hawa asks, pulling her from her thoughts.

"I just ran," Marjan says. Then Marjan sits straight up.

Mina's skin prickles, as it does when she detects breaking news, a story worth telling.

You doubt yourself, my niece. But how do you think you got this far? It is her khala Shaima's voice, a voice she has missed more than her own mother's. *Go on. Let your daughter see your lion heart.*

"I have an idea. But we'll need Hawa's help. And it means tomorrow you'll have to broadcast one more interview to your viewers, Mina. Are you up for it?" Marjan asks.

"Always," Mina says, with the unwavering commitment of a best friend. Maybe her presence here is Soraya's doing, a gift from an uncharted station. "But who am I interviewing?"

"Me," Marjan replies.

61

2017

"Oh, the things I do for you," Soraya whispered.

"I wanted to tell you."

"So you knew your sister was there before we left? My God, of course you did. No wonder you were acting so strange," she said, exhausted. They'd completed the mission debrief, eaten a quick meal, and returned to their quarters to sleep. They were sitting on their cots, at no risk of anyone overhearing them, and still Soraya dared not speak at a normal volume.

"I wasn't sure," Marjan explained. "I haven't seen her for years."

"That could have gone so badly," Soraya said, shaking her head.

"But it didn't, thanks to you," Marjan said. "I don't know how to . . . how to . . ."

"How to thank me?" Soraya filled in. "How about you tell me why you never mentioned this sister?"

Marjan had learned so much from her military training and yet she'd missed one essential lesson—no mission was successfully conducted by only one person, no matter how elite or well-trained. Marjan had been charging forward on her own for too long. She needed a sister, a friend, a confidante. A platoon would be ideal, but for today, Marjan would take even one sister in arms.

"A thousand years ago, I was one of five daughters. We were nothing special, just a family." She told Soraya the entirety of her story, starting from the day she became a bacha posh.

"Your aunt was right. You are a warrior," Soraya said when she finished, with an arm around her friend. "You just didn't have the uniform before."

Something light floated upward in Marjan's chest, slipped through the thick knot of her throat. She blinked rapidly, allowing the tears to fall.

"It breaks my heart that you had to survive that life, but I'm so grateful that you did."

How had she held all this in for so long?

"If you ever want to talk about it . . ." Soraya began.

"I won't."

"I don't mean today or tomorrow," Soraya said.

Marjan shook her head. "It is behind me," she said.

This wasn't true, of course. Seeing Shahla proved that.

Who had been with her mother when she took her last breath? Had her father ever felt remorse for giving his daughters away? What did Rohila look like now? Did anyone pray over Khala Shaima's grave?

How foolish she'd been to write her number on the cotton of Shahla's dress! What if her husband saw it and asked her about it? Her husband was not like Abdul Khaliq, but he was still a man. Men did not take well to wives keeping secrets tucked in the folds of their dresses.

Marjan knew that Soraya would not disclose her past to any of the other women in the platoon. But Marjan had not anticipated that her friend would treat her exactly the same once she'd learned about her past. Marjan saw no pity in Soraya's eyes. Marjan realized this was part of why she had been so reluctant to talk about her history—she could not have stomached being treated like a wounded child.

They went about their work and missions as usual, traveling back to Kabul together. In the city, Soraya visited often, spoiling Hawa with small gifts and the bubbly conversations that occur between a vivacious aunt and her admiring niece.

Until the day, almost a full year later, when Marjan's phone pinged with a new text message.

Salaam. I don't know if this is the right number.

Marjan thought nothing of it at first. There were plenty of wrong numbers. Some men even had enough idle time on their hands to text a string of digits at random looking for a woman to chat with. Marjan ignored the message and only bothered to respond two days later, when the dawn azaan had woken her from a restless sleep.

Who are you looking for? she wrote back.

The response came later that day.

A visitor traveled far to give me this number a year ago. I'm looking for her.

This message made Marjan's heart pound. Was this Shahla? Did she dare ask? If she replied, she might put herself in danger. She thought long and hard before she typed out a reply.

Sister, I am not sure who you are. Maybe I would recognize your voice.

A few moments later, Marjan's phone lit up with an incoming call from the same number. Her finger hovered over the screen, unsure if she should pick up. What was the worst that could happen? This individual already had her number. And if there was any chance this was Shahla, she had to take it.

"Yes?" she said timidly.

"Rahima? Is it you?" Shahla whispered, and Marjan's fingers tightened around the phone.

"Oh, Shahla. I didn't know if I'd ever hear from you. Are you all right?" Marjan asked, whispering as well.

"I wasn't sure if I had the number right," Shahla said.

"Whose phone is this?" Marjan asked. She'd seen her sister's living conditions. She had married into a family that had enough to feed everyone, but in rural homes, there was one phone, and that phone stayed with the husband.

"It belongs to my son," Shahla said. "His father has given him one now that he's been helping with his work. Jameel is a good boy. I've told him that I wanted to get in touch with my elderly aunt. My husband did not think very highly of our family and sees no use in me contacting any of my relatives."

Marjan pressed her fingers to her forehead. "You were so ill when I saw you. I was worried . . ."

"Oh, that was a terrible time. I recovered, thanks be to God. And Sitara. She helped nurse me back to health."

"How is my little sister? Did you ever tell her it was me that night?"

"She's well. Her children are well. She's a good girl but I don't trust her to keep you a secret just yet. She is still trying to find her way in this home. Some days she says she wishes I would not have brought her into this family. Other days, she's grateful. The sky changes colors by the hour and so do we."

Marjan sat by her apartment window. She ran her finger along the serrated edge of a mint leaf growing in a rectangular planter. She wished she could bring her sister into this world, to have her sit beside her on the floor, their backs against the cushions and two cups of tea between them going unfinished because they had so much to say to each other.

"But, Rahima, we had so little time that night and my head was woolly with fever. I can barely recall what I said and what I asked you. Where are you? Tell me everything."

"I go by Marjan now," she explained. "I live in Kabul, in an apartment. I have been a soldier for a few years now. It's been . . . the best thing for me."

"I dreamed so many times of seeing you again but never could I have imagined you would appear in a uniform."

Marjan had to ask. "The one taken in that night, did he return?"

"He did. After three weeks."

"Does he run with insurgents?"

Shahla took so long to respond that Marjan wondered if the call had dropped.

"I am not privy to his business." This was possibly true. It was also possible that Shahla did not want to invite another midnight visit by soldiers. "You are happy with the work you do?"

Marjan considered this. She was no fool. She knew the government had its flaws, its corruptions and vices. She had heard the sordid stories about which appointments had been bought, the lucrative mining contract that went to a cousin, the sexual exploitations committed by men one rung above their victims. There was too much money in the country. There was so much poverty. What was the alternative? A country led by terrorists or greedy warlords? At least in this version of Afghanistan, the girls had a fighting chance. At least there were good people in Parliament and the ministries as well, fighting for the country's soul.

"If we never see a woman do anything but marry and have children, it's easy to believe that is all we can do. Women have all kinds of jobs in Kabul and other cities. I want my . . ."

Marjan paused, unsure if she should say more. Her eyes fell on her daughter's sneakers by the apartment door.

"I want my daughter to know she can choose what she wants to do with her life."

"You were pregnant with her when you ran away?" Shahla whispered.

"Yes. She is bright and sweet and reminds me of our beloved Parwin," she said.

"Sweet, sweet Parwin. Oh, Rahima, you are really like no other woman," Shahla exclaimed, erupting into laughter. "I have to keep my voice down."

Finally, they could connect with each other. Shahla would, from time to time and when she was sure no one would see what she was doing, borrow her son's phone to send a message or make a quick call to hear her little sister's voice. Marjan warned her to delete the messages after she sent them, so they would not be seen by anyone else. As eager as they were to reclaim their connection as sisters, they could not do so often. Shahla lived in a home with many other people. She had little privacy and was almost always in full view of at least three or four people—her children, her husband, or her in-laws.

Marjan did not send messages; she only replied. She was terrified she would cause her nephew's phone to ping while it was in the hands of his father or someone else.

She wanted so much to tell Hawa about her khala Shahla, but she did not. Every time she thought about introducing Hawa to the truth about her family, she struggled with where she would draw the line. How could she talk about Shahla without talking about why they could not visit each other? And what if she wanted to pick up the phone and call her aunt?

It was a doomed mission.

Marjan did not sit still, even when she was home. She cleaned, reorganized, and tended to three pots of flowers and herbs on her windowsill. She was in motion at all times, resisting the undertow.

Provinces away, Shahla did the same. She sometimes found herself lying awake in the precious stillness of night, and if she was certain no one would notice, she draped a shawl over her shoulders and slipped out of the compound. On those nights, she walked far into the valley, golden jackals yipping in the dark. She would sit on a rock by a willowy stream and dip her fingers into the cool waters, trying to divine where the water had come from and where it would go.

Two nights after speaking to her sister, Shahla went on a moonlit pilgrimage. This time, she stepped into the stream and sat in its cool waters and cried. The blood, sweat, and cooking oil from her clothing seeped into the rippling flow. She watched the water welcome her tears, knew they would join a river she could not see and cross this country. There, in the cradle of ancient mountains, she let God alone hear her laugh.

62

AUGUST 29, 2021

"Good evening, dear viewers. Today, I come to you from outside the studio. Like many of you, I have been struck by the takeover of our beloved city, of our country by the Taliban, the so-called Islamic Emirate. We continue to see hordes of people making their way to the airport, desperate to board one of the last outbound flights before the Americans officially end their twenty-year occupation of our nation, a period marked by countless casualties, civilian and military. It was also a period marked by progress and growth in various economic sectors but also mired in corruption at all levels of government. As always, we must connect events to the impact on people."

Mina clears her throat. She gives an almost imperceptible nod, a signal to Hawa to zoom out so that viewers can see a woman standing beside Mina. The woman looks up. She holds one end of her headscarf by her temple, concealing most of her face.

"I have with me a woman with an intriguing story. For her safety, we will not reveal her identity. This brave woman overcame incredible life challenges and went on to serve in the Afghan National Security Forces. She was a member of an elite squadron of women trained to carry out missions targeting insurgents. The Taliban have claimed, since their takeover, that there will be no reprisals, no punishment of those who served in the army. Khanum, do you believe these promises?"

"Of course not," Marjan replies. "For years, I wore a uniform and defended my country, my people from these terrorists. They are disorganized. Many of them have only known a life of war. They have already begun hunting down anyone they see as their enemy. They nearly kicked down the door of my apartment."

"And why were they at your home?"

Marjan looks beyond the camera, to the children and their mothers, a live audience to her confession.

"They assumed the soldier they were looking for was a man. They didn't realize I was the soldier."

"An assumption many would make," Mina admits. "And since they came to your apartment, what have you been doing?"

Hawa tries to keep the camera steady. It's a challenge even though the handheld device weighs next to nothing. Marjan still holds the end of her headscarf by her temple.

"I have been on the run, hiding."

Marjan lowers her headscarf, lets her hand drift from her temple to her earlobe, revealing half her nose.

"And do you have a husband, Khanum?"

"I did once, but I had to leave him. He was a violent man, one who cheated and stole. He was morally corrupt at home and at the highest levels in this country too."

"This must be a terrifying time for you, then. Have you tried leaving?"

Marjan nods again, and her headscarf drops another centimeter, revealing her upper lip. She's exposing herself to the camera, and it is akin to shedding a coat in the dead of winter. The Taliban are already hunting Afghan soldiers, and a video by the notorious woman behind Metra Media will certainly be on their radar. Could they use the data and the technology they've inherited to track her down? Who knows? And while Marjan's wanted nothing more than to be invisible to Abdul Khaliq, she needs him to see her now so that she can lead him astray.

With her other hand, the one that hangs at her side, she signals Hawa to come closer. Hawa takes a step toward her mother and Mina, keeping them both in the frame.

"The airport was a nightmare. I don't see any hope there, and the flights are ending. It's a matter of hours now."

"What are your plans, then?"

"I do not have many options," Marjan says. Viewers can see most of her face now. They need only to invoke symmetry to fill in what is missing. "I will try to leave by land, as many others are doing."

"Are you not discouraged or afraid of the dangers of traveling through territories now controlled by the Taliban? What if you are stopped along the way?"

"God is merciful."

"Mm," Mina says. "And you will be leaving behind friends, family, a life you have built. How does this feel?"

Marjan's eyes are pink and wet. A knot forms in her throat as she thinks about Shahla, Rohila, and Sitara. She thinks of her sisters in uniform, at least a few of whom will not find a way out. She thinks of her neighbors, the shopkeepers, Hawa's classmates and teachers, the midwives and beggars. She thinks of the women in the shelter, of Kobra and these brave women living on this noble hill with their bright-eyed children. She thinks of the promise she made to her daughter, that the music wouldn't be taken from her. Every mission was a fight for all of this, the innocents and the innocence of her homeland. What is it like to turn her back on all of this?

"It is . . . it is dying without death."

63

AUGUST 30, 2021

Mina's back is stiff from sleeping on Kobra's floor. There is little room to move around. She's been spoiled by the comforts of her own home, a plush mattress. Proper windows. A bathroom. But in their desperate situation, the space Kobra has made for her is generous to the point of embarrassment.

Kobra and her children are already out, fetching water and preparing dough and playing outside before the sun makes it impossible to do so. Today is just another day for them.

Mina pops a new SIM card into her phone and checks on her post anonymously, as if she's a performer who's taken a seat in the audience. She would rather not do this, but it's better she review the comments than subject Marjan to them. The interview Hawa recorded has now reached twelve thousand views and has hundreds of responses.

Serves these women right working with Americans. Nothing but whores to their Western masters.

My brother served in our army. He wasn't paid for months and then died in combat. Do you give a damn about him or is it only women you care about?

Long live the republic. These monsters are a plague.

The Taliban will bring peace. Shame on a government that puts women on a battlefield. God is good.

Mina, why don't you respond to my messages? You are my queen.

Screw your mother.

The real value is in the sub-comments and the sub-sub-comments, the digital bickering and self-righteous accusations and contrarianism by zealots and bots and souls seeking souls. Their interactions trigger an algorithmic boost, a feeding frenzy in which scorn and rage are the chum, in an abyss turbulent with thrashing sharks, some real, some imagined.

There is one comment that she needs to show Marjan.

"You're back," Mina says, a hint of surprise and relief in her voice when Marjan walks through Kobra's door in the morning. Hawa stands up and puts her arms around her mother, closes her eyes when she feels her mother press her to her chest. "Did you find everything you need?"

"I think so," Marjan says, trying to catch her breath. This is no time to be out of shape. "How's your post doing?"

"My viewers don't disappoint. And before you ask, yes. I've removed the SIM card in case anyone tries to track my location."

Marjan chews her lip and runs through any other precautions they should take. They cannot afford a single misstep.

"Lots of people are seeing the video. I need you to look at this comment. The user goes by Pious One. Does it mean anything to you?" Mina says, as Marjan kneels beside her.

This woman deserves what is coming to her.

Pious One has tagged four other people, and each have responded to his post with a thumbs-up. One has a locked account. The others haven't posted much. There are pictures of a lake, religious calligraphy, a sports car. Marjan clicks around, scans the photos on their timelines until she comes across one that stops her heart.

It is a picture of a man standing in front of a black SUV. He is looking into the distance, but behind him, Marjan makes out the front of the compound she was dragged to as a thirteen-year-old bride. Marjan looks more closely at the man's face, recognizes him as one of the men who used to drive her and her sister wife to Kabul.

Marjan looks at Mina.

"It worked," she says.

Hawa looks at the ground, ashamed and afraid of the father she's never known. She's also ashamed of how much she's longed for him. She feels as if she needs to repent.

"Let's give you some time to work on what you've got. Hawa, come with me. You and I have some work to do," Mina says. Hawa picks up her flute and follows her outside, where they sit under the dappled shade of a plane tree.

Kobra stands in the doorway, watching as Marjan empties the contents of two plastic bags onto the rug, items that have cost her nearly all of the remaining cash she had. Kobra takes stock of the pieces and starts to understand her visitor's plan. She shakes her head, convinced this is a doomed mission. Then again, Kobra knows better than most how foolish it is to underestimate a woman. This raised city, this hidden uprising, was built by underestimated women, and the city stands. Her children laugh and learn. The summers are too hot and the winters too cold but they are warm in between.

She leaves so that Marjan can have a few moments to herself.

Marjan's phone pings. It's a reply from Jenna.

Okay. I've let our guy know. Today is the final day. Let's make it happen.

Marjan once asked Jenna about their training. What had she gone through to qualify as a CST?

Jenna had laughed.

She'd undergone basic training five years before she'd even heard of the CST program. For the Special Forces support role in Afghanistan, she and the others had to make it through a rigorous assessment and selection process, grueling tests of their physical, mental, and intellectual capacity, with little feedback in between. For five intense weeks, they trained in search and seizure, room clearing, insertions and extractions, checkpoints, dismounted patrols, tactical movements, general medical care, scenario training, reporting, software use, and with weapons including M4, M9, M203, and 0.5 caliber firearms. There was more, of course, including a crash course in Afghan culture and languages. The CST recruits had been required to carry a fellow soldier on their backs while in full gear to prove they would leave no one behind.

That was the code they lived by, Jenna had told Marjan. That was why she was still fighting for them.

Jenna tells her to stay tuned for gate instructions. She does not tell her whether her contact, a sleep-deprived and overwhelmed official at the State Department, has agreed to signal his colleagues at the Kabul airport about this particular FTP or if he's even responded to her middle-of-the-night message. Marjan decides against asking her. She has no choice but to proceed with blind faith.

Marjan removes her purchases from the bag. She wraps the elastic bandage around her chest as tightly as she can, trying to flatten her breasts. It is not as easy as it was a decade ago. She slips into the tunic and baggy pants. She wishes she had a vest to conceal her chest, but this will have to do.

She looks down at her body, tries to imagine how she will appear to others. She opens the door a crack and sees Kobra standing on the other side of the threshold. She opens the door wider, and Kobra enters the room, looks her over.

"What are you going to do about your hair?" she asks.

Marjan touches her hair, makes a decision.

"Do you have scissors?"

Kobra reaches into a tin and pulls out a small pair of stainless-steel scissors, a hint of rust on the blades. She offers them to Marjan.

"Can you do it, please?" Marjan asks.

Kobra obliges, leading Marjan outside and behind her home. She makes the first cut just above the elastic hair tie. Marjan reaches back to touch the back of her head and feels the shaggy, uneven ends. She takes the bundle of hair, still bound by the elastic, from Kobra and puts it in the plastic bag. This process, her undoing, feels familiar, and that brings her some strange sense of relief.

Kobra continues clipping and snipping until it is almost all gone. She steps back to assess her work.

"Well, all I can say is it will grow back," she says.

"I know," Marjan replies.

"Not bad," she says. "But you're still too . . . pretty. Let's go back inside."

Marjan does as instructed. She needs all the help she can get right now. Kobra examines Marjan's face with one hand on her hip. Then she kneels on the floor and retrieves a red tin from behind one of the floor cushions. She sets it down and goes outside. Two minutes later, she returns with a pinch of cooking fire ash on a leaf and a lump of steel wool. She sits cross-legged in front of Marjan with her tools arranged beside her.

"Tilt your face to the sky," Kobra says, reaching first for the pen. With tiny strokes, she thickens Marjan's brows, gives them a bushy, untamed shape. She extends them so they come close to meeting in the middle and reach out toward her temples. She touches the tip of her pinky finger into the ash and brushes it across Marjan's new brows, darkening the skin between the pen strokes. She picks up a rag, walks outside, and returns seconds later. She touches the rag to Marjan's cheek, drags it across the skin below her cheekbones and toward her chin, then smudges it with her thumb. Marjan can smell the ash on her face, wonders what the dust was before it met fire. Kobra does the same across Marjan's forehead and then in the hollow beneath her browbones.

"Have you done this before?" Marjan asks.

Kobra chuckles. "I used to study my husband's face as if I were a religious scholar and he was a holy book. I could tell from the shape of his mouth, from the way he arranged his brows, if we were going to have an uneventful day or if I needed to make sure the children didn't test his patience."

Next, she dabs the steel wool into the ash and then touches it twice, lightly, to the angle of Marjan's jaw. She picks up the pen again, stipples across Marjan's upper lip, her chin, and the contours of her jaw. She withdraws her hand and considers the effect.

"I'm sorry I wasn't forthcoming with you when we first arrived," Marjan says softly.

Kobra dabs a bit of ash onto the back of her hand, then rotates her hand for a different view.

"I don't blame you," Kobra says. "And if it makes you feel any better, I lied to you too. I told you we had no room for you, but there is an empty room. I could have sent you there but I needed to keep you close so I could figure you out."

Marjan chuckles. "And what did you figure out?"

Kobra rests her hands on her lap. "I didn't guess the soldier bit. But I did know you were in danger. I guessed that if we turned you away, there was a good chance one or both of you would end up on another kind of hill in this city."

Marjan looks down, thinks of the freshly tossed soil on Soraya's hillside grave. She doubts her mother will be able to afford a dignified headstone.

"Let me try something," Kobra says as she adds a bit more ash to the steel wool and covers Marjan's chin. She pauses again to bite her lip. She cannot decide if the effect is convincing or ridiculous. She has Marjan turn her head left and right.

Kobra hands her a small mirror, no bigger than the palm of her hand. Marjan holds it at arm's length to see her face. She turns her head side to side. Kobra's work is not perfect, but it might just do the trick. She puts on the cap she purchased, tilts the rim down to hide her face.

When she steps outside, she sees Hawa and Mina beneath the tree. Even from this distance, she can see Hawa's mouth fall open and Mina's shoulders pull back, and she knows she is transformed. She walks to them in her sneakers, shoes she plans on darkening with the same ash Kobra has applied to her face, to blur their feminine shape.

"You look so different," Hawa says. She sounds spellbound. Marjan looks to Mina.

"It's good. It's . . . it's actually very good," Mina says, peeking under the cap for a full view.

"Why do you sound surprised?" Kobra huffs. "I could make an ugly man out of your pretty face too. Your viewers would never know."

Mina smiles.

"I appreciate the offer but I need my viewers to recognize me," she says.

One hour later, they bid the widows farewell, some skeptical that this trio of visitors will be leaving for good. Even Mina has her doubts, but she keeps them to herself. The ride to the airport is quiet, each of them anxious about this plan that requires them to separate once they are out of the car. Marjan braces herself, watches Hawa. Her daughter stares straight ahead. Marjan dares not ask if she is afraid. She doesn't want to poke holes in Hawa's courage.

They approach the long road to the airport and encounter a Taliban checkpoint manned by two men younger than Marjan, men who were once little boys, she reminds herself.

"Show your documents!" one of them barks.

"Here. I have an official letter by email," Mina replies, showing him her phone screen. He looks from her to the small writing on the phone, shields his eyes from the sun's glare. He squints then looks at his companion. The second boy comes over. He drags a grimy finger along the phone screen, closing out the email.

"Where is it?" he says, glancing into the car. He looks at Marjan curiously. She clears her throat roughly and tries to avoid his gaze.

Mina looks at her phone, realizes what he's done, and reopens the email she's received from the organization committed to protecting journalists. It is addressed to her because she is on their mailing list, a declaration of their commitment to help journalists trapped in a crumbling Afghanistan.

"Here it is," she says, and seeing the way the boy's brow furrows at the screen, she takes a leap. "As you can see, it says very clearly that I am to make my way to the airport with my brother and his daughter. Our travel has been cleared by the Americans and our names are on their lists."

The first boy has lost interest. He moves to speak to the driver of a car approaching behind them, one full of men in collared shirts and pants. They look like government officials, puppets of Western masters, and he's eager to wave his rifle in their faces.

The Talib pounds on the hood of the taxi, and Marjan sees Hawa's head sink forward in relief as they are allowed to proceed. When they reach the airport limits, they step out of the vehicle. Marjan exits from the passenger side. Hawa follows Mina and exits on the driver's side. The taxi drives away, kicking up a cloud of dust between mother and daughter just before they step onto a most treacherous stage to give the performance of their lives.

64

AUGUST 30, 2021

"Dear brother, which way do we go?" Mina says without an ounce of mirth. It is her turn to be shrouded today. She's pulled her headscarf around the lower half of her infamous face, a makeshift niqab. She pulls her sunglasses out of her handbag and starts to put them on.

"Mina, no," Marjan says.

The sunglasses are black with gold embellishments. They look expensive.

"Fine. I'll go blind," Mina says gruffly, and stuffs her shades back into her bag. "Hawa, take my hand. It's more believable."

Marjan checks her phone once more to confirm the directions she's received from Jenna. What would she do without these women behind the scenes to help them escape? They have sacrificed so much, showing up for missions on principle, not politics.

"This way," she says, and they start to make their way to the gate where the marine, a friend of a friend of a total stranger, is stationed. They move lightly today, having left their bags behind. At least their belongings would go to good use, distributed among the women and children of the City of Widows.

Marjan keeps her head bowed, tries to avoid anyone's gaze. She worries what the heat and sweat will do to the ash and ink that are her disguise.

They press forward through crowds of people and scan their surroundings, still far enough from the gate that they can see Taliban circulating in the area, rifles at their sides. In the distance, closer to the gates, Marjan knows the area is secured by a small cadre of Afghan men, the notorious special forces unit of the national army carrying out their final duty before they too, will be allowed to board a flight leaving the country. Atop the walls of the airport, American marines stand guard. It is a most bizarre triangulation of enemies and allies.

Marjan reaches for Hawa's hand, then stops herself. She focuses on forging ahead and carrying herself as a man might, arms at her sides, space between her feet, leading with her torso. She wears a frown, furrows her heavy brows beneath the cap.

"Hold on tight," Mina says to Hawa. "Everything's going to be fine."

Hawa nods. She is less afraid than she should be. She watches her mother's new silhouette, her pulled-back shoulders and squared-off hips, and understands that in this woman, she has an army fighting on her behalf.

"Why did I listen to you?" a man shouts at his wife. "We shouldn't have come here."

A girl with wide eyes and a pink shirt trips and falls to the ground. For a moment, Hawa mistakes the girl for Layma, her classmate. A passerby stumbles over the girl, nearly crushes her.

"Watch where you're going!"

There are more angry shouts, the bubbling of blame as temperatures creep up around them.

Marjan darts left, wanting to steer clear of the situation. Mina follows her lead, dragging Hawa behind her, but it is hot and crowded. Her hand slips away from Mina's. Hawa looks over her shoulder, tries to see if the girl, who bears an uncanny resemblance to her friend, is back on her feet. And in this distracted second, Hawa steps on a man's foot.

She looks up, ready to apologize, but freezes.

Behind the man is a face she last saw at this airport. Her father. There is hardly any distance between them.

Marjan feels a prickle on the back of her neck. She turns in time to see Hawa within arm's reach of Abdul Khaliq. Would he recognize himself in her face?

Marjan pushes through people and grabs her daughter's hand roughly, as an angry father might, pulls her away from these five men, Abdul Khaliq and his entourage. She looks up briefly, despite herself, and their eyes meet.

"Forgive her," Mina says, her voice soft and quivering. She steps between Abdul Khaliq and Marjan, envelops Hawa in the long caftan she's wearing, and keeps her back to the men. Without her makeup and in this shrunken pose, Mina passes for a nondescript woman.

They move away, expecting at any minute to feel something lash at their backs, or at the very least to hear a shout. Marjan is trembling, but with adrenaline, not fear.

"Keep going," Mina whispers to Hawa.

When there is sufficient distance from the men, they pause to take a breath.

Marjan holds her daughter by the shoulders, looks at her face. "Are you okay?"

Hawa nods, though she feels like she's breathing through a straw.

"What do we do?" Mina asks.

Marjan needs to think. Her plan to draw Abdul Khaliq away from the airport has clearly failed. He either didn't see the video they posted or chose not to abandon his post here in Kabul as a deputy Talib. Do they proceed with the rest of their plan now? Do they dare draw attention to themselves while he is here?

"They haven't chased after us, so I don't think they recognized me. I think we should do what we came here to do," Marjan says.

They move closer to the gate. Mina does not tell Marjan that, as she's feared, the beads of sweat on Marjan's forehead have dampened her new brows.

They are as close as they can get to the gate. Marjan reaches under her tunic, removes the tula that she has tucked into the binding holding down her breasts. She hands it to Hawa and nods at her. It is her time now.

Hawa takes in a deep breath. Mina and her mother stand on either side of her, protecting her space. Hawa brings the wooden flute to her lips, arranges her fingertips over the oval openings of the cylinder. She draws a breath of exhaust-filled air, turns that air into breath and breath into sound and sound into a song she has been practicing since yesterday, a song that she has committed to memory.

My homeland,
Without hymn, without melody
My homeland
On you suffer without remedy

Heads turn, but Hawa plays on.

More heads turn, but still not the marine's who stands over the wall. Marjan looks back at the hordes of people behind her, at the ground they have covered. Could she have gotten this far if she weren't fighting for Hawa? She doubts it. There is a parting in the crowd, a narrow splitting of the sea. Marjan sees Abdul Khaliq in the distance. This time there's no mistaking it's him.

Hawa looks at her mother, who signals her to continue. Hawa takes a deep breath and plays again, another forlorn verse.

The marine takes two steps in their direction. It is impossible to read his face, his gaze hidden behind dark sunglasses. He has been vigilant since the day of the bombing. He can still feel the weight of the fallen in his arms. He is more tired than he has ever been, and he is counting down the final hours of this mission. He wants nothing more than to sing happy birthday to his wife next month, to put all of this behind him.

He commits all five senses to his duty. What is that sound? His lips are dry, cracked by this desiccating heat.

Marjan sends a message to Jenna, and the reply comes almost instantly.

Tell her to keep playing.

Hawa takes in another breath, sends it through the flute.

The marine focuses on the crowd to his right, homes in on the source.

Marjan and Mina wave their arms like bodies fighting to stay above water. They dare not shout. They need the sound of Hawa's flute to reach the marine. She needs this music to save her now as it has saved her before. The music does just that, knowing that Hawa will spend the rest of her life repaying the favor.

Epilogue

"Come on. We'll take Hawa to the children's tent for her classes and then we'll check out the women's space," Mina says.

"I'll take Hawa, but I'm really not in the mood for the women's group. Besides," Marjan replies, waving at the large tent they are standing in, the rows of green military cots, "every day here is a women's group."

"And every day you come up with some excuse. I don't know how long we're going to be stuck in this place. Let's make the best of it."

Of course Mina wants to go. Her reporter's blood craves stories, details, testimony, context, confirmation.

She also loves an audience.

"They promised they won't force anyone to share," she says. "You can go and not say a word."

Marjan groans. "Why go if I'm going to sit there like a stone?"

"To listen, Marjan. What good is one person speaking if no one is listening? Come and be someone's patience stone."

"You should go, Madar," Hawa says, sliding her feet into her sneakers. She laces them quickly, her eyes already on the door.

They walk across the tent, large enough to host a town hall. This tent has been their temporary home since they arrived in the United States a month ago. Marjan watches Hawa's ponytail bounce. Last night, she dreamed they were once again in the airport and Abdul Khaliq grabbed her daughter from her and disappeared into the thick of people. Marjan tried to scream for help, but she couldn't make a sound. Another night, she dreamed that she was back on the hill of Zanabad watching the last flight take off.

They were so lucky.

The marine who waved them in had plucked from Mina's hand the letter she waved around, the one awarding her special recognition for her courageous reporting on corruption. He admitted to them later—when they were waiting for the plane's doors to open and boarding to commence—that Hawa's music had caught his attention.

I don't even know how I heard it. Felt like the sound cut through the noise at just the right frequency or something.

Hawa held on to her tula for the entirety of their journey, the flight across the globe, until they disembarked in the gray and cold airport somewhere in the United States, a city with too many syllables to its name. Phi-la-del-phi-a. From there, they boarded another flight, one that took them to a desert.

Who knew America had deserts?

They stood in lines, were processed by uniformed soldiers who walked them from the plane to a cavernous tent, then directed them to other soldiers seated behind folding tables equipped with bottles of hand sanitizer and boxes of pale blue face masks. Their names were entered into laptops. Marjan looked over at Mina. Exhausted and famished, Marjan hadn't heard the first question asked of her. The man behind the computer signaled to someone, and an Afghan man in a plaid shirt and khaki pants appeared. He introduced himself as an interpreter. Marjan had shaken her head and declined, not wanting to reveal anything personal to him.

She gathered her remaining energy and assured the interviewer she could speak and understand English.

And are you married?

Marjan had looked to Hawa then. They would start fresh in this country, writing Abdul Khaliq out of their stories. He existed in their past, and that could not be changed. But Marjan would not carry him with her, not one step further.

"I am a widow," she told him.

They were taken to another area, where they sat in chairs behind a curtained barrier and bared their shoulders for vaccines. They answered more questions. They confirmed more information. And then they were shuttled to the village.

The village, Marjan learned, was a tent city erected in two weeks by American soldiers on this hot and tawny earth. Each tent holds up to one hundred cots. Families, accustomed to the privacy of high walls, hang sheets to separate themselves from their neighbors. Marjan, Hawa, and Mina live in a tent for single women.

The camp is run by soldiers and civilians. There is a medical team, kept busy with pregnant women, skin rashes, aching teeth. Hawa asked one doctor if she had any medications to make her taller, which earned her a smile and a laugh.

The base hums with activity, with people wearing laminated badges on lanyards and others in military uniforms. Instructions were given by word of mouth initially. The evacuees had questions, too, but theirs went unanswered. The people with badges didn't seem to know what was going on mostly. But within days, routines and systems were created.

Slowly, order replaced chaos. The process became clearer. They will be resettled somewhere in America. No, they cannot choose where they will go unless they have family there willing to take them in. They will have permission to work, and they will receive assistance for three months. After that, they'll be on their own.

Marjan and Mina pass by the clothing tent, full of cardboard boxes and tables buried under fabric. So much of it cannot be used. Shirts that are nowhere near a respectable length. Sweatshirts with faces of strangers or loud logos. They dig for clothing in their sizes, for pieces that might match, for items that might make them feel a bit more like themselves.

Today, Mina is wearing a rare find—a blouse the color of pomegranate juice with dainty gold buttons. It has a small grease spot on the left cuff but is in otherwise good condition. The collar is spilled open, revealing a heart-shaped patch of Mina's skin.

"Let's stop in here for just a moment," Marjan says as they pass the clothing tent. "I want to ask that lady one question."

"I'll wait for you here. I don't have the patience for that place today," Mina declares, so Marjan pops in alone. She emerges a moment later, beaming.

"Why are you grinning like that?" Mina asks suspiciously.

Marjan holds out her hand, raises her brows, and signals for Mina to take what she's offering. Mina does so, her brows furrowed as if she doesn't trust Marjan with her life. Marjan drops a silver metal tube into her friend's hand.

"You little devil. How did you find lipstick in that mess?"

Marjan had gone in there a couple of days ago with a request. The woman she spoke with had scoffed at her, explained that they were providing essentials only. Marjan had nodded, almost embarrassed that she'd asked, but another woman had stopped her on the way out.

I can't even count how many women have come in here looking for makeup and tweezers. But I get it, sweetheart. I feel better when I get a little dolled up too.

Mina opens the tube, twists the perfectly angled lipstick up. It is a shade somewhere between ruby and cherry. Mina takes off her sunglasses, looks at her reflection as she pulls the lipstick across her lips then smacks them together.

"Khala Mina! You look so beautiful!" Hawa exclaims. She is cheerful during the day, but Marjan can see her retreat into her thoughts when no one is looking. She curls up next to her mother at night, close enough that Marjan can feel her daughter's heartbeat. Like pendulum clocks sitting side by side, one pulse quickens, one pulse slows. It helps to keep the nightmares away.

And Hawa looks forward to her time in the children's tent. She's made friends there, children who delight at her flute playing.

"There she is, our brilliant and camera-ready journalist," Marjan teases.

"God save you, you're a resourceful friend." Mina smiles broadly.

Marjan feels her breath catch. Hawa leans into her mother. She must see it too.

"What is it?" Mina asks.

"This is Soraya's shade. When you smile, you look so much like her."

Hawa nods, her eyes welling with tears.

Mina scoffs. "If only I were so lucky," she says softly. She touches her fingertips to the tender skin beneath her eyes, presses away the tears. "She should be here with us."

Marjan says no more. She still cannot talk about Soraya without choking up, without fearing she will fall apart. She needs to change this, though, because she plans on telling a lot of people about her best friend, the most courageous and glamorous soldier in their whole platoon. Mina links arms with Marjan.

"Maybe you'll let me get a little of this lipstick on you too," she teases.

"On me? No . . ." She's never been one for vanity, but the past few weeks have made her self-conscious. Her skin is irritated, and the pants she's found here are too long for her legs. Marjan touches the back of her head, feels the shaggy, uneven hair beneath the headscarf. It will take a long time for her hair to grow out.

"I think your short hair suits you, Madar. Maybe I'll cut mine too," Hawa says as she pulls back the flap door of the children's tent. Inside, it is bustling with activity, with children delighting in half-broken crayons, books they cannot yet read, and a haphazard collection of used dolls, toy cars, and building blocks.

Mina and Marjan watch her take her place on the rug with a woman who has come to teach them English. Marjan utters a silent prayer for her daughter, for this miracle of a child.

They go on to enter the community tent, where seven women are seated in folding chairs arranged in a circle. There are two thermoses of tea and a plate of fanned-out graham crackers in the center of the circle. The tea is a simple comfort, despite the awful squeaks made when a Styrofoam cup is pulled from the sleeve and the chemical smell of the foam.

A woman walks in, a volunteer. She carries a plastic bag heavy with fruit, a rare treat. The women watch as she looks for a way to arrange a dozen peaches and plums on a table. Two plums roll off. She catches one before it hits the ground. One of the women in the group takes the other plum off the floor, wipes it clean with the sleeve of her shirt, and takes a bite. The others follow her lead. One by one, they take two steps toward the center of the room, pluck out a fruit. Only a few actually eat them. Most are saving it for their children.

Marjan picks out a plum, slightly bruised but ripe enough that she can feel the juices ready to burst through the dark skin.

Most of the women are reluctant to talk. They've been so trained to be secretive that they spend a lot of time sitting in silence. Many are still stunned that they made it here, to this country that managed to build a village for three thousand in a matter of days. This country that spent twenty years in their homeland trying to do the same. The women share many questions. *Where will I live? How can I learn English? How will I take care of my children? How can I get my college credits accepted here? What will happen to my family back home?*

Sometimes they are tired of asking such heavy questions when they already know the answers will not satisfy. Instead, they fill the silence with trite complaints.

The food here is terrible. The machines are too noisy. I'm getting back pain from these cots.

On a group chat, the other women from Marjan's platoon share the same grievances. They are scattered across the United States, sheltered at different military bases. They've been told that if they step foot off the base they will lose the help they've been promised—finding housing, three months of rent, legal assistance. They are here on humanitarian "parole," a word no one in the platoon was familiar with. Marjan typed the word into the search box on her phone and a definition appeared.

The release of a prisoner temporarily or permanently before the completion of a sentence on the promise of good behavior.

I do feel like a prisoner here, Elaha admitted.

Good behavior? That might be hard for some of us, Zarifa replied. She added a wink emoji.

Oh, girl. What have you been planning for when you get off this base?

A lot, Zarifa says. *I want to be a soldier here. Or maybe go to school and become a lawyer.*

Jenna and the others have been rallying them, checking in often and promising to help them get settled once they are released from the bases. Marjan and the others are grateful, ready. They are soldiers still, and will soon be forging ahead on their individual missions, carrying out their own orders.

After hearing two women complain again about the food, Mina leans forward in her chair. Marjan recognizes the serious look on her face. She is becoming her public self, the competent and unflappable persona.

"Sisters, sisters," Mina calls out with authority. "Your complaints about this guesthouse are valid. Truly, the bread cannot be called bread. But I'm reminded of a verse from Mawlana. If you'll allow me? I may not remember it whole."

The women nod and Mina begins, her eyes closed as she summons the lines.

This body is a guest house,
Every morning, a new visitor.
Do not bemoan the burden,
He will retreat into non-existence.
Welcome, entertain them!
They are guests from the unseen world.
Sorrow may spoil your joy,
Even as it sweeps your house clear
And readies the way for a new delight.

There is a moment of quiet deference for the poem. Mina waits a spell, then breaks the silence.

"But then again, Rumi didn't have to eat this cardboard chicken or chase after five children," she says, one eyebrow cocked.

There is laughter then, and it is hopeful, a splash of water in a desert. Marjan whispers to Soraya sometimes, when no one is around. She tells her how much she misses her, how empty this world is without her. When she floundered as a mother, Soraya saved her. She helped her survive the guilt and filled in the gaps, making sure Hawa felt beloved. Soraya saved her a thousand times over, and yet Marjan failed her. For this, she will never forgive herself.

Marjan wonders, those who knew her as a girl—her sisters, her mother, her aunt—what would they think of her now? She prays, in her own way, for Shahla. For the people she's loved and lost. She hopes she does not lose them all, though she feels the grief of having lost everyone.

And what about Marjan? She thinks of her own being, considers herself as a guest house. She has been so many women in her life. Will she ever be a soldier again? And if not, who will emerge? Who will she be from now on? The hardheaded girl? The child bride? The nervous mother? The lion-hearted survivor? The hopeful romantic?

All of them, she decides, because that is the only way to feel whole.

At the end of the hour, she and Mina walk back to the children's room. Hawa looks up from her drawing, as if she has sensed her mother's eyes on her. She races to the door, her artwork flapping in her hands. It is a crayoned picture of a potted flower sitting on a windowsill. Stems bending toward the light. It is clearly a child's work, but Marjan can almost feel the petals, soft as an infant's cheek. She takes the drawing and trades it for the plum. Hawa giggles as juice runs down the corners of her mouth, and Marjan laughs too. They walk back to their quarters, fingers sticky. Mouths sweetened.

Hawa takes one last bite of her plum and tosses the ridged pit into a metal bin. It lands with a *clink*, a solitary note to mark the end of the season of stone fruit.

Acknowledgments

This story began to take shape when I learned about the Afghan women who served in the Female Tactical Platoon, a unique and covert special forces unit trained by U.S. Special Operations.

There are kernels of truth in this story. There is a hill of widows in Kabul. The Female Tactical Platoon and the Cultural Support Team existed and played critical roles in military operations. There was a horrific bombing at the airport; the casualties increased when American marines fired in retaliation. Seven children and three adults were killed in an erroneous drone strike. And as I write this, the Taliban continue to ban girls' education beyond sixth grade. Women are banned from public parks and gyms. Every week, new edicts are announced that rob girls of even the simplest dreams, their basic rights denied in a state of gender apartheid.

I owe a debt of gratitude to the people who so generously shared their time, expertise, and personal experiences with me. They have enriched the story with authenticity. Thank you, Mahnaz Akbari, FTP Commander, for the conversations, insight, and inspiration. Much thanks to Army Officer Malia Carson, who served on the Cultural Support Team and as an advisor to the FTP. Malia went on to cofound Sisters of Service, a partnership between the CSTs and the FTPs resettled in the United States. And thank you to Naheed Bahram, U.S. Country Director for Women for Afghan Women, for sharing insights on the goings-on inside a women's shelter in Afghanistan. Enormous thanks to the very talented Negin Khpalwak, who studied at the Afghanistan National Institute for Music and went on to become Afghanistan's first woman conductor with Zohra, the first all-female orchestra in Afghanistan. Negin generously shared her experiences both in music and in recruiting children from an orphanage to study at ANIM.

I've taken some liberties, of course, and any inaccuracies are my own, intentional or otherwise.

To my agent, Helen Heller—our conversations always keep me loyal to the story first and foremost. To my editor, Rachel Kahan—your insights have sharpened each and every story, and this one is no exception. Thank you for elevating this book and believing in these stories. And to the team at William Morrow, I am so grateful. Copyeditors, you are incredible. From spotting typos to fact-checking events and even weather details, you have saved me many times. I'm so grateful to the many people I don't get to meet but whose work and energies are invaluable; thank you for the designs, marketing, publicity, and everything in between. Special thanks to Brittani DiMare, Hope Breeman, Andrea Molitor, Hope Ellis, and Alexandra Bessette. And a huge thanks to Mumtaz Mustafa for another gorgeous cover. This one made my heart soar!

I'm also fortunate enough to have these stories reach readers across the world. Thank you to Jemma McDonagh for building those global bridges and to my many international publishers—the translators, editors, designers, and marketing teams who give my books wings.

And to all who have been patiently (or not so patiently) awaiting this story, thank you for choosing to spend your time with a book. Special nod to Shikha Lambda for championing these stories and alchemizing fiction into humanitarian aid.

Writing is a solitary process that requires space, time, and sanity. I could not do this without my village—my parents (the world's greatest grandparents) and my extended family. I'm lucky to have friends who keep me breathing, laughing, climbing, and dancing—Basima, Fahima, Wida, and my forever koukla, Laura. To Zoran, Zayla, Kyrus, Cyra—my days are brighter and better because of you. To my husband, Amin, none of this is possible without you. All my love, always.

For more about the work of the FTP and their journeys upon arriving in the United States, look for "The Untold Story of the Afghan Women Who Hunted the Taliban" by Amanda Ripley, *Politico*, April 8, 2022. And for more about 1st Lt. Ashley White, whose life was taken by an IED while serving with the Cultural Support Team, check out *Ashley's War: The Untold Story of a Team of Women Soldiers on the Special Ops Battlefield* by Gayle Tzemach Lemmon. The research for this book was informed by far too many articles to list here but those interested can check out my website.

About the Author

Nadia Hashimi is a pediatrician turned international bestselling novelist and the daughter of Afghan immigrants. She is the author of four books for adults, as well as the middle-grade novels *One Half from the East* and *The Sky at Our Feet* and the young-adult novel *Spilled Ink*. She lives with her family in the Washington, DC, suburbs. Visit her online at nadiahashimibooks.com.